Mary Horlock was born in A... Guernsey in the Channel Islands... in contemporary art at Tate Liv... first novel, *The Book of Lies*, was longlisted for the *Guardian* First Book Award. She lives with her family in London.

Praise for *The Stranger's Companion*

'A compelling and unusual novel'
The Times, A Top 10 Historical Fiction Book of 2024

'Such a wonderful, distinctive cast of characters.
The narrative voice is brilliantly original'
Zoë Somerville, author of *The Marsh House*

'A mesmerising historical mystery. Delectable'
Anna Mazzola, author of *The Book of Secrets*

'An atmospheric, haunting story full of evocative, swirling myths. Gloriously gripping'
Liz Fenwick, author of *The Secret Shore*

'A fascinating mystery [and] a truly transporting read'
Woman's Weekly

'Highly original, intense and captivating'
Jenny O'Brien, author of *Roses for the Dead*

'Daphne du Maurier meets *The Trouble with Goats and Sheep* – an enthralling, intriguing mystery'
Katie Lumsden, author of *The Secrets of Hartwood Hall*

Also by Mary Horlock

Joseph Gray's Camouflage
The Book of Lies

The Stranger's Companion

MARY HORLOCK

BASKERVILLE
An imprint of JOHN MURRAY

First published in Great Britain in 2024 by Baskerville
An imprint of John Murray (Publishers)

This paperback edition published in 2025

1

Copyright © Mary Horlock 2024

The right of Mary Horlock to be identified as the Author of the Work has been asserted by her in accordance with the Copyright, Designs and Patents Act 1988.

Map drawn by Barking Dog Art

All rights reserved. No part of this publication may be reproduced, stored in a retrieval system, or transmitted, in any form or by any means without the prior written permission of the publisher, nor be otherwise circulated in any form of binding or cover other than that in which it is published and without a similar condition being imposed on the subsequent purchaser.

All characters in this publication are fictitious and any resemblance to real persons, living or dead, is purely coincidental.

A CIP catalogue record for this title is available from the British Library

Paperback ISBN 9781399813174
ebook ISBN 9781399813181

Typeset in Sabon MT Std by Manipal Technologies Limited

Printed and bound in Great Britain by Clays Ltd, Elcograf S.p.A.

John Murray policy is to use papers that are natural, renewable and recyclable products and made from wood grown in sustainable forests. The logging and manufacturing processes are expected to conform to the environmental regulations of the country of origin.

Carmelite House
50 Victoria Embankment
London EC4Y 0DZ

www.johnmurraypress.co.uk

John Murray Press, part of Hodder & Stoughton Limited
An Hachette UK company

The authorised representative in the EEA is Hachette Ireland, 8 Castlecourt Centre, Dublin 15, D15 XTP3, Ireland (email: info@hbgi.ie)

For my mother, who is Paddy, but is also Nona.
Possibly a witch, but a good one.

Cast of Characters

Elise Carey – Sark's postmistress, the widow of Phillip Carey

Phyllis (Phyll) Carey – only child of Elise and Phillip

Maud Pratt – Sark's midwife (now retired) and Phyll's godmother. The widow of Albert Pratt

John de Carteret – Sark's chief constable, married to Marie

Edith (Edie) de Carteret – youngest child of John and Marie

Major Earnest Hyde – lives part-time at Beau Regard, Little Sark, and owner of the Bungalow Hotel

Everard Hyde – son of Earnest and ex-wife Hermione

Nancy Dolbel – housekeeper to Major Hyde, married to Harry

William Toplis – landscape painter, long-standing resident of Sark

Muriel (Mule) Toplis – daughter of William Toplis

Reverend Louis Severy – Sark's vicar

Gilbert Baker – fisherman, resident of the Barracks, Little Sark.

Small George Vaudin – son of Big George Vaudin, Sark fisherman

Eric and Lisl Drake – artists and owners of Sark's art gallery

Paul and Ann Cecil – artists and summer residents

Miranda Cecil – daughter of Paul and Ann

Dr Percy Stanhope – Sark's doctor from 1899 to 1932 (deceased)

Dr Stephen Greener – Sark's new doctor

Dolly Bihet – housekeeper of the Bel Air Hotel

Sarah Williams – English visitor, widow of Cyril Williams, honeymooned on Sark in 1913, returned yearly until 1922

Sylvie Price – art student and one-time associate of the Cecils

Frederick de Carteret – Sark schoolmaster, no relation to John

Jim Remfrey – deputy police constable

The Stranger's Companion

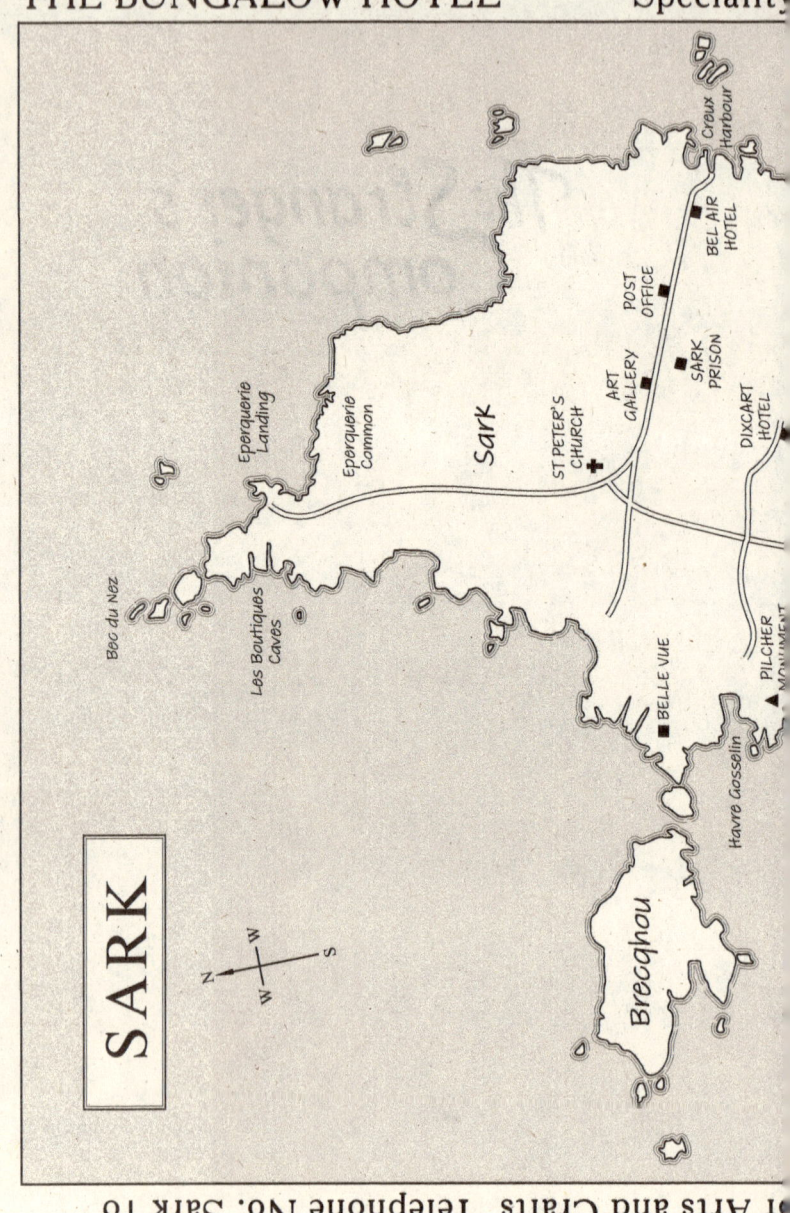

THE BUNGALOW HOTEL — Speciality of Arts and Crafts   Telephone No. Sark 18

SARK

- Croux Harbour
- Bel Air Hotel
- Post Office
- Art Gallery
- Sark Prison
- St Peter's Church
- Dixcart Hotel
- Eperquerie Landing
- Eperquerie Common
- Sark
- Bec du Nez
- Les Boutiques Caves
- Belle Vue
- Pilcher Monument
- Havre Gosselin
- Brecqhou

Afternoon Teas Telephone No. Sark 14

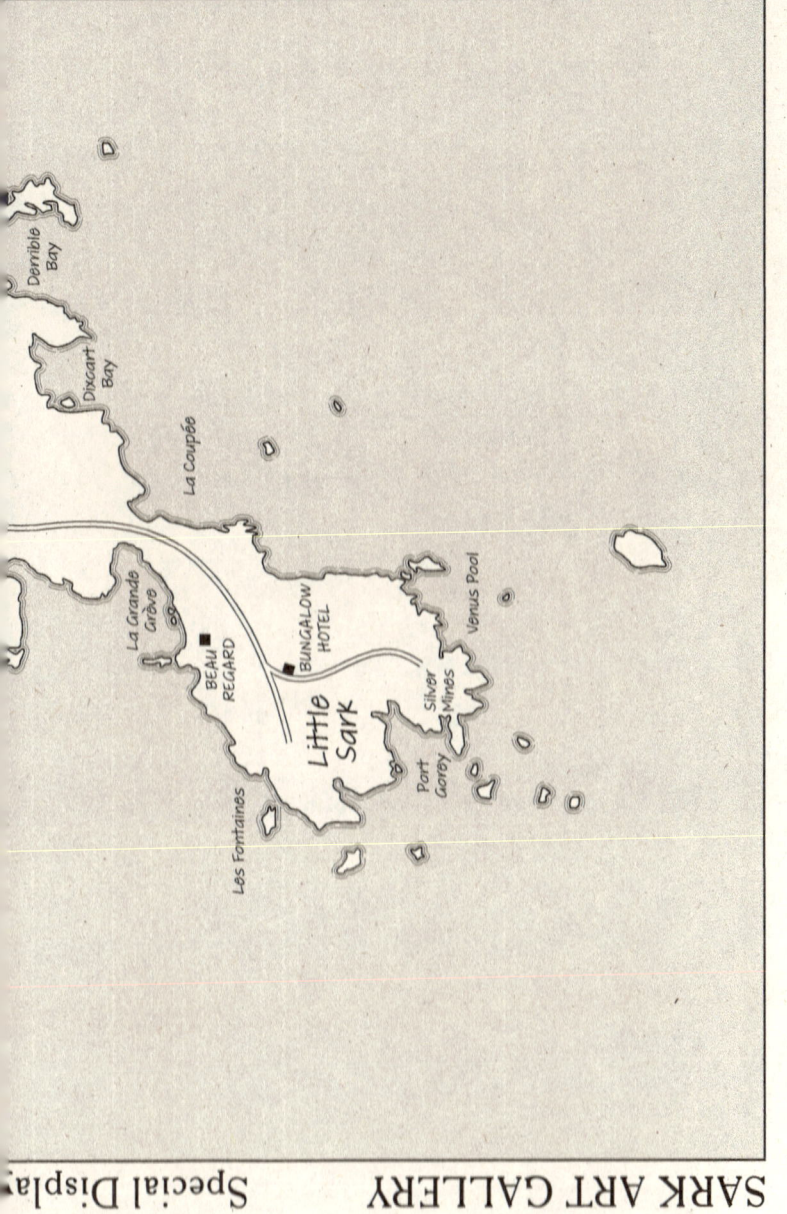

Dernible Bay
Dixcart Bay
La Coupée
La Grande Grève
BEAU REGARD
BUNGALOW HOTEL
Little Sark
Venus Pool
Silver Mines
Port Gorey
Les Fontaines

SARK ART GALLERY   Special Display

Prologue

THE WEATHER THAT summer had been especially fine – not since 1919 had Sark enjoyed such brilliant sunshine and cloudless skies – but September brought a sudden drop in temperature, which was later taken as a warning.

When the coat was first spotted on the rocks, nobody rushed to raise the alarm. It looked as if it had been spread out to make a picnic blanket, as if some visitor had, moments ago, been sitting there, relaxing, reading, or simply admiring the view.

There are several postcards of Port Gorey where the tragedy occurred. It has long been a favourite spot for artists. This was one of the reasons Gil Baker didn't worry. He was taking a fishing party around the coast in his small boat, and it was one of his passengers, peering through binoculars, who first noticed the coat. Little is known about this fishing party, but they were businessmen from Jersey, the largest of the Channel Islands, and had drunk too much in Sark's various taverns the night before. Gil therefore didn't pay them much attention. He was also struggling against a strong current and turning tide. Anyone familiar with Sark's south coast will know there are razor-edge rocks dangerously close to the surface. In Gil's mind, it seemed likely that the coat belonged to one of Sark's newest inhabitants, members of a self-proclaimed 'artists' colony' who had passed the summer painting and bathing in the nude.

So the tide came in and the coat remained. It was Harris tweed, we learned later, its colours blending neatly with the mineral-veined rocks and rust-topped bracken. It lay open with its arms splayed, one cuff flapping despondently. There was a moment when the wind almost picked it up, and we feared it might be swept away, but then the heavens opened.

After several hours of rain a young man came scrambling down the path. He was himself wearing only a jumper and scarf but the coat did not belong to him, and he seemed rather startled to find it there. He stared at it for a short while, standing very still with his hands on his hips, and then he walked further down the cliff and began to search the slopes and drops and ridges. In a matter of moments, the other clothes were found. They were arranged in two piles, pressed flat and neatly folded. There was a woman's blouse, jacket and skirt and a man's suit, shirt and even a set of cufflinks.

They were left on a bank of rock, on an area just above the tide mark, apparently still waiting for their owners to return.

There was always that hope at the start.

PART ONE

I

GUERNSEY EVENING PRESS

Monday, 2 October 1933

'ISLAND RIDDLE'

Sark, our Most Serene And Unperturbed Island, has been rocked by a startling development this weekend. After welcoming a regular stream of visitors these past months, two have apparently vanished. The mystery began with the discovery of two sets of clothes, belonging respectively to a man and a woman, left on a cliff edge. It is reported that these clothes are of good quality and appear almost new. But where are their owners? How could two persons, evidently a man and a woman, have disappeared? What have they done and where have they gone?

And so it is that Sark, The Island Where Nothing Ever Happens, has made front page news.

The clothes were collected and delivered to Chief Constable John de Carteret and he now faces the queerest problem of his career.

We therefore welcome the co-operation of our readers in the hope that someone may be able to offer some answers.

WELCOME, STRANGER, to Sark, the wildest and most neglected of the Channel Islands, and once you see it you'll understand why. It lies some seven miles east from the larger island of Guernsey, and is surrounded on all sides by sheer, steep cliffs. In the past visitors have stared up at these bare walls and decided the island is too barren and inhospitable for any civilised person to live there. It is often said none do.

But today, please persevere. If you navigate the lethal rocks round the northernmost tip, the aptly named Bec du Nez, you will come to a harbour, the smallest in the world. Here is a decent stone breakwater where local fishermen gather to stare cryptically. Just ignore them. Head for the hole in the cliff. Yes, to enter Sark you must literally let her swallow you. You will find yourself climbing a steep hill shrouded by bushes and trees, then you will reach an open plateau and breathe a sigh of relief.

Here is the Avenue, a grandly inappropriate name for what is a dirt track bordered by low-lying hovels. Note the quality of silence. There are no motor-cars on Sark, which explains the roads that are not really roads, and we hope your shoes are sensible. To your left is the Bel Air Hotel, part-thatched, with a public bar so damp and dimly lit it must surely be authentic. On another day we'd recommend you rest here and sample Dolly Bihet's excellent scones.

Maybe that's what they did.

But nobody knows for sure just yet, because it is Monday, 2nd October, and two sets of clothes, newly discovered and heavy with rain, lie in the island's prison. Everyone is waiting, so you had better hurry up. Walk briskly on until you reach a signpost. It points left to the prison and right to the post office. Beneath it stands a squarely built woman with aquiline features and short grey hair. This is Elise Carey, the postmistress. Like all women in their forties she won't discuss her age. She wears small, round glasses she doesn't need and stiff wool breeches she makes herself. Today, on account of the rain, she has pulled on a full-length oilskin. Quite the Grim Reaper chic. The post office remains shuttered and she marches off in the other direction, wading through the small crowd that's formed outside the prison.

Sark's prison is like all Sark buildings, miniature, as if built for a child. There is no crime on Sark, since everyone knows everyone else, their habits and their business. Why commit a crime when you'd be so quickly caught? But that makes what has happened more peculiar. The discarded clothes have been spread out on a trestle table and their musty, vaguely rotted smell invades the space, mixing with sharper notes of stale tobacco and fresh sweat. Over the course of a few hours everyone has come to look, and since the prison is next to the schoolhouse, a cluster of children now assemble. Word has spread. It has also jostled, nudged, skipped and elbowed.

John de Carteret stares down at the clothes and scratches his chin. To the newspapers he is Chief Constable de Carteret, but we just call him John. He has cheeks that bear a fresh-scrubbed glow, eyebrows that meet over his nose, and a moustache his wife Marie hates. He grew it in 1914 to make him look older and finally it has the desired effect. John nods to Elise Carey as she enters, then goes back to the scratching of chin.

It is truly baffling. The passenger ledgers of the ferry boats have now been consulted, and the registers of the four hotels have been checked. No visitors are unaccounted for, no guests reported missing. Sark has a population of 500 souls, a number that swells by several hundred between May and September. After that, the tourist season turns off like a light. Just now people are battening down the hatches, as the coming weeks turning into months will see Sark cut off from everywhere on account of walloping south-westerlies. Sark is a different island in the winter, as everyone will tell you, its isolation being part of the appeal and the horror.

'I don't understand this,' John says to Elise. 'And I don't like things I don't understand.'

But for the assembled islanders the mystery of the clothes and their missing owners makes a welcome change from talk of the weather and the behaviour of mackerel. The tiny prison has become crowded, transformed into a point of interest, a stage upon which a small chorus can gather to offer their opinions. As is typical of these situations, people who know the least say the most. The schoolchildren, wide-eyed and fidgety, have already agreed it is witchcraft. The belief in the supernatural is a firm feature of island life even now, and it was a full moon on Saturday night, a time when witches are most active. A large coven are said to meet at low tide on Grande Grève, which is the largest beach on the island and excellent for swimming.

As is clear, the clothes have a strange and powerful effect on all those gathered. Even lying flat they are determined to communicate, to plead their cause. The lady's jacket has one button missing. The man's coat is mud-stained with the labels torn out. What could possibly have happened to their owners? Perhaps Phyllis Carey knows. She has pushed her way into the prison to stand beside her mother. By the way, we must only ever call her Phyll. She hates her name and blames her mother for it. She blames her mother for many things but we will get on to that later. Phyll is twenty-two and willow-thin with thick brown hair recently cut short. (A mistake, we all agree.) She has just returned to the island, having left what was a perfectly respectable job in Southampton for some less respectable reasons she is not yet willing to disclose. She is wearing a cotton dress the colour of daffodils. It's short-sleeved with pearl buttons down the front and too flimsy for October. This could be one reason why she's paying close attention to the abandoned clothes. The woman's jacket and skirt are a beige flecked tweed, they bear an Edinburgh tailor's label. The blouse is peach silk with a double-edged collar. Phyll runs her hands over both and then takes the blouse and holds it out in front of her. For a moment she's a woman in a shop about to try it on.

She doesn't look at John de Carteret as she answers his questions, but she assures him that no, she didn't see two strangers arrive off a boat in the last few days, nor has she seen these clothes anywhere before. Phyll turns the blouse this way and that, a dreamy look in her eye, and her mother clears her throat, as if embarrassed. Elise has already assured John that she didn't see this vanished couple. John considers it a great pity, since Elise has a knack for knowing things before they happen and if she had seen the couple, he's sure his problems would be solved.

Phyll turns and shows the blouse to her mother. 'Isn't it pretty?'

Elise raises her eyebrows even further up her forehead. She appreciates fine clothes as much as the next person, but she would advise female visitors to wear something hard-wearing. Sark hedges are as bad as Sark rocks and Sark furze-bushes are of the most penetrating description. If you must wear a dress then free it of any superfluous trimmings, otherwise you will leave mementoes of yourself all over the island, though that could come in handy if you get lost.

The rain beats heavy on the roof, the wind whistles down the chimney. Elise checks her watch. *The Courier* is late bringing the mail, and now she is worried it will bring something else. Representatives of the press are no longer welcome on the island. Last month an article in the *Daily Star* claimed that Sark people had grown too reliant on the extorting of innocent tourists for an income. What scandalous tosh! Our lawyers will be in touch. Let's be clear about one thing: life here is hard for those persons who aren't 'free of the sordid responsibility of making a living' as per the part-time English residents, nor are we inclined to 'swim naked and sleep in tin huts' like members of the new 'artists' colony' described in July's edition of *Studio* magazine.

Small George Vaudin has seen the naked artists just the once, when he was collecting lobster pots with his father. George has bright red hair, intense blue eyes and wild freckles, and he is standing at the prison window, jostling for space beside an excitable girl with short bobbed hair and an upturned nose. This is Edie de Carteret, the daughter of the Chief Constable, who so far ignores her. When John isn't keeping the peace he works as a farrier and blacksmith. Most islanders have more than one job. Frederick de Carteret, for example, is schoolteacher and island magistrate, both posts secured through the sole qualification of legible handwriting. Despite John and Fred sharing a surname they are not related and they do not like each other. There is a great deal of feuding in Sark, especially in the winter when there is little else to do.

Phyll Carey, as already stated, is local. Her flimsy excuse for a dress is not. It belongs to Miranda Cecil. The Cecils are typical summer visitors and also, sadly, artists. They own a small studio on the western edge of the island. Mrs Ann Cecil RA, RSA is a real presence and Mr Paul Cecil RA, RSPCA, has great vitality of personality. Yes, these descriptions are deliberately insincere but they aren't here so it doesn't matter. Phyll is very good friends with Miranda, their only daughter, who is extremely pretty and far more sensible than her parents, which honestly doesn't mean much.

Sark has always attracted artists. There's nothing we can do about it. They jump off the boat and think it's a world made for them. It isn't, but why argue? They never listen. Sark's most famous artist has now entered the prison and comes to stand beside Elise. Mr William Arthur Toplis is known for his meticulous landscape paintings that are frequently rejected by the Royal Academy, who don't appreciate his genius. He is a serious, elderly artist and not the naked kind, and as he is deaf he shouts: 'They are dead. They are drowned. Bloody fools!'

Phyll turns rather stiffly. 'We don't know that yet.'

She lifts up the woman's jacket with arms extended, then crocks her elbows and draws it close so it falls against her chest. She tucks the collar under her chin and runs a hand over the buttons. It would fit her perfectly, she thinks, and for a few seconds she imagines another version of herself finding the clothes on the rocks, and swapping them with her own. It's an odd thought and she bites down hard on her lip to block it out.

'The woman was my size,' Phyll tells John, and she lifts her chin so the jacket folds forward. She wonders how much a woman must love a man to cast off her clothes on the rocks, and what has he done to her, and why, and exactly as she thinks this she senses a new face peering in at the window, taller than the others. She stands rigid, holding her breath, aware of this shadow on the edge of her vision.

Edie de Carteret isn't aware of the young man standing behind her. If she were to turn now, she would see a face that is very pale, with brown eyes bruised by tiredness, the brows above them sharply arched. But Edie cannot tear her eyes away from Phyll, who has touched the clothes, which surely means she will die. Edie shuts her eyes and starts muttering what might be a protective spell, and this clearly works as Phyll releases the jacket and rubs her hands together.

'What an odd business,' she says, and as she says this her eyes skitter to the open window, but the face she thought was there has gone.

'The fact is,' John announces, 'no one on the island recognises the clothes and nobody has reported anyone missing, so at the moment I don't have much.'

'At the *moment*,' Elise repeats. Her eyes have also drifted to the window, sensing someone there. A threat perhaps. She struggles to refocus her attention on John. 'You will have to search the cliffs.'

Everyone groans. Despite being only three miles long Sark has nearly forty miles of coastline, a mixture of sandy bays and lethal drops, fissures and caverns and all that fun stuff. It's often said the worst mistake any Sark child can make is to walk backwards close to a cliff edge – well, there are other things, but let's move on. The islanders will happily quote stories of how someone lost their footing or was swept away by a wave. Best not ask.

But, those who visit Sark will always make some inquiry as to its discovery and early settlement, and since so little has been put on record we can always make it up. Before there was a school or a prison or a harbour, Sark was a plateau of rock beaten into shape by the sea. On a map it looks like two islands joined and divided by a narrow ridge of rock called La Coupée. The northern, larger part is Great Sark and the southern end is Little Sark. (Very original, we know.) The first incident to be recorded with any certainty was the founding of a monastery by a Welsh monk named St Magloire in AD 565. After that things went downhill and for a long time the island was under the control of smugglers or pirates and wreckers, a criminal underclass frequently decimated by violent massacres. This might explain why so many areas are said to be haunted and dangerous to visit at night. The drama rumbled on until 1565, when Helier de Carteret arrived with the authority of Queen Elizabeth I to colonise the island. He founded a feudal state and became the Seigneur, and most of the laws date from this time, although now we have a Dame, which is a vast improvement.

According to the law, there must always be two serving constables. This is so they can arrest each other to pass the time. As a joke, it never gets old. John has been Chief Constable since 1919. Until now, he's only dealt with very petty incidents, invariably perpetrated by the island's last Seigneur, but that is a whole other story.

Our point is, he will need all the help he can get.

Unfortunately Small George Vaudin is the only person to volunteer, thrusting his arm in the air. 'I know the west coast better than anyone. I can start searching *now*!'

Edie de Carteret nudges him viciously. 'Me too! Me too! I can do the east!'

The schoolchildren all now shout at once and John finally notices his daughter and raises his hands in horror. He doesn't want Edie involved, but if he says it's too dangerous she will just want it more.

Luckily Elise swings round, hands planted on her hips. 'Enough! We don't need help from silly young children who should be in school.'

Her voice is high but firm, and the silly young children, including Edie, who pouts the way her father hates, fall silent and disperse. They are more scared of the postmistress than the chief of police, and in this their instincts are entirely correct. John wants more words with Elise for this reason, but as everyone moves outside she is busy with her daughter, speaking sharply into her ear. John doesn't want to intrude as he knows things have been difficult.

Elise has always been supportive of Phyll, her bright, ambitious child. She spent a lot of money getting Phyll off the island, paying for secretarial courses and a boarding house in Southampton. The last anyone heard, Phyll had found herself a post as an assistant to an assistant at a publishing house specialising in nautical subjects, which was surely very thrilling. Then suddenly Phyll was back, a bedraggled figure standing at the docks, clutching a suitcase that turned out to be a typewriter. A Bluebird Portable, we are told. It had cost her all the money she'd made. Phyll now says she wants to be a writer and 'make it on her own', which is all quite alarming.

Elise turns back to John and her gaze is so fierce it startles him. 'I've an idea. We should get Phyll to type up a description of the clothes, send that to the *Guernsey Press*. It is a way of staying in control of what's being said. You use it to appeal for information.'

Phyll's mouth drops open. She has strong features: thick, straight eyebrows, a long nose, a large mouth. It is the kind of face people call handsome so her mother thinks it's a shame she is always scowling.

'Wait,' she says. 'I didn't . . . '

But John is already surrendering his notepad. 'It would help me, Phyll, can you? You can write better than me and you . . . er . . . know about clothes.'

Phyll smooths down Miranda's cast-off, which flutters like a curtain in the breeze. She wonders if she should be offended by that last comment, but she has been offended by so many things recently she's not sure she can accommodate more. She glowers expertly at her mother and then at John, who has adopted a lunatic grin.

She takes the notepad. 'This isn't exactly what I had in mind when I said I was going to write . . . But if I *must*.'

She is aware she sounds like a sulky child and kicks at some gravel, which, as she is wearing sandals, is a mistake. With pebbles now wedged under toes, her scowl only deepens.

Elise digs into one pocket of her oilskin. 'And Phyll can also go and check on the Cecils' studio, and then we can be sure the clothes were not Ann's . . . or that anyone else has been there. I have a spare key.'

Phyll clamps her arms tightly over her ribs. Her mother is using the calm, reasonable tone that never fails to enrage her and she feels a familiar mix of frustration and indignation, the kind specifically formulated for daughters whose mothers do not understand them. She doesn't want to go to the Cecils' studio, but she knows what will happen if she refuses: her mother will lift her eyebrows haughtily and enquire what *else* her dear daughter has to do, and Phyll has nothing else to do, which is quite her own fault. She thus rolls her eyes elaborately, takes the key, and stomps back into the prison. But then she stops. She is wobbling on the threshold, her head bent over John's notepad. She lifts the page closer and studies it. She blinks and blinks.

'Everard Hyde,' she says sharply, turning back to John. 'Everard *Hyde* found the clothes?' She takes care to enunciate each word, and then she looks down at the page again to check.

John tells her yes.

Phyll doesn't lift her head.

His full name is in fact Everard George Hyde and moments ago he had been standing at the prison window. Go back further, and he was the young man scrambling over the cliffs at Port Gorey. Phyll takes a deep breath and walks directly to the man's coat and lifts it up, holding it level with her eyes, like it's another person facing her. She shuts her eyes and she is suddenly twelve years old again and Everard is standing beside her. He is draped in his father's old coat, waving a torch under her chin.

'Woo-hoo,' he whispers. 'I'm a ghost, do you see?'

But this is not where it starts. We need to go back, right back.

Lucky for us, nowhere is far on Sark, and time is a relative concept. Come, walk out of the prison, take a right on the Avenue and turn back ten years.

There is a side gate into the gardens of the Bel Air – did you notice? It still squeaks when you open it. Come, let your feet sink into the grass. The lawn slopes down towards the harbour, but ahead, because it is summer, all the roses are in bloom. Feel the heat in the sun and picture two children sitting on the verandah. A boy and a girl trying hard to ignore each other.

Soon one of them would disappear.

And yes, it was a game.

2

The Bel Air Hotel and Public Bar, Harbour Hill.

(Centrally located with charming gardens and a fine sea view, comfortable rooms.)

1 August 1923

THE BEL AIR'S VERANDAH, freshly painted, gleamed white in the afternoon sun. It almost hurt our eyes to look. It was a tea party for summer visitors. Like we said, there are always summer visitors to Sark, but it was worse in the years after the War, when the island became popular with people who wanted to escape or find themselves, which was different but equally hard. To quote one newcomer: 'We are all just slightly mad.'

Major James Earnest Jolyon Hyde MC, DSO would not have called himself mad. He would've preferred respectable, educated and possessing family money. He was resident of Beau Regard, the only modern house on Little Sark, where he also owned the Bungalow Hotel. He sat, by choice, on the least comfortable chair, sipping hot, watery tea. His son, who he secretly believed was not his son, sat beside him. Everard Hyde wore his short brown hair neatly parted to one side, which was how his mother liked it, and he was still at that age when he liked to please his mother. He had come to Sark for the summer, the whole unbearable summer, because she said it was important he spend time with his father, despite whatever else she said about him. Everard would have preferred to have no father at all, or a dead one like all his friends.

On the opposite side of the table sat Phyll Carey, but she refused to look at Everard or even acknowledge his presence. She did not like boys although she also wanted to be one, which explained the shortening of her name. Her dark hair was unwashed and unbrushed and she wore crumpled shorts with socks that bagged over her boots. She had only come because Miranda had invited her. Miranda Cecil was then fourteen and very pretty with hair so blonde it surely couldn't last. Unfortunately she was sat at the other end of the table next to a glamorous lady talking French. Phyll was furious: she had assumed the tea party was just for her. She often made the mistake of thinking things had been arranged for her, especially if it involved the Cecils, since they made a lot of fuss and noise. If we remember rightly, the party was to celebrate the Cecils' completion of their studio. They now planned to spend three months of each year on the island, and when Paul wasn't painting the cliffs he'd make a bit of money teaching small groups. Paul was handsome and witty and popular with women, which was useful as there were a lot of spare women since the War.

Phyll thought of the Cecils as characters from a book. She read a lot of books, even the ones she wasn't meant to, thanks to her habit of wandering into one of the island's hotels and picking up whatever guests left behind. A cursory glance about her bedroom floor would reveal a guide to common seaweeds, seven copies of *The Gentleman's*

Magazine, some detective novels of questionable quality, a catalogue of girdles, a very battered *Wuthering Heights* and the collected poems of Emily Dickinson. There was also a *New Oxford Dictionary of British Artists*, a gift from Paul to her mother. 'To prove to me he's in it,' Elise muttered somewhat grudgingly. Elise Carey, not long widowed, had no time for art and literature, but Dolly Bihet, the Bel Air's kitchen maid, let Phyll read aloud to her while she baked. Phyll dreamt that she would travel the world like the Cecils and write the kind of books that might be left behind in hotel lounges.

Phyll didn't know this yet but Everard Hyde also had a good imagination. He was picturing the verandah as a boat, beached on a lawn of boiling hot lava. He was wondering how to escape, when suddenly and without warning, the table erupted. Phyll had picked a large scab off her knee. Even she was surprised by the amount of blood.

'It was just a scab!' she said afterwards, kicking up dust in her wake.

Everard jogged to keep pace, head down and hands deep in his pockets. 'And *everyone* picks scabs.'

Well, no, not everyone. One of the ladies present, a Mrs Sarah Williams of Sunny Banks, Northampton, had cringed and twisted her head away as if she were about to faint, causing Ann Cecil to clap her hands and suggest Phyll show Everard 'the delights of the town'.

There were no delights, there was not even a town, and Phyll was quite indignant. Then Everard asked how she'd hurt her knee in the first place and she turned to look at him properly.

'I was climbing a cliff.'

Everard puffed out his cheeks, genuinely impressed. 'I climb trees, but I've never climbed a cliff.' He hesitated. 'Is it hard?'

Phyll thought that was the world's most stupid question. '*Extremely.*'

Undeterred, Everard started to unbutton the cuff of his shirt and straightened out his right arm, twisting it round. 'Look at this – I fell out of a tree two weeks ago.'

We are sad to report that the large bruise, which had previously been the shape of North America, had shrunk and faded, transitioning from several shades of overripe plum to something reminiscent of wilted lettuce. Everard, conscious it had underperformed, would later blame the harsh sunlight, but Phyll took his arm and turned it this way and that, as if forgetting it was still attached to the rest of him. She was secretly fascinated to see someone so pale and she wondered if he was dying of an interesting disease.

'Break any bones?'

Everard shook his head and Phyll let the arm drop, but before she walked on she glanced back over her shoulder to check that he would come.

It was late afternoon and the last of the day trippers were hurrying in the direction of the harbour. Everard turned around to watch them go and felt a pang. He wasn't sure how he'd fill the weeks ahead.

'Do you think *I* could climb a cliff? I would like to try.'

Phyll stole another look at him. She was going to say no, not a chance, but something made her hesitate. He was watching her, waiting, and she rather liked his anxious frown. She lifted one shoulder and let it drop.

'If I can do it, I bet you can.'

So maybe this is where it starts. *If I can do it, I bet you can.* A few words like a promise or a pact.

Nobody saw them walking along. The door of the general stores was propped open but empty, and the surgery and the post office had both closed for the day. Phyll picked up her pace as she went past the post office.

'My mother works there,' she whispered. 'But whatever you do, don't look. She thinks it all very odd because your father said he wasn't married when he first got here, and *then* he said his wife was dead, and he *never* mentioned you.'

Everard twisted his mouth into a grimace. 'My mother is in France. She ran off with my father's best friend and they had to get divorced and it upset everyone and I am not allowed to mention her when I am with him.' The words had come out in a rush and he stopped and looked up. 'Please, please don't tell.'

Phyll wore the same serious expression she had worn all through tea. She lifted her left hand and made a small motion as if to button her lips together. They had now left the Avenue and were walking down a narrow lane bordered on both sides by trees, whose branches and leaves mingled and met over their heads, making a shady tunnel. Everard gazed up wonderingly at the different greens.

'So you are at boarding school,' Phyll said. 'Is it *torture*?'
Everard sighed. 'No. I like it.'

He thought it better to be honest. Boarding schools are supposed to be terrible places, but if your parents are terrible then they're a port in a storm. Everard had been sent away when he was four years old and he was used to it. He liked the routine and the noise and he'd made a few good friends, whom he often went to stay with in the holidays. When he'd first been told he had to spend a month with his father he'd gone into a panic and formed a plan to do something shameful and get sent away in disgrace.

Perhaps, now we look back, that is how it starts, but we can spend a long time searching for a seed, and a seed can't grow on its own: it needs water, light, a fertile habitat.

'I'd rather be *there*,' Everard said eventually. 'I don't like my father.'

Phyll lifted a single eyebrow. '*All* the *best* men are dead.'

They had now reached the entrance to the church. The graveyard spread out on both sides of the lane, with an old stone boundary wall broken by an arch. Phyll positioned herself under it and looked around. She could hear the chirping of small birds and somewhere in the distance a dog was barking. There were no people about. They were completely alone.

She smiled. 'So, you like climbing,' she said, 'I bet you can't climb *that*.'

She raised one arm straight, pointing to the ancient elm tree that grew out behind the arch, its thick, knotted branches stretching over the lane. It was not a tree that she'd ever tried to climb, which was why she suggested it. She waited as Everard looked it up and down, then he took a deep breath like he was about to dive into water. Without a word he marched quickly under the arch. Phyll followed him, wading through the hydrangea bushes to reach the base of the tree. But he had already pulled himself up onto the wall, and stood with his hands pressed flat on the tree's trunk. He was sizing up the lowest branches, then he wrapped his arms around one and kicked up his legs.

He made it look easy, which was annoying. Phyll thought about telling him to stop and come down. He was right under the wall and she was worried he'd fall. She watched as he stood up on the first branch and reached for another, and pulled himself higher. Phyll held her breath, not quite believing it. Any minute he was going to fall and break his neck. She imagined it happening, but she didn't tell him to stop. She walked back onto the road. There was still nobody about. No witnesses, she thought. She was tempted to run back home and leave him there, but then what? She stared up into the leaves until there were circles in front of her eyes. She was sweating so much her shirt had stuck to her shoulders. She wriggled them and danced from foot to foot, then she bent to inspect the dried blood on her leg. She tried to clean her wound by spitting and wiping, but that made it worse. Now she had the taste of blood in her mouth. She spat into the side of the road and stood up too fast and felt dizzy. The tree came towards her and the leaves were a dazzling green. It was so quiet she wondered if Everard had climbed back down.

'I can't even see you!' she called up. 'Everard? Where have you gone?'

He didn't answer. Phyll walked back into the churchyard and paced around the tree trunk. She listened for a rustle of leaves or a giggle, and the waiting made her throat twitch. She heard only the distant sound of horses' hooves, a fly buzzing around her. She lowered her eyes and folded her arms. What if he'd slipped back down when she wasn't looking, and now he was crouched behind a headstone, ready to jump out? She walked the length of the wall, turning her head from left to right, braced and ready to fight. How dare he trick me, she thought, and then she made a wider circle, weaving between the closest headstones. She had almost had enough. *Oh, he just vanished*, she said, in her head.

She walked back out onto the road.

She was about to say, 'I'm leaving,' when three leaves fluttered down. She reached out and caught them and laughed. 'Very good.'

But she still couldn't see him. Phyll turned a full circle, frustrated, and then noticed a gap in the opposite wall. It was slightly lower than on the church side, with uneven stones that stuck out to make footholds. She went over and started to climb. The tree on this side was covered in ivy with a few stunted branches lower down the trunk. She used them and pushed herself up, and once there were branches beneath her she felt better. Then, from somewhere far below, she heard a trio of voices. It was Major Hyde, with Ann Cecil and Mrs Williams, the woman who'd made such a fuss about the blood. The Major was bringing them to see his personal pew inside the church.

'Sark is my home now,' he was saying. 'I couldn't abide London: the sound of a car horn, the screech of brakes. I need the peace and quiet and I shall use my time to write.'

'Oh, to write, how marvellous,' said Mrs Williams. 'Yes, you must. I don't know any writers, but I do admire them . . . '

'And Sarah, *you* must take lessons from Paul,' Ann added. 'It is important to have hobbies, now more than ever.'

Phyll held her breath and watched them walk under the arch, then Mrs Williams stopped abruptly, turned round and touched her shoulder.

'I felt something.' She tilted her head back. 'The oddest thing – it felt like someone just tapped me on my shoulder.'

Ann walked back to join her and both women looked up and down the road. 'Perhaps a butterfly,' Ann suggested. 'I saw some gorgeous Red Admirals in the hedgerows.'

They walked on, and Phyll lifted her head and stared through the leaves. Everard had to be over there, hiding in the tree, but why couldn't she see him? She straddled a branch and lay flat on her stomach, feeling the thump-thump-thump of her heart against the bark.

The church door slammed and there was the crunch of footsteps along the path to the road. Phyll glimpsed the bustling shape of Marie de Carteret, John de Carteret's wife. She was humming to herself as she came out from under the arch, but then she let out a sharp yelp, as if she'd been stung by something.

Phyll smiled, because now she understood.

Perched high in the elm, Everard plucked another bud and rolled it between finger and thumb. He was enjoying this new game. He was like a bird looking down on everyone, aiming his missiles very carefully. His next victim was Sark's doctor, Percy Stanhope. The poor man almost lost his hat and stumbled back against the wall. Everard had to stifle a laugh. He was having so much fun he didn't notice the sky change colour, darkening by degrees, but after a while he wondered where Phyll had got to. He supposed it was his fault for not involving her. He was too used to playing on his own, getting lost in his own world. He sighed inwardly. He would find her tomorrow and say sorry. He supposed climbing a tree wasn't nearly as good as climbing a cliff.

Then he heard the creak of a branch, very close, and something struck his brow. He blinked and jerked forward, raising his hand to his head. It was a shock to see her just above him, staring down through the leaves. She had somehow climbed across from the other tree and now peered over the branch with her cheek resting on one hand. She was trying to look relaxed but her dark hair was plastered to her cheeks, which shone from the effort.

She eyed him proudly. 'Got you,' she said.

The relief rippled through him and broke into a laugh. He nodded. 'Yes, you got me.'

So. At last. Here it is.

The start of something secret and special, but possibly also terrible.

It really just depends on your viewpoint.

3

GUERNSEY EVENING PRESS (LATE EDITION)

Monday, 2 October 1933

'SARK MYSTERY: APPEAL FOR WITNESSES'

As some of our readers will be aware, the clothing of a man and a woman were recovered from the cliffs of Little Sark this weekend. As yet nobody has come forward to claim them, and to aid identification we can print this description of the items:

The woman wore a jacket and skirt of beige flecked tweed, the jacket had seven nickel buttons, one of which is missing. Both were a small size eight. The blouse was peach-coloured and tailored to the waist with a two tier, pleated collar. The shoes were dark brown leather and square-heeled with a single strap and gold buckle.

The gentleman's overcoat is dark navy blue. The label has been torn out. His suit was from Montague Burton and dark brown check. He wore a pin cotton cream-coloured shirt and brown brogue shoes, size nine. He would be around six foot tall.

The clothes were found on the cliffs close to Port Gorey, a spot that requires good climbing and a little care in its approach. Readers familiar with Sark will recognise this as the site of the old silver mines, and its rugged, remote beauty attracts day trippers during the summer.

Locals are naturally worried for the safety of this couple and John de Carteret, the Sark Chief Constable, would be glad to hear from anyone who might have any information.

IF YOU LOOK AT A MAP of Sark you will see the main thoroughfares run north to south and east to west, leaving the rest of the island as unlined as a child's palm. It is a fairly straight line south from St Peter's Church to La Coupée, then over to Little Sark, with the road only stopping at the Bungalow Hotel. After that, there's footpaths over the common to the cliffs and Port Gorey.

The guidebooks call Port Gorey 'delightful' and 'picturesque', which shows how little they know. It lies on a hunched and barren stretch of headland where no tree can ever grow. At the height of July there's a bracing walk to be had, we promise, but not today. Today, it feels like the end of the earth.

Everard Hyde, all grown up, has walked with two men along the path to the rocky ledge where he found the clothes. His dark hair is long and unruly and sticks to his cheeks. His eyes are red, his lips turning blue. In front of him the sea is petrol-dark, spitting up high walls of foam. The wind pushes him back but he leans into it, drawing his shoulders up. John de Carteret follows with his head bent, and he's brought along his assistant constable, Jim Remfrey, to help. John picks his deputies year by year. Jim didn't want the job but couldn't refuse without a medical certificate, and since Dr Stanhope had drunk himself to death there was nobody to ask.

There is a steep drop close to the zigzag path, where the cliff was dynamited to make a beach and slipway. Above it is the crumbling, ivy-clad ruin of a mine shaft. It was called Sark's Hope, which now seems unfortunate. A century ago Peter Le Pelley, the then Seigneur, invested his savings in silver mines. He brought over hundreds of men from England to dig the shafts and for a few years there were more people living on this shredded stretch of cliff than on the whole of Sark at any time before. It was quite the tourist attraction, but it seemed so improbable it was maybe always doomed.

The mine didn't yield a high-quality ore, and in 1839 Le Pelley was drowned on his way to Guernsey. His brother invested more money, but then the ceiling of Hope shaft collapsed, and ten men were trapped and drowned.

People talk about houses being haunted, as if ghosts need four walls and a roof. Cliffs can be haunted. Whole islands, too. John stands with his cap pulled low and his collar turned up. He is numb with cold. They have spent half the day scouring the common, which is mostly heather and gorse with a few tracks beaten through it. Closer to the road there's a half-derelict shed. They took shelter inside it when the rain picked up and found a bed of trampled ferns and a strip of blue material, frayed and torn along one edge. John has stored it in his pocket and checks it now and then.

He stares down the cliff. He doesn't want to think the worst, but everyone is saying the two people have drowned. Everyone drowns at Port Gorey, they tell him. Harry Dolbel could name three men in recent memory, including Phillip Carey, the husband of Elise, although nothing is known for certain about that and no body was ever found.

John stares out to sea and thinks about the currents and the tides. He doesn't understand why two people would come here in such awful weather and he wants to talk some more to Elise about it. He also wants to ask her about Everard, as she made such a sour face when his name was mentioned. John has a faint memory of Everard from before, and if he squints he can still see the boy in the man. Was this really the same lad who caused so much trouble?

Everard lifts his eyes, conscious of John watching him. 'Should I have left them? The clothes, I mean.'

John shakes his head. 'Of course not. You were right to bring them to me.'

Everard nods and then frowns. He looks much older when he frowns. 'Why did Phyll Carey have them? I saw her in the prison. She was holding them up . . . '

John turns his back to the wind. He remembers how Phyll kept touching the clothes, the odd look on her face. He wonders what has happened to make her so unhappy. 'She's the same size. That's all.'

Everard nods again and John studies his face. He wants to ask him why he's back now, after all this time, but he's never been good at small talk and the rain feels like pins on his face. He turns around, giving one last look to the rocks down below them, where at low tide there will be a beach.

'We'll have to come back tomorrow,' he sighs. 'I have no idea what this is about. If it were June or July, I'd say they'd been swimming . . . But now?' He shakes his head. 'Not a chance.'

As we've said, Sark in the summer is a lovely place, but come September the cool breeze turns to ice and bites. The hotels and guest houses close one after another, and even the part-timers dig out the dust covers and hurry for the harbour. Visitors often ask how we cope with the harsh winter months. Our standard reply is that we grow our fur, sharpen our claws and run about on all fours.

It guarantees they don't ask again.

There is a fine postcard of Port Gorey currently on sale at the post office: a watercolour sketch by an uncredited artist, showing the ruins of the silver mine with the cliffs beyond. Elise has it pinned to the noticeboard next to her counter, but tourists generally prefer the view of La Coupée or the one of an old woman milking a cow. The post office is closed, in any case, and Elise is back at the prison, which John never locks. She lifts up the woman's jacket and holds it under her nose. She can smell earth and gorse, salt and cheap soap. She closes her eyes and tries to block out the voices of the children reciting their times tables.

Sark's prison and schoolhouse were both paid for by the money from the silver mines. The old tombstones from St Magloire's chapel were used to build the walls of the new playground. Maybe that's why the Le Pelleys were cursed. Or maybe they weren't cursed, maybe they were just unlucky. It's useful to have the prison close to the school: Fred de Carteret regularly threatens rowdy pupils with a night's incarceration, and since the prison is said to be haunted, it has the desired effect. The story goes that a servant girl who stole from her mistress was held here for three days and became hysterical on hearing a phantom sobbing voice through the night.

The Reverend James Cachemaille told that story. He was the vicar during the era of the silver mines and wrote articles for *Guernsey Magazine* about 'wild and beautiful' Sark. He was less complimentary about the islanders, however, and some of his more colourful anecdotes are now endlessly repeated in those not-to-be-trusted guidebooks. It gives the impression that Sark's finest families are gullible clog-wearing simpletons who cast spells and charm warts.

What nonsense.

We don't wear clogs. But we do respect the natural world and its cycles. We put great faith in signs, too, and if an animal falls unwell there are certain rituals we adhere to.

A piece of pierced flint is often seen dangling from the key to stable doors as a safeguard, and it is a much noted fact that the chimneys of Sark cottages are still built with a witch's seat, just in case one wishes to take a rest, since you would not want her slipping down into your hearth.

By all means go ahead and laugh, but the good Reverend Cachemaille developed such a fear of the sea he would devise daily walks so he never came in sight of it. Of course, that was after he saw Peter Le Pelley drown, but our point is, it is very easy for a routine to become a ritual, and from there it is only a hop and a skip and you have a superstition. If it helps, where is the harm? When life is hard, we all need a few rules to tame the randomness of fate.

So please remember it is very bad luck to give anyone parsley although to steal it is perfectly fine, and if the first person you meet on leaving the house is a woman, always stand back and let her pass. Elise would argue that is basic good manners. Elise is not a witch – please don't use the word – but she has what some call 'the hidden knowledge'. It used to be said that such powers came from the Devil, and although it feels right to blame a man we think it was her mother, a lovely lady called Alice Tanquerel who died tragically young.

Elise can't explain how it happens, but she famously lost the power of her legs when Harry Dolbel was blown up at Delville Wood, and she also felt the bullet that brought John de Carteret home from France. Unfortunately she told everyone he was dead, and John's wife, Marie, drove herself insane with grief for three whole weeks before receiving notice of his return on a hospital ship. There was also a troubling incident when Elise warned a tourist of impending danger and the poor woman was so terrified she ran into the road and was trampled by a horse.

Let's move on. Elise leaves the prison and stands for a moment looking up and down the Avenue. She walks towards the still-closed shutters of the post office. It was previously the vicarage and its two rear walls date back to the 1500s, being at least a metre thick. Sark people are very proud of the thickness of their walls. It means a person might be murdered in their kitchen and no one outside would hear. Albert Pratt, Sark's postmaster for some thirty-five years, adapted a front window to make a fold-out counter, and he paved the courtyard and gave it a border of pink and red geraniums. Albert was terribly fond of geraniums, though it's a mystery why anyone would be. Elise was his assistant and took over when he had his stroke. She remains devoted to his widow Maud, who was for years the island midwife, and Maud loves Elise like a daughter. Elise now feels quite ambivalent about her actual mother due to the 'inherited curse of sadness and knowledge' as she cheerfully calls it.

Maud lives on the Rue de Sermon, in a little cottage that Albert was fixing up before he died. It was the shelves that killed him. They are, we all agree, excellent shelves. They cover an entire wall of the kitchen and are crowded with herbs, powders and syrups. There remains a great reliance of natural remedies on Sark as for long periods there was no doctor resident on the island, and then we had Dr Stanhope, and the less said the better. Maud can pluck any plant and tell you how to use it. She forgets other things, but that's the island's fault. After all, Sark is The Island Where Time Stands Still, and if nothing around you changes, then you expect that you, too, will stay the same.

But we all age and we all die, and some of us do it horribly.

Elise stomps inside the post office, pausing to check her reflection in the hall mirror. She is, as usual, appalled. She has two deep creases between her eyebrows and lines all round her mouth. She tells herself to frown less, but, really, what's the point? She started wearing glasses after her husband died, which was also when she cut her hair. The death of Phillip Carey was number three in 'Fatal Accidents around the Coast', in the *Guernsey Magazine* of 18 January 1920. It was reported that he was checking on his boat and was swept away during a storm, though there were rumours of suicide brought on by war neuroses.

Elise thinks again about the clothes in the prison. It is meant to be very unlucky to keep the clothes of a drowned person. It is said they will come back, inhabit the clothes and haunt you. Elise has kept all of her husband's clothes. She would quite like to see Phillip again. She has some words for him, in fact.

Three sharp knocks and she lunges for the door, pulling it open so fast the man behind it jumps back in fright. This is Peg Godfray, who offers a feeble shrug and gestures to the sodden, half-filled sack he's just abandoned on the doorstep. Sark's post is shipped over from Guernsey and often arrives in a questionable state, either dropped in puddles or trampled by livestock. Elise picks up the offending sack and marches into her office to sort it. With the counter pulled up there is just enough light to see the small desk on which sits a ledger and a set of scales. Behind that, running the length of the back wall, is an old ship's cabinet that Albert restored.

Elise rifles through the sack. It should be pointed out that her knack of knowing things before they happen was established before she took this job, but now, it helps. She reads a postcard to Nancy and Harry Dolbel from their son, makes a note of what must be a bill for Eric Drake at the art gallery, and rattles a packet of what's surely pills for Major Hyde. Before John went to Port Gorey, he asked her to look out for any odd-looking letters. Elise doesn't find anything like that, but she turns the sack inside out and shakes it over her desk to check. A cream-coloured envelope flutters free. Eyes narrowed, Elise bends to pick it up. The paper is stiff and expensive-looking, the address handwritten. 'Phyll Carey'. Not 'Phyllis Carey', not 'Miss Phyllis Carey'. Elise bristles and turns the envelope over, rubbing her thumbs along the edges. Then she walks to the door and holds it up to the light. Now, she thinks, now, now.

Everyone keeps asking her why Phyll has come back and Elise has no answer for them. Just yesterday Mr Toplis had leant right over the counter, shouting, 'Not a chap is it?'

Elise told him not to be ridiculous. Of course it wasn't – it couldn't be. Her daughter is far too clever for that. But it is hard to have a clever daughter if you don't feel clever yourself. Elise wonders about Everard Hyde. It's an odd coincidence that he is also back and it makes her uneasy. She is still holding on to the letter when she reaches into her oilskin for her keys. She has a lot of keys, likes the weight and feel of them, and there is a dainty, silver one for the top drawer of the old ship's cabinet. A special space for 'private matters'. Elise fits the key in the lock and tugs. The drawer only comes halfway out, snagging on a bundle of postcards and letters. She reaches a hand inside to push them down and then the drawer comes free.

Elise doesn't receive much post herself. Phillip was not a man for the written word, which was a shame considering how much time he spent away. Elise got over that particular disappointment, but what she still can't forgive is the lack of letters from her daughter. Phyll could scribble away for hours in her diary, fill pages to Miranda and that boy she hardly knew, but she barely ever bothered to drop a line to her dear mother.

Elise shuffles through the bundle. If she were to spread them out you could scan them and see how Phyll's handwriting has improved from something curved and clumsy to an even, elegant slant. She wrote to Everard Hyde every year, a mixture of postcards and letters. She sent the postcard of Port Gorey that Elise stocks, and a lovely view of Derrible Bay.

Phyll wanted to stay in touch. She probably still thinks she has.

Elise takes this new envelope, still sealed and stares at it. If she needed to be sure she could dig in the back of the drawer and pull out some of Everard's letters and compare the handwriting, but the kitchen door slams loudly and she jumps. She lays the envelope on the top of the bundle and shoves everything back in the drawer.

'Phyll, is that you?' She turns the key in the lock.

'Who else would it be?' Phyll appears in the doorway, her hair wet from the rain. 'I went to check on Maud. She's not there.'

Elise folds her arms. 'And did you see anyone else?'

Phyll glowers at her mother. 'No, of course not.'

She tramps up the stairs and Elise holds herself still and waits for the slam of the bedroom door. As it happens she presses a hand to the locked drawer. She lowers her eyes and glares at it.

Everard Hyde, she thinks to herself. Everard Hyde. Now there is a body she is not wanting back.

4

St Peter's Church

(First road to the right after passing through the Avenue.)

3 August 1923

ST PETER'S CHURCH WAS built in 1820 by two Peter Le Pelleys, father and son, in an attempt to civilise the Sarkese. An earlier guidebook called it 'ugly from all aspects', and we don't disagree. It has a few interesting plaques but we personally prefer a walk through the graveyard, which is as rich in wildflowers as it is history.

Phyll had steered Everard into the oldest section, by the crumbling, moss-covered wall, where the gravestones were sinking back into the earth. She was currently describing the death of Peter Le Pelley III, the man responsible for the silver mines, and had raised both hands dramatically,

'The boat smashed into the water and never resurfaced! The expedition *doomed*!'

She could deny it all she wanted later, but aged twelve, Phyllis Carey wanted to be just like her mother. She wanted to cut her hair short and issue dramatic pronouncements. In her diary she described herself as 'very ugly' and 'always staring'. She wasn't ugly but she did stare: she liked to focus all her attention on one person and predict what they would say, and since she conducted these experiments in secret she considered them highly successful. If she was an unusual child it didn't matter because there weren't many children her age for comparison. This was another reason why she read a lot of books, and she sometimes copied out long passages and claimed them as her own.

Phyll was also very interested in death, which we consider normal and healthy in children, especially in the years after the War, when death was close by all the time, like a next-door neighbour, though obviously not a friend.

They found a comfortable spot in the Baker family plot, where the cow parsley grew high and hid them. Phyll breathed in the sweetish scent and sprawled on her back with her hands cradling her head. Everard rolled onto his stomach and caught a ladybird in his hands, making a hole between his thumbs and first fingers so that Phyll could take a look.

Whatever people said about Everard Hyde afterwards, he was not a boy to torture small animals or pull the legs off insects. His school reports called him conscientious, thoughtful, even 'a team player'. Of course, they could have said that about any student, and perhaps that was the point. What Phyll wanted most of all was to stand out, what Everard wanted was to blend in.

She leaned right over, cupping her hands around his. Everard was shocked by how close she came, but he liked the sensation of her hair tickling his cheek. He didn't dare move in case she did, so he waited and waited, holding his breath. When she drew back he opened his hands and the ladybird fluttered off.

They watched it go and then he turned to look at her, 'So, is your father buried here?'

Phyll stretched out flat on her stomach, nestling her head on her arms. 'They never found his body.' She paused. 'No body, no grave . . . '

Everard lay down on his bent arms, copying her position. 'How . . . how did it happen?'

Phyll took a blade of grass and held it in front of her. 'It was the night of a terrible storm,' she began, which is how a lot of good stories begin.

Phyll would always say she remembered the night very clearly, even though she'd been asleep. The noise had woken her. The rain sounded like nails being flung hard and fast at the window. Or perhaps it was the wind. She thought the roof had been blown off the house, or the house had been blown away. She had jumped out of bed and run onto the landing, but the wind here was worse. It hit her full in the face and she worried the front door had been blown open, but as she hovered on the edge of the landing she saw very clearly, even in the dark, that the door was shut and the bolts drawn across. It made no sense. She did wonder if it was a dream, because time slipped and shrank, which happens in dreams. Then she heard noises downstairs – crashing and rattling – and she crept down one step to look. She had to press herself into the wall because the house seemed to rock. She felt for the next step, curling her toes, feeling for the skirting, but then it happened. A voice spoke into her ear. Very clear and close. 'Don't come downstairs!'

Phyll drew herself up and said it straight into Everard's ear. '*Don't come downstairs!*'

Everard shrunk back. 'No.'

Phyll nodded. She could almost feel it: the deathly cold breath in her ear. She watched his face, enjoying the horror.

'So what did you do?'

Phyll pursed her lips. 'Well, I didn't go downstairs – silly!' She lay back on her side. 'I ran back to my room and climbed into bed.' She hesitated. 'But *in the morning*. Oh! The house was a mess; the branch of a tree had smashed a hole in the roof and broken two of our shutters and a window. There was water and glass everywhere. My mother went down first and called up to me, and do you know what she said?' Phyll sat up a little, leaning close again. '*Don't come downstairs!*'

Everard looked shocked, then blinked fast. 'So wait, *she* said it?'

'Yes, but not before.' Phyll hesitated. '*Before* was a *premonition*. My mother has them all the time. Everyone said the storm had got in but . . . ' she lowered her voice. 'It wasn't rainwater . . . it was salty like the sea, and there were footprints. *Men's footprints.*'

Everard seemed to think about this for a minute. 'So . . . it was your father?'

Everard stared so hard at her she had to look away. Phyll turned onto her stomach and let her eyes drift out of focus. She thought back to the night of the storm, picturing herself hovering on the stairs in her nightdress. Maybe if she'd gone down she might have seen her father.

'You *could* have been dreaming,' Everard said, after a minute.

Phyll didn't look at him. 'You can't be that cold in a dream.'

But in all honesty, she couldn't be sure. The next morning she'd woken up in her mother's bed, snug and warm, with no memory of how she'd gotten there. Maybe she *had* been dreaming, or maybe she was muddling it with the morning after.

When she told her mother about the voice Elise had looked at her strangely and said it was perfectly possible that she had heard something. She didn't seem remotely surprised or worried, but then she was busy mopping up the water. It was later that she made Phyll show her the spot on the stairs, and she went to stand there herself, and closed her eyes and lifted her nose, like a hunting dog tracking a scent. It was unclear if Elise sensed something, but she shook her head and frowned as if she couldn't understand it. She then warned Phyll not to tell anyone about it.

'You are very young and people might say you are telling tales.'

Phyll promised her mother she wasn't, and Elise stroked her hair very tenderly after that and said not to worry, that she'd always believe her.

It was a good moment. Phyll didn't really miss her father since he'd never been there much before, but every so often she'd walk around the downstairs rooms with her fists balled and her eyes closed. She sometimes heard sounds after dark – footsteps or a door slam – but it was mostly Maud. Maud was always in their house because it used to be her house, and she knew every inch of it. One night, after Phyll had mentioned the noises, Maud had lifted up a loose floorboard on the landing and pulled out an old shoe. Burying shoes in houses was to safeguard the occupants against evil, Maud explained. Phyll thought that was interesting and developed her own rituals. She made a box of charms, filling it with things like her father's old shaving brush, a shilling from his jacket, three of the smoothest pebbles he'd ever given her. She also found a rusted watch that was broken at one o'clock, the time she imagined he'd died. Later came a shrivelled orange, a Roman coin and silver ring, all of them salvaged after storms. None of these items belonged to her father, but they'd come from the sea, which seemed important. She touched them nightly, counting down from ten.

The sun sank behind the trees, stretching out all the shadows around them. Phyll wondered what other stories she could tell Everard. She would ask Maud. Maud would be pleased to hear she'd made a new friend.

'Did you know,' she said, 'all graves have to be dug in the shape of a cross. If they aren't, the coffins get up and follow you.'

Everard had propped himself up on his elbows. 'Walking coffins?' He looked about.

Phyll rolled onto her back. 'The whole island is haunted. It is because there's nowhere for the dead to go.' She circled her hand in the air. 'They just wander round and round.' She waited a moment. 'There's a ghost in the prison and a ghost in the schoolyard and a ghost in the Seigneurie.' She was going to say that there was a ghost in Little Sark but she decided to save it for another day. She turned onto her side, resting her hand under her head. 'A few years ago some visitors even swore they heard *chanting*.'

Everard lifted his eyes. 'Chanting?'

Phyll nodded. 'There were monks here.' She sat up and pushed her palms together in front of her. '*Requiem dona ei, Domine . . .*'

Everard looked wonderfully serious and also started singing: '*Et Jesum, benedictum fructum ventris tui . . .*'

Neither of them had noticed Reverend Severy returning from his rounds. Louis Severy was in his fifties, a tall, stooping man with pillowy grey hair and a beak of a nose. He was all in black and sweating hard, exhausted from an afternoon with Nancy and Harry Dolbel. Harry had lost both of his legs in the War and spent all his time perched on a window seat in his kitchen, calling out abuse at passers-by. The sight of him there, with the stumps where his legs should be, made Severy feel weak. It was as if he lost the power in his own legs, or became ashamed of them. He mopped his face. During the War there had been something to pray for, but now, what was there? Harry had told him frankly. *Sorry, you have lost me, Vicar.* Severy shook his head. Surely no one was lost. He took a deep breath in and looked about.

The dying sun fell in patches through the trees, creating arrows of light that fell across the gravestones. The air was still and warm, and everything was quiet. Had the world ever felt this quiet? Severy clasped his hands behind his back and stood in a kind of trance. He realised he could hear singing. Soft voices floating through the air. He turned slowly, head cocked. It wasn't coming from inside the church, but from over the fields. It was Latin, he was sure, and the sound was both distant and close. He moved through the grass, walking in a slow, deliberate fashion, putting one foot in front of the other. He felt his whole body pulse, it was as if even the ground had a heartbeat. The grass grew thicker and higher and soon his fingers skimmed foxgloves, but he carried on until he reached the boundary wall. Here the air was cooler and he bowed his head and laid a hand flat to his chest, feeling his heart jump. The singing had stopped, though, and now he only heard the chatter of small birds. Was that all he had heard? He took two slow breaths and peered into the next field where a few sheep grazed. There was nothing. There was no one.

Sighing, Severy turned and started back to the church, but as he looked up he saw two shadows, two figures, standing straight. His legs nearly gave out under him and he lifted a hand, as though to ward them off. Then he realised they were children. Only children. The sun had stretched their shadows. His eyes now struggled with the depth of focus, the splintering of sunlight through the leaves.

'Oh!' He let out a startled laugh. 'You children! Oh! What *was* that noise? Did you hear it?'

Everard was too stunned to speak. 'H-hallo, Reverend. Excuse me, what noise?' His words came out in a rush and he turned to Phyll, whose eyes were glazed and fixed.

Severy blinked anxiously and looked at Phyll, a paralysed smile on his face. 'Someone was singing in Latin.'

Phyll firmly shook her head. 'No, we would have heard.' Her voice was deep and serious. She turned towards Everard. 'I didn't hear anything, did you? I'm not sure I know Latin.'

Everard concentrated hard and said, 'Sorry, no. I also didn't hear a thing.'

5

JERSEY POST

Wednesday, 4 October 1933

'SARK MYSTERY: INVESTIGATION OPENS IN GUERNSEY'

Nobody has yet come forward to claim the clothes found on the cliffs of Little Sark this weekend, and nobody has been reported missing. A search continues of the surrounding coastline and the clothes have been transferred to Guernsey, where Chief Inspector James Langmead of the Guernsey Police has opened an investigation.

As all members of Sark's population have been accounted for, we must presume that the clothes belong to visitors. It is most likely that they came from Guernsey, but whether they were local to Guernsey or had arrived at an earlier date from England remains to be seen.

Since nobody has been reported missing from the regular passenger boats, the police speculate that they used a private charter. There are a number of moorings and landing points around the coast aside from Creux harbour, so it is possible they came and went from another part of the island.

Any persons with any information regarding this case are asked to make themselves known to the Island Authorities.

PROTECTED BY STEEP CLIFFS ON ALL SIDES, Sark likes to look impregnable, but a boat trip round the island will show you otherwise. There is a good landing point at L'Eperquerie in the north, and decent moorings on the eastern side, at Dixcart and Derrible Bays.

When Sark was first popular with day trippers they'd disembark at Havre Gosselin on the western cliffs. Here, they'd have to climb a ladder that extends out from the rock, and scramble the rest of the way using a rope. All part of the thrill, we are sure. Young men came to hunt and fish, which may have been a euphemism. The island's taverns were always open, even on the sabbath, and so Sark developed a reputation for paganism and debauchery – we promise they aren't the same. There's a story about a Guernseyman who came hunting, but despite being an excellent shot and seeing a great number of wild ducks, failed to fell a single bird during his first visit. He consulted a wise man who told him it was the work of witches. He thus armed himself with silver bullets, since silver is the one material known to be effective against witches, and it worked because he managed to shoot one bird just here, on these cliffs, and sent it spiralling into the bay. Unfortunately he never found the body. Perhaps he imagined it, perhaps he was drunk, but on the return boat to Guernsey he noticed a young woman with a bandaged hand giving him thoroughly filthy looks. He tried to speak with her but she turned her head away. He later learned this young woman had a 'reputation' and thus deduced that she was the bird he had shot, and that she was, naturally, a witch.

That's some stunning male logic: it is easier to believe that a woman is a witch than to accept she doesn't care for you.

Edie de Carteret, being twelve years old, would like very much to fly. She flaps her arms and imagines what it would be like to swoop over the headland. It's a bright afternoon: there has at last been a break in the rain, and the sky is pearly white with small clouds rippling over it. Edie flutters as far as the Cecils' studio, a simple wooden cabin set back from the path. In summer it's an ideal spot: the wide windows let in light and the sea, and the sun dances off the floorboards. But Paul made the mistake of cutting back all the trees so that now, in October, it feels bleak and exposed.

Edie presses her imaginary beak to one of the windows and spies Phyll Carey on her knees, sifting through the contents of an old tea chest. Seen in profile Phyll has an interesting, angular face, the kind an artist might like to paint. She's still wearing the yellow dress but a sensible blue cardigan covers it. Edie watches for a minute, then raps hard on the window and makes Phyll jump.

Phyll stands up quickly and slams the trunk shut. She looks tired, a little furtive, like a criminal caught in the act. We suppose she has her reasons. After she typed up a very detailed description of the clothes, she added a short note to the editor of the *Press*, introducing herself as a 'journalist visiting family' and offering to send further updates. She signed off as 'P. Carey' so they'll assume she is a man.

For those interested, Phyll was only ever a very lowly publishing assistant, typing up other people's words. She won't yet discuss what happened, but she had dreamt about going to England for so long it's hard to admit what a failure it was. Later, she might say that she couldn't adjust to the grey streets teeming with people, or the tall buildings that blocked out the sky, or she will moan about the deadening routine of the office, or the fussy little man in charge of it. In time she will find her excuses, but for now her eyes roam over the studio and she lets out a wistful sigh. She remembers when Miranda gave her the dress she now wears, bundling it into her arms, and she can picture Paul stretched out on the daybed, kicking out his long legs.

He would curl up one side of his mouth and call them 'my da-arling girls'. He was always kind. He told Phyll she had the brains to do anything. She screws her eyes shut. It feels like a lifetime ago.

'Here you are!' Edie swings through the door. 'I have been worried about you!' She puffs out her cheeks and can't remember why, and then her eyes widen. 'Oh yes! You touched those clothes.' She curls up her fingers. 'What if they are *cursed*?'

Phyll shakes her head, half-sighs. 'Oh Edie, really?'

'Yes!' Edie paces the length of the studio, enjoying how her new shoes sound on the painted floorboards. She whips a hand round in a flourish. 'They might have belonged to witches.'

'Witches?'

'Yes!' Edie clasps her hands behind her back, nodding wisely. 'Witches shapeshift, *as I am sure you know*.'

Phyll rolls her eyes and folds her arms. She does indeed know. She knows all the stories. 'But . . . if witches shapeshift . . . they won't *need* clothes.'

An excellent point and Edie swings around with her nose in the air. She can tell by Phyll's face that she is not taking this seriously. She looks her slowly up and down. '*Or* they could just do what *you* do and take Miranda Cecil's clothes.'

Touché. Phyll feels the colour rise in her cheeks. She would like to make it clear she doesn't *take* Miranda's clothes. Miranda gives her the things she's grown out of or grown tired of, so it was a pattern in their friendship that repeated over years. It probably won't happen ever again, but Phyll's not ready to admit that. She turns away, reminding herself how much she hates children. Elise was once very keen for her daughter to become a teacher, and Phyll was made to babysit half the island children. Just between us, it's a miracle they all survived. Marie de Carteret found Edie tied to a tree in Dixcart Valley and had strong words with Elise on the subject.

But Edie enjoyed the experience and thinks Phyll secretly adores her and is playing hard to get. She comes to a halt by the shelves and starts picking up odd bits of bric-a-brac and putting them back, like someone in a shop who can't decide what to buy. She examines first a seashell, then some sea glass, then an empty bottle. She wanders over to the canvases stacked in the corner. There's a painting of Miranda: fair-skinned and fair-haired with wide, blue eyes. She remains a great beauty.

Edie pivots back, eyes narrowed. 'So, what are *you* doing here?'

Phyll is standing poker-straight. 'I could ask *you* the same question.'

It is an interesting stand-off and since they are both very stubborn we might be here for some time. Thankfully there's a knock at the door and Edie lunges to answer it.

'You!' she cries. 'You were following me, I knew it!'

Small George stands, blinking on the doorstep. He wasn't following Edie, for heaven's sake. He was continuing his reconnaissance of the cliffs heading north from Port Gorey, following the tides and currents indicated in his dad's *Channel Islands Pilot*. Small George thinks the missing persons have drowned and so hopes to find a dead body. He wants to find a dead body in the way only someone who has never found a dead body could possibly want such a thing.

He envisages a corpse with skin as pale and cold as marble. He'd prefer to find the woman, though obviously the man would do. This will be better than all the adventure stories in his *Boy's Own Paper*, which are frankly utter tosh.

But as Small George scoured the cliffs for a dead body he happened across a live one. Standing behind him is a tall woman with white hair falling from a once-neat bun. She stands with her hands clasped in front of her, a slight smile on her flushed face, hazel eyes wide and alert. Although she is old she stands very straight, as if to attention, and almost skips into the studio. This is Maud, of course. Everyone knows Maud. She is the woman who knitted the cardigan Phyll wears, and who put Phyll to bed most nights of her childhood, and who taught her the Latin names of every Sark plant. She also taught her how to stew limpets, which was pointless as they are disgusting. Don't worry, she has other recipes. Maud is an excellent cook, much better than Elise, who boils everything to death.

Maud takes a regal turn about the studio, her grey dress swishing at her ankles. 'So this is where you got to!'

It's unclear who she means and Small George looks proportionally embarrassed. He mumbles that he found Maud at Port és Saies without a coat. Maud makes a tutting sound and flaps a hand. She doesn't need a coat, she has an excellent constitution and is known to walk for miles each day. But her fingers are red with cold and she flexes and presses them together.

'I wanted to see you,' she turns to Phyll, 'to tell you . . .' Her eyes skitter across every surface. She wanted to say something about coats, but now she's forgotten. She frowns. It keeps happening and the only thing she remembers is how people look at her afterwards. They stare at her expectantly and she has to arrange her face and summon something else, like a performer pulling a rabbit out of a hat, which she saw when Chapman's Circus visited Guernsey. She had wanted her ears pierced after that. She scans the room and tries to jog her memory – objects often help – and moves closer to the shelves by the window. There is a black-and-white photograph of Paul and Ann on their bicycles.

'The man,' she says, 'was very *rude*.'

For a second Phyll thinks she means Paul, but then Small George, who is standing rigid, almost shouts, 'The missing man and woman! Maud says she saw them. They were walking over La Coupée. They were going to Little Sark!'

George has turned so red his freckles have vanished.

Phyll folds her arms and looks first at him, and then at Maud. 'Maud, is this true? You saw the missing man and woman?'

Maud raises a hand and pats her hair self-consciously. 'Do I look awful? My hair . . . is it very untidy? I suppose it's the wind . . . '

'It makes sense!' Small George blurts. He looks at Edie. 'Your dad, I mean Chief Constable de Carteret, he found a bed . . . Well, not a bed . . . there's that old shed on the common at Port Gorey. Jim, as in Deputy Constable Remfrey, said someone had laid ferns and furze on the floor and it was all trampled on, so the man and woman must've slept *there*.'

Edie is outraged that George knew this before her.

'How awful,' Phyll says. 'They slept in that shed?'

Small George nods. 'And they went to wash in the morning and got swept away on the beach.'

Maud is still trying to fix her hair. 'No, Albert was soaked through, but he came back.'

Small George snaps his head round. 'What?'

Phyll resists the urge to cover her mouth with her hand. She takes a step between George and Maud and thinks very carefully about what to say next. Albert has been dead for twenty-odd years so he can't have been anywhere recently.

It is Edie who punctures the silence. She gasps theatrically and lifts herself up onto her toes. 'Albert? Your husband, Albert? But he's *dead*. Did you see his ghost?'

Maud turns and looks down at Edie, whose small eyes bulge.

'Did he look *dead*?'

Phyll grabs Edie by the elbow and pulls her aside. 'Stop it,' she hisses. 'Maud gets confused sometimes . . . she's *old*.'

Edie makes a huffing noise. 'Like my parents, you mean. My parents are *prehistoric*.'

Phyll grits her teeth. 'No, it is not like that.' But she doesn't have the patience to explain what it *is* like, and she goes back to Maud, who is pressing her knuckles to her mouth.

She lays a hand on Maud's shoulder and tells her not to worry, but she wonders if they should. It is perfectly possible that Maud saw the missing couple, since Maud is forever roaming about the island and stopping people to talk to them. Now she is older, tourists have less patience with her.

Phyll glances up at Edie. 'We should probably go and tell your dad.'

Edie nods happily. There is nothing better than bothering her father.

Phyll ushers everyone to the door and then hesitates at the threshold, casting a final look about the studio. She can't get over how desolate it feels, just a husk of a thing, really. Or maybe that's her.

Outside the sky is churned up like murky water, rippling with grey clouds now threatening rain. It feels as if the afternoon has ended before it began. Phyll locks the studio door and stands for a moment with her back to the others. She moves as if to put the key in the pocket of her dress, but first she removes a photograph from the pocket of her cardigan. She quickly transfers it, with the key, to her dress and then turns and slips off the cardigan to give to Maud. Maud shakes her head but Phyll insists.

As they head towards the road Edie hangs back, eyeing Phyll furtively. '*You're* sad,' she says. For a self-absorbed child she's annoyingly perceptive. 'Is it because you want to be in France with the Cecils?'

Phyll ducks her head so that her hair falls over her face. She lets out a long sigh. Every summer Paul and Ann would say, wouldn't it be lovely if Phyll came and joined them, and they'd talk about how nice it would be for Miranda to have company and they'd describe all the things they would see and the fun they would have. But it was always too complicated, or the timings were wrong or their lodgings too small.

'I was never going to go,' Phyll admits.

Her mother had always said as much, dismissed it as make-believe. She had warned Phyll not to fixate on the kind of people who couldn't earn a wage between them. No, Elise wanted her daughter to direct her energies into something respectable and reliable, etcetera, etcetera.

A mother's advice is always right, especially when it's not taken, which mostly it isn't.

'Well, *I* should like to go away with them.' Edie makes a small pirouette on the path. 'But at least now you are back you can see this Everard Hyde person.' She stops spinning. 'My dad says he *knows* you.'

She says that last bit slowly, eyes fixed on Phyll, but Phyll pretends to be distracted by the wind. It's whipping up the hem of her dress and she shoves her hands in her pockets and presses them flat to her thighs. But she's really just checking the photograph is there. Only later, when she is alone in her bedroom, will she take it out and look at it again. She will hold it in both her hands, up close to her face, and study it like a relic, something precious and long lost. She found it in the trunk along with Paul's sketches. She took it out before Edie noticed. Now she has it, she will keep it.

It's not even a good photograph, as Paul would tell you. It's over-exposed because the sun was too bright and bounced off the sand, and the three children are off-centre, too cramped together. Phyll and Everard are squatting in swimsuits, Miranda standing behind them, holding out her skirt as if to curtsy. Everard scrunches up his eyes because he's blinded by the sun, and Phyll leans so close to him their forearms blend together.

Phyll can't remember what they had been talking about. She wishes she could. She turns and looks at Edie. 'We played together one summer,' she says simply, 'and I wouldn't know him now if I saw him. Not at all.'

6

Derrible Bay

(From Creux harbour take the first path to the left of the road, and proceed across the common until a gate is reached.)

6 August 1923

EVERYONE THINKS DERRIBLE IS A MISPRINT, that it should read: *terrible*. Terrible Bay! What an idea. It's actually from the French, meaning a funnel-shaped earth fall, a natural shaft or chimney cut into the rock. The beach itself is one of Sark's finest, though the path over the cliffs is very steep and the lower sections only negotiated by means of iron rings driven into the rock. It was for this reason that Major Hyde suggested they take his boat.

Look closely at that photograph Phyll has: Everard isn't squinting because of the sun, but tilting his head and turning towards her. Miranda is the only one posing for the camera. She stands with her shoulders back and a smile ready. But they aren't the only people in the frame. In the distance behind Miranda, there is a woman in a long white dress. It has a square-neckline and full sleeves and she looks almost Victorian. Her dark hair hangs in a single braid and her hat is tilted so we can't see her whole face. This is Sarah Williams, and she is not paying attention to the children, but turning to talk to Everard's father, the Major, who isn't even aware he's in the picture.

It was one of those days when the sky was so bright they couldn't even look at it and the sea sparkled like it had been cut from diamonds. Paul Cecil was excited as he had a new Kodak camera and spent the whole boat ride peering through the viewfinder and talking about 'glorious effects'.

Phyll hadn't been allowed on the boat. The Major had looked appalled when she turned up on the quayside and he'd had to tell her no, there simply wasn't room. Phyll was careful not to act upset and Ann Cecil suggested they meet for lunch later.

'Mule is bringing a picnic to Derrible,' she said. 'You can meet her halfway.'

Mule was Muriel Toplis, the youngest daughter of William Toplis, and Ann's great friend. She was in her thirties and still lived with her parents. In his diaries Paul described her as 'an honest and unspoilt phenomenon' and joked that if being the daughter of William Toplis hadn't put her off men, then Sark's male islanders would finish the job.

Phyll met her at eleven o'clock and helped her carry food down, so they were waiting when the boat came into the bay. Everard was the first into the water, wading to the shoreline holding his towel above his head, and Phyll, who was already in her swimsuit, ran to meet him. She laughed when he took off his shirt because she still didn't understand how he could be so pale. It was as if the sun had never touched him. She grabbed his arm and held it to hers.

'Look at that! You are like something straight from Dickens!'

Phyll said it loudly because she wanted everyone to hear. She had only read *Oliver Twist* but she was about to start *David Copperfield*, and if they'd asked she might have told them so. After Major Hyde had humiliated her about the boat trip she had strolled up the cliff, slipped through the French windows of Beau Regard and taken his own copy. Everyone remembered when the Major had his crates of books delivered to the harbour: they were all gilt-edged and bound in red leather, bought by the yard from Whiteley's. Phyll didn't think he'd miss one. She also didn't care.

She ran with Everard along the first stretch of sand, tugging his arm. That's when Paul stopped them.

'A photograph!' he said. 'Just one!'

They crouched for a second and Miranda stood behind them, and Mrs Williams, who had come on the boat and was feeling slightly queasy, didn't realise she'd be in the picture. She turned to the Major and said, 'It is marvellous to see children happy.'

They were happy. Phyll was trying to pull Everard back into the water. At first he leaned away, resisting, but then he dived down and Phyll shrieked and fell backwards. He swam fast and she chased him, hands snapping at his ankles. He spun around and splashed her and she ducked under, and it went on like that for quite a time. They were making a lot of noise but the adults didn't notice. Miranda liked her new dress and so stayed on the beach, dancing over small waves. She was pretending to be a dancer at Covent Garden, and after executing two perfect *petit jetées* Paul clapped and tossed her an imaginary bouquet. The French woman from the tea party was also there. Her name was Sylvie Price and she had offered to give Miranda lessons in exchange for paintings lessons with Paul. She was younger than the other women and had short bobbed hair and a wide lip-sticked mouth. She wore a sleeveless muslin dress and Paul posed her against the cliffs and said she looked 'wonderfully modern' against the backdrop of ancient shapes.

Ann and Mule stayed close to the rocks in the shade of the cliff and started to arrange the picnic. In addition to pâté, bread and apples, Ann had brought a basket of strawberries picked fresh that day, but everyone was the most delighted with the Major's contribution: a meat pie made by his housekeeper Nancy Dolbel and two bottles of champagne that he floated off the side of his boat to keep cool.

Everard found it surprising that people liked his father. 'I'm really sorry you couldn't come on the boat,' he said.

Phyll floated on her back and smiled at the sky. 'Don't worry, at lunch I will list Sark's worst boating accidents and let's see if I can make that Mrs Williams faint again!'

The tide went out quickly and Paul walked about, exploring the beach. He laid his arm around Sylvie's waist and guided her into the next cove, waving and smiling at Ann as he went. 'I want to show Sylvie the Creux,' he called out. 'And the other entrance is easier.'

Phyll lay back on a sun-warmed rock and draped an arm over her eyes. 'When it's very low tide I could take you to some better caves,' she said. 'They are called the Boutiques, because smugglers stored treasure there.'

Everard climbed up to sit beside her and they waited as Miranda jumped over the rocks to join them. She moved lightly, as if her legs had springs, then pivoted back to wave at her father. Paul raised a hand as he guided Sylvie round the side of the cliff. Miranda watched them go then made her way over to Everard.

'What's your mother like?' she asked.

Everard opened his eyes and the sun made him frown. 'She's beautiful . . . and American. My grandparents live in a place called Boston.'

Phyll turned her head. 'You've *been* to America?'

Everard rested his elbows on his knees, making a cradle for his head. 'Yes. One day I might go to live there. I mean, after school and everything.'

Miranda was balancing on one leg. She raised her arms over her head and smiled brightly, a smile she had been practising in the mirror for some time. 'You'll get away sooner than us,' she told him. 'It's easier for boys.'

All three children turned then and looked back at the beach. The Major was walking beside Mrs Williams, but she had said, 'Please call me Sarah,' so we shall. They were talking about the Army and the War and who they knew had died and where. In some ways it made things easy, to have these common subjects. Sarah and Cyril Williams had come to Sark for their honeymoon in 1913. Cyril was declared missing in 1916, and missing, presumed dead a year later. His personal effects had been lost but Sarah found some consolation in revisiting the places they had been to together.

'So many died,' she sighed. 'I still can't fathom it.'

Everyone said that as more time passed she'd feel better, but it was a wheel turning constantly at the back of her mind. She asked herself the same question: where had they gone? She had read books about life after death, and Cyril's mother had gone to meetings with a medium. Heaven was just another country, she said, and they had to find a new way to make contact. Sarah didn't like to think of Cyril being far away, she preferred to imagine him here. The dead are all still with us, she'd think, and she'd often see his face in the street.

'Wouldn't it be lovely if it was an island like this, a place where all our boys could be together?'

Hyde stopped walking and turned to study her profile. He found it a thoroughly odd idea, but he remembered sections from the *Odyssey*, one of the few books he'd read as a lad. 'You mean like an underworld?'

They'd walked round the cliff and now stood in front of the mouth of the cave. The Major stepped inside and let his eyes adjust to the darkness. The temperature dropped, which was quite a relief, and the sounds from the beach – the turning of the sea on the shore – were at a distance. Hyde took off his hat and smoothed down his hair. The ceiling of the cave was very high in this part and Sarah turned her head slowly, staring at the sharply jagged planes of rock. She looked very appealing in shadow, with her eyes showing up dark in her pale face. They moved forward, but it was hard to find an even footing as the floor of the cave was a mix of shingle and larger, irregular stones.

Sarah complained about her shoes but the Major took her by the elbow. 'You really must see this,' he insisted.

A short way ahead of them was a clear, bright shaft of light, like a spotlight on a stage. The roof of the cave had collapsed, giving way to a perfect disc of bright blue sky.

Hyde pointed. 'Do you see it?'

Sarah cried out, 'Oh yes!'

Their voices echoed off the rocks, and they walked towards it.

'You know,' Hyde said. 'When Odysseus went into the underworld he saw the ghost of his mother, but when he tried to embrace her, she slipped from his grasp.'

Sarah turned suddenly and almost lost her footing, but he reached out with both his arms and steadied her. They smiled at each other, then Sarah stepped in front of him, feeling her way along the sharp-edged rocks. There was enough light to guide them and soon there was a stretch of flat sand. Sarah walked under the light and looked up, staring directly up towards open sky.

'How incredible! Goodness!'

Her white dress took up all the light, as if it were phosphorescent. Hyde wanted to stand beside her but the sun was too dazzling and bright. He pulled out his handkerchief, blotting his face. 'You know, I saw my brother the night he died . . . '

'Really?' Sarah had turned to look at him but he kept his head down.

'I was in hospital. I had caught my leg on some barbed wire and the damned thing had become infected.' He paused. 'I had a very high fever, and Evelyn came to my bedside. I was delirious and I asked him what he was doing and I thought it meant that I was dying.'

'But you weren't?'

'No.' Hyde ran a hand through his hair and felt the sweat trickle down his back. He could smell iodine and disinfectant. Hospital smells. Evelyn was there, watching over him. He straightened up. 'No, I wasn't dying, but he had. He was sniped at close range while helping to repair some wire.

He . . . he shouldn't have gone out. It was a full moon, and he should have known. He was killed at one o'clock. One of the nurses said someone had come and told me the news and so I must have dreamed my brother there. Yet there is still a part of me that wonders . . . the timing of it all, how both of us were caught by wire . . . '

Paul had walked out of the shadows with Sylvie and was struck by how wonderfully tragic Earnest Hyde now appeared. Even Sylvie was transfixed. Hyde loosened his collar and was inspecting the sloping walls of the cave.

'I mean, what are the chances?' he muttered. 'I had been *caught* on wire and he was killed by it.'

There was an uneasy silence, and when Hyde glanced back he was surprised to find everyone staring at him. He stood very straight, clasping his hands behind his back. There was something strange about this cave, about the stillness of the air. It seemed to hold him in place. He was about to say something else when two dark shapes darted in from the side, and Sylvie and Sarah both turned and gasped.

It was only Everard and Phyll, climbing over the boulders from the narrowest entrance. Everard straightened up and folded his arms over his chest, tucking his hands into his armpits. He shivered a little, embarrassed by how everyone looked at him, but Phyll just grinned. 'It's lunchtime,' she said. '*Nearly* one o'clock. Mrs Cecil says to come.'

7

THE TIMES

Thursday, 5 October 1933

'SMALL ISLAND MYSTERY STILL UNSOLVED – MISSING PERSONS OR MURDER?'

An astonishing mystery has lately unfolded on the quiet Channel Island of Sark. Last weekend two sets of clothes belonging to a man and woman were found on the southern cliffs, but so far no individual has come forward and claimed them, nor have any islanders been reported missing. Sark's part-time police force has sought the help of neighbouring islands but are still no closer to solving the riddle.

The man's suit bore the Montague Burton Ltd label but, to add to the intrigue, all other labels had been purposefully torn out. The manager of Montague Burton in Guernsey sold a suit to an English gentleman last week, but after viewing the discarded clothes was unable to confirm if it had been purchased at the Guernsey branch.

It is likely that the couple slept in a derelict shed whilst on Little Sark, as some broken ferns were found arranged on the ground. A silver button that matches those on the woman's jacket has also been found, along with a shred of blue material that might have come off a petticoat.

A search of Sark's extensive caves and bays has borne no fruit, but one local woman has come forward to say she saw a man and woman last Saturday. They were talked to on La Coupée, a narrow bridge of rock that is one of the finest tourist sights of the island. The man was of sturdy build and taller than the lady, but little more is known.

The Police are still appealing for information to help solve this mystery but with each passing day the hope of finding these people alive seems to fade.

IF SARK WERE AN ANIMAL then La Coupée would be its spine: a ridge of mineral vein that extends down the body of the beast, narrowing to a knife-like bridge that divides and unites the two unequal halves. Over time, the wind and sea will do their work and Little Sark will be set free, but for now day trippers flock to see La Coupée, and marvel at how it exists. But not everyone who comes this far will dare venture across. It is only three feet wide and rises some 300 feet from the sea. On the eastern side is a lethal drop to knife-edge rocks and a cave, while on the western edge there's several million steps to Grande Grève.

On any day a stranger should take care: it slopes down and then there is a sharp climb up, and before railings were installed in 1900, people often crawled over on all fours during high winds. If the weather is bad Little Sark is best ignored – and certainly no one should try to cross at night.

Furthermore, it's said La Coupée is haunted, although there remains much discussion as to what or who by. The one thing we all agree on is the scream. It is only heard on stormy days: an agonising shriek that starts from high up and sweeps down by degrees to the sea. It was noted by an islander in the winter of 1731, who believed he was hearing someone fall to his death. The next day a man really did fall. This is what we call an '*avertissement*', a warning of a tragedy still to come. A ghost from the future, if you will.

It is wrong to think of ghosts as part of the past, as their return shapes the present and future. Maud believes she saw the missing man and woman on La Coupée, but it is possible she saw another young couple at a different time. Time is compressed, like air in a cave, which is by the way the explanation for that fearful sound. It is the waves rushing into the cave deep under the cliff on the eastern side. It forces out the air with such speed that it screams. You hear it once and then it repeats, a terrible echo.

The young woman crossing now stops several times to lean out over the railings. She stares down the cliffs towards the sandy beach of Grande Grève, then she backs up and peers over the eastern edge. It's a bitter-cold day, so we are pleased that Phyll has opted for sensible trousers and a tweed coat, even if the coat is old and has lost several buttons, so she must grip it at the collar. The mail bag slung over her shoulder looks empty, but then the people who live on Little Sark are not the kind to get post.

Little Sark is generally considered a place beyond the pale. People from the main island tend to shake their heads and say it is just *too* quiet, *too* empty, and *too* strange. But Phyll has come here for a reason. She is tracing the last known route of the missing couple. She will thus cross La Coupée and follow the road as far as the Bungalow Hotel, then pace over the common and see this derelict shed. If she happens to meet anyone on the road, she will be ready. She has no ulterior motives, she is sure.

As Phyll goes into battle with the wind, Major Hyde is warm in his drawing room in Beau Regard. The house remains a solitary white beacon on the cliffs, although the French windows that Phyll once slipped through have been reglazed with smaller panes, and the Major's desk has been moved in front of them so they can't be opened. There is also a thick layer of dust on the mantelpiece. Nancy Dolbel is still his housekeeper, but there are certain things she's not allowed to clean.

The Major has a guest. John de Carteret has taken a large sherry and settled himself in the other armchair beside the unlit hearth. He feels he has earned this drink. Having completed his tour of all the island homes, he has acquired a fennel paste for a bad tooth and a fresh octopus for supper, but no further information about the missing couple. Phyll did come and report to him what Maud said, but Maud is now unsure.

The Major picks up some newspaper and starts shredding and twisting it, making ready for a fire. He pauses over a headline, shaking his head. 'No common sense, this government!' Major Hyde is a great admirer of Sir Oswald Mosley, as are all the fashionable people just now. He can talk for hours about British foreign policy, but we'd rather he didn't, so let's move on.

'You know, it could be suicide,' he looks over at John. 'Times are hard.'

John hasn't ruled it out, but he's read enough reports of suicide to know that people wanting to drown themselves leave their clothes on, to add weight. He thinks there have been more suicides in the last few years, but maybe he's looked for them. He picks up a loose page and reads six lines on the 'Sark Island Mystery'. Until now, Sark has never made the headlines ('Man Falls off Bar stool: Breaks Thumb' doesn't count).

John feels a creeping dread, envisaging hordes of journalists trampling his crime scene, and he doesn't yet know if it *is* a crime scene. A few broken ferns in an old shed, a button and a scrap of fabric is hardly conclusive.

He takes a long sip of his sherry and lets the sweetness sit on his lips. 'We did wonder if they came as far as the Bungalow and found that it was closed . . . '

The Major almost drains his glass. 'Hardly my fault.'

Hyde bought the Bungalow Hotel just after moving to Little Sark. It has seven double bedrooms and is advertised as 'a haven for honeymooners', but is only open for half of the year. Hyde will soon be leaving for Alassio, where he has another house and like-minded friends. He has a special relationship with Italy, harking back to a childhood where the sun always shone. Looking back on events, or perhaps looking down, as if peering through water. The ripples cause confusion. He peers into his glass.

'I still can't understand why Everard didn't bring the clothes to me.'

John frowns. 'He did the right thing. He wanted to reach me before the light was gone, in case we could get a boat out.'

Hyde seizes on the words with a kind of greed. 'I have a boat. I could have organised a search.'

Eighteen years in service, need he remind anyone of that. Earnest Hyde was the life and soul of his regiment, a man who would not send any of his men out to do anything he himself would not do. If you see anything suspicious, give me a nudge. Always report to the officer in charge. His men said he had a boy's heart and a lion's courage, or maybe that was the brother who died at Ypres. We would need to check Hyde's memoir, *The War as I Saw It*, which took seven years to write and was eventually published privately and pressed on unsuspecting friends. John scans the mantelpiece, noting the photographs of young men, tall and haughty in their peaked caps and uniforms. Any one of them might be a younger version of Major Hyde, but it's more likely the brother who was mentioned in Dispatches.

Hyde eases himself out of his chair and paces over to his desk. He is currently trying to write an adventure story, like the kind he read as a boy.

'Perhaps I should write a mystery. *The Lost Clothes*. We should contact Agatha Christie, hmm?'

John doesn't seem to hear and the Major turns and glares at him, quickly impatient.

'Did I give you a copy of my book, John?'

'Oh yes.' John sits more straight, suddenly alert.

Hyde smiles, reassured. He is not a great writer but he shares with a great many writers an inflated sense of self and a constant need for approval. He read somewhere that writers require routines and thus he wakes at dawn to an icy wash and black tea before winding all his clocks and walking around his property. Only then will he sit at his desk and stare blankly at the view.

He is doing that now, gazing out of the window. He refocuses on his reflection in the glass. On good days Earnest Hyde assures himself that he's still handsome. He has those classic features that age well. His hair is greying, but as with most fair people it doesn't show much. It remains thick and full, parted just off centre. He has blue eyes and all his teeth. But on bad days he thinks his face is collapsing. He will keep having to check his features and he's even had to ask Nancy if she sees anything amiss.

Behind him John clears his throat. 'It must be nice to have your son visiting.'

Hyde doesn't turn back. 'Not exactly.'

He lowers his eyes to the papers on his desk. Since Everard turned twenty-one he is entitled to benefit from various family trusts, and he has brought contracts to be agreed and signed. Hyde finds himself caught in an interesting bind: he wants Everard to leave, but in order for that to happen he must sign the papers, and that will give his son a good deal of money. It is all quite problematic. Hyde strolls to the waiting decanter and pours himself another glass.

'We don't get along. It's his mother's fault. You know how it is with women.'

John refuses more sherry and stares at his lap. He does indeed know how it is with women. He has a great respect and sympathy for all women, and considers them superior to men, because he is a sensible chap. We were all in awe of his mother: Edith de Carteret, the original model. She was widowed young but raised three sons and rented rooms to tourists in the summer whilst also running the island stables. We can still hear her saying that mothers were blamed for everything because the fathers were never there. A fair point, you would agree.

John thinks about Everard. He seems like a nice lad, a little awkward but eager to help, which is more than can be said for his father. John has only a vague recollection of Everard from the last time he was here, and he guesses it was when Edie was very small and screaming through the night. He shakes his head, a soft smile forming. John had two sons and then Edie came along, conceived in the weeks after he came back from the War. She is still surprising him. She has been muttering non-stop about witches since the clothes were found.

Little Sark has a bit of a reputation for witches, as it happens. During the 1600s a whole family were accused, one after the other. The women were carted off to Guernsey and strangled and burned, the men were maimed and mostly banished. It was a travesty, of course. These people didn't meet with the Devil or fly through the night. They were just a little different from their neighbours.

What this shows is that living life on the fringes is not without its risks. Perhaps we should warn Major Hyde.

Perhaps not.

John has retraced his steps over La Coupée by the time Phyll reaches Beau Regard. She has spent a desolate hour walking around Port Gorey and she stands for a moment, staring at the windows and the terrace and the lawn. It doesn't look as grand as she remembers – the trees swamp the house and there are weeds in all the flowerbeds. She scans the windows of the upper floor and thinks, and she's thinking so hard she doesn't notice two figures coming up the path. Then she turns and it's too late.

She was braced for this moment, but even so. He looks nothing like the photograph she has, nothing like the little boy squinting on the sand. Everard carries on walking towards her and she's surprised by his height and how his hair curls at his neck. His features have settled and hardened but the eyes are the same: they are dark brown, sombre, the skin beneath them ringed with mauve. She takes in all these things and then she notices a streak through the right eyebrow like a line drawn through sand. And there is stubble on his chin. The cold wind shakes her and she realises she's staring.

He is now very close.

'Hello stranger,' she says, and then he smiles and he's not a stranger at all. The mouth curls and the dimples appear in each cheek and she almost laughs. She knows that face.

It has been in her head for years. She's spent a long time mapping those features onto other people. You search every face for the right one, the exact arrangement. It's here, she tells herself, and she breathes out. 'So it *is* you.'

Everard nods and opens his mouth, but he can't think what to say. He is struck by how strong she looks.

Small George waits beside him, then politely clears his throat. 'Hello Phyll,' he says. 'Have you met my friend.'

Phyll lets out a laugh and lifts one eyebrow. '*Your* friend is he?'

Everard looks down, embarrassed, and lays his hand on the gate. 'Hello Phyll,' he manages, and his smile wavers. 'Do they still call you Phyll?'

Phyll finds it impossible to look at him up close. She stares at the gate, at the sign that reads, 'Private Property'. She folds her arms over herself. 'What else would they call me?'

Small George stands back with his head slightly cocked. He can't decide what's happening here. He met Everard on the day that the clothes were found, and since then, they have shared many sandwiches and walked the cliffs, in search of the missing couple. They have talked about lots of things but never Phyll, so why, George wonders, are they acting so familiar? A few seconds pass and nobody speaks. George sighs and turns his attention to a hedge thick with blackberries.

Phyll watches George, knowing Everard is watching her. The wind buffets her hair and she tries to tuck it behind her ears. She looks up at the sky and down at the path. She waits for Everard to speak, and when he doesn't she's annoyed. She reaches into her bag, pulling out a crumpled package.

'I brought the post . . . for your father.'

She wants to make it clear that she hasn't made this journey just to see him, that she had many other important things to do, such as deliver the post, which admittedly isn't that important. She opens her mouth and closes it. She should say something about how she came to see Port Gorey and walk the cliffs because she is writing about the missing couple.

Everard stares at the package, eyebrows slightly raised, arms hanging slack at his sides.

She pushes it against his chest. 'Take it.'

She wants to appear brisk and efficient and not show that she cares. Everard raises his hands and for a second their fingers touch. Phyll pulls away quickly. She thinks she might cry. There are tears brimming under the surface. She swings round to look at George and blinks and sniffs.

'Any new developments?' she asks sharply.

George stiffens and spins round, wiping blackberry juice off his mouth. 'Nah.' He swallows. 'But that doesn't mean I think *you* are right.'

'Oh?' Everard tilts his face towards Phyll. 'Right about what?'

Phyll tucks her hands into the sleeves of her coat to keep them warm. She is still turned towards George, away from Everard and the house.

'I had a theory that the man and woman weren't dead.' She turns now to face Everard. 'Perhaps they were in love but couldn't be together,' she swallows and looks down, 'so . . . so they've staged their suicides as a way of escaping . . . ' she pauses, 'as a way of escaping whatever past had trapped them. They have run off to start a new life.'

She thinks it's a good theory and Everard bends his head. 'Oh Phyll,' he says. 'You always did have the best stories.'

He says it lightly but Phyll feels it like a slap. She stiffens and jerks her head up. She glares at him. The anger is bubbling up under her ribs, it's been building and building, waiting for this.

'You used to like my stories,' she says bitterly. 'I mean, do you have any better theories?' She waits a beat. 'Or maybe these two people will turn up after ten years and tell us what happened! How does that sound?'

Everard blinks quickly, mouth tightly shut and Small George gawps and takes a step back. Phyll looks between them and wants to scream. But instead she swings her bag over her shoulder and storms off down the path.

'Forget it!' she calls out, then she stops and turns back. 'But we'd better not be seen together, Everard.' She lifts her hands and gives a theatrical shrug. 'People might think we were up to our old tricks, like before!'

8

Les Fontaines, Little Sark

(Follow the one road on Little Sark to its end, then fork right
onto the cliffs before Port Gorey.)

6 August 1923

LES FONTAINES IS A CHARMING, hidden corner of Little Sark, so-named after the nearby natural springs, a once-prized well. There is safe bathing at high tide and at low tide you can scramble over the rugged boulder-strewn shores as far as Grande Grève. A number of local fishermen keep their boats here in the summer, so for Earnest Hyde it was an easy walk home.

Rather than take the steep path to the Bungalow, he opted for the shady route that wound around the cliff to the house. Here, the brambles grew high so as to block out the gales in the winter. Hyde liked how enclosed it felt. He was relieved that the day was over. He normally could not cope with groups of people and long conversations in the open air, but it had all gone off very well and everyone had thanked him profusely.

Earnest Hyde wanted people to look up to him. He found Paul Cecil amusing and harmless. He was vaguely curious about the arrangements within the Cecils' marriage, but he had no particular interest in Ann. Hyde knew he would never remarry. He didn't understand women, nor did he need to. He did sometimes think about sex, but that could be paid for, like everything else. He'd paid for it before, during the War, and felt no shame about it.

A simple business transaction.

He felt a sharp pull on his knee and stopped abruptly, gasping at the shock of it. He had been walking too fast, forgetting himself. He took a few breaths and looked about. The sun fell in patches on the path, creating a dappled effect. It was rather like being underwater. He carried on, taking slow, deliberate steps. He couldn't tell how far he'd walked, how much time had passed. The air was cooler now, and his mind drifted back to the cave. He was a little unsettled by how much he'd said. He tried not to talk about his brother and now it felt as if he'd given too much away. Of course, everyone had a war story, but it was a risk to show weakness. Earnest Hyde had never pretended to be close to his brother. Evelyn was the favourite younger son, the one everyone preferred, and Earnest's earliest memory was of feeling replaced. It was why he had refused to let him join the same regiment, or share his Duke Street apartments, or even meet his fiancée. 'So *this* is your famous brother!' Hermione had drawled on their wedding day. Hyde winced at the memory and stopped walking again. He pulled out his handkerchief, pressing it to his lips. It smelt briny, like the cave. He'd come into a clearing and the sun fell in bright, thick shafts ahead. He lifted his eyes and looked at the sky. When he'd first heard that Evelyn was killed he hadn't believed it. How could he? It still felt like a dream, a childhood wish fulfilled.

He looked down at the path. He preferred this fractured light, not total darkness but something in-between. And what a relief to be alone. He'd left Gil Baker to secure the boat to its moorings. Gil was a local fisherman, the salt of the earth, entirely trustworthy. Hyde had ordered the boy to stay behind and watch, suggesting he might even learn something. Hyde called Everard 'the boy', never his son. If there'd been any likeness between them it might have stirred some sentiment, but Everard had Hermione's eyes and that same weak mouth. It felt like another betrayal.

He carried on up the path, forcing his mind in other directions. He reminded himself that the day had gone smoothly and how everyone was probably still talking about him. He was sure Ann Cecil was trying to matchmake. He did find Sarah attractive, of course – he'd been struck by her delicate wrists and neck – but it felt like such an effort.

He was tired now, with the beginnings of a headache. The champagne had been a great success but he preferred whisky, and he'd go to see old Dr Stanhope tomorrow, have another treatment with his galvanic-faradic battery. Hyde had spent some time at a well-known London clinic and was now very proud of his tolerance for pain. He liked to apply the electrodes himself, working them up and down his leg. It wasn't an entirely unpleasant sensation, a little like being stung by a jellyfish.

Soon be home, he thought. Then someone called out and he spun back unsteadily.

'I told you to stay behind!'

He was expecting to see the boy, but the path was empty. Hyde blinked and waited, but nobody came. He took a step back, annoyed, confused. He was sure he had heard Everard and his eyes scanned the high hedges. He was struck by the intensity of the colours, especially the golden-green of the leaves. He listened carefully, but the only sound was the shrill cry of a seagull. It swung high over his head and reminded him of the whistling of a bomb. He felt himself tense and stood very still. Far down the cliff came the gentle suck and sigh of the waves hitting rocks. He flexed his fingers. It was possible he'd heard someone's voice from a distance. He was reminded that sounds could carry far around the coast. Quite often he would be in his garden and hear passengers on a passing ship. That must have been it.

He started again up the path, except now he felt that it was too quiet: there was no buzzing of bees or chatter of birds. He walked a little faster, even though his knee ached. He was gripped with a tremulous feeling, a thrumming in his throat. The silence seemed to build and build and he consciously moved his eyes over the ground, as if looking for traps. When he saw the roof and chimney of Beau Regard he should have felt relieved. Here, the path flattened out and widened, but it took him out into the open and that made him waver. His chest and throat felt tight and he stopped walking and looked about carefully, his eyes raking over the white fence and the gate and the trees beyond it. It was all familiar and yet it felt wrong. Off-kilter.

He dug inside his blazer for his father's pocket watch. He wanted to check the time and he craved the familiar weight of it. He squinted at the glass and saw his own face in miniature, then he checked the hands. The time read one o'clock. A cold horror washed over him. He pressed the watch to his ear. He had wound it this morning, when he wound all his clocks. It never stopped. It never let him down. He felt unsteady, as if he'd been tricked. He was back in the cave at low tide and saw again the patterns in the rock.

'Major Hyde!'

Nancy Dolbel was walking down to meet him, wiping her hands on her apron. She had come to see what they'd caught for supper and her round, flushed face held that question. Hyde straightened up to tell her no luck, but as he did her expression changed. Her eyes opened wide and her jaw went slack. She staggered forward and Hyde saw her rough, red hands come towards him. He reared back instinctively, revolted by the thought of her touching him, but then he realised she was pointing. He wheeled around, bracing himself, ready to strike out. It was a woman. She was watching him through the branches of the bracken. Her gaunt, pale face was as still as something carved in marble. Her eyes were sunken yet alert and searching, thick, black hair hung close to her cheeks. She seemed to float there.

Hyde felt something pressing on his chest. He couldn't breathe or move or speak. He was very afraid, and he also felt something deeper, a damp cold that spread through his body, from his fingers and toes to his torso. He tried to lift his arm to touch her, since she seemed very close, but he was held down by weights, pinning him, and the fear of it, and the coldness of the air made him think of ice setting. He was paralysed. Time splintered and split. He and this woman were locked together and her hollow eyes drew all the strength out of him. Then he realised Nancy had fallen at his feet, and her screams brought him back. He saw his own hand raised up, trapped in the bracken. He jerked it towards him but it caught on thorns, pricking and snagging his skin. He tugged harder but the branches held him. He couldn't understand how that could have happened and he cried out in pain and frustration. With another firm jolt he pulled his arm free but the skin was shredded and bleeding, with thorns still embedded in his palm. He stared at it in disbelief. His heart was beating hard and fast, like a fist banging against his ribs.

He looked up then and the woman was gone. It was empty space: shadows and branches and leaves where she'd been.

'In God's name!' Gil Baker was rushing up to meet them, his old face shiny with sweat. Once he reached Nancy, he bent over her, then he looked up at the Major. 'What have you done to her, man?'

Hyde blinked and blinked. What had *he* done to her? What had *he* done? The words would've stung more but he was turning this way and that, staring at the path and the thick hedge of brambles.

'Come back here!' he cried. 'Come back!'

Gil straightened up to face him but was a good foot shorter. 'What's going on?'

Hyde gripped him by his shoulders. 'Did you see her? Did you see her?'

Although Gil was small, he was strong. He pushed back against the Major's weight. 'See who?' he cried. 'I only see Nancy at your feet!'

As if on cue, Nancy groaned. Gil bent down on one knee and tried very clumsily to cradle her head and shoulders. 'Nancy, girl?' he cooed. 'Talk to me.'

Nancy blinked and for a second she stared into space, then she gasped. 'Oh my God, she was here, Gil! It was the Lady!'

Gil drew Nancy towards him. 'The lady?'

Nancy nodded frantically and Gil held her, rocking her slightly, his small, red eyes roaming over the scene.

Hyde glared down at them impatiently. 'A woman! Some woman.' He was saying the same words over and over. 'She was here, she looked . . . well, I don't know . . .' He stared back down the path. It was darker now and small insects clouded his vision. He batted at them. The woman. How would he describe her? White dress, dark hair. He couldn't remember her face and for a second he was not sure she had one.

'What is she doing here?' he asked. 'What does she want?'

Nancy had sat more upright. 'Oh, Sir. She hasn't come for years. We don't know why she does.'

Hyde stepped back, swallowed hard. He needed his heart to slow down. 'What *do* you mean?' He spread out his hands. 'I have never seen her before and yet she was here, waiting for me!'

Gil shook his head. 'She's not of this world, Major.'

Hyde let out an involuntary snigger. *Not of this world.* He wanted to tell them to be reasonable, talk sense, but he was too angry. Not of this world! Of course the woman was real. What else could she be?

'Are you insane? It was a woman.' He turned his head and stared into the thicket, focusing on small details to check his eyes still worked. 'You must know her. Is she local? What was she doing?'

But as he stared into the brambles he realised she could not have been there. The branches were thick and thorny, criss-crossing, quite impenetrable. He wanted to say something but his tongue had stuck to the roof of his mouth. He swallowed. He told his heart to slow down, and he ordered his pulse to steady. Remember your place, man. You have been to War. You have watched men die. You have seen bodies blown apart, towns destroyed. He pulled his shoulders back and took two deep breaths in.

'She was in the bushes,' he said calmly. 'All in white. A wedding dress.'

'A nightdress.' Nancy mumbled, pressing a handkerchief to her face. 'She was hiding. We disturbed her.'

'I believe she is harmless.' Gil nodded. 'I myself have never seen her.'

Hyde drew out his handkerchief and held it to his palm, watching the blood seep through, then he tried to tie it in a knot. He thought about the woman, how pale she had looked, and he stared into the bushes, unable to take in what it meant. He was trembling and sweating, the fear pouring from him. He bent down beside Nancy and the pain shot through his knee. 'We must stay calm,' he spoke through his teeth. He was back in the trenches, under attack.

He looked Gil in the eye and made his voice hard and level. 'Let's help her up to the house.'

Together they lifted Nancy back onto her feet and guided her up the path.

'The lady used to live in the house,' Gil said. 'The house that was there before yours. I am sure you were told.'

Hyde searched back in his mind. Was this a trick? The house, his house was new and he took great pride in that. He stared up at the smooth white walls and gleaming windows, and then he lowered his gaze to the stepped terrace onto the lawn. It was all clean lines and cared-for. He would not be afraid.

'The . . . the old house burned down *years* ago,' he stuttered. 'I remember that.' And he felt exhausted with the effort of remembering.

Gil nodded. 'You could see it for miles.' He tilted his head up and sniffed the air. 'Just now . . . I thought I could smell it.'

Hyde smelt only his roses. The sky was turning pink and quite free of clouds. He blinked and shook his head. It was all too much. Nancy was hysterical, babbling incoherently, and Gil was no better. Hyde staggered back, repulsed by them.

'I am going back to search the path,' he said. 'You go inside and pour yourselves some brandy, I must just check.'

The terror he'd felt had given way to something else. He was keyed up, fired by adrenalin and fury.

'You have nothing to fear but I demand you come out!' He wheeled down the path, turning left and right.

He felt better for shouting. He would drive this creature out. She was real, there was no doubt about it, and he would not be made a fool of. He would find her and challenge her. A woman on his grounds, by *his* house, half-dressed. How dare she! Who was she? He started along the path. He would get his cane and thrash the brambles. 'Come along,' he shouted. 'Come back!'

9

DAILY MAIL

Friday, 6 October 1933

'SARK'S MISSING COUPLE: THEIR LAST JOURNEY'

Last weekend the discovery of a man and woman's clothing on a beach on the remote island of Sark sparked a search that has spread across the English Channel. The owners of these clothes remain a mystery, although several members of the public have now come forward with information. A key eyewitness is an elderly fisherman of Little Sark, a Mr Gilbert Baker. Mr Baker, who had been off the island for several days, travelled to Guernsey to examine the clothes now being help at the police headquarters. Although Mr Baker was unable to say for certain, he did recognise the overcoats as those worn by a man and a woman who he encountered during a downpour of rain on Saturday. Mr Baker told local reporter P. Carey that he briefly took shelter in a shed and it was here that he met the couple. He guessed that they had also been caught out by the rain.

The next day Mr Baker was taking a fishing party round the coast when one of his group mentioned seeing a coat on the rocks. He didn't make the connection to a day earlier, and he is certain that there was nobody in or near the water at that time, as the sea was then becoming rough. He had forgotten the matter until he was contacted by Jersey's Port Authorities with a message from Sark's Chief Constable about two possible missing persons.

Meanwhile, several other people have been interviewed by police. A Colonel J. L. Forrester and his wife travelled from Sark to Guernsey on the *Joybell* on Friday morning and believe they saw the couple arrive at the Creux harbour. The man had short, dark hair and a moustache. The woman was smaller than him and very attractive. Also, a housemaid at one of Sark's hotels believes she served the missing couple on Saturday afternoon. A full report will come in the evening edition.

THE 'SARK MYSTERY' CONTINUES to grow. It has sprouted limbs and many heads. It is attention seeking, money grabbing. It has jumped from the regional to the national newspapers, from page four to page one, creating a solid appetite in the English reading public, a craving for something they didn't know they needed. Everyone thinks they know what happened, although they also admit they may be wrong. It is like a piece of detective fiction, the kind that is so popular just now. A man and a woman, unnamed and unknown, came to an island and vanished from a cliff.

To islanders, however, it sounds a lot like folklore.

And we do love our folklore.

For centuries it was the custom to gather in each other's houses on long, winter nights. This was known as the Veille, when everyone would share the warmth of a single hearth and comb and card the wool, and to ward off boredom we'd tell stories. Unrequited love was a popular theme, as were tales of vanishings or transformations. There was always a twist and it was hard to beat a murder, and it didn't matter if someone died, since they invariably came back.

Doesn't everyone love a ghost story? It means the ending is never that, because life continues, just in a new shape or form. We could argue that every story is a ghost story, because once a tale is told, it is over, it is past. All we can do is keep going back over it, to go from the end back to the start.

So. Two people. A man and a woman. According to Maud, they walked over La Coupée on Saturday afternoon, but Gil Baker says he met them in the morning. Poor Gil. The business of newspapers is train crashes and government scandals, and he still cannot conceive how this has anything to do with him. He is a shy man, now aged sixty-five, with cheeks the colour of boiled beetroot and eyes fixed in a squint.

'I do not want anyone taking my picture,' he says testily. 'It's bad enough with that Mr Drake and his arty lot trying to paint me.'

Gil is currently installed in the kitchen table of the post office, drinking a cup of Elise's over-stewed tea. He is not one for long conversations, but Elise is one of the few people he trusts as he spent many years fishing with Phillip.

'I had only gone to check on Major Hyde's boat,' he explains, 'the boats in Little Sark must all be brought out of the water come October.' He sighs. 'It's too rough. But Major Hyde has been putting it off. He is getting lazy.'

Phyll, who sits at the head of the table, carefully jots this down and Gil turns to her, panicked. 'No, no. Don't put that in your article!'

Gil remembers when Phyll was younger, when she'd come to the harbour and throw stones at the breakwater. She was always alone and scowling and Gil wasn't sure what to say to help. He assumed she was missing her father. To this day Gil feels bad about Phillip and how he died. A few times he was tempted to ask Phyll out on the boat, only it is bad luck to have a female on board. They are as unlucky as priests. Gil has certain rules that he sticks to, as do all Sark fishermen. Never mention rabbits or offer him fruitcake. We have no idea why.

Gil didn't get a good look at the couple. He is not what we'd call a people person. They were in the shed ahead of him so he felt like he was intruding. He remembered the lady had long dark hair because it was wet and she brushed it out. The gentleman was smart and might have been younger, he also had a moustache.

'That's it?' asks Phyll, clearly let down. 'Think hard, Gil. How did they act towards each other? Could you smell alcohol on them? Had the woman been crying? Did the man seem angry?'

Elise glowers at her daughter with nostrils flared and lips pursed. She is not happy about Phyll writing for the newspapers (even if it was her idea, as John so helpfully reminded her). Of course she wants Phyll to have a project, but this, she feels, is dangerous. Phyll has a habit of getting carried away. She has always been a dreamer – all that novel-reading as a child didn't help – and now reality will never match or fit. Elise is sure this is why Phyll left her job in Southampton. She knows she wasn't fired as she made discreet enquiries. The firm reported they were sad to see Phyll go and that she'd made a good impression although 'had a habit of overstepping herself.' Elise sets her teeth together. Oh, what to do! On the surface there are many things Phyll could be: she has brains and guts and an excellent vocabulary, but she is also impatient, quick-tempered and terribly tactless.

Here's an example: Phyll has just asked Gil if he thought the man and woman were lovers. As if Gil would know!

'Now, Phyll,' she sighs. 'That is quite enough. Leave Gil be, he is exhausted.'

She wants Phyll to tread carefully – it doesn't do to look for scandal – but within seconds of dispatching Gil, her daughter is pulling on her coat.

'I have to go and talk to Dolly,' she says. 'She served them at the Bel Air, she might have got a better look.'

Elise shakes her head. She thinks Dolly Bihet is the type of woman who would say anything to anyone to get her name in a newspaper.

'You know it could all still be nothing.' She makes her voice casual. 'And there are journalists from England arriving, there will be a lot of competition . . .'

Phyll spins round, eyes flashing. 'You don't think I can cope?'

'It's not that,' Elise replies (although it is, partly). She is tempted to pin Phyll by the shoulders and stare deep into her eyes. She waits a beat. 'You don't think it is a little too convenient that Everard Hyde found the clothes? That this all happens just when, suddenly, *he* is here?'

Phyll blinks rapidly. 'No,' she replies. 'I think it's pure chance.' She rears up, turning. 'And I frankly don't care. Everard is irrelevant. I haven't seen him for years. Why would I care?'

Elise says nothing but she knows Phyll is lying. She knows that she went to see Everard – pretending to deliver the post, how obvious! – and she found the photograph from Derrible Bay in Phyll's pocket. (Yes, Elise was going through her daughter's pockets – she has been doing this for years and she thinks this is normal behaviour.) The photograph made her heart squeeze. She stared long and hard at the three children on the sand, but she also studied the people in the background – the woman in the white dress, so young and pretty and smiling. That poor woman, she would not forget.

'It's got nothing to do with Everard,' Phyll says, picking up her notepad. 'It is about these two people . . . They were living and breathing when Gil met them, and Dolly saw them too.' She pauses at the door, turning her head just a little way back. 'It's not just about writing a story or getting my name in some byline. These people are real, flesh and blood. Maybe they had problems and they need our help. They aren't a trick or a hoax,' she hesitates, 'they aren't *ghosts*.'

But maybe they are. Two people. A man and a woman. They were here and now they are not, and some islanders saw them and some didn't. It is like a game of hide and seek with the very recent past, a past that is still within reach. Phyll thinks if she follows the clues she will find them. It will solve a puzzle and give her the ending she needs.

That's another thing about a ghost story: there is always the chance to go back.

But Everard and Phyll can't return to the children they were – they will never again sit on those creaking wicker chairs on the verandah of the Bel Air. It's the only hotel that stays open past October and here we are again. The chairs outside are long gone, though Dolly salvaged one and keeps it in the kitchen just for Phyll. It's where she sat and read aloud on all these dark weekday nights. The verandah is no longer painted white. Mr Frith, the proprietor, had it stripped back to the original wood and varnished a rich brown. Today, it's rather wet. Phyll enters by the side gate and takes the path through the garden. The flowerbeds are a haze of colour in the summer, but now they are all drooping under the weight of the rain. The grass is too long, but it was here, by the steps, that Miranda would sit and have her French lessons with Sylvie Price.

'Je m'appelle Miranda,' she'd purr, twirling her hair between her fingers. '*Il fait chaud aujourd'hui, n'est-ce pas?*'

Phyll strides up the steps, dropping her notepad on a table. She stands exactly where a young Everard once sat in his blue shirt with his hair slicked, but she turns away from the memory and stares out to sea. The garden is wide and long, leading down to a shrubby border, and beyond that there is a footpath to the harbour. In the summer children run up and down it and hide in the bushes. To the right, through a wooden trellised archway, there's a vegetable garden with carrots, potatoes and green beans arranged in neatly tended rows. There's also an old stone outhouse but we won't talk about that yet.

Now it's October everything needs pruning, and Mr Frith is often seen in his shirt sleeves brandishing a pair of rusty shears. He says next summer he will get rid of some flowerbeds and put out more tables to cater to the day trippers. But he says that every year. Phyll lowers her eyes. There is one round, wrought iron antique table, too heavy to move. It stands apart at the bottom of the garden, with four matching chairs, which, because of all the rain, have been tipped forward to rest on the table's top. They look like people with their heads bent.

The smell of the earth is sharp and vital, fresh as blood. The woman has gone now, but that's where she was, that's where she sat. She chose that table to sit at, the one that has been washed clean by rain. Or perhaps the man steered her towards it. They didn't come inside or look in the lounge for somewhere warmer, somewhere comfortable. They didn't want to be cosy. Instead they sat with their backs to the hotel so nobody would notice them. It almost worked.

Dolly hadn't had a spare minute to go to the prison and see the clothes but she read Phyll's description in the *Press*.

'I couldn't believe it,' she says huskily. 'I still can't.'

Dolly is small and broad with brown hair that curls all around her face. She is only five years older than Phyll but has always acted motherly towards her. She stands very close, shaking her head. 'They came in Saturday afternoon, around three o'clock. I remember because I had just made a fresh batch of scones and I was sitting out the front and suddenly they appeared.' Dolly gestures to the table. 'I only spoke with the gentleman. He came and asked for black coffee. I took it out to them.'

Phyll lifts her notepad and starts to write. 'What did he look like?'

Dolly thinks for a minute. 'Late twenties. Brown hair.' She waves a hand around her chin. 'A moustache but a proper one, not like that Hitler chap.' Dolly rarely reads the newspapers but she does look at the pictures. 'Piercing eyes,' she says suddenly, and nods as if she likes the phrase. She scours her mind. What else, she thinks, what else. She sees the two people in outline with their backs turned to her. 'The woman had lovely long hair and she fussed over it a bit, tidying the pins. They were looking down towards the harbour, as if waiting for the boat, but it was a rough old day and I was wondering if that's why they only wanted coffee.' She pulls back her shoulders and stares into space. 'There was something about how they were together. They weren't *arguing* but . . . ' she lifts her chin and struggles to find the right words. 'They weren't really talking, either. They seemed a bit depressed.' She turns her head just an inch. 'Like you.'

Phyll stops writing and looks up. 'Oh Doll. I am not depressed.'

But Dolly isn't stupid, whatever people think. She pulls down the corners of her mouth. 'You were all excited when you went away to England and now you have a face like you fell in a puddle. What happened? Or should I ask *who*?'

Phyll blinks smartly and inspects her shoes. 'Nothing. Nobody. It doesn't matter.'

Dolly leans close. 'You *can* tell me, you know.'

Phyll could, in fact, tell Dolly, because Dolly out of everyone would understand. Dolly has a habit of attracting the wrong men and believing what they say. She tells herself she won't do it ever again, and then she does. Regular as clockwork.

Phyll shakes her head quickly, flicking her hair away from her cheeks. 'It doesn't matter now: I have to get this copy in for the late edition. Don't you dare talk to those English reporters. Only talk to me.'

Dolly flushes. 'That's my girl!' she says, then her smile falls. 'But I can't *not* talk to them – they are booked in here.' She checks over her shoulder. 'I will tell them very little, though, as long as you remember I am now *housekeeper* not housemaid.' She lifts both hands and makes little speech marks with her fingers. '*Dolly Bihet, housekeeper.*'

Dolly has worked at the Bel Air since she was fourteen. She tried two summers at the Bungalow – Major Hyde offered her more money and her own room – but she couldn't settle. She found the nights too eerie and although she slept well she had awful nightmares. She dreamt about being buried alive, which she decided was something to do with the miners. She'd also wake with headaches. Her mother called her a silly goose, but she came back to the Bel Air and Mr Frith was so thrilled, he promoted her.

'Why would they go to Little Sark?' Dolly shudders. 'I wouldn't go back there for love nor money. Oh, the atmosphere. I never felt right the whole time I lived there . . . it's *cursed.*'

Phyll is standing on one leg, inspecting the frayed lace of her left shoe.

Dolly blinks. 'Are you even listening?'

Phyll straightens up. 'Of course I am.' She circles a hand. 'But we have to stick to the facts, I'm not getting drawn into the whole *atmospheres and curses*.'

Phyll no longer believes in witches or ghosts or curses, and she's embarrassed to think she ever did. A childish phase, she'd call it. She straightens her shoulders. 'We need to focus on this man and woman. Obviously they were lovers and I think they were running away. Maybe they were married to the wrong people and this was the only way they could be free. *I* think they faked their deaths.'

Dolly opens her eyes wide. 'Oh, that's an idea! Like something out of a book!' She looks up and taps at her lip. 'Wait. Did we ever read one like that?'

Phyll clears her throat. 'No, Dolly, we did not.' But she wonders if they did. She imagines it making an excellent plot. Phyll wants so much for the man and woman to be alive. She wants to find them and save them, and make everything better. She can't do it for herself, but she could try and do it for someone else.

Dolly checks her watch. She has to get back to work, but as she turns to go she lays a hand on Phyll's arm. 'It's a shame your mother didn't see them. Elise would know what happened, wouldn't she?' She puffs out her cheeks. 'I don't know how she does it!'

Phyll lifts her head high and holds herself rigid. She wants to say she knows exactly how her mother does it and she is sorely tempted to turn to Dolly and say, don't be fooled! But instead she bites her tongue and tips up her nose, as if sniffing the air. Down the garden, beyond the trees, there is a line of glittering sea. She walks down the steps and onto the grass, letting her shoes sink into the soft ground. The clouds move quickly overhead. There'll be another storm, she is sure of it. She walks to the table where the man and woman sat, placing herself behind the woman's chair. At the bottom of the garden there is a gap between the hedges with a path down to the harbour. If the man and woman came this far, then they were waiting for a boat. Phyll pictures the woman sitting here, fussing over her hair, making herself presentable for the journey home.

She instinctively reaches up to touch the nape of her neck. It feels so bare it's still a shock. Phyll lets her eyes drift out of focus, and she notices a dark shape. There is a man walking up from the harbour. He is wearing an unbuckled overcoat and a hat pulled down over his forehead and Phyll thinks for a second that this is the missing man. This week has looped back and tripped her up.

But if she were really looking, she'd see that this man's face is lined and there are deep hollows under his eyes. He comes closer and lifts his hat in greeting, but Phyll is already distracted. She'd dug her hands into her pockets and has realised that the photograph is missing. Her throat tightens and she has to pull both pockets inside out to check. How can it be gone? Where has it gone? She stares at the grass and turns around to see if it's fallen out.

The man stands on the other side of the table, looking amused. 'Hallo, there. Lost something?'

Phyll looks up. 'Oh, it's nothing.'

The man reaches into his own coat pocket and produces what looks like a business card. He mutters his name and says, 'I am gathering information about the missing persons . . .'

Phyll feels the hairs on her head standing alert. She looks at the card but makes no move to take it, and she glances round the garden one more time.

'Our readers can't get enough of it,' the man continues. 'You local? Anything you can tell me? I'm sure a pretty girl like you must know all the gossip.'

It seems suddenly very dark and still. Phyll shakes her head and steps back. 'No, sorry,' she says. 'I am a stranger here myself.'

10

'A Famous Sark Ghost'

8 August 1923

'WE CALL HER THE STRANGER LADY,' she said, and everyone went quiet.

The sun was shining through the gaps in the trees and it felt very much like a spotlight. *I am on stage*, she thought, *it's the opening act*. Phyll looked at Major Hyde, who was sitting with his bad leg stretched out straight, then she smiled at Ann Cecil and Mule Toplis, who'd arranged themselves around him. They had carried the bench so that it was in the shade of St Peter's. A little distance away Paul was conducting one of his art classes and there were various ladies perched on folding chairs. Everyone had stopped to listen and Phyll thought it was better than brilliant.

'The Stranger Lady. What a name!' Ann lifted a knee and laced her fingers around it. 'So *why* do they call her that?'

Phyll gripped her hands together. 'Nobody ever found out her name.' She rose up on tiptoes. 'She was only on Little Sark for a few months before she died.'

It was Sark's most famous ghost and Phyll was bursting to tell them the whole story. She was getting good at telling stories and she'd even written some down in her diary. She opened her mouth, her lips slightly pursed, but then she felt a flutter of doubt. It might be better to go and fetch Maud. Maud had heard the story directly from the wife of the last Seigneur, who had been alive when it happened. Phyll also knew that adults generally only listened to other adults, and Maud, she conceded, was a kind of adult.

Maud was, of course, aware of the recent drama at Beau Regard. Within the space of a day, half the island had heard some version of it. That both Nancy and the Major had seen the Stranger Lady made it an event worthy of discussion, and Nancy was an excitable woman given to garbled monologues most of the time. Maud was in the process of fixing her a tonic for her nerves when the children knocked. Maud didn't mind the interruption. It was good to meet the boy Everard, who she'd heard so much about. For what it's worth, Maud liked him. He'd bowed his head very low and said, 'How do you do, Mrs Pratt?' and then offered her his arm, which she refused with a mocking pout.

'It's quite all right, young man,' she replied. 'I am not that old. I can walk.'

Maud was then seventy-eight, for those keeping count. But age was a state of mind and her state of mind was fine, thank you kindly. She was fit and healthy and she looked younger, she thought, with her pink cheeks and thick hair, which she wore in a single braid like a schoolgirl. Maybe the hands gave her away – they were thin and sun-spotted, the veins standing proud – but that's why she wore gloves, especially for gardening. You never know what you might rub up against, she always warned.

So they wanted to hear about the Stranger Lady? Now, that was a story for a dark night and a warm fire, but it could also be told in a churchyard. Maud was headed this way later, in any case. Albert had a lovely plot in the western corner with a wide space around him, just how they'd agreed. She had recently planted forget-me-nots, blue coneflower and irises. They looked glorious against the thick bank of foxgloves.

But when she reached the churchyard she felt suddenly embarrassed. She was still in her apron with her sleeves rolled and here were all these people! If she'd known she was going to have such an audience she might have worn a better dress. Too late.

'Hallo Mrs Pratt,' Paul called out, coming towards her. 'So we believe you know all about the Major's Ghost.'

Maud noticed the Major sitting in the shade. He looked rather dazed and raised his bandaged hand.

'Do excuse me for not getting up,' he said, gesturing faintly to his leg.

Maud smiled. She didn't know the Major well, but she knew about what was politely dubbed 'his troubles'. She had once seen him kick a dog across the Avenue just because it yapped. She could have offered him a tonic for his nerves but he was the sort who would laugh at her and call it poison. All very ironic considering the amount of whisky he drank.

But anyway, where was she?

'I know as much as anyone,' Maud said, which wasn't strictly true. 'It was a long time ago.' (That *was* true). 'The woman appears very rarely. She came with her husband and they rented a house in Little Sark. The property was on the same plot of land where Beau Regard stands. It was called Petit Regard and was only ever rented out to visitors.'

She spoke these words directly to the Major, who nodded as if he were grateful.

'The gentleman was an artist. He left his wife alone all the time and she would wander the cliffs. She was obviously unhappy and she was also afraid. If anyone tried to talk to her she'd run off in distress. It was assumed that she was foreign and didn't speak English. Some people said she was mad.'

'The artist and his mad wife,' Paul said, stretching his arms over his head. 'What a cliché. Of course, male artists are the *worst*.'

'Raging egomaniacs,' Mule cut in, eyebrows arched. 'They think the world revolves around them.'

Paul chuckled and focused on the Major. 'But it is an odd sort of coincidence . . . that day down at Derrible we had been talking about ghosts, hadn't we, Earnest?'

Hyde flashed him an irritated look. 'There is no connection.'

Several of Paul's ladies had come to listen, and Maud recognised the young widow, Mrs Williams, who was often on her own and looking sad. There was also the French girl with the strong perfume. She smiled and nodded to them, making a bit of space between her and Paul.

'So what happened to the lady?' asked Mrs Williams.

Maud cocked her head. 'We believe her husband killed her.'

There followed a silence, and Maud was conscious of their shocked, still faces. She waited. It was as if even the silence turned towards her.

'The husband *said* his wife had died in her sleep, and there was no doctor on the island.' Maud gave a little shrug. 'An old woman was asked to lay out the body and the lady was buried the next day. It happened very quickly and because nobody *knew* them, nobody questioned it.'

Paul pursed his lips and folded his arms. He might as well have tapped his foot. 'So there's no actual proof he killed her?'

Maud frowned. She didn't like interruptions, it rather ruined her flow.

'Well, Mr Cecil,' she sighed. 'It was what happened afterwards that was so strange. The husband arranged to have a cross put on her grave – an ugly, elaborate thing – but each morning it was found uprooted and lying flat on the grass. It would not stay upright. This happened a few times so the husband had a spike put in the base. Even that didn't work. In fact, it made it worse. The next morning, it had been pulled up and *thrown* some distance from the grave. The whole thing was extraordinary.'

Sarah Williams was casting her eyes about. Her husband had no grave and it bothered her terribly. 'But how could you pull up a gravestone?'

'How indeed.' Maud sighed. 'And *that*,' she paused, 'that was when she first appeared.'

Sarah snapped her head round. 'Oh.'

Maud held her gaze, nodding. '*Oh*, indeed. She was seen at twilight, always dressed in white, as she had been on her deathbed.' Maud turned her attention back to the Major. 'She always looks wretched, I am told, but if anyone tries to get close, she vanishes.' Maud stopped talking and looked down. 'It is very sad. In life and in death it is the same cycle repeating.'

'Fascinating,' said Ann through half-closed eyes, 'as if she is trapped in that moment.'

Maud nodded.

'Well, it's a good story,' Paul stifled a yawn. 'But who was this artist?' He clicked his fingers briskly. 'Do we even have a name, Mrs Pratt?'

Maud shook her head. 'Nobody remembers the man's name, and it doesn't appear on any records. Either he erased it, or someone else did. He fled the island and died not long after.' She opened her hands and frowned at them. 'That's all I know.'

But Paul was shaking his head. 'So we don't even know if the husband *did* kill her.'

'We do so!' Phyll had stuck up her hand like she was in school. 'The old woman who laid out the body later admitted she'd seen marks around the woman's neck . . . she'd been too scared to say at the time.'

'Really.' Paul lifted his chin. 'How convenient.'

Phyll scowled. It wasn't convenient. It was just what had happened. She was going to say something else but she couldn't think what and her throat was dry. Why was Paul laughing?

The Major stood up. 'The thing is, Nancy, *Mrs* Dolbel has got it into her head the house is *haunted*. She is complaining about windows being left open, doors slamming unexpectedly when nobody is home, and this morning a glass was broken in the kitchen. She said that must have been thrown at the wall to create such a mess.' He shook his head.

'You had better watch out,' Paul said. 'That could get expensive.'

Everyone laughed and Sylvie raised her perfect eyebrows and said, 'This husband. He was obviously not a good artist.' She shrugged. 'If nobody remembers him.'

The laughter carried on and Phyll stepped back into the shade of the trees. She was feeling very flustered. It had been going so well and now they'd ruined it. The Major was complaining about Nancy and Ann was saying, 'The things I have heard!' Phyll chewed at her thumbnail and Paul started telling a story about Italy. Phyll tugged at a thin strip of skin. She wanted Maud, but Maud had vanished. She couldn't see Everard, either. She retreated further under the trees and was surprised by how much cooler it was. She shut out everyone's voices and began to look for her shoes.

'Here,' Miranda called. She was sitting in a patch of sunlight near the archway, making a daisy chain. She looked up at Phyll and smiled. 'I hope you see that Maud is completely *mad*.'

Phyll folded her arms very tightly and frowned. She wanted to say that Maud was not mad, and that lots of people had seen the Stranger Lady, including her mother, but she decided such information was wasted on Miranda. She waited in the shade until the Major had left and then spent some time glowering at Paul, who didn't notice. She told herself she didn't care what anyone thought, but she did care about Maud. She found her tending the flowers at Albert's plot.

His gravestone was a fine thing – a thick slab of local granite. 'Albert Adolphus Pratt' it read. 'Son of Sark. Beloved Spouse and first Postmaster.'

Phyll squatted in front of the foxgloves. 'I am sorry I made you tell them now.' She hugged her knees. 'They just don't understand.'

Maud sat back on her haunches and shielded her eyes with her little trowel. 'When people are scared they make jokes.' Then she pointed with the trowel. 'But *he* is taking it seriously.' She was gesturing to Everard, who paced between the older graves, bending down to read each inscription. Maud smiled. 'He asked me where the grave was. Said he didn't want to tread on her. Very polite. I *like* him.'

Phyll felt suddenly better, as if she were sick and had now been cured. She ran over to join Everard, grinning broadly. Of course, she could have told him not to bother – every inch of St Peter's churchyard had been searched by all kinds of people to no avail, the Lady's grave remained unmarked – but Phyll thought it could be a game they could play together. They walked side by side and she waited for him to speak. When he didn't, she wondered if he was worried. He'd been quieter today – distracted – and she assumed it was connected to the ghost. She supposed that it was fair enough that he was scared. He didn't know as much about ghosts as she did. She plucked a long stalk of grass and waved it in front of her, sending a cloud of insects into a frenzy.

'Try not to worry,' she said with some authority. 'The Stranger Lady is harmless, she won't hurt you.'

Everard shot Phyll a look of pure anguish and she noticed for the first time a red mark on his cheek. She raised her hand to touch it, but he jerked away.

'It's nothing.'

Phyll froze with her hand in the air and Everard walked on without looking back. She felt her heart stall. She didn't have to ask what had happened because she knew straightaway. Her father had hit her mother, and that was another thing she wasn't meant to talk about. She lowered her hand and clutched her sides, and she tried to fight the effervescence bubbling under her ribs. It felt very close to her skin and she stared at the grass and remembered standing on the stairs at home. She could hear a chair hitting the floor and a sort of dull gasp. She made herself think about something else.

'Did you know,' she began. 'The water in the wells turns to blood on New Year's Eve! Yes. And a piece of silver in the butter churn helps it set.' She caught up with Everard and swung her grass. 'What else, what else? Oh! When you are going down to the beach, pick up a stone and take it with you, then you get good luck.'

Everard turned and smiled. 'Do *you* want to hear something funny?' He lowered his head and leaned in. 'I thought the ghost was *you*.'

Phyll laughed although she wasn't sure why. 'You thought it was me?' She stopped thrashing. 'How could it have been me?'

Everard shrugged and carried on walking, but Phyll slowed to a halt and stared at his back. 'Wait a minute. Did you see the ghost? Did she look like me?'

He turned, blinking in the sunshine. 'No,' he lowered his gaze. 'No. I didn't see anything.'

Phyll batted a fly out of the way. The sun felt very hot on her head. 'So you thought, what, that I was playing a trick?'

Everard walked back to face her and they stood very close. 'Yes. I thought it was the sort of thing you might do and I laughed.' He smiled again. 'And then,' the smile faded, he looked to one side, and shrugged. 'Father hit me because he thought I was laughing at him.'

Phyll dropped her stalk. 'I'm sorry,' she said. She felt that it was her fault. 'Oh, I am sorry.'

They had completed a full circuit of the graveyard and were now close to Albert's plot. Maud had left so Phyll sunk down onto her knees like she might say a prayer, then rested back on her heels and patted the grass beside her. After a moment's hesitation Everard sat down. He crossed his legs, pushed his elbows into his knees, and rested his fists against his temples.

'I know it was stupid.'

A butterfly darted between them and Phyll followed its path. 'Nothing you tell me is *ever* going to be stupid.'

Neither of them spoke again until Miranda came over to join them, swinging a daisy chain from her hands. Miranda was the best at making daisy chains because she didn't bite her nails, and the daisies in the graveyard were pink-tipped and perfect. She knelt down beside Phyll, who plucked some flowers and half-heartedly plopped them into her lap.

Miranda knew she'd upset Phyll, but she sometimes found her to be such a baby. She sighed and smiled over at Everard. 'You know I *did* see a ghost once. Do you want to hear about it?'

Everard looked up at Miranda, his face blank, and then glanced across at Phyll to see what she thought.

Miranda frowned at that and tilted her head to the sun. 'I spent two terms at a convent just outside Venice.' She closed her eyes. 'It was a grim place. There was a dead nun who was meant to roam the corridors.' She opened her eyes and looked over at Everard. 'Of course, schools must be full of unhappy ghosts . . . all those miserable children and their more miserable teachers.' She patted her daisy chain. 'This one time after morning prayers I had to take a message to the Mother Superior and her office was down a long corridor with all these statues of the saints lined up. It was a bright, sunny day but as I walked along, the light dimmed.'

She paused and her face changed completely, and she looked back and forth between Everard and Phyll. 'I felt terribly cold and my pulse started to race but I carried on walking steadily, and then, just I was just reaching the end . . . a black shadow passed by, right in front of me.' Miranda leaned over and wafted her hand in front of them, making a breeze. 'Just like that,' she said, blinking. 'I was petrified.' She bent her head forward and gave a small shudder. 'It scares me now just to think of it.'

Everard drew his knees together. 'Was it really like that?'

Miranda lifted her head slowly and her eyes met his. She burst out laughing. 'No! Of course not. I am joking.'

It took a second, maybe two, then Phyll started laughing, and Everard felt a stab of panic and laughed along with them. 'Oh, that's good!' he said.

Miranda leaned over and prodded his bare knee. 'We used to have competitions to see who could tell the scariest story after lights out.' She tilted her head. 'Don't *you* do that?'

Everard bent his head. His cheeks had turned bright red, hiding the mark his father had made.

'Of course,' he lied. He stared at his knees. 'But the thing is my father was really angry about it. He went white as a sheet and I honestly thought his eyes would pop out of his head. He even got his sword from the house and started thrashing at the bushes.'

Everard pictured his father's face up close, his big hand gripping him, screaming at him. He hugged his legs and stared downwards, and nobody said anything and the silence was a relief. Then Ann Cecil's glossy voice broke over their heads. She was calling Miranda for her French lesson, and Miranda made a show of rolling her eyes but jumping up quite readily. Before she turned away she held out her chain of daisies and laid it on Everard's head. He blushed again and Phyll felt uneasy. The minute Miranda's back was turned she snatched the daisies off his head.

'I hate your father,' she said.

Everard exhaled slowly, relaxing his shoulders. 'It's fine . . . I got my own back.'

Phyll frowned. 'How?'

Everard looked over his shoulder and then looked back at Phyll. 'I opened the windows after Mrs Dolbel shut them *and* I slammed the door, *and* I broke the glass.' He smiled. 'It seemed only fair. I wanted to scare them. Well, no . . . I wanted to scare my father . . . I like Mrs Dolbel.' He frowned. 'Don't tell anyone.'

Phyll bit into her bottom lip. Of course she wouldn't tell. She thought for a minute. 'I could help.'

Everard looked slightly stunned. 'What?'

Phyll leaned over, lowering her voice to match his. 'It is very easy to scare people,' she went on, a small smile spreading over her face. 'About the Stranger Lady . . . Some people say *the islanders* pulled up the cross because they knew the husband had killed her, and they wanted to scare him and drive him away.'

Everard still didn't speak and Phyll plucked some petals off a daisy. 'Of course we'd have to be careful. We couldn't tell anyone, not even Miranda.' She frowned a little. '*Definitely* not Miranda because she might tell her parents.'

Phyll felt suddenly better. She liked the idea of having a secret, since secrets tied people together. They were the cornerstone of any proper friendship, she was sure.

'But there must be rules.'

'Rules?' Everard repeated.

Phyll nodded and held his gaze and because she was smiling, he did, too.

She stood up and laid the crumpled daisy chain on the top of Albert's headstone. 'We must be respectful of the real ghosts,' she said.

11

THE DAILY RECORD

Saturday, 7 October 1933

'STARTLING DEVELOPMENT IN SARK MYSTERY'

The mystery of the discovery of a man and woman's clothing abandoned on the rocks on Sark cliffs took a dramatic turn last night. After a week of intensive searching and speculation, there have been reports of the body of a woman seen floating in the sea. Initially the body was seen close to the rocks by the lighthouse, but further investigation was impossible since the sea was judged too rough.

The area is especially perilous and has been the scene of numerous shipwrecks. The Chief Constable would not let any men go out as it would have been a matter of great risk.

This discovery, which Sark fishermen definitely connect to the mystery of the abandoned clothes, is a tragic outcome, if it proves to be true.

A careful lookout is being kept until the weather improves.

FOR THOSE WHO WISH TO SEE SARK BY BOAT, it is vital to use a local man as a guide, and even then, the lurking rocks and lunatic currents pose a constant threat. Consider the sad demise of Peter Le Pelley, the Seigneur behind the silver mines. All hands were lost on that ship, and the same fate befell another crew in 1868. The grieving widow of one, a Mrs Jane Pilcher, commissioned a striking but frightful granite obelisk that sits on the cliffs above Havre Gosselin. It bears the inscription, 'Caution and Warning!' But we would like to point out that there is usually a warning. Most of the shipwreck stories follow a pattern: the locals shake their heads and mutter about a coming storm and some soon-to-be-dead person says, 'Oh no, I know better.'

As regards local guides, we recommend Christmas Vibert, Peg Godfray and Gilbert Baker. But even Gil might have been wrong about today.

They are suspended in mid-air, floating in space. There's a held-breath moment of stillness and quiet and then they tip and plummet. The hull slaps the water so hard it jumps. Everard gasps in shock as an icy wave drenches him. His father, who is peering over the gunwale, doesn't flinch. Everard thinks he is going to die, although he might be remembering the last time he was on this boat with his father, when he lay crumpled and bloodied in the stern, unable to see out of one eye.

But let's focus on what is happening now. How did this come about? Why are they here? It's Gil's fault, in fact. He had marched round to Beau Regard and told the Major straight that they had to move the boat. He said that it was now or never and they had a few hours before the storm hit. Gil was genuinely worried, which is why he asked Everard to come and help. Gil considers three a magic number. It's another one of his rules.

Major Hyde only agreed because he didn't want Everard left alone in the house. It is a day when Nancy comes to clean, and he doesn't want the two of them talking. He had already made a mental note to have some words with the old girl. Nancy needed to be reminded of the trouble Everard had caused. Wide berth, yes, wide berth.

Another wave hits, flooding the deck, and Everard blinks and shakes his face, gulping air. The cold is astonishing but he forces himself to think of something else. He reminds himself this won't take long: they only have to get the boat round to the harbour, and then he will go and see Phyll. He wants to apologise for upsetting her. He has shaken the water out of his eyes but as fast as he does this another wave hits them. He holds tight to the sheer-line but his fingers are turning to ice in his gloves. His father is pointing to the headland, saying something, and Gil nods his head like this is fine, like this is nothing they haven't seen before.

The inky-black sea is far too close, tipping up to meet them. Is it meant to be this close? Everard tells himself Gil knows what he is doing. The fact that Gil is here is the only reason he came. Gil won't kill them. He says it again, Gil won't kill us. The boat heaves up. Everard doesn't mind the feeling of weightlessness but it's what happens after, when they dip. His feet lose touch with the deck and it feels as if his insides have been wrenched out of his body.

They have made it past La Coupée but now they're fighting waves from all sides. Gil turns the boat closer to the rocks, which is what they need to do. He says rolling is better than pitching, and Everard nods because he understands. The cold bites, the wet seeping through. He looks down at the wooden deck and feels the pressure of the water under it, threatening to break through at any minute.

Ahead of them is the harbour and the white column of the lighthouse, though it is hard to judge distance when the boat keeps lifting and falling. It's like being caught on a fairground ride. Everard tells himself it will stop soon and they'll be safe, and maybe he should close his eyes. No, that makes it worse. He scans the surface of the water.

In Sark and Guernsey, right up until the last century, there was a strong belief in sirens – those women who sat on the rocks and sang before a storm. In Sark they were meant to be young and beautiful whilst in Guernsey they were wizened old crones. They'd lure the ships to the rocks and then the storm would do the rest, and whether they were young or old, ugly or fair, the women would come for the sailors, drag them down to the ocean bed and eat them. A lot of fishermen never learn to swim as they believe it means a slower death. They also won't recover a dead body from the sea. Honestly, there are so many rules. Gil's father, Samson Baker, was seriously neurotic about them.

They are nearing the harbour when it happens. Everard is clinging to the side when a pale shape pitches out of the foam. He glimpses a human head and a tangle of black hair. It's a woman, facing downwards. The wave buffets her and an arm rises up, and he sees her whole body lifted in the swelling water, cresting on a wave, and then she's gone. He shouts out but his voice is lost in the wind. The boat lifts up and he falls on his back, face turned to grey sky. His mind is blank but he manages to roll onto his knees and swivel round, pinning his chest against the side of the boat. Another wave rises up and the sea is like a screen in front of him. The woman is there, held like a rag doll.

Everard snaps his neck. 'It's a body!' he yells. 'There is a body in the water!'

But Gil doesn't hear. He is in the eye of the storm, putting all his energy into keeping their course. He hunches over the wheel, eyes fixed on the breakwater, willing it closer. This is all he cares about.

Everard skids and slides over the deck, grabbing at his arm. 'Mr Baker! There is a body. I saw a body.'

Gil turns to him, raw eyes blinking slowly, but doesn't seem to register. The boat pitches and he has to hold her steady. He is gritting his teeth, using all his strength.

'Major Hyde,' he shouts. 'Boy says he saw something.'

Let the Major deal with it, he thinks, and Hyde, who is right by his side, turns without understanding.

'A body!' Everard repeats over Gil. 'I saw a body.'

Everything seems to be happening too slowly. Everard is desperate. They have to look, they have to see.

Gil keeps his hands glued to the wheel. 'Seaweed!' He mouths the word more slowly: '*Sea-weed*.' He shakes his head, as if to say, *not to worry*.

Everard uses a hand to shield himself from the spray and moves around Gil so he's in front of his father, closer than they have been in this whole week.

'Over there! I saw something. Dark hair, a head! *It's a body!*'

A smaller wave catches them and they topple and fall back on the deck. Hyde bangs his elbow hard and yells in pain and Everard pulls himself up and crouches over, offering to help.

His father lashes out. 'You!' he shrieks. 'There's nothing out there. God damn you. What is wrong with you?'

It always comes back to that, the thing that is wrong with him. There must be something wrong with him. Everard doesn't know what it is, but he scrambles backwards, the soles of his shoes sliding on the wet deck. His whole body is shuddering and he thinks he's going to be sick.

'I saw a body!' he says desperately. 'Out there! I saw her!'

But Gil can't turn back. He has to get them safely in to the harbour. It is the job he's paid to do and the Major's boat is not built for this weather. It is what he says, over and over, even once he is safely installed at the bar of the Bel Air.

'It would have been murder to go back.'

Dolly wipes a glass and stares at him. 'But what if that Everard is right? Peg and Big George both thought they saw something out past the lighthouse. They came in earlier and told all the reporters and caused a right fuss.'

Gil pulls his cap right down over his brow. He doesn't think it's possible. But what if it is? He presses his fingers into the worn joints of the bar. He should find Everard and say sorry. The truth is, he was scared. The waves were too strong, and the Major was shouting over everyone. Gil doesn't like Major Hyde. He takes his money, but that doesn't mean he likes him. He remembers the last time Everard was here, when he was just a little boy, helping him tie up the boat and wanting to name all the knots. Gil remembers what happened after the Lady appeared. Nancy was in such a state he'd taken her into the house and given her a brandy and he'd gone to the window and watched the Major thrash at the brambles. Everard had wandered up the path to watch and then his father spun round and slapped him so hard it sounded like a whip crack. Shocking, it was.

Gil turns his glass round and round. He has no children so he can't imagine what it's like, but he is sure if he had a son he wouldn't hit him.

'There is nothing I could've done,' he says, but it's unclear who he is talking to.

The wind is still raging when he staggers home alone, his head muzzy with drink. Gil never normally drinks this much, which is why he swears that he will go out tomorrow, whatever the weather. In his own boat, with a crew of his choosing, he will find this woman and bring her in. The sky is pitch-black but it's a straight, flat road. Gil knows the way. This a man who has lived all his life in Little Sark, in his family home, now too big for one person but crowded with a century's worth of objects. He can't get rid of anything because none of it is his, and the clutter is a comfort. It reminds him of his mother and his father and his sister, who is frozen in his mind at ten years old. He sometimes imagines they are all there, waiting.

His chest feels tight as he reaches the start of La Coupée. Until now the high hedgerows have protected him from the worst of the wind. He pulls his cap over his ears and braces himself for it. La Coupée never feels very stable and he hates to cross it at night. It's like walking on a tightrope. He can hear the sea on either side and he hunches his shoulders and tries to walk fast. The wind hits him, pushing him to the left, so that it's an effort to stay upright. He presses himself into the railings and starts to make his way along.

His mother used to tell him stories about La Coupée. Of course they were just stories, but stories always start in truth. Gil pulls himself along steadily. It's so dark he can't see more than a few inches in front of him. He hears the sounds of wailing from the caves. He knows it is only the caves, but he thinks of the woman in the water, if she *is* in the water. He knows he has to force out this thought, this fear, but doubt is like a trapdoor and now it's wide open.

He stops for a moment and peers out over the cliff. He thinks back to that Saturday, being caught in the rain. Again, he is running over the headland to the shed. Again, he meets the man and woman. The woman's hair is wet and falls in ribbons down her face. Gil thinks, if he goes back enough times, it will change. He could ask them if they are in trouble, if they'd like some food. He pictures himself letting them into his house and sitting them by a warm fire. But he'd never do that, would he? He just wanted to get away.

He pulls back from the railings and picks up his pace. He is yearning for home now and he keeps his eyes down, focusing on the space just in front of his boots. The path curves up so he has to work a little harder but he's aware, without lifting his head, of the dark mass of Little Sark ahead. The end of La Coupée is carved into the cliff so it's like entering a trench. The wind drops away and the sky becomes a pale strip above him. Gil lunges like a sprinter for the finish line and then he senses something ahead. Something waiting. He tells himself it's his mind playing tricks but his heart's fluttering like a bird in a cage. Trapped: it's too late and too far to turn back.

He lifts his head and there she is. She stands with her head bent and the hair falling over her face. Her shoulders are bare and hunched: she's only wearing a slip and she is turned away from him. Gil feels his heart stop. He stands a few feet away from her, close enough so he knows that she's real. He feels the cold of her, and there is an odd musty smell like the smell from the shed. Her hair looks like strands of seaweed, catching the wind. Gil cannot breathe or move and everything is suddenly very quiet. She is shuddering from cold. He wants to touch her but he can't lift his arms.

He clears his throat. 'Come back and get dry,' he whispers, and then he wrenches his eyes away from her and stares up the road. 'I can show you the way. I should have offered before.'

The woman doesn't turn round and he wonders if she has a face. The bodies of the drowned wrinkle and bloat. The skin peels away. As Gil thinks these things his body jerks awake. He takes one step and then another. He realises he's walking away and he doesn't want to leave her, so he waits to see what will happen. If she comes along with him, he can help her. He thinks he might still have some of his mother's things. He could make some soup. He thinks of all these things quite rationally. Then he remembers he should say sorry, too. He owes her that. He should not have left her. He turns stiffly, the word forming on his lips, but before he can say it he sees that she's gone.

12

'Haunted Places'

13 August 1923

SARK ISLANDERS ARE REARED on the belief that the spirits of the dead are allowed to revisit the places and people they knew when they were alive. Considering its history, you'd expect the island to be full of drowned sailors and pirates, men with bloated skin and frosted lips, or soldiers with their bloodied tunics. Not so. In fact the ghosts are nearly always women. There is a woman in the prison, as we've mentioned, and another one who lingers in the graveyard after dark. There is another on the Rue Lucas and yet another seen round Dixcart Valley. There's even one who paces the floors of the Seigneurie, but only if a certain door is locked. And they are not the same woman, if that's what you're thinking, because according to reports they are different heights and ages, and their dresses vary in length and style. What do these women have in common, we might ask. All appear anxious or upset, as if anticipating some woeful event or finding themselves the victim of it.

Maybe the women come back because they have a stronger link to the living, or maybe the women come back because they still have work to do. They are, after all, the ones more routinely ignored and abused in their lifetimes.

They have been dismissed, belittled, not trusted, not seen. Sorry, we don't mean to go on, but haunting could be a form of revenge. It's ironic that once a person is dead they might have more power.

This was the attraction for Everard. He wanted just a bit of power, to feel that he had an effect.

He was happier since meeting Phyll and he was waiting for her now, sitting in the tree by the church. His father had left the house early, telling him to 'make himself scarce'. Everard thought that was funny, since all he did was make himself scarce. He could literally make himself invisible. He sighed and stretched out his legs. He felt safe up here; he loved the dappled pattern of the canopy of leaves, and the sound the birds made. He really could live here. Years would pass and everyone would wonder what had happened to Everard Hyde and he'd throw little missiles down from time to time.

Only Phyll would know. Everard smiled. She had taken away some of his loneliness, although he hadn't realised that he had been lonely. It felt as if they'd known each other for ages, but everything was still fresh and new. Phyll wasn't afraid to take risks and she said whatever came into her head, and she hadn't been horrified when he had told her about his tricks. Everard felt bad for upsetting Mrs Dolbel, but he was glad that Phyll was going to help. Since everyone wanted the dead to come back, it would be a good game to play. It could be their secret, like his place in the tree: somewhere nobody knew about, where the adults couldn't reach.

Everard wondered where his father had got to. He had trailed him as far as the Avenue and then given up. He knew it was wrong to spy, but since his parents' divorce no one told him anything, so there didn't appear to be another option. He leaned out of the tree and stared down along the lane, the sunlight playing tricks at the edges of his vision. That's when he saw her.

Sylvie Price was very striking: her short black hair shone like a helmet, and she had a wide mouth and almond eyes. She wanted to be an artist but she was also an excellent model. There was one photograph Paul took of her where she stared directly at the camera, her eyebrows arched so perfectly they might have been drawn with a compass. It's a shame Ann tore it up. Sylvie wore these little silver bangles on both her arms, so Everard should have heard her coming. She was tilting her head back, but she hadn't seen him. He was sure she hadn't seen him.

Everard plucked a leaf from the closest branch and held it out in front of him, rolling it between finger and thumb, debating whether to let it go. Sylvie might like to be tricked by him, but Sylvie was clever and it would be a shame to get caught. He hesitated, weighing up the odds, because this was a game he wanted to keep playing.

'There you are!'

The leaf fluttered down, spiralling quickly, spinning round and round. Everard didn't see it land because Paul Cecil, Mr Cecil, had run up to Sylvie and grabbed her wrist and pulled her under the arch. She let out a short laugh and then it went quiet. Everard stayed perfectly still with his arm outstretched. He stared at two pairs of feet pressed together, toes touching. Tentatively, he leaned out further. Mr Cecil and Sylvie were kissing. Sylvie was kissing Mr Cecil, or Mr Cecil was kissing Sylvie. Everard wasn't qualified to judge.

He was suddenly very cold: a chill spread through his body, reaching up to his shoulders and his neck. He closed his eyes and felt his heart skip and jump. It seemed to be turning somersaults. When he opened his eyes again, Mr Cecil and Sylvie were gone. He breathed out in relief and then he frowned at the space they'd left. Mr Cecil and Sylvie. That wasn't right. He leaned back against the trunk.

Had he not been so shocked he might've climbed down the tree and run straight to the post office. But Everard knew he couldn't do that, because Phyll had told him under pain of death never to call for her at home.

'My mother will see into your soul,' she had warned, fixing him with her most penetrating gaze. 'She will read your innermost thoughts and guess what we are up to . . .' she leaned forward, 'we'll be *done* for.'

Everard didn't want anyone to see inside his brain so he stayed still and waited with his hands pushed between his knees.

He would have found the post office closed, in any case. Elise Carey was, at that moment, standing in the middle of her darkened parlour, hands clasped and head high.

'You feel as if you don't trust your own eyes,' she was saying.

She was talking to Major Hyde, which was a bit of a surprise. He had turned up just as she'd finished with the post, looking furtive and asking for a 'private word'.

'This is all very embarrassing, but Nancy mentioned that you had seen her, too . . .'

He was referring, of course, to the Stranger Lady Nancy had told the Major about Elise and her abilities. She may even have called her 'psychic'. So here they were, alone together in the front room of the post office. Elise always kept these front shutters closed in the summer. It meant the air stayed cool, although now it added atmosphere. The sunlight fell in narrow stripes on the floor and dust danced in-between them. Elise stood very straight, balancing her weight on both feet. The Major drew a little closer. She was surprised by how close he came. She peered into his eyes, which were a very pale blue. She reminded herself she didn't like handsome men. She did not like handsome men because they always knew they were handsome and therefore exploited it. She cleared her throat and told herself to focus.

'I was with my husband,' she said. 'We had been walking around the island before he joined his regiment. He had gone on ahead and I was looking at the view.' Elise rocked back on her heels, transported to that moment. 'She was just *there*, beside me. It was such a shock. The world went quiet. The sky, the sea, the ground under my feet, it all just fell away. I looked at her and she looked at me.' Elise paused and looked down, as if searching for something lost. 'I don't think I have ever felt so scared.'

The Major bent his head. He was so tall he seemed to fill the whole room, even as he tried to make himself small. 'And what did she *look* like?'

Elise held her hands together, then drew them apart. 'She had dark hair that hung around her face, like it was wet. She wore a white dress. I did think perhaps a wedding dress.'

The Major nodded and stared at her intently and she wanted very much for him to blink. She looked down. Maud had warned her this might happen — well, not this specifically — but Maud had made a lot of noise about how Nancy was in such a state that she might hand in her notice. 'She swears blind Beau Regard is haunted, and she can't carry on working there, but Nancy *has* to work now Harry can't. They won't manage on his pension.'

Elise had not responded so Maud had sighed several times, very loudly, and twisted her mouth into a series of odd shapes. Oh, Elise had tried to refuse. She felt for Nancy, she really did, but she didn't like involving herself with anyone who wasn't local. It was one of her rules, especially since the lady visitor getting trampled by a horse. She reminded Maud of that whole miserable episode, but Maud jutted out her chin and muttered about responsibilities, that it wasn't about the Major, it was about the Lady, and Nancy.

'We women stick together!' Maud said, which is what she always said – she could literally bang a drum to it. Then she began to list all the times she'd looked out for Elise, and where would they be now without each other, etcetera.

Back in the parlour, Elise refocused on the Major. 'But this was *years* ago,' she said. 'Phillip never even saw her. I wondered if it was a sign that he was going to die, but he didn't . . . not in the War.' She glanced away to the side. 'One of life's great ironies, you might call it.'

Major Hyde nodded. 'Yes.' A hesitation. 'But was he injured?'

Elise frowned, trying to find the words to reply. She felt they were wandering off course. She folded her arms and forced herself to look at the Major. 'Perhaps *you* could tell me exactly what happened . . . *to you.*'

That was more like it. Elise was a very good listener. Years of staying silent honed her skill. But maybe it wasn't a skill, rather the absence of one. All she had to do was ask a question and wait. She sometimes pictured herself digging a giant hole for people to fall into. Silence was space. She maintained eye contact, keeping her expression neutral, and oh, how people talked, especially about themselves. It helped that they always assumed she knew more than she did, and so told her more than they should. The Major was no exception. He was soon pacing the room with his arms behind his back, talking about the cave at Derrible and his boat and the Cecils. He even mentioned a Greek myth, which Elise found quite baffling. He said the woman had appeared out of nowhere by a clearing close to the house. He'd heard a noise and there she was. She'd seemed so real to him that he'd searched the grounds afterwards, determined to find her. It had been a dreadful shock. But that wasn't all. Ever since then the house felt different. It was as if someone had taken up residence alongside them. He'd walk into a room and sense that someone had been there just ahead of him. Doors were left open and then suddenly slammed. A glass had been smashed, books moved. 'Small things, I grant you, but unsettling nonetheless.'

Elise watched as the Major ran his hands through his hair. It was thick, with streaks of ash blonde. She imagined he used some kind of oil on it.

'Maybe it sounds foolish,' he concluded, 'but the house feels,' he hesitated, '*occupied*.'

Elise kept her hands together. 'You have the sense you are being watched.'

The Major nodded. He was again very close to her. She could smell the tobacco and whisky, both of them expensive.

He turned and paced over to Phillip's chair. 'May I sit?'

Elise felt her whole body tense. Only Maud was allowed to sit in Phillip's chair, but she didn't know how to explain that, and now she was too late, he was already making himself comfortable.

She walked over and sat down facing him.

'The Stranger Lady,' he said. 'It's an odd name.'

'Well.' Elise opened her hands. 'I didn't know her, and you are sure you never saw her before . . . Maybe you would prefer to see a ghost you know.' Elise paused. 'Like your brother.'

Hyde's eyes jumped. 'My brother?'

Elise looked down at her hands. 'It would be understandable to see someone you know, a family member, or one of the men of your regiment, or even one of the Germans you killed. Seeing familiar faces would make sense. You could think of them as resurfaced memories or remnants of dreams.' She looked up. 'Or the work of a guilty conscience.' She allowed herself a small smile. 'We want to *know* our ghosts, so that we can feel a bit more in control. We can't always.'

The Major appeared to give this some thought. 'But she appeared to *me*. She wanted *me* to see her and I have to believe there is a reason. She looked so terribly desperate. I mean to say, does she need my help?'

Elise's smile widened. How typical of a man to assume a woman needs saving. 'She's dead, Major. I think you are a bit late.'

The Major let out a short, startled laugh. 'You are right, of course!' But then he drew his eyebrows together. 'Perhaps she thinks it is *her* house still.' He leaned over, resting his elbows on his knees. 'I was talking to Dr Stanhope about it. He thought perhaps, because of the War, my senses are heightened. There is all this *energy* we don't normally see, and the people who have had a great shock are more able to see it.'

Elise swallowed. 'An affinity.'

Hyde nodded. 'And if the woman *has* come back, then others might.' He looked up as he said that. 'Once a connection is made . . . I was wondering if you would come to the house, Mrs Carey? Would you come and have a look around?'

Elise frowned and sat back. 'If you want a medium you'll find them at the back of the newspaper, Major Hyde.'

'Oh no!' He lifted his hands. 'No, nothing like that. I . . . I . . . I just mean, well, it's very helpful to share this with someone . . . It would help Nancy, too. If you just walked around the house.'

The Major leant so far out of the chair he was almost in her lap. Elise reached out and laid a hand on his arm. She gave a single, almost imperceptible nod. 'All right then. We will see.'

It was always something to feel that power flow towards her, like a stream coming down a slope towards a river.

As he left, the Major took both her hands and held them. 'I am really very grateful,' he said.

It gave her a warm feeling. Elise liked how he'd looked at her. She would go to the house and walk through each room and she thought, yes, I can do this. No promises, but perhaps I will sense something. What would be the harm? She paused in the hallway and looked in the mirror. She had been avoiding her reflection for months, but now she smoothed down her eyebrows and pressed the flesh on her cheeks. People used to call Phillip handsome, but they said it with a sly glance her way, as if their looks didn't match. Why should looks match? Elise frowned and then stopped herself and instead lifted her chin and turned her head slowly. She wondered if the Stranger Lady would know her if they met again. Her hair had now grown out enough to skim her shoulders.

When Elise first cut her hair, everyone was mortified. Maud had thrown her hands up. 'Your best feature!' she cried. 'Your lovely hair!'

It was in the weeks after Phillip vanished, so people put it down to shock. Elise never said otherwise. What use would it be to tell them the truth, that Phillip had wrapped her braid around his fist and pulled so hard she thought her neck would snap? Her lovely hair, a lovely noose. Elise exhaled slowly, watching her shoulders fall. She told herself it wasn't his fault. Like the time when he cracked her ribs and broke her nose. No, it was her fault. She should have been better prepared. There'd been warning reports in the newspapers, about how men returning from the Front were subject to odd moods and violent outbursts. Elise told herself that couldn't be Phillip, even when it was, even when he woke in the night, arms flailing, raging.

But what use was it to think on that now? She wanted to remember the man she'd married, the quiet man from before the War. She closed her eyes and counted back. A clear day coming into autumn. The sky a deep, pure blue. Elise could even smell the gorse. Then she felt another presence: the Stranger Lady beside her, close enough for her to touch. Elise opened her eyes and looked again in the mirror. She made a noise somewhere between a shout and a sob and clamped her hands to her mouth. She had only seen it for a second, but now she understood. That afternoon on the cliffs it had been like seeing herself on her wedding day. It was not so much a realisation as a recognition, like uncovering a fact that she'd known all along. Of course, she thought, *of course*, and she wanted to sink to the floor and fold herself over.

The warning had been for *her*, not for Phillip, of the terrible things to come.

PART TWO

13

GUERNSEY EVENING PRESS

Monday, 9 October 1933

'WOMAN'S BODY TAKEN FROM SEA'

The body of a woman was recovered late yesterday from the entrance to a cave under Port Gorey in Little Sark. Something had been seen in the water on previous days but a positive sighting was confirmed by a young islander, George Vaudin, who had been keeping watch from the cliffs. He spotted the body and promptly alerted the Chief Constable John de Carteret, who visited Port Gorey. It was not at the time thought necessary to put out to sea as it was believed that the body would come ashore in the half tide, but after much deliberation it was agreed that a recovery by sea was safest.

Assistant constable Jim Remfrey accompanied Gilbert Baker and Alfred Hamon on Mr Baker's motorboat *Vigil*. They were able to locate and remove the body and return to Creux harbour. Mr Baker, it will be remembered, had encountered the missing man and woman in a shed a week earlier. Mr Baker was unable to say definitively that this was the same woman, such was the state of her disfigurement, but he did recognise her hair.

For many islanders the discovery of the body has confirmed their worst fears. It now falls to our newly appointed island doctor, Dr Stephen Greener, to examine the body and confirm cause of death. More details to follow in the evening edition.

PHYLL SITS AT THE KITCHEN TABLE, staring at the words 'cause of death' on the page. She has moved her typewriter in here because the desk in her bedroom – two tea chests pushed together – was giving her a stiff neck. She sighs and slams the carriage back. She knows she has to write more. The woman's body has been found, so this is her big chance, but it's too hard, too devastating. She shivers and rubs her toes together. Her socks are still wet from when she stepped into one of the ever-widening puddles on the Avenue. She should take them off, but she wants to stay cold.

She was waiting on the breakwater when the *Vigil* rounded the cliff, and as she braced herself against the wind, she remembered other days she'd walked there, when she'd watched Gil go out, looking for any trace of her father or his boat. Gil never spoke to her, but when he saw her he'd often give a little shake of his head. The memory shocked her, and for a minute it felt like time was twisting round to trip her up.

Of course today was different: today they had a body.

'Is it her? You are sure it is her?' Phyll called out.

Who else would it be?

She was hidden under a crumpled sail tarpaulin, a body like a landscape in miniature. Phyll stared at the pits and troughs and backed away, unable to hold back her tears. She didn't wait to meet the new doctor, who was shivering under a large umbrella.

Stephen Greener is a bachelor in his thirties. He worked in Guernsey for many years but took the post in Sark on a whim, idealising a simple state of society and customs handed down.

'I was expecting the odd fish hook and horse bolting,' he said, gulping the tea Dolly offered. Dr Greener accompanied the body up to the Colinette, and it was here time played another trick. His eyes, which were jumping nervously over the crowd, fixed on Everard Hyde. The doctor felt a sudden jolt. Did they know each other? Had they met? Stephen Greener thought so, but when Everard caught him staring, he quickly looked away. He was then guiding Small George back to the comforting arms of his mother.

Small George, we can report, was pleased to have found his dead body, but the excitement didn't last. From a distance the woman looked like a shop's mannequin, floating with her face down, but George can't describe what he saw when they turned her over. Such gory details won't go in any of the news reports, but they shall give him nightmares for months and years to come.

Back in the kitchen, Phyll yanks the page out of the typewriter. She reads it over, frowns and rubs her temples. She stands up and walks in her wet socks down the passage, leaving little damp marks on the flagstone floor. She pushes open the front door and leans out, inhaling deeply.

It is that quiet moment before dark, and the rain has stopped too late for it to matter. A fine mist coats and cushions everything. Phyll rests her head on the doorframe. She is still holding the sheet of paper. She hasn't counted the words but she knows there aren't enough. For the past week she has imagined this runaway lover, this fugitive creature. She has pictured her slipping onto a steamer bound for France, and boarding a train for Italy, and arriving at a busy port in Spain. She has dressed her in all kinds of new clothes, something fashionable but not too daring, and she's cut her hair into different styles. This mystery woman was going to change her name and start again. Phyll has thought up all these possible endings, all these alternatives, and now none can happen. The prison door slams shut and she jumps, looking up. Just a gust of wind. Phyll hasn't believed in ghosts for years, but sometimes she misses them.

Back in the house, the shoe is still under the floorboard on the landing. Phyll never asked, but it actually belonged to Albert. He put it there just after he became postmaster. Albert had a great respect for the old ways, though he wasn't a fan of ghost stories. He believed the girl in the prison who heard weeping most likely scared herself with the echo of her own sobs. Similarly, the housemaids who saw the pale woman at the Seigneurie were confused and grief-stricken after their beloved Seigneur drowned. They saw themselves, that was all. Albert liked to offer a practical explanation. The ghosts are just us, he said, nothing less and nothing more.

It's a good point. We think the clothes we wear, the words we write, the things we build are what makes us real, but they are just the leftovers. It's what we feel that makes us real, and what we love and fear and hate and miss.

But the leftovers give others comfort. Albert loved every inch of the post office and so his mark is everywhere. He sanded down the door that Phyll rests her head against. He also built the shelves in the kitchen. They are not as elaborate as the ones he built later. Here, he opted for a single shelf that runs around the whole room just below the ceiling. He did this because he was worried about some of the things Maud kept. 'They should be out of the reach of children,' he told her, back when he thought they might still have some.

Maud bustles in through the back door, just as she's done for the last forty years. Some days she expects to find Albert waiting there. She is carrying a basket of freshly cut rosemary. She's not sure why. She remembers walking with Elise to the Colinette and then the rain drove them back. Maud forgot her coat so she borrowed Elise's oilskin. She slips it off, frowning. It feels too heavy – like wearing a tent – but in one of the pockets she's found a photograph. The picture of Phyll, Everard and Miranda as children. Ah yes! That took her back. Maud thinks Phyll looked better with long hair and will have to tell her. She tuts. The shock of her cutting it! So like her mother! She lays the photograph on the table next to the typewriter and spreads the rosemary out to dry. She does this very carefully.

Phyll wanders back along the hallway, sniffing the air.

'I love that smell. Rosemary for remembrance. Is it for the lady, Maud? That's nice.'

Maud smiles and then nods because she's sure it was.

Sark doesn't have a morgue – there has never been a need for one – so the woman has been laid out in the old outbuilding of the Bel Air. It's the custom on Sark that a body must not be left alone in a house overnight and so our two constables, John and Jim, agree to watch over her. John takes first shift, setting up camp in the open doorway. He's cold and wrapped in his coat, sitting on an old camp chair, but because he's exhausted he falls asleep quickly and then he hears noises and wakes in a panic. Time is circling back. He is in the trenches. He lurches forward, arms outstretched. He swings round, calling out. 'Who goes there!'

A stooped figure turns towards him and his heart stutters and stops. The woman is in front of him, she has come alive. He splays his arms against the doorframe. 'God in mercy!'

'No, John. It's me.'

He knows that voice and time slows down. The shadow takes on substance. It is Elise, but she looks strange. He realises she's wearing Phillip's greatcoat. John clutches his heart and staggers back, then he bends forward, resting his hands on his knees. 'Elise! What are you doing?'

Elise has had just enough time to brush the tears off her cheeks. She has come to see the body, of course. It's been years, but still she wonders. When there isn't a body you always wonder. She has long accepted that her husband has gone, but where he's gone, she cannot say. There are still nights when she stands in the courtyard and looks up and down the Avenue. We live in anticipation of certain moments, those watersheds or whatever you want to call them, when there will come a burst of clarity, of sudden understanding, when things just fall into place. But what if that moment never comes?

John finally straightens up and catches his breath. Elise shrugs at him. 'I just thought you might want company,' she says, as if this is quite normal.

John, still only half awake, lifts his scarf over his nose because the smell is terrible. 'I thought it was rats. Come away. Why didn't you wake me first?'

But Elise doesn't move. 'I left a flask of coffee outside. But bring me the lamp, please. I need to look at her properly.'

John does as he's told but turns his own face away. He will not look at the woman again. It is a too-terrible sight. The front of her skull has collapsed and there are no eyes or nose, just a hole where they should be. It is as if her whole face has become one wide, petrified scream. It looks worse in the lamplight but Elise doesn't blink. She pats at the hair, which is brittle with seawater. She wishes she could tidy it. She looks down the length of the body. The arms are pale and slim, and she sees no cuts. But there is a wedding ring.

Elise feels a little unsteady as she walks outside and she stands beside John, not saying anything, just clearing her lungs in the fresh air. John has unscrewed the flask and the bitter smell of the coffee rises up. He pours out a small cup and offers her his chair.

John is the only man, other than Phillip, that Elise has ever loved. They've known each other all their lives. They went to school together, played together, learned to swim together. There are so many things she can list on her fingers. Then it got to the point where they knew each other too well, like a brother and sister. That's what she tells herself, anyway.

There comes a shout, then a peal of laughter from the Bel Air, the sound of a door slamming.

Elise draws her shoulders back and stares straight ahead. 'He killed her then.'

John crouches low beside the chair, his knees cricking painfully. 'Is that what you feel? I did wonder if she might have fallen forward. You can easily lose your way on the cliffs at night.'

Elise tilts her head to count the stars. 'It was a full moon.'

John doesn't say anything for a moment, then he turns his face towards her. 'So you think he killed her? Sorry to ask . . . but can you use your gift?'

Elise swallows hard and shakes her head. 'I'm going on common sense only. Maybe it is because I didn't meet them.' She takes another sip of coffee and hands him the cup. 'At least we have a body. Phyll had it in her head that the woman wasn't dead. She was driving me mad with her silly theories. I suppose it was wishful thinking. When there isn't a body . . . you always wonder.'

John stares into the cup. 'You're thinking about Phillip?' He doesn't wait for a reply. 'I think about him, too, all the time. I wish I had done more. I should have tried to talk to him, but we all had our struggles.' John takes a sip of coffee. 'I don't know what was in his head, going out in a storm like that.' He pauses, waits some more. 'But maybe it was his solution.'

Elise turns her head very slowly. 'Solution? What do you mean? *Solution?*'

John, uneasy, clears his throat. He stares down at the ground and then up at Elise. Her face is very still. He hands her the cup. 'That time he was blown up,' he says. 'Everyone else in his group got killed. He told you that.'

Elise leans over to pick up the flask and refill the cup. 'He didn't *need* to tell me. He'd wake up thinking all this stuff was on him. He was clawing at it, pulling it off him, but it was his own skin, I told him . . . I told him.' She stops. 'He could not even hear me.'

John takes the cup then sets it down because it is too hot and his fingers burn. 'About the other men: he said there was nothing left of them to bury. It was all mixed up, and he said that was better . . . He said there was nothing worse than the smell of a rotting corpse. We all knew that smell.' John glances over his shoulder. 'I remember he said it was better to be, ah, what's the word? Obliterated.'

Elise finds she has to fix on something to steady her mind. She makes out the furrows in the vegetable patch, the low shrubs beyond. 'Are you saying that Phillip went into the storm so that he *could* be destroyed?'

'I don't know. We repeat things, don't we?'

Elise holds herself steady. She recalls how Phillip would talk through the bars of his fingers, holding his face in his hands. The same hands that tried to choke her, that dragged her by her hair.

After a minute she clears her throat. 'When he was angry it was like the house couldn't hold him. I . . . I . . . ' she stops. 'I was worried for Phyll.' She stops again. 'I used to find her huddled on the stairs, listening out . . . She'd listen to him stomp about and wait until it was safe . . . '

John doesn't say anything and Elise knows she has to leave. She stands up quickly, but her whole body has started to tremble. 'I told him to go.'

She blurts out the words and John straightens up to meet her and reaches out an arm. She takes it. 'I told him to go,' she whispers. 'I *had* to.'

Elise will always say she loved her husband, but the truth is more complicated, as the truth often is. She stares at the ground, at her feet, and she blinks fast to stop the tears.

'I just needed him out of the house, away from us. I didn't mean for him to leave the island, to take the boat that night . . . I just wanted space.' She wipes her eyes and gulps a breath. 'I didn't mean it.'

But she can't even remember what she said to him. She was wrung out, exhausted, and when she found out the boat was gone, she didn't panic. She told herself Phillip would be fine. He had made it through the War, so surely he could make it through a storm. Elise would do the same thing again – she does believe that – and she often opens the wardrobe and tells it to his clothes. She tells it to the night when she stands at the open door. She tells it to his shoes, and she tells it to his chair. She would tell it to his face if she ever saw him.

But she's never said that to Phyll, and it's a secret Elise carries inside her. When she comes home later, she can hear the clack-clack-clack of the typewriter in the kitchen. She takes her time to bolt the door and pats her eyes so that Phyll won't see she's been crying, but Phyll has come into the hall and is holding something up. 'Why did you have this? Tell me. Why?'

No hello, how are you or where have you been? Elise cranes her neck and sees the photograph of Phyll with Everard and Miranda at Derrible Bay. She feels her chest tighten. Not this, she thinks, not now.

'It was in *your* coat pocket,' Phyll goes on. 'Why would you go through my things?'

Elise leans back on the door, sighing. 'I suppose *he* gave it to you.'

Phyll cocks her head. 'Do you mean Everard? No. He did not give it to me.'

Elise turns to look at her face in the mirror. Her eyes are red but Phyll hasn't noticed.

'It is a nice photograph of you children,' she says bitterly. 'But when I saw it I just saw the people behind you.' She points to Sarah Williams, so pretty and young-looking in her fitted white dress.

Phyll looks down at the photograph. 'What?'

'Remember *her*,' Elise jabs a finger. 'You did not care for her feelings, did you? What are we all to you, Phyll? Are we just like characters in one of those books you read? You want to move us about, make us act how it suits . . . '

Phyll's eyes snap up and she stares at her mother. 'It wasn't like that!' She breathes. 'You know it wasn't like that.'

She is blinking fast, real tears pricking her eyes, and for a second Elise feels terrible, as if she's crushed something precious. She wants to say sorry but she cannot think how.

She slips off the coat. 'I don't know anything,' she replies wearily.

That, at least, is true.

14

The Venus Pool, Little Sark

(A charming tidal rock pool nestled in the cliffs of Little Sark, only
exposed an hour before low tide. Take the grass track over Gorey Common.
Sensible shoes advised.)

13 August 1923

MANY SARK STORIES concern thwarted lovers. Young men fought each other, often brother against brother. They loved some girl passionately, with the ardour of a child for a butterfly, pursued, adored, then forgotten in an hour. There were misunderstandings aplenty, since young men are notoriously inarticulate. One chap jumped off a cliff to his death, another was pushed by his friend.

But the Venus Pool is not named after any such story. Earlier guidebooks have credited William Toplis with both discovering and naming it. Wrong! It was originally called 'Feeney's Bath' after Peregrine Feeney, a lesser-known artist who showed it to Toplis, and 'Feeney' became 'Venus' because someone wasn't listening, or because Old Toplis mumbled.

A lot of people never find it because even if they make it over La Coupée they take too long marvelling at the views or they scramble down the wrong path and then forget the tide, which moves like a monster freed. It took Toplis twenty years to paint, which is some indication of his obsessive genius and possible madness. He could only work when the light was right and tide was low and the rocks exposed, and this only happened on rare days and for a few hours at a time. Actually, now we think about it, maybe the name is right, since love is like that: equally hard to capture, only caught in glimpses, impossible to keep.

The plan that day was for Phyll and Everard to meet the Cecils and find the pool together, but the tides were wrong and Phyll was late. She did have an excellent reason.

'You won't believe what *I* just heard!'

Phyll had been collecting her swimming things when she'd eavesdropped on her mother talking with Major Hyde. 'He has asked her to come to your house, to see if she can make contact with the Lady. Your father asked her especially. Everard! This is *perfect*!'

It was too good a chance to miss. Phyll ordered Everard onto her bicycle and made him pedal as fast as he could. Beau Regard was close enough to the Venus Pool so they could go there first and 'set the scene'. Everard wasn't sure what Phyll meant but he did as he was told, standing up on the pedals and leaning over the crossbar. Phyll sat on the saddle and held tight to his belt. She screamed as they crossed La Coupée and a group of tourists pinned themselves to the railings, looking on in horror. You weren't allowed to cycle over La Coupée ('We broke the law! Ha ha!') But Phyll only told him afterwards, once they'd reached the house.

Back then Beau Regard was still well-kept, with tidy borders and an immaculate lawn. Clematis hung over the windows by the kitchen and the doors didn't creak. The air smelt of wood polish and every surface gleamed.

Everard waited, willing his heart rate to slow, counting time with the grandfather clock in the hall. He was hot from cycling, the sweat trickling down his face.

'We should hurry,' he said. 'Just to be safe.'

Out on the grass Phyll's bicycle lay abandoned, one wheel still spinning on its own. Everard hovered by the door, trying to still the panicked thumping in his chest. After a minute he heard an odd, shuffling sound and turned his head to look.

A hunched figure came staggering out of the drawing room. Everard jumped back in terror. Then he realised it was Phyll. She was wearing his father's old mackintosh and had pulled the collar over her head so she looked like a hunchback.

She stuck her hands out straight. 'I've come to get you!' she croaked. 'Watch out, little boy!'

Everard forced a laugh. 'That is not remotely frightening.'

Phyll dropped her arms and emerged from the coat. 'I know. Must try harder . . .'

They walked into the drawing room and stood for a moment, looking about.

It was perfectly neat and tidy. There were pale pink roses in a vase between the windows, a sofa and two chairs upholstered in dark velvet, cushions with gold tassels plumped up on them, a stack of books on the writing desk. Everard followed Phyll's eyes, trying to see what she saw.

'Perhaps we could knock over the vase?' He pointed.

Phyll frowned and pressed her lips together, then she shook her head. 'Too obvious.'

She did not like this room, she found it cold and impersonal, and the clock on the mantelpiece ticked down like a bomb. Aha. The mantelpiece. There were lots of photographs all crowded together, in ornate frames and set behind glass. She drew a little closer and saw ladies in dark, flouncy dresses and children with big eyes and white collars and young men in peaked caps. She remembered afterwards that there hadn't been a single one of Everard, but it wasn't about that. She only had one small photograph of her father, his face the size of her thumb. It hadn't bothered her before, but now it did. She saw all these people lined up, looking at her, and they were proof of something she didn't have. She reached for a family group: a mother and father and their two little boys. They looked stiff and unhappy, as if they'd been stitched into their clothes.

'Those are my grandparents.' Everard was standing close, whispering, as if they could hear.

Phyll nodded and put it back very carefully. She stepped sideways and selected another frame. It showed the same two boys, but older now. They stood on a shingled beach in front of a boat, bare-chested and suntanned, each clutching an oar. She pulled the picture close enough to see her own face in the glass, with Everard just beside her. She saw his ear and one eye and she watched him blink.

'My father and my uncle,' he whispered. He was acting like they were in a museum. He pointed to another frame. 'And this is my uncle in his uniform. He is dead.'

Phyll barely glanced at it. She was still holding up the picture of the boys by the boat. She recognised the Major, his nose and his eyes. The younger brother was darker, smaller, with his chin tilted up. Phyll set the frame down but kept her hand on it and then, quite suddenly, she jerked it forward. The frame toppled and fell, hitting the hearth so the glass smashed. It made a very satisfying sound and Phyll stared at the back of the frame and the small shards of glass scattered around it. It looked quite natural. Everard had uttered a small noise like a gasp but she made a point of not turning to look at him. She was going to be brave for both of them, or at least that's what she thought.

Of course, a bit of broken glass wasn't enough. Phyll had a better idea. She crouched down and stretched her arm inside the chimney and patted the brickwork with her hand, coating it in soot. As she pulled it out, powdery black granules scattered onto the carpet.

Everard was still staring at the broken frame, and when he saw the soot he stepped backwards, afraid of leaving footprints. He followed Phyll into the kitchen. She grabbed the handle of the back door, and then made four fingerprints on the wooden frame beside it. She stepped back, cocking her head, like an artist assessing her work.

'I think that's good,' she gave a nod. 'Not overdone.'

Everard swallowed hard and looked at the smudges. 'But do ghosts leave handprints?'

Phyll swung round and looked at him squarely. 'If they fully materialise then yes, they can leave hand or footprints.'

Everard felt he had to nod, and Phyll smiled and looked again at the doorframe. She lightly smudged the soot marks, then gave a little shrug. 'After all . . . how else do they knock on doors or push things over?'

Everard accepted she was right, that she was, after all, the expert.

He said, 'Perfect, let's go.'

The Venus Pool is eighteen feet deep and almost circular. Some days the water is turquoise blue, other times khaki green. Toplis's painting of it is now in the Guernsey museum. It is the only work where he added a human figure, which we feel was a mistake. The original model was hired by the artist when he was in London and he paid her sixpence for the trouble of perching on a box, but she didn't quite fit with what he desired and so he later painted her out and copied a model from a magazine. Ann Cecil found that hilariously funny: the quest for an ideal that didn't exist. Ann had sat for Paul when she was younger and was now encouraging him to paint Miranda, 'a more perfect specimen of English girlhood' who wouldn't cost a thing.

Phyll and Everard had gone directly to the pool and were already treading water when Ann and Miranda appeared. Ann looked annoyed.

'Sorry we were held up. Have either of you seen my husband?'

Everard shook his head and sunk lower in the water so she couldn't see his mouth.

'Sorry!' Phyll cried. 'We walked the *whole* way on the cliffs from Grande Grève . . . '

Miranda went behind a rock to change and Ann stood for a while with her hands on her hips, studying the cliffs on either side. She talked constantly, almost to herself, muttering about angles and light, and then settled with her sketchpad.

Phyll swam in a small circle around Everard. 'Please don't look so scared,' she whispered. 'If anyone suspects, I'll take the blame, I promise, I swear.'

She meant it very seriously because she thought he was worrying about what they'd done. She knew he was afraid of his father, and she remembered what that felt like. She wished she could take it away. She dived down, kicking up her legs and swivelling round so she could stare up through the water's surface to the blue sky above. She let her body sink lower and stretched out her hands to touch the boulders at the bottom. They were smooth, worn down over the years, thickly coated with seaweed. She stayed there for a minute with her arms splayed, and she let out a breath and watched the small bubbles of air rise up to the surface. She felt calmer under the water and she wondered how long she could stay down. Everard was floating above her, his pale legs marbled with sunlight. She wanted desperately to reach out to him. Until this point Phyll had only loved a certain number of people whom she'd known all her life. It made things simple. Now, that was changing. She felt the blood pounding around her body, she'd almost run out of breath. She willed Everard to look down; she decided if he looked down now it meant he loved her, too – and she kept her eyes trained on him and waited and waited.

But he didn't and Phyll let herself be lifted up. She broke through the surface and swam fast to the other side of the pool. Never mind, she thought, and she distracted herself with an image of her mother marching over to Beau Regard and finding the soot and the broken frame. She smiled and turned around. Everard was still treading water and Miranda had changed into her swimsuit. She twisted her hair to one side and moved to the edge of the pool, delicately lowering one foot into the water and gasping at its coldness. Phyll realised with a jolt that Everard was staring at Miranda. She gulped in a breath so fast it stung. Kicking off from the side she swam a fierce backstroke across the pool, then spun around in time to snatch at Miranda's foot. She made it look playful but she tried once and then twice, and because her hand was wet she couldn't get a grip. Miranda kicked out at her, annoyed.

'Stop it! Phyll. Don't be silly!'

Ann looked up from her sketchpad. She wondered what was going on, but she didn't wonder for long. She had already noticed the looks Everard was giving Miranda, and in her head it made perfect sense. Miranda had really emerged this summer, she was a rare flower coming into bloom. Phyll was bound to feel jealous. Ann smiled a sad smile, because three would always be a difficult number. She misunderstood the scene perfectly, just as she misunderstood a great many things. Phyll misunderstood it, too, but she had youth as her excuse. She struck out into the middle of the pool, windmilling her arms over her head. 'Fine then, strike your poses,' she said. 'Little Miss Artist's *Model*. I can't think of anything more *b-o-r-i-n-g*!'

Everard wanted to say he quite agreed but he didn't trust his own voice. Nothing was happening as he thought it would. He felt uneasy being here with Mrs Cecil and Miranda. He focused on the rippling surface of the water. The sun felt very hot on his neck and shoulders, like it was holding him down. He flipped onto his back, stretching out his arms and his legs, but the sun was too bright and made him frown. He closed his eyes. He had told himself not to think about it but his mind kept jumping back like a scratched record. Sylvie and Mr Cecil. Mr Cecil and Sylvie.

He turned his head and watched Miranda ease herself into the pool. He felt sorry for her now, knowing what he did. His mother's affair had been this terrible thing. He'd only understood a little of what had happened, but he remembered lots of slammed doors and everyone being embarrassed. He had felt to blame for it, which wasn't right or fair, but it was easier for him to blame himself than anyone else and the guilt had been like an object he could pick up and put in his pocket. It weighed him down and he felt the weight now. He was angry at Sylvie and Mr Cecil for adding to that. He liked Mrs Cecil much more than her husband, and he didn't want her to be upset. But he couldn't risk telling anyone, not even Phyll. It wasn't about trust, because he did trust Phyll, it was about guilt and blame. He watched a single cloud pass over. I have forgotten, he told himself, it's fine.

The minute the tide was out, it started to come back. All three children lay in the sun to dry off and watched the sea reclaim the pool and flood the rocks. Everard and Phyll chose to take the long route over the cliffs and were saying goodbye to Miranda and her mother just as Mr Cecil and Sylvie appeared at the top of the path. Paul jogged down the path to meet them.

'Sorry, sorry!' He waved his hands. 'Got held up.' He reached Ann first and kissed her lightly on one cheek. 'Darling, I've come to fetch you for drinks at the Bungalow. I just saw Earnest. Huge drama at his house. Mrs Carey confirms the place *is* haunted.'

'*Really?*' Ann's voice rose up an octave. She twisted her head round to look back at Phyll. 'Do you hear that, Phyll?'

Phyll had scaled a boulder a little way off and paused with one foot above the other. She hauled herself up and gave her best nonchalant shrug. 'Well, my mother would know.'

She turned back and grinned at Everard, who was glaring straight at Paul. He didn't say anything and they carried on up the track together, walking away from the others.

Phyll waited until they were out of sight, and even then she took care. 'Aren't you pleased?' she asked quietly. '*It worked.*'

Everard didn't answer straightaway. He stopped walking and looked out to sea. 'It's great.' He didn't seem happy, though. He narrowed his eyes. 'Let's show them all. What next?'

15

GUERNSEY EVENING PRESS

Tuesday, 10 October 1933

'DISAGREEMENT AT SARK INQUEST'
BY OUR OWN REPRESENTATIVE

As reported yesterday, the body of a young woman was discovered off the coast of Little Sark. This follows a week-long search of the island after the clothes of a man and woman were found abandoned on the cliffs of Little Sark. The identity of the couple remains unknown, but it is believed that they had arrived on Sark on Friday or Saturday, and were talked to by a handful of islanders. Although there is no clear evidence linking the dead woman with the clothing found on the rocks a week earlier, everyone on the island feels the sense of an inevitable connection.

Our Sark correspondent, P. Carey, was present at the inquest, and can now offer a full account of what is surely the most mysterious drama in recent history.

It was a most sombre occasion. At three o'clock this afternoon, in the fading light of the Sark schoolroom, with desks pushed to one side of the room and small children sent home, island officials and members of the public came together. Mr Frederick de Carteret, acting as coroner, began the enquiry, opening with the customary Sark ritual of Our Lord's Prayer spoken in French.

The first witness was then called. Mr John de Carteret, Chief Constable of Sark, confirmed that the body of a woman had come in with the tide. It had been found in the shallow water close to where, a week ago, two sets of clothes had been found at Port Gorey. The body wore only undergarments: a pair of blue knickers and a slip-over. There was also a gold wedding band on the third finger of the right hand. The hair was dark, the face badly disfigured. The body was ultimately recovered by boat and brought round to the Creux harbour.

Dr Stephen Greener, the island doctor, was then called to give evidence. He had examined the body that was now being stored in the old stone store adjacent to Bel Air Hotel. He could confirm that it was a woman of five foot five inches with dark hair. He estimated her to be in her twenties. The body was already in a state of decomposition. There was no sign of injury to the spine or limbs, but the skull had been shattered, the nose and part of the jaw was missing. Dr Greener stated that the extent of the injuries could not have been caused by the action of the waves. In his opinion they were probably caused before death.

Mr Frederick de Carteret asked if they could have been caused by a fall from rocks. Dr Greener replied that it was possible if the woman had fallen forward and her head hit the rocks first, but there were no other injuries or broken bones. Frederick de Carteret then asked the doctor to consider whether it was likely the woman took her own life, as this might explain the absence of other injuries. Dr Greener accepted that this theory needed consideration, but without any knowledge of the woman's state of mind he could draw no conclusions.

Mr Gilbert Baker, a farmer and fisherman of Little Sark, was then called to give evidence. Mr Baker, it will be remembered, had met a man and the woman sheltering in a shed on Little Sark the previous Saturday. He was asked to repeat details of their conversation and give an indication of the 'mood' between them. Mr Baker felt he was unable to offer an opinion. He deduced that they were together and that was all. They discussed the weather and he helped them hang up their coats on the rafters to dry.

Another witness, Miss Dolly Bihet, the housekeeper of the Bel Air Hotel, was then called. Miss Bihet had identified the clothing of the man and woman from press photographs and could offer a clear recollection of serving the couple. They only drank black coffee and did not speak to each other. Miss Bihet sensed they were depressed, and possibly had had an argument. It was Saturday afternoon and she presumed that they were waiting for the return boat to Guernsey, although she did not see them leave.

There followed various lines of discussion about what might have happened. Several members of the press expressed the view that it could not be a case of suicide as there were no letters of explanation or farewell. It was also noted how the clothes were neatly folded and left above the tideline, as if to suggest a bathing accident.

The coroner put it that the likely explanation was the unfortunate couple had run out of money and after a night of sleeping out in the open, had gone into the water to wash. As they were strangers to Sark they would not have known about currents and the danger to swimmers, especially at this time of year. It is possible the woman got into trouble and the gentleman tried to save her, and both have tragically perished. There is still every chance the man's body will come in with the tide.

The coroner ruled that as the woman's companion has not been found, and as there are no other witnesses, there will be an open verdict of 'an unknown woman is found drowned'.

This was considered inadequate by many present, and there followed nearly an hour of heated debate. Some parties were eager to frame the death as accidental, yet others argued that this was in no way consistent with the woman's injuries. The word 'murder' was spoken more than once, first in a murmur, then with greater passion, and questions have been asked as to whether Scotland Yard should have sent over detectives to assist in the investigation.

In light of all this, Dr Greener has recommended that the body be sent to Guernsey for further tests and investigation. Much as we wish to lay the lady to rest, for now, the funeral must wait.

'OH MY HEAVENS, you have been stirring the pot.'

Dolly's milky-white face has flushed a rich pink from all the alcohol. She hands the newspaper back to Phyll, who drops it on a table crowded with glasses.

'It's not just me,' Phyll says defensively. 'And I am only reporting the facts.'

Dolly nods. 'Of course, and it's good there will be a second opinion.'

But not everyone agrees. It's been a day since the inquest and the island has split itself apart. Plenty of people think it's a fuss for nothing, but others are muttering about 'foul play' and a cover-up. Fred de Carteret blames the newspapers for turning the whole thing into 'a cheap whodunit'. Phyll worries about that. She and Dolly have read quite a few of them, after all. It is how they spent the last three winters. And Dolly is now calling herself a 'key witness' after Dr Greener declared her observations 'most astute'. Dolly cranes her neck, hoping to see him.

They are at a party at the art gallery. Yes, we know it is poor taste to have a party the day after an inquest, but Eric Drake swore he planned it weeks ago. This is his third exhibition and he wants to mark the end of what he calls 'the season'. Plus, there will never again be so many journalists on Sark, so it is too good an opportunity to miss. Eric has already asked Phyll if she would review the show for the *Press*. 'A change from dead bodies,' he said happily. 'Light relief!'

The gallery stands at the end of the Avenue. It is a concrete structure with pillars and a dome-shaped roof, built in a matter of weeks this summer. Elise considers it a blight and an eyesore and won't be in attendance. Lisl, Eric's wife, did invite her. Lisl is twenty-nine, blonde and American, having married Eric in New York after knowing him a matter of weeks, which is the kind of thing we warn against in stories. Never leave your family and home for a man you barely know, but an adventure is always exciting at the start.

Lisl lights a cigarette and sucks hungrily, shivering in the cold. The gallery, so light and airy in the summer, is proving a Devil to heat. Behind her, Eric slops more lethal punch into mismatched glasses. Candles have been pushed into empty bottles and shoved in corners where they flicker erratically, under threat from constant drafts. Although pleased with this arrangement, Eric has made no effort with himself. Just the other day Elise asked him if washing and shaving were other aspects of modern society against which he was rebelling. He laughed heartily and said, 'Don't forget to mention me in your Black Mass, Mrs Carey!'

Charming, really.

'God, I love your mother,' he tells Phyll, filling up her glass. 'She's bloody funny.'

Phyll frowns. 'I don't think she means to be.'

'She's cursed us,' says Lisl, who kisses Phyll on both cheeks then wipes off the lipstick smudge she made. 'I keep seeing rats. She's sent us a plague of rats!'

Phyll sips her drink and winces at the sweetness of the punch. 'I doubt it. There have always been a lot of rats on Sark.'

Lisl laughs, snorting cigarette smoke through her nose. She is very beautiful but there are faint fault lines appearing around her mouth. 'What about this poor woman?' She sighs. 'Obviously the chap killed her. Eric wants to go to London next week and I've told him I shan't be left alone. There could be a murderer on the loose.'

'Oh for heaven's sake.' Eric makes a circling gesture with one arm. 'Don't be so dramatic. He is long gone, I bet.' He turns his attention to Phyll and bows grandly. 'Shall I take you round the show? You are going to write it up, I hope, now that you are a *gentleman* of the press!'

Phyll cringes and glances left and right. 'Does everyone know?'

'*I* think it's brilliant,' Lisl touches her elbow. 'Good for you! Paul would be proud . . . He always said you could write.'

Phyll feels the colour rise in her cheeks. 'Paul? Paul really said that?'

But her words fall into empty space. Both Lisl and Eric have turned away suddenly to greet new guests coming in. She takes a long sip of her drink and turns to look at the pictures, which are unframed and abstract, then she notices Fred de Carteret standing a few feet away.

'All this fuss.' He is glaring at her over his spectacles, 'I am sure it *was* an *accident* . . .'

Phyll wipes her mouth. 'You are entitled to your opinion, and I am entitled to mine.'

She turns away and drinks more of the punch, heart thudding fast. She's still thinking about Paul. So he talked to Lisl about her. The idea makes her skin prickle. Paul was the only person she had shown her writing to and he'd always been encouraging. She'd like to think that that, at least, was real. She finishes her glass and hurries into the second room, looking for somewhere to set it down.

'Phyll!' Mule Toplis waves frantically. 'Come here. I *must* talk to you.'

Mule is clad in a green evening gown cut on the bias, and for a woman who never dresses up, it's quite a transformation.

Phyll goes to her, smiling, and Mule grabs her by the arm. 'Have you heard the news about Paul?' Phyll blinks. Why do people keep mentioning Paul? She shakes her head. 'No . . . I . . . er . . . what *about* Paul?'

Mule covers her mouth with her free hand. 'He's had an awful accident. He *fell* out of his new studio window.'

Phyll thinks it is a joke. It sounds so implausible. Her mouth widens into a smile and she's about to laugh. 'He fell out of a window?'

Mule nods. 'Yes. Silly fool . . . '

Phyll is confused by Mule's off-hand tone. 'Wait – is he . . . is he dead?'

'Oh no.' Mule has grabbed two crackers off a tray and dispatches one swiftly and speaks through the crumbs. 'Back is broken, though.' She swallows, covering her mouth. 'He was at the new studio in Paris, trying to get a look at the view. He leaned out too far and some masonry gave way.'

She pauses, the second cracker held by her mouth. 'These artists and their views!'

Phyll stares into space. Paul has spent ten summers climbing all over the cliffs. He isn't afraid of heights and he's never once lost his balance. 'He was looking out of the window?' She's dazed. All she can do is repeat the words she heard, as if she's learning lines.

Mule swoops to the drinks table and returns with two glasses. Phyll takes one and drinks almost all of it, then presses the cold glass to her cheek. Mule watches her thoughtfully, sucking crumbs off her fingers.

Phyll shakes her head. 'How could that happen?'

Mule's eyes shine like wet stones. '*Who knows?* You would have to ask Miranda.'

'Miranda? Why Miranda?'

'He was *with* Miranda.'

Phyll has to concentrate hard on staying upright. Paul was with Miranda. Of course he was with Miranda. This time, finally, she had planned to go with them. She had handed in her notice and even bought her ticket. She was so excited, it had all seemed so perfect, but then everything fell apart. She can still feel Paul's hand pressing into the small of her back, curling round her waist. She hears him whisper into her ear, and now he is stroking her hair. She swallows and squeezes her eyes shut. She is ambushed all over again. It was wrong, all wrong, and she had written to Miranda and told her. She had to explain why she couldn't go away with them. She told her exactly what had happened. *We had promised there'd be no more secrets.*

'Isn't it strange?' Mule says loudly. 'When did you last see Paul? Didn't he look you up in Southampton before he sailed?'

Phyll thinks of the last time she saw Paul, when he called her a child and slammed out of the door. Her eyes start to swim. 'He had some galleries to visit . . . ' her voice quavers and fades. She wants to tell Mule everything, but she's stunned by the shame of it.

Mule leans in. 'No Miranda?' She watches Phyll's face closely.

'No.' Phyll has dropped her head, letting her hair fall like a curtain in front of her. 'I . . . I didn't see her.'

'Ah.' Mule folds her arms and stands very still. She lets the noise of the party swallow them for a moment, and then the penny drops. 'Oh my dear,' she says tonelessly. She lifts a hand and touches Phyll's shoulder. 'Oh my poor dear girl,' she says quickly. 'He didn't, did he?'

Because Phyll is just the right age, and Mule knows what Paul is like. It took her a few summers to see the pattern and then it was all she saw. He likes them at twenty and twenty-one, when they are fresh-faced, unattached and easily flattered. He charms and teases, offers 'an education'. Mule never understood why Ann put up with it, but she assumes they had rules. Not your daughter's friends, for example. She peers into Phyll's face, her dark eyes turning liquid. She wants very much to hug her, but instead she reaches out her hand and lets it fall in the space between them.

Phyll is already backing away and she pivots so fast she bounces against Mr Frith, who slops his drinks and cries out in alarm. She ignores him and fights her way towards the door, then she sees Everard standing outside, half in shadow and turning away. She's so shocked she freezes. Bodies push against her and she feels like she's surrounded. She uses her shoulders to weave outside.

'Everard!' she calls, but she can't see him anywhere. A few huddled figures turn and glance at her, but he's not there, so she starts quickly along the road, in the direction of Little Sark, almost running. 'Everard! Wait. Come back!'

The darkness swallows her but by the time she's past the church her eyes have adjusted. She slows her pace to a brisk walk, stopping occasionally to check her surroundings. Clouds have blotted out the stars but she can see the outline of the road ahead and the high earth banks on either side. She keeps going because she wants to talk to Everard, and it might be easier in the dark with a bit of alcohol inside her. She wants to ask him why he went away, why he never came back and why he never wrote. Yes, she will ask him all of those things. She's a bit giddy, but she walks steadily, listening to the crunch of her shoes on the road, turning her head slowly from side to side.

'Everard?'

Her throat is starting to hurt. She folds her arms. She wishes she'd brought a coat, but at least Mule hasn't followed her. She doesn't want to talk about Paul. She doesn't want to think about him, either. She remembers him unpinning her hair and draping a scarf over her shoulders, and how he sighed and said, 'ah, better.' She sets her teeth together, makes her hands into fists.

'No,' she says aloud.

She doesn't know who she's talking to, but there is a reaction – a darting movement in the bank to her right. She swings round to face it, arms out. Her heart's jumping and she waits another minute, holding her breath. Someone is there. What if it's the man? She remembers what Lisl said about a murderer still on the loose and she pictures him there in the dark. She's tensed, ready to run but one minute passes, maybe two. All is still.

She stamps her feet, kicking up gravel. If it's a rat, there'll be an answering rustle, but there's nothing, no sound at all. Phyll wonders if he's there. She scans the road ahead, and then looks back the way she came. There is nobody about – is it safe? She's not scared. She tells herself she is not scared.

She can't have seen Everard in the doorway. She must have imagined it. How sad to see his face everywhere, to be thinking about him so intensely he just appears. Like a ghost, she supposes, but she doesn't believe in ghosts. Not any longer. She hunches her shoulders and stares at her feet. Perhaps Everard was there, but didn't want to talk to her. She's been so angry at *him*, she hasn't considered the possibility that he's angry with her, and he has every right to be. That summer ten years ago she promised she'd take the blame and in the end, she didn't. Everard was blamed and sent away, and she never spoke up. She didn't try to help. She was too scared and too selfish.

She let him down.

The night air is prickling her skin, making her numb and she rubs her arms quickly. Better to go back. 'I am sorry,' she says into the darkness. 'If you're there, I am really sorry.'

Then she turns and starts to walk back the way she came. She stares at her feet and walks in a straight line but she still has the feeling she's not alone. She walks quickly, tucking her hands under her armpits to warm them. She thinks about running back to the gallery. She'd be safe there and she could explain to Mule about Paul, and make her promise not to tell anyone. Mule cannot tell anyone. No, Mule wouldn't. Phyll groans out loud.

She is almost by the church and she can hear the noise from the party: there's music and laughter and the sound of a glass smashing. She breathes out in relief and slows her pace. She reaches the archway and waits a minute, debating what to do, and again she has that feeling, that someone is watching. She glances into the graveyard. Did Everard come here? She hovers on the edge of the road, peering in, but she feels uneasy. The skin on the back of her neck crawls as if something cold and wet is gathering there. She smells the sweetness of damp earth and rotting leaves. She turns very slowly and steps back. It is very dark under the trees: not like the shut-in darkness of a room, but a more deep and natural darkness. She reminds herself she's not afraid of the dark but her heart squeezes painfully. She tilts her head back and stares through the branches to the sky. The leaves that remain are thin and shifting. Then it happens: something small and sharp hits her shoulder. She pauses mid breath, the air in her mouth. She lifts her hand and brushes her shoulder, feeling only the fabric of the dress.

When she hears a branch crack, she doesn't hesitate. Maybe it's all in her head, but that doesn't make it better. She runs hell for leather towards home.

16

'Some Odd Superstitions'

13 August 1923

'FIRST YOU MUST open all the doors and windows and burn some herbs – sage is best, very cleansing – in the hearth. Then put some herbs in a great bucket of water and wash down every floor and surface. If someone wants to do you harm, or you feel there is evil in your house you must *cleanse* the space.' Maud was pulling the comb through Phyll's damp hair and she paused to tease out a small knot. 'Then,' she lifted the comb, 'you must go round and shut all the windows and doors one by one.'

Maud had given Nancy the usual instructions: an old trick that she'd learned from her mother, who had heard it from her mother, and so on.

Phyll leant forward, tensing her neck. 'And that works?'

Maud was about to reply when she noticed Elise standing in the doorway. She turned her head and smiled.

'Of course,' she said quietly. 'If you ever feel someone wishes evil upon you, you must not talk to or look at them, don't even open your mouth. You must lock them out, so close everything: shut doors, windows and gates, you must even plug the keyholes. *That way* you deny the evil access.'

Elise came into the room and settled in the chair facing them. She clasped her hands in her lap and watched Maud go to work on another knot, taking a handful of Phyll's damp hair and pulling the strands apart. She marvelled at Maud's patience. Elise was not the sort of woman to bother with knots. That's what scissors were for. She consciously avoided meeting Phyll's gaze and instead bent over to unlace her boots, then she took a while rubbing her ankles and rotating them. She was very tired. The walk back from Little Sark had finished her off and she had the beginnings of a headache – her own fault for drinking the Major's brandy. But at least she'd been able to reassure Maud and Nancy. She'd made it clear that the 'weird energy' at Beau Regard was down to the Major's brother, hence the photograph being smashed in the hearth. She reported no trace of the Stranger Lady in the house and no threat to Nancy. Good to have the matter over with.

She straightened up and closed her eyes, but still she could feel Phyll watching. Elise braced herself. She had never known a child to ask so many questions. The sign of an active mind, Maud said, but as far as Elise could see, Phyll changed her mind constantly. Just two months ago she'd threatened to cut all her hair off with a kitchen knife and truly, Elise had been thrilled, yet now here Phyll was: resplendent in a freshly starched nightdress, long hair shining like oil. Elise was tempted to say, 'To what do we owe the honour,' but she didn't want to start a conversation. She assumed Phyll was trying to impress Miranda Cecil, which was not the worst thing in the world.

She rested her head back, and minutes passed in what she considered a companionable silence. Well, at least one minute passed. Elise heard her daughter sigh and shift position, then Phyll began to tap her foot on the edge of the grate. Tap-tap-tap. *Here it comes*, Elise thought.

'Major Hyde called it *uncanny*!' Phyll blurted. 'You went into a trance and sensed the presence exactly where the woman appeared! Did you see her? Mr Cecil was very excited. He said they should *hire* you for a séance . . .'

Elise snapped her eyes open. Séances she had heard about. Locking women in cabinets. 'Never,' she said crisply. 'Hire me out? Like a carriage?'

Phyll lowered her eyes and bit her lip. 'No. Of course.'

Elise arched her eyebrows. 'I won't discuss what went on. You *know* my rules, Phyll.'

Her tone was harsh but the child needed reminding. If people were to trust her then she had to honour that trust, and this was a small island. Elise didn't want Phyll fuelling gossip.

She looked across at Maud, who seemed to take the cue.

'Yes, and if things get any worse,' Maud said lightly, 'we could get a sheep's heart. You have to pierce it with iron nails and hang it in the chimney and set a good fire.'

Phyll shrieked and Maud laughed. 'It's true! They did it all the time when I saw a girl. You will still find a few shrivelled hearts stuck up chimneys, believe you me.' She laid her hands on Phyll's shoulders as if holding her in place. 'Now, let your mother rest . . . She's done enough today. Let's get you upstairs.'

Elise relaxed and let her mind drift, and she must have slept as the next thing she knew, she was alone in the parlour. She heard Maud's low voice and then a ripple of giggles from the floor above. Elise didn't always approve of Maud's stories, but it's not like Phyll was easily scared. Elise looked across at Phillip's chair. Well, not anymore.

She leaned forward, holding herself rigid. 'So,' she said in a whisper. 'Is this it?'

She waited a moment, gripping her knees. It was still possible to see the dent Phillip's body had made in the upholstered back of the chair. Elise stared hard at it, and waited, and as usual nothing happened. She blinked and sat back, slumping her shoulders. 'Fine! Have it your way.'

Let's be clear about one thing: Elise had never for one minute thought Phillip would take the boat out. She had wanted him out of the house, that was all, and she assumed he'd take shelter from the storm and calm down. When he didn't appear the next morning, she thought he was calling her bluff. But days became weeks and we all know the rest. Was he dead? She didn't know.

That's right. She didn't know.

Elise only said Phillip was dead so that people would stop asking. She was the woman who had all the answers, so how could she *not* know? She said it as a test, really, and she assumed something would happen, and she waited for a sign. She kept his chair by the fire and his shoes by the door and she watched them. She thought she'd feel something, sooner or later. But she sat facing his chair and felt nothing, and she stood at her post office counter and felt nothing. She cut her hair and wore his coat. Still nothing.

What was wrong? What had changed? If he was really dead, wouldn't she know? Maybe it was the shock, maybe it was the grief, but Elise had no reaction. She felt numb and dumb. It was as if the sound had been turned down on the whole world. She told herself to give it time. Phyll asked where her father had gone and Elise said, 'He is right here,' but it was a lie. Then other things happened, like Sally Vaudin fell pregnant and Pat Hamon's nephew was killed and Elise had no inkling. Where were the dizzy spells, the buzzing in her ears, the lucid dreams? As if losing a husband wasn't bad enough, she had also lost her power, her gift, her curse, her burden.

Of course Elise blamed Phillip – the shock of him leaving – and she didn't tell anyone, not even Maud. She thought if she was patient then it would come back, and in the meantime, she watched everyone carefully (hence the glasses), and she listened to every bit of gossip, and yes, she prised open some post. Where was the harm? People had come to rely on her, they needed her, and she didn't want to disappoint.

So she had gone to the Major's house and walked through all the rooms, touched his papers, pictures and books, and she'd even held his hands and looked deep into his eyes. And she had felt absolutely nothing. The thing about the dead brother was a guess. The smashed frame in the hearth would have been a gust of wind, and as for the soot marks, anyone could have made them. She had been tempted to say as much, but there'd been something about how the Major clasped her hands. She had wanted to shake him off but her muscles went slack and there was no strength in her arms, and then he'd said they had both lost people they loved.

She'd held his gaze and noticed the symmetry of his cheekbones and the straight line of his nose. Men aged better than women – why was that? The way he'd stared at her. It had been quite some time since anyone had paid her such attention. Was it wrong to feel flattered?

'Are you awake?'

A small, cold hand on her arm made her start. Elise opened her eyes. She was still downstairs and someone blocked her view of the chair. She swallowed – her throat felt dry as sand.

'You need to come upstairs.'

It was Phyll. She was speaking quietly. 'There is something in my room.'

Elise grasped the arms of the chair. My daughter, she thought. It still surprised her, that rush of love. She had been so pleased to have a girl. She remembered Maud saying, 'It's a girl,' and breathing out in relief, and Phyll squinting up at her, her puckered face so serious even then. Later on, people said she was lucky because boys grow up wrong without their fathers but a girl would be fine. Elise said she was lucky full stop.

She reminded herself to breathe. 'Something in your room?'

Phyll nodded and brushed the hair from her eyes. A face as pale as her nightdress. Elise thought she must be dreaming since Phyll never brushed her hair, then she remembered. Maud had been here. Maud had put her to bed.

Phyll lifted a hand and was pointing to the rafters. 'I think it might be Dad.'

Elise's heart lurched. She pulled herself up and reeled about the room. 'In *your* room?' She was standing up now, swaying a little. She picked up the lamp and swung into the hall. She took the stairs two at a time. *So this is it*, she thought, *he's here*, but then she pulled up short on the landing. Was she dreaming? Her heart was crashing against her ribs and she had to rest her hand on the wall. She thought she might be physically sick.

'It is in my room,' Phyll said quietly, coming up behind her, her voice high and breathless. Elise stared at her for a minute, still not adjusting to how she looked with her hair loose. Elise shook off the thought as irrelevant, took a deep gulp of air and stepped over the threshold. The room flickered in the lamplight. It looked the same as always. Phyll's books were stacked upright along the floor, on the window ledge, on the chest of drawers beside the door. So many books, Elise thought, they seemed to make a frame for the whole room. The bed was crumpled with the sheets pulled back, the mattress sagged in the middle. Elise scanned the cabinet beside it, all the objects. She stared hard at everything and then she stretched out her arms. She was waiting to feel something: a tingle down her spine or a change in the air. She paced to the far corner and set down the lamp, then she ran her hand through space, spreading her fingers, watching the shadows she made. She turned away from the wall and took a breath and then another, and the pause between the end of one breath and the beginning of another contracted and expanded. She felt nothing. She saw nothing. She edged forwards and the floorboards creaked so she stopped again and waited, and then she turned just her head to look at Phyll, who stood waiting patiently on the threshold. Her face glowed in the lamplight but Elise couldn't make out her expression. She walked lightly to the bedside table, pressing her fingertips down on the wood. She felt curiously like two people: one version was standing beside Phyll, and the other was in the room, performing. She sighed deeply and then Phyll walked across the room, took her hand and tugged her to the bottom of the bed. '*Here. Here,*' she said quietly.

Elise stared into space. She wanted to sit down, to give up, but Phyll clung to her fingers. 'Don't you *feel it? Here.*'

Elise felt only an extraordinary anxiety. She looked down into her daughter's eyes and thought she might cry. She lowered her head. She was going to say, 'No, he is not here', but the words dried up. Going back over it later, she wasn't sure what she was thinking. She focused all her weight in the balls of her feet and reminded herself that children need certainty. It had to be black or white, yes or no. Then she told herself she would do anything for her daughter.

She raised her head sharply. 'Aha! I do feel something.' She gave a nod. 'Yes, I really do.' Then she smiled at Phyll and waited for her to smile back. It was enough, wasn't it? She shut her eyes and imagined light and warmth, not horror, not pain. She swallowed, waited. 'He meant no harm. He was checking on his little girl.' Then she released Phyll's hands and stepped away. 'Well, Phillip. Come and sit in your chair. Let's not scare each other.'

In terms of irony it was second to none. All over the world, as night draws in, parents tell their children not to worry about ghosts, and yet here was Elise inventing one. But it was more a wish than a lie, since she did want Phillip to come back. Only she wanted him back to the man he was before, the one who didn't scare her. So it was actually a lie.

And she didn't question for one minute whether her daughter was doing it, too.

17

THE PEOPLE

Wednesday, 11 October 1933

'POLICE SEARCH FOR MISSING MAN'

The body of the unknown woman found in a cave in Sark and on which the verdict of 'found drowned' was returned at the inquest has been brought to the sister island of Guernsey for further inquiries under police orders.

The body was removed from a stone outhouse where it had been stored and brought to Guernsey on an old lifeboat. It was hard not to feel pity for the few passengers on that vessel, conscious as they were of their sad cargo. The captain reported boisterous seas between the islands but the body was safely delivered to St Peter Port and taken to the sanatorium to be viewed by medical experts.

Various lines of investigation, hoping to identify the young victim, are being pursued, and the search continues for her companion, since the clothing of a man was found laid out on the rocks beside those of the woman.

If that is the case, there is still the man to locate and it seems quite extraordinary that there remains no trace of him at all.

PEOPLE COME TO SARK TO DISAPPEAR. It is, after all, very easy to slip off the beaten track when there are so few of them, and if the visitor tires of cliffs and beaches, they'd do well to explore those narrow paths inland. The sheltered valley of Dixcart is the perfect place to hide. Here the different kinds of trees knit together, blotting out the sky, and the ground is a forager's heaven, rich with edible plants and herbs.

It is early and Maud is walking. She collects sprigs of lemon balm to rub between her fingers. Good for colds. Has she had a cold? She doesn't think so. She is walking alone, following the path of the stream down to the beach. Well, she is not entirely alone – every so often a small child with short dark hair peers out from behind a tree or a shrub. But who is this child? For half a minute Maud thinks of Phyll. But Phyll would be barefoot and filthy and this child wears smart new shoes. 'I am invisible!' she whispers. 'Can you not pretend?'

Maud smiles and straightens up. Of course she can pretend. She is very good at that. She brushes the soil off her hands and tilts her head back, tapping two crooked fingers to her chin. 'Who is that talking? Is it thin air?'

In the seventeenth century, Sark islanders believed that the spores of ferns could make a person invisible. The vicar at the time wrote about it. He said young men used it to communicate with the Devil and commit wicked acts. But then, islanders also believed that if a young girl went to the church on midsummer's eve she would see the ghosts of whoever would die the following year. Why anyone would want to see *that* is beyond us, but there was one young lady who was extremely stubborn. She was called Marie or Isabelle or Edith, and she had no patience with these old wives' tales. Her young man, however, was very upset because he did believe the warnings. He wanted to go with his beloved, but there was *another* old saying that any young *man* who went to the church on midsummer's eve would promptly die! Thus, the chap hit upon the clever plan that he would fill his pockets with fernseed and follow his girl in secret, which he did.

Midnight arrived and there they were, standing together, although the young woman had no clue her lover was present because the fernseed worked and he was invisible. Then everything else worked, too. The young woman saw the ghosts of those who would die, including her *own* ghost and (more horror), her beloved. She fell down in a faint, and her young man, who was still invisible and utterly nonplussed, picked her up to whisk her home. The girl came round and naturally screamed her head off – she thought she was being kidnapped by the Devil himself – but the young man wouldn't let go. She died of fright, or maybe the chap didn't know his own strength and killed her. When he leaned to kiss her he found her lips cold as marble, and there was no breath between them, because he had died, too.

'Maud! This is a terrible story!' Edie stumbles backwards into damp moss. 'Why are you telling me this?'

'Because you wanted to be invisible!' Maud wafts a frond of lady fern over Edie's face. 'The next morning the islanders found the young woman's body floating in the air . . . They tried to lift her down, but she couldn't be moved, so they agreed to wait another day, and sure enough in the early morning there were two bodies. The young man was lying crossways under his girl, as now midsummer day was past, and he was visible again.'

It is a good story, but let's be serious. Ferns in any form won't make you vanish. They will, dried into powder, soothe a bad stomach, and if stuffed in a mattress they will banish nits. It's not black magic, it's Mother Nature, and all Sark women know the basics. Today, Maud has been digging up roots. October is the right time for roots, as the goodness goes back underground.

Later Edie is installed in Maud's kitchen, staring in wonder at Albert's cause-of-death shelves. She scans the bottles and jars and Maud explains how a tincture of hawthorn lowers blood pressure and fennel is good for sore gums. Edie is not really listening. She just wants to find a pickled frog or lizard's eyeball. Now that would be something.

The island children persist with this notion that Maud is a witch. Hilarious we are sure, now that we live in times when women aren't burned at the stake. Let's clear this up with no further to-do: of all the poor persons accused of witchcraft in the Channel Islands not a single one was a midwife. Midwives need to be trustworthy and reliable individuals, calm in a crisis, a safe pair of hands. Not the sort of people to go round kissing the Devil's naked rump or worshipping goats. (Not that those poor women ever did that, they were just tortured to admit to daft things.) Yes, yes, Maud knows a fair few incantations pertaining to pierced hearts and old shoes. Does she believe them? Not a bit. But they give people a sense of agency, and doing something is always better than doing nothing.

Edie makes a begging gesture. 'Please can I have potion to poison Walt Hamon?'

Maud chuckles. 'I am afraid I can't help with that.'

But actually she could. Just look on the top shelf. There is henbane (Latin name, *Hyoscyamus niger*). The seeds eaten alone can cause wild hallucinations, giving you the sensation that you are weightless and travelling from one place to another. It's likely that this was the ingredient used in those so-called 'magic brews' of so-called witches, those poor souls. During several of the scandalously unjust witch trials on Guernsey, a number of women reported that the Devil had appeared to them in various guises and induced them to rub some suspect ointment over themselves and they were 'transported through the air with extraordinary velocity' to a place where, sadly, more than their credulity was abused. What this tells us is that unprincipled and designing men drugged some women, not that they were witches. But the women were the ones who were strangled and burned, with their ashes scattered to the winds. Not fair, is it? But the world is a dangerous place for women, so it's worth learning a thing or two about plants.

Maud used to make a mixture of poppy and henbane to relieve the worst labours. Rather shocking, but it wasn't that different from the 'Twilight Sleep' touted by German doctors at the time. Maud hasn't had the best experience with doctors. Before Dr Greener they had Percy Stanhope, a total quack, even before he started drinking. A sad business. Maud would actually have to sneak into his surgery at night to clean and sterilise everything.

She warms the tea she made earlier. A blend of mint and basil, which is good for clearing the airways. Did she have a cold? She clears her throat as if to test it, laying a hand flat to her chest. She does forget things, which is hardly a crime, but then she forgets what she forgets, so it's fine. When you reach a certain age there is just too much to hold on to, so who can blame her if she prefers to pick and choose. Today she feels fine. The drama over the dead woman has brought everything into focus. She knows what happened before and she knows what's happening now and she sees everything clearly, like jars lined up on a shelf.

'Did you *hear* about Mr Cecil?' Edie chimes. 'He fell out of a window and broke his back.'

Maud eases herself into a chair facing Edie. 'Which means he fell backwards.'

Edie hadn't really thought about it. 'We still have to find this missing man,' she says. 'Do you think he's dead?'

Maud purses her lips. 'I am sure.'

'But how can you be sure?'

Just then the back door swings open, letting in a gust of icy air. Elise stomps into the kitchen and glares at Edie. Elise, for the record, looks worse than usual – her eyes are ringed and raw and her hair sticks out at angles, as if she's been electrocuted.

'What's this?' she barks, leaning over a chair and glowering ominously at the child.

Maud pours out more tea and says, 'Well, isn't this nice', which it obviously isn't.

There is a painful silence.

Elise glowers at Edie. '*Why* are you here?'

Edie gulps and presses her thumbs into the table. 'I am in hiding. Mum says I brought shame on the family . . . again.'

Elise folds her arms and sits down, her oilskin creaking stiffly. She'd quite like to hear what has upset Marie de Carteret, since normally that is *her* job. She lowers her head. 'What happened?'

'I was with Small George after school. I was trying to comfort him about finding a dead body. We were just talking, but Walt Hamon came over and started to tease us and said, "*Ooo Edie's in love with George*".' Edie sighs. 'So I kicked him with my new shoes.' She pauses. 'In the bit where it hurts.'

Elise can't stop herself smiling. She does not condone violence, but Walter Hamon is a notorious bully who is known to throw small children into cow pats.

Maud shakes her head, tutting. 'Walter Hamon. He had an *enormous* head as a baby . . .'

Edie grins delightedly. 'My mother says *I* was a very difficult birth! She says I nearly killed her.'

Maud and Elise exchange a look and lift their cups to hide their mouths. We should clarify that Maud did not deliver Edie. Marie de Carteret was by then thirty-three (and therefore 'ancient') and convinced herself something terrible was going to happen. Thus she took herself off to Guernsey, where the labour was as difficult and protracted as she had predicted.

Edie digs in her coat pocket, fishing out her father's notepad, which she may have borrowed or stolen. '*Because* I am in trouble,' she says, 'I am going to help Dad find the man.'

Elise snatches the notepad and starts leafing through it, frowning at John's impossible handwriting. Edie waits a few seconds before she tries to take the notepad back, but Elise won't let go and they have a tug-of-war, then Maud clears her throat and Elise realises she is fighting with a child. Edie reclaims the notepad, smiling.

'There *was* one thing . . . ' She is flicking through the pages and glancing at Maud. 'Small George told me that when he found you at Havre Gosselin you mentioned "two men on the beach", and one of them was Albert. But then, you told Dad you saw the couple on La Coupée. Was there another man, though?'

Maud feels a little fluttering in her throat. She scans her mind for something to fix on. Something safe. She pictures Albert on their wedding day and the carriage decked in flowers. She smiles. She honestly thought she saw him on the beach, but now she accepts she was mistaken. Albert never fought anyone. Albert abhorred violence.

'Oh Edie,' she gives a little shake of her head. 'You will have to excuse an old lady. I do get confused.'

Elise nods and lifts herself up. 'Your mother must be wondering where you are. I can walk you home.'

But Edie isn't giving up. She stares at Maud. 'I thought maybe you saw someone who *looked* like Albert. Did the man look like Albert?'

Elise is frozen into an oddly bent shape: half-standing, half-sitting. She turns her head slowly to look at Maud, who swallows and lets out a long sigh, her shoulders sinking.

'No, I don't think so. Sometimes my mind jumps and I see Albert. Of course it's not him, it's an echo of him, and maybe that's what ghosts are. If it's hard for you to understand, then think of it as a daydream.' She smiles. 'Don't you ever daydream?'

Edie twists her lips thoughtfully. Just recently she has imagined herself in court, with Fred de Carteret looking down at her, asking for her whereabouts on the night of 2nd October. She refuses to answer and smiles enigmatically and she is about to be sentenced when Small George, watching from across the schoolroom, flings himself across the teacher's desk and screams, 'She was with me! She was with me!' It's really quite brilliant.

Edie stares into space. 'But ghosts *can't* just be daydreams. Gil Baker saw the ghost of the dead woman on La Coupée. He said she was as real as you or me. I told him he should have asked her what happened. Honestly, it is so unfair. I would love to see her, then I could ask.'

Maud raises her eyebrows. 'If only it were that simple.' She lifts a bony finger and taps lightly at the table. 'Remember my little story of what happened to the girl in the churchyard? You shouldn't ever wish to see a ghost, unless you are ready to see your own.'

18

'The Phenomenon of Pousseresse'

18 August 1923

SO. A BOY AND A GIRL in a churchyard. Half past midnight on a warm summer's night. The girl wore her best white nightdress and when she swung round her dark hair spread out like a fan. She felt weightless and free, which was how she imagined a real ghost might feel. Back then, Phyll did believe in ghosts, and she didn't see the problem in pretending to be one. Everard wasn't sure what he believed in, but the games and dares were a way to find out.

The sky was dark lapis, with a few clouds to blot out the stars. It was Phyll's idea to sneak out after dark. Since convincing her mother she'd seen the ghost of her father, she had that giddy feeling of there being no rules. She didn't seriously expect Everard to come. She said it as a dare, to test the limits, and as she crept out of bed and ran along the Avenue she told herself she'd wait twenty minutes, then give up.

But miracle of miracles, Everard was even there ahead of her, hiding under the archway to the church. When he stepped out of the shadows she could only see the whites of his teeth and his eyes, and she had to cover her mouth with her hands to stop herself from laughing. They both looked different in the darkness. Everard wore his father's old coat and normal clothes underneath, and he held up a torch that he shone under his chin. They stood for a minute, grinning at each other, then Everard turned the torch on Phyll and looked her up and down.

'Why are you wearing *that*?'

Phyll tugged at the dress self-consciously, turning round. 'It's white. I am a ghost, don't you see?'

She also thought she looked quite pretty, though she'd never dare say it.

Everard shifted from one foot to the other and mumbled that it might be too obvious. There followed an awkward silence where they both looked elsewhere.

'Perhaps . . . ' Everard slipped off his father's coat. 'Put this over it. Like you did before. I have an idea.'

A short while later a strange shadow wobbled along the Rue Lucas. It swerved and then steadied itself and appeared to pick up speed. It was Everard on Phyll's bicycle, standing up on the pedals, except this time he was mostly hidden by Phyll, who perched on the crossbar in front of him. She wore his father's coat pulled up over her head and buttoned up to hide her face, and in one hand she held the torch out in front of her. She twisted her other arm behind her to keep a grip on the handle. This was quite a complicated arrangement and Everard was impressed by how still she stayed. He couldn't see much, but he imagined the effect was frightening, and the plan was to blind anyone they met with the torch, so they were dazzled and didn't understand.

Everard had to cycle fast and he was soon very hot, swaddled by the coat, but he liked cycling fast and they sped through the lanes by Dixcart, swerving twice to avoid people. At least one man cried out in shock. After that they headed for La Coupée. Phyll didn't say a word and the road was very flat for a long time, then Everard felt her tense and tip back. He expected her to tell him no, it was too dangerous in the dark. He thought about the brakes or swerving into the bank, but by the time he thought those things it was too late. The road dropped suddenly and it was like they were falling. He gritted his teeth and froze on the pedals, bracing himself for impact. He did briefly wonder how he'd tell Mrs Carey that her only daughter had died doing a hundred miles an hour in the dark off a cliff, then he felt Phyll's hands on top of his and he told himself he wouldn't let that happen. She was locked in place like a shield in front of him and there was terror and excitement and a moment of speed and balance where he didn't remember what they were doing or why, and they were just free. It felt like a near-sheer drop but it only lasted seconds and they flew, and then he had to start pedalling again to propel them up the other side. He was buzzing with adrenalin, burning with the effort. He couldn't believe they had managed it, and after a few seconds he wondered if Phyll had died of fright because she didn't move or make a sound. Then she suddenly threw back her head and let out a blistering scream. She screamed at the sky and the sound carried around them and splintered into echoes.

Everard laughed and carried on pedalling. He didn't want to stop, even though he was exhausted and they were well clear of La Coupée. Phyll kept her hands clamped firmly over his and they cruised along, pressed close. They saw nobody but he didn't mind. He wanted to keep it like that. They were the only people in the world, caught in its very centre, at that moment. It was completely strange but completely right.

Eventually he steered them gently into a bank. Phyll tumbled off the crossbar and started to laugh. She was on her knees, arms outstretched. 'I can't believe we did that! We did it! We flew!'

Everard lifted himself off the bicycle and collapsed on the hard, brittle grass. He lay flat on his back and stared at the stars. They seemed to spin like they were caught in a whirlpool. He was sweating hard, breathing fast. After a minute Phyll crouched down beside him.

'I am really sorry,' she said. 'But I lost the torch.'

Everard shook his head, smiling. 'It doesn't matter. I am just glad we didn't die.'

I am just glad we didn't die.

Phyll repeated the words later, alone in her bedroom. Her face was still flushed with excitement, gleaming with sweat. They had become ghosts without dying, which was really something. She wanted to pinch herself to check she wasn't dreaming, but there was the smell of dried earth on her hands and a streak of black oil on her nightdress. Proof, she thought. She sat down on the edge of the bed. She felt a little guilty and shocked at what she'd done, but she couldn't stop grinning. She reached down and pulled out her box of charms, and as she held it in her lap the door creaked open. It was nothing, just a breeze, but she stared long and hard at the shadows out in the hall and then in the corners of her room.

The other night she had lied to her mother about sensing her father, but sometimes, if she stared long enough, outlines would blur and new shapes emerge, and she really could convince herself of anything. It was one of the dangers of a good imagination. Like a good story, it could trick you into thinking it was not a story at all, and it became so real it was like a person sitting beside you.

And what if it *was* a person? 'Pousseresse' is the Sark word for a nocturnal disturbance. It is interesting that Sark has its own name for it, suggesting it happens a lot. The vicar who noted those facts about fernseed included it in his journal. 'Pousseresse' was when a person was either woken by a noise in the night or suddenly felt a presence close by in the dark, a spirit preying on them. They compared it to a creature like a cat or dog prowling about, and in some cases it would jump up and pin them to the bed. It was mentioned in at least one witch trial as most sufferers felt that witchcraft had to be involved, since it came and went so quickly.

Alone in his surgery, Dr Stanhope jerked awake. He felt something waft over him, a cool breath on his face. He tried to open his eyes but it was black, then he heard a sharp noise, like the clink of metal or glass. He could not sit up: there was a solid weight on his chest. Even when he was fully awake, he couldn't lift his head. There was the smell of vomit at his collar, the taste of acid in his mouth. He was sprawled on his bed, still fully clothed.

His mind spun and raced and the night returned in flashes. Major Hyde had been here, raving about his ghost.

'I believe it is a chain,' Hyde had said. 'One ghost appears and prepares the way for others, once the connection is made. It is like opening a door. The woman appeared to me for a reason, and now she has let my brother in. Last night, I felt someone was in the room with me: a dark but menacing presence. It *had* to be Evelyn. It had to be . . . '

The brother. Evelyn. Of course.

There came another sound from next door: the groan of a floorboard. Stanhope focused on the ceiling, which was low and close. These old houses, he thought, with their creaks and their sighs. The surgery was another one of Sark's oldest cottages, further along the Avenue on the opposite side to the post office. Its two front rooms dating back to the 1600s. It was here that Sark's first vicar had lived, writing his journals about witches and fernseed. Stanhope knew that vaguely.

He was still flat on his back and his heart bounced against his ribs. He slowly moved his head and stared at the door. He pictured the dead behind it. There was now a terrible pressure building on his chest, like a lead fist pressing down. He gulped air. Was he dying? He was sweating like a man with a fever. He moved his shoulders very slightly, feeling the fabric of his blazer shift about him. He needed help, some chemical assistance. His usual trick was Chloroform – dabbed on a handkerchief it always calmed him down – but he had given Major Hyde his last bottle. Damn it.

Stanhope generally preferred the milder months, but this summer had been impossible. They had gone weeks without a drop of rain and the heat had been relentless, driving everyone to the edge. He slowly lifted his hands and laid them on his chest. Now he remembered. After dealing with the Major he had gone to the Dixcart Hotel, to attend a case of sunstroke – his third in a week. He'd stayed on to listen to the wireless, but then he'd drunk too much and dozed off and when he woke the connection was broken and there was only this faint buzz and hiss.

What a day, what a night. Stanhope struggled to unbutton his shirt and lifted his chin. It had been a long walk home and he'd lost his way twice because the roads all looked the same in the dark. Then this light had swung at him: a yellow light that had come out of nowhere. It sent him reeling into a hard earth bank, filling his mouth and eyes with dust. His back still ached from the impact.

Stanhope winced in pain and levered himself forward, then he rolled and squirmed until he was almost sitting upright on the edge of the bed. He stared at the floor and took a few more breaths before he tried to stand. He rubbed at the base of his spine. There were no more sounds from next-door, so perhaps he'd imagined them, or perhaps it was a dream. He had said the same to the Major, explaining how if one sleeps very deeply and then wakes, there is always that strange in-between. 'A waking nightmare,' he called it. 'You dream and then wake and the impression left behind is so deep it seems real.'

Stanhope couldn't remember getting home, but he obviously had. He raised his hands in front of his face and moved his fingers one by one. He blinked and turned his head from left to right. He told himself he was fine. The Major's ramblings had unnerved him, that was all. 'I wasn't dreaming,' Hyde had insisted. 'I was awake when I saw the woman, and Nancy saw her, too.'

If Stanhope had bothered to write notes he would have said that the Major hallucinated this woman, that hallucinations were a symptom of nerve strain. Hyde had heard about her from somewhere and repressed the memory. As to why she re-surfaced now, well, it could be that she represented his own disguised desire. Ghosts were always about what we couldn't have. Just consider poor Nancy: a woman in the crisis of mid-life who must care for an invalid husband. Yes, a delusion could spread like any illness, and now Elise Carey had gone to Beau Regard and told the Major whatever he wanted to hear. He would have been better off trusting a gypsy at a fair! Stanhope recalled Phillip Carey sitting in the Bel Air, muttering about his wife putting a curse on him. He'd caught her burning herbs or something. And now Nancy was the one burning herbs. Poor, gullible Nancy. Stanhope shook his head. He blamed the War. It had left so much empty space for people to fill. And Sark was all empty space. Yes, there was such a thing as too much peace and quiet.

He found his matches and lit the lamp by his bedside.

'I am coming,' he called out, though he wasn't sure he could.

Silence now, apart from his heart thudding loudly. He wanted to sit back down, to sleep, but he propelled himself towards the door. It was madness to be scared in his own home. He heard another click and he lunged into his office. 'Well? *Well?*'

The orange glow of the lamp spread to his desk and the two leather chairs by the hearth. The room was empty, of course, and he breathed out in relief. He took two more steps into the room and turned a full circle. Everything looked normal, but then he stopped. Something had changed. He blinked, as if that might help him to understand. He paced to the fireplace, moving his eyes over each surface. He had the strangest feeling. There was more space between the chairs and the air smelt fresh. He walked to the basin and saw droplets of water. Had he washed? He touched his head, his collar. Then he noticed a piece of paper pinned under the ashtray on his desk. He picked it up.

> *Forgot to mention – Paul Cecil is proposing a night of 'ghost-watching' at the house, next full moon. Should be interesting. Hope you can come. EH.*

Stanhope stared into space. EH. Earnest Hyde. So the Major had returned. He felt both relief and frustration, because it *was* all nonsense, but now he'd have to go, if only to settle the matter. He breathed in deeply, filling his lungs, and something cool rippled down his spine. A breeze? So a window *had* been open. He turned and walked to the window to check, and saw his own reflection in the glass. He frowned and went to pull the shutter across, but then he lowered the lamp to peer out. He wondered about that bright light on the road. What sort of thing was that? He sighed and drew back, but the reassurance he needed fell away. He saw his face again, overlaid with something else. There was a stain where his nose should be, and the eyes looked wild and angry. He dropped the lamp in horror but his eyes clung to the window, to the face looking back at him.

'My God!' he cried.

He lifted his hands to his cheeks, but the face regarded him steadily, then turned and walked away.

19

DAILY MAIL

Friday, 13 October 1933

'SARK MYSTERY: MURDER OR MADE TO LOOK THAT WAY?'

An extraordinary story that has gripped our reading public these last weeks has come from Sark, one of the smallest and wildest of the Channel Islands. Two weeks ago the clothes of an unknown man and woman were found on the cliffs, but there was no sign of their owners. So began what many newspapers are calling 'The Sark Island Mystery'.

After extensive searches the body of a woman was discovered in the sea, her head and neck badly mutilated. The evidence suggests she was the victim of a murderer, yet we still do not know her name, nor do we know how she came to be there. It is believed that she arrived on Sark with a man – either her husband or her lover – who remains at large, and her body was either thrown into the sea or left on the rocks to be swept away by the tide.

The islanders are naturally appalled by the tragedy, but some have become equally enraged by the media interest in the case. These are very private people who guard a traditional way of life. They say there has never been a murder on Sark, and yet with only two volunteer policemen, no motor cars or street lights, and only two telephones, it could be argued that Sark is the perfect place to commit such a crime and even get away with it.

There are rumours, too, of some supernatural influence. It is said that the cliffs where the clothes were found are cursed. On any night you might encounter a ghostly woman in white, or perhaps a witch. Certainly, on a dark night, it is an eerie place to visit. One must ask why these two people came and stayed here at such an unseasonal time.

The mystery, however, might soon be solved. The dramatic discovery yesterday of two suitcases left in the cloakroom on the jetty from which English mailboats sail has added weight to the murder theory. One of the suitcases contained women's clothes and the other was half-filled with men's items. The theory was that, after killing the woman, the murderer left some of his clothes on the rock, as if to suggest a suicide pact, and then donned a fresh outfit which he had brought from the suitcase.

The first mate of the steamer *Acceptance* told a reporter that a man returned to Southampton from Guernsey two days after the clothing was found at Port Gorey. He was a tall man in a brown suit, carrying a mackintosh. 'He said he had visited Sark and found nothing of interest there.'

A further remarkable statement was made today by one of the porters in the Guernsey harbour cloakroom. He stated that the dead woman landed from the Southampton boat a fortnight ago, with a man. Some time later he saw this same man board the steamer for England alone.

DURING THE LONG NIGHTS OF SARK VEILLES, after the stories were all told, islanders like to play a little game. This involved a man donning the false head of an animal, or in some cases using an actual skull. He'd then cover his body in a sheet and make the jaws of the head open and shut. He would run about, growling and braying and trying to bite anyone who took his fancy. People either found it hilariously funny or fainted from horror and fright, and things quickly descended into 'acts of immorality and promiscuity' according to a certain vicar, who obviously wasn't there. The game was duly banned, although as with all things, the islanders carried on in secret, which made it far more fun.

Scholars have speculated that this odd game was connected to the legend of Tchico. Tchico was a spectral hound, a dog of the Devil whose eyes burned red, who was said to haunt certain areas of Sark. There were similar beasts in Guernsey and oddly enough, Guernseymen also had this bizarre ritual of dressing up. They would drape themselves in hides and go on sprees, raiding houses and molesting women. This was called going '*en varouverie*', which essentially means 'werewolvery'.

Well, well.

It does make us wonder what is worse: the wolf, or the man who dresses up as one.

But we have no concerns about Dr Greener. He has an earnest, eager-to-please manner and is also teetotal, thank heavens. A vast improvement on his predecessor, whose surgery he is now taking over. We find him supervising the arrival of his furniture, which can barely fit through the door.

'Rather poky,' he muses. 'But perhaps I can knock the two front rooms together.'

Maud raises her eyebrows. 'A family of five once lived in those two rooms . . .'

Maud is off on another walk because the atmosphere at the post office has given her a headache. She stops to inspect the doctor's furniture, which is now lined up along the Avenue. As usual she's forgotten her coat and Phyll hurries after her, holding it up.

Phyll looks quite hungover but Dr Greener is oblivious. 'Oh, Miss Carey!' he calls out, brandishing the *Daily Mail*. 'Did you see this? Quite a hysterical piece. I'm not rattled by the threat of white ladies and witchcraft, but I didn't know about the suitcases.'

'What suitcases?' Phyll takes the newspaper and reads it slowly whilst Maud peers inside a leather valise.

'Huh,' she says after a minute. 'No. Neither did I.'

Her voice sounds small and flat. She sighs and hands the newspaper back and Dr Greener folds it over and tucks it under his arm.

'I must say, when I applied for the job of island doctor I didn't anticipate such drama!'

He is trying to make a joke.

Phyll glares down the Avenue towards the harbour. 'Well, everybody here seems to think I have *added* to that drama. Even my own mother. So maybe it is better I don't write about it anymore.' She lifts her head and takes a deep breath. 'I've actually written a piece about the new art gallery.' She pauses. 'Although I am sure that will upset my mother *just* as much . . . '

Dr Greener looks confused but nods and smiles. 'Fascinating, I am sure.' There is the sound of crashing from inside the surgery. He winces and shrugs. 'One must adapt, diversify! And if you require other projects, might I request a more up-to-date guidebook? One with a decent map and recommended walks. I do feel there is a gap in the market. I keep getting lost!'

Maud snaps her head up. 'Now *that*,' she turns to Phyll, 'is an idea.'

Stephen Greener beams delightedly. He really is a good sort, trying his best to fit in.

'You've written about the gallery? *That tosh!*'

Phyll turns to find Mr Toplis glowering spectacularly. 'All this modern stuff,' he growls. 'Too much slackness, too little detail. Not like in my day . . . '

He shakes his head and jerks away from Mule, who has brought him to the surgery to have his blood pressure checked. Mule pulls a face, clearly embarrassed, and Phyll remembers their last conversation and looks away.

'Oh it's not that bad!' Dr Greener chuckles. 'A more savoury topic than *murder*!' He says the word like he wants it for dinner. 'The *Daily Mail* thinks the chap killed that poor woman and escaped.'

'Well, that's men for you,' tuts Mule. 'They always slip through the net.'

Phyll keeps her head down, praying for the ground to swallow her. She wonders if Mule has told anyone. Maybe not, not yet, but soon the whole island will know. Phyll already feels like it is branded on her forehead: 'Paul Cecil's Latest Conquest'. She keeps going back over it. She was so naive. That was even the word Paul used. *How could you be so naive?* But what else could she be? She's spent her life on a tiny island – what did he expect?

She'd do anything to turn the clock back and start again. She shuts her eyes and folds her arms tightly. When she was younger, she would smash stones down at the harbour. Other children practised throwing stones out to sea but she always found it more satisfying to hurl them at the breakwater. Her anger still feels like a physical thing, something she needs to expel out of herself. She should not have written that letter to Miranda, but she was so angry, and she felt she had to explain, and they'd promised each other there'd be no more secrets. It was a bit like throwing stones and not waiting to see where they land. Now that was *naive*, she thinks, and she sighs loudly.

'Are you all right?' Mule is watching her closely. 'I am sorry about the other night . . .'

'You do look dreadful!' Mr Toplis interrupts. 'Did you go to that party and drink their disgusting punch?' He shakes his head. 'Can't stand these young artists. Playing at "life in the rough". Mark my words, they won't last the winter.'

Dr Greener looks worried. 'Oh? What will happen to them?'

Mule chuckles. 'Don't worry, Dr Greener. As long as you don't drink too much you will be fine. The last doctor,

Percy Stanhope, died of drink, did anyone say? He lost his mind completely . . .'

Dr Greener glances back at the surgery. 'I did hear something.'

Mr Toplis peers at the article in the *Mail*. 'That poor woman, too. I am sure she came to Sark before. I keep thinking we must have met, one summer past, at the Bungalow or at Dixcart. Perhaps she stopped to admire one of my paintings. Perhaps she had thought how wonderful it would be to live on such an island, and now she's died here and she's trapped. Another ghost!'

Phyll lets out an exasperated gasp. 'There *are* no ghosts.'

Toplis puffs out his cheeks. 'You know there are . . . I'm often on the cliffs on my own and I feel it and there are always odd sounds late at night . . . '

'Please,' Mule sighs. 'Can we change the subject?'

Phyll ignores her. 'There are no ghosts,' she says firmly. 'It's just silly rumours and people are sucked in. Do you know Everard and I used to climb the tree by the churchyard and throw things at anyone who walked past? Because of that, Marie de Carteret thought the graveyard was haunted. She even talked about a cold spot!' Phyll talks fast, her words unspooling. 'And another time we cycled around after midnight and I wore Major Hyde's coat over my head.' She stops and lets out a bitter, clipped laugh. 'We scared the life out of Dr Stanhope, blinding him with a torch. We were awful, but we were children, and it was a game – that's all!'

Maud blinks slowly, her mouth puckered shut and for a moment no one speaks.

'Oh! Everard *Hyde*!' Dr Greener lifts a hand, nodding to himself. 'Major Hyde's son. I *knew* I recognised him.' He shakes his head. 'Small world, small world. So he was a bit of a risk-taker, eh? Well, that explains it . . . I met him as a boy . . . treated him, in fact. Gosh, this was a decade ago . . . I had just qualified and I was at the town practice in Guernsey and the Major brought him in.'

Phyll turns stiffly. 'You treated Everard?'

Greener nods, swallowing. 'Poor lad. Nasty cliff fall, wasn't it?' He presses his right hand to his mouth and stares into the middle distance. 'I mean, credit to him for trying to climb a *cliff*. And actually, that is interesting when one considers these things in terms of cliff falls. He must have fallen forward and raised his arm to protect himself. I was terribly worried he'd lose the sight in his eye.'

Greener folds over his fingers and says a little more about Everard's injuries, but his voice loses momentum as his eyes dart left and right. He senses something amiss. He had assumed that everyone knows everything, that Sark is so small there can't be secrets, but he's unnerved by the looks he's getting. It occurs to him a little too late that the Major had brought his son to Guernsey so that people here wouldn't know.

Everard needed six stitches above his eye, for anyone asking. Sometimes, when he is upset or anxious, he feels a gentle throbbing there. It reminds him that it happened, but not how. His memory is fractured with parts broken off. At first he wasn't meant to talk about it, and now ten years have passed and he can't. He's out walking again, scouring every inch of the coast. He wants to find the man, the man who hurt that woman, because he thinks there is still a chance. The clouds are darkening, threatening rain, but he carries on regardless.

Maud is also undeterred by the weather, and after saying goodbye to Dr Greener she drags Phyll to Eperquerie Common. L'Eperquerie is in the far northern tip of Sark. It was from these rugged cliffs that Reverend Cachemaille watched Peter Le Pelley's boat split apart. Phyll could put it in her new guidebook, if she was so inclined. But Phyll is despondent, not saying a word, and Maud stalks ahead, braced against the wind.

She is the first to see Everard coming up the path, and she notices how he takes the steps with a certain doggedness, pushing down hard with each foot. Although she can't see his face there's something very familiar about the way his shoulders slope. He is the right height and the right build and his hair is the same colour. Aha, she thinks, and something clicks back into place inside her head.

She lifts her chin and leans into the wind. She decides she won't look at him too closely because she wants to draw out this feeling. It is like being suspended in a dream. It is only when he is really close, about to lift his head that she can't resist.

'Albert!'

Everard doesn't hear the word clearly but looks up and sees Maud, and then, confused, he turns round to check there isn't someone else coming up the path behind him. There's nobody there, just the grey sea spitting up whitetops.

He turns back and faces Maud. 'Mrs Pratt?' He nods. 'Perhaps you don't remember me? It's Everard Hyde.'

Maud looks puzzled for only a second, then draws in breath. 'Of course! Everard Hyde.' Her eyes flicker slightly then open wider, acknowledging something. She lifts a hand. *Now*, she thinks, it is making sense. She rotates her hand, uncurling her fingers. 'But call me Maud, we are old friends. And look, you are soaking wet.'

Everard nods and looks down at his trousers, which are drenched below the knee. 'I climbed down to look in the caves.'

Maud takes the next step down to meet him and tucks her arm through his, drawing him towards her so they stand together with their backs to the wind. She lowers her voice and speaks into his ear. 'You have to watch the tide. Funny thing . . . we were talking about you earlier. Do you remember a Dr Greener?'

Everard looks up, suddenly anxious, his mouth making an 'o', then he sees Phyll standing on the grass beyond them.

She doesn't even acknowledge him. 'Maud, we should be going,' she shouts. She nods towards the horizon. 'It is going to rain.'

It's true, there is a thick bank of grey rolling in over the sea, but Maud doesn't care.

'Look who I found!' She holds tight to Everard and steers him up the steps so that he is soon level with Phyll. 'He went to the caves.' She turns her head to examine him again. 'Were you looking for the man?'

Everard can't think what to say, and Phyll's harsh look makes him awkward. 'Yes and I remembered these caves. I came here once before . . . ' He meets Phyll's eyes and for a moment the wind and sea are quiet. 'With Miranda.'

Maud huddles closer to him, smiling benignly. 'Well, I am glad to see you all grown up, but . . . ' she tilts her head. 'I must ask you a difficult question.'

Everard looks a little panicked. 'Oh?'

'Yes,' Maud nods. 'I want to know why . . .' she pauses. 'Why did you never write back?' She says the words slowly and watches Everard's face. 'My Phyll sent you all those postcards . . . she wrote to you twice a year, didn't you, Phyll?' Maud nods to Phyll, who looks appalled and then glances back at Everard. 'I remember you as this boy with such lovely manners, so I didn't understand why you never replied. She was so upset.'

Phyll resists the urge to cover her face with her hands. She didn't think the day could get any worse and now she wants to die. She holds her breath and prays for the ground to swallow her. Again.

But Everard is looking at her. 'What postcards?'

Phyll sets her teeth together. She tells herself she doesn't care. 'The postcards I sent.' She thinks her voice sounds quite normal and she waits a beat. 'But it doesn't matter.' She has to repeat herself. 'It doesn't matter.'

Everard gulps, his Adam's apple bobbing. He gives a small shake of his head. 'I never got any postcards, Phyll, I don't know what you mean.'

Phyll looks up and studies his face. She wants to say, don't lie, but his expression is too strained and he doesn't blink. 'I posted them to your school. I used the directory to get the address right. I got the address right.'

Everard holds her gaze. 'Phyll, I promise, I swear, I never got any postcards. I never got anything from you. I wrote *to you* and I never heard back and I thought that meant you didn't want to hear from me.'

Phyll opens her mouth. Her eyes are burning and the wind is getting stronger. She feels like it might blow her away. She draws up her shoulders. He wrote to her? How is that possible?

Maud thinks she knows. She is tapping a crooked finger to her chin. 'I suppose it *could* be a problem at the *post* office.'

She speaks slowly and deliberately and Phyll turns her head. It takes a few seconds for her to realise. 'My mother,' she says flatly. 'My mother?'

Everard starts to paddle his hands. 'Oh well, I don't blame her.'

Phyll snaps her head round. 'I do!' She glares at Maud. 'Maud. Did *you* know?'

Maud gives a flurried shake of her head, but then she wonders if she did. Her eyes skitter anxiously down the cliff to the sea. The wind is picking up. The man's body may come in with this tide, she thinks. Maybe tomorrow or the next day. She squints at the horizon, to the point where sea and sky merge.

'You have to be careful in the water. Once you're in, you can't get back.'

It has started to rain properly now and Phyll is turning away. Everard wants to stop her but he can't. They are repeating something and this time he has to let her go, so he holds on to Maud and as he does this, he senses someone coming up behind them. He turns around, and Maud does the same, and it is a perfect synchronised movement, as if someone has called out to them. For a second there really is someone and Everard rocks backwards, not understanding.

'What was that?' he asks.

His voice sounds faraway and small, and Maud looks at him strangely, as if she looks right through him. 'You and Phyll and the tricks you played. Tell me *exactly* what you did.'

20

Dixcart Hotel, Dixcart Valley

(The oldest and most secluded of Sark's hotels. Situated close to La Coupée, with easy access to the harbour. Hotel porters will meet the boats.)

21 August 1923

ALTHOUGH SARK ATTRACTS day trippers some of you may wish to stay longer. The Bel Air is convenient for the harbour, but Dixcart Hotel has long been favoured by writers and those craving quiet. Algernon Swinburne and Victor Hugo both stayed here and had rooms named after them. Perhaps Cyril Williams deserves one, too. He was a tall, bookish man who dressed well. He wore waistcoats and neckties with the collars pinned, very proper, and these thick horn-rimmed spectacles. We did wonder how he passed the medical for the Army, considering his terrible eyesight, but there is nothing we can do about that now.

Cyril Williams brought to Sark a great suitcase of books. Maybe a person should not bring books on their honeymoon but Sarah didn't mind. Cyril was a shy man who had overcome a stutter as a child by reciting rhyming couplets. One of his books was lost, dropped and then trapped between shelves in the residents' lounge. It was a 1910 edition of *Collected Poems* by Emily Dickinson, an unusual book for a gentleman but a gift from a favourite female cousin. It had a green cloth cover and languished, gathering dust, until a carol concert in 1918 when a certain beetle-browed child was sprawling on her back under some chairs and claimed it. She read aloud now:

> *I'm nobody! Who are you?*
> *Are you nobody, too?*
> *Then there's a pair of us – don't tell!*
> *They'd banish us, you know.*

It was the first poem in the book and Phyll often imagined it was written for her. Now, she imagined it had been written for *them*. She smiled across at Everard. 'Do you see? It is us. We are the pair of nobodies. We are the nobodies nobody knows!'

They were lazing in the vacant spot beside Albert's grave. Everard lay on his back with his hands cradling his head and Phyll was sitting up with her legs bent. She rested her head on her knees. She wanted to close her eyes but the minute she did the world started to spin. Everard might have been sleeping so after a minute she twisted round and lay beside him, propped up on one elbow. She made a careful study of his face – the pale forehead, the crooked eyebrows, the slope of his nose – she tried to memorise everything. To feel things for the first time was to feel things intensely, like finding a new colour or flavour. He was the one she'd compare all others to.

'So what shall we do tomorrow?'

Everard groaned and rolled onto his side, opening his eyes slowly. 'I have to play tennis with the Ladlows. There is a picnic, too . . .'

Phyll squashed the petals of a buttercup between her fingers. She didn't play tennis and she didn't know about the picnic, but the Ladlows were English visitors, so what did she expect? She breathed in deeply, as though in need of air. 'Well, *I* thought we could go to those caves I told you about. The Boutiques.'

Everard nodded lazily, eyes closed again. 'Miranda was asking about that.'

Phyll chewed her gum. She kept forgetting Miranda, and she felt a little guilty, but not enough to do much. 'I suppose we could *all* go,' she sighed. 'But you have to promise, you have to *swear* . . . we don't tell her a *thing*.'

Everard snapped his eyes open. 'I never would.'

Phyll smiled. 'Good.'

She pushed the book through the grass towards him. 'And on that note, there is something I have to show you.' She kept her fingers pressed down on the cover. 'I've had this book for ages. I found it at one of the hotels and I had never really thought about who it belonged to before me . . . '

Everard frowned and picked it up, examining the spine with one eye shut. 'You found it?'

Phyll sat up. 'Yes.' She took the book back and flipped open on the first page. The feel of the paper sent a shiver right through her. She took another gulp of air and handed it back, tapping at the top righthand corner. 'Read whose name is written there. I was never sure before, and it's not like I knew him . . . I mean, it didn't matter.'

Everard had propped himself up and was frowning now. He followed the path of Phyll's finger. It was not a very legible inscription – the handwriting was small and slanted left, and the 'ams' of 'Williams' smudged. Phyll waited as

Everard lifted the page closer and moved his lips. He shook his head and looked up at her, perplexed.

'Williams?'

Phyll nodded, eyes wide. '*C. E. Williams!* The dead husband of Mrs Sarah . . . the lady staying at the Bel Air.'

This was the moment Phyll would go back to later. She would spend other summers lying alone in the churchyard, staring at the space Everard had left. She would imagine snatching the book back, telling him to forget it, or not showing him at all. It would have been easy to think of something else, a different trick. If only, she'd think. *If only*. But we are all of us haunted by our mistakes.

This was how it happened, according to Marie de Carteret. She had been tidying the altar flowers in the church when she heard a gentle sobbing. At first she tried to ignore it. The night before she'd been packing up the hymn books when someone had started knocking on the main door. She had gone to look but found nobody there, and the silence afterwards unsettled her. Children playing tricks, she suspected, but it set her nerves on edge. Marie liked the peace and quiet of the church, especially now she had a baby at home, except recently even the church felt strange. She had told Reverend Severy there was an atmosphere and now who was this weeping? Eventually she went outside to look.

'What is it? *Who* is there?'

There was a woman on the path. She stared at Marie and Marie stared back, and after a second they recognised each other. It was Sarah Williams, the young widow who came to evensong.

She was holding a book, which she brandished in front of her as she walked up to Marie. 'The most extraordinary thing! This book belonged to my husband.' She waved it under Marie's nose. 'I haven't seen it in *years* and I just found it on the bench where I have been sketching just round the side of the church!'

Marie didn't follow. The nice lady was talking too fast in a high, thin voice and then she laughed a little manically and brushed tears off her cheeks. 'We thought it might have been stolen!' She cradled the book like a child, then she flipped it open and tapped at the page. 'It was my husband's book. He lost it. *And then I lost him, and well, it's been so hard.* But now it just appeared! It has come back.'

Marie stared at the book. She thought of the knocking last night and felt suddenly faint, but Sarah Williams was too excited to notice. She wanted to write and tell her mother straightaway. She wanted to tell everyone. She wanted to shout it down the street. It was nothing short of a miracle. All these years she had been coming back to the places she'd been with Cyril, and it sometimes felt as if she were going backwards through her life, but this, this precious book, meant everything stopped. She had her moment of clarity, of sudden understanding.

She stopped at the post office, placing the precious book on the counter in front of Elise.

'Oh, Mrs Carey. You will never believe what has happened!'

Elise, who had been watering Albert's geraniums, put down her jug and frowned at the book. Elise knew Mrs Williams as a kind, sad lady who'd been widowed far too young. Elise even remembered the husband, who had once bought the full range of Sark postcards, something that had never happened before. She took hold of the book and listened to the story of how it was lost and now found.

'Isn't it incredible?' Sarah cried. 'How is it possible?'

Elise opened the book and stared at the first page, and although she stood very still in the full glare of the sun, she felt as if ice-cold water was pouring over her head and down her arms.

'Extraordinary,' she managed.

Sarah nodded. 'I am just so happy, I cannot tell you. I *was* looking for something I didn't know was there!'

Elise smiled stiffly, feeling sweat run down the sides of her face. She fished out a handkerchief, which she balled in a fist and pressed to her lips. She was glad for Mrs Williams. Didn't the poor woman deserve a bit of happiness? She bit into the soft cotton and kept her eyes down.

'Well, it is a sign,' she said eventually. 'A gift.'

'Isn't it?'

Elise swallowed hard as she thought she might be sick. As we've mentioned, Elise was no great reader, and she was by all accounts an appalling cook, but she always kept a tidy house. How many times had she lifted her daughter's books off the floor, dusted them off and returned them to a shelf? How many times had she ordered them according to size, or stacked them so the colour matched? We don't know the answer to those questions, but we do know Elise recognised this book. She remembered the delicate lettering and the feel of the soft cloth. She had even read a few pages, wondering if she might like poetry since it seemed to involve fewer words.

Fewer words, Elise thought, and she stood very still in the heat of the day, staring at these pages until they faded to white.

'He is watching over you. He wants the best for you. It is proof.'

Empty words, but their impact was electric. Sarah was already in tears and Elise found she had to cry, too. They embraced with the book wedged between them, and Elise closed her eyes and tried to think. The book. Where had it come from? Where had Phyll found it? Who else might know? She was sifting through memories, trying to stay calm.

She couldn't believe Phyll had done this, but she knew without a shadow of a doubt that she *had* done this. Soon she was pacing Phyll's bedroom, scouring the shelves, searching the drawers. She hated this feeling of panic, the groping and the loss of control. What else had she missed, she wondered. She pictured Phyll in her nightdress pointing to the shadows in the corner. 'Here, just *here*.'

Elise slumped onto the bed, gripping the edge of the mattress. No. The betrayal was so personal it stunned her. She folded herself over, pressing her fingers to her eyes. Phyll had led her upstairs and lied to her face. Elise had lied, too, but that wasn't the point. She gulped in a shuddery breath. My own daughter, she thought, and she stared at the floor and tried to make sense of it.

Then she caught sight of Phyll's beach towel tucked under the bed. To be more exact, she saw a streak of black soot along one edge. She bent down and picked it up, and the soot transferred to the tips of her fingers. She remembered the marks on the door at Beau Regard, and she stood up so quickly she almost fell over. She lurched to the window and flung it open.

Outside the sun was still very bright, the sky a faultless blue. She heard birds singing and watched a carriage pass. And there was Phyll. She was with her little friend, the Major's son, and they walked so close their shoulders rubbed. Phyll was whispering something, cupping her hand over Everard's ear and then they burst out laughing. They were actually laughing.

This was the moment that Elise would go back to later. She would stand at Phyll's window at other times, years later, and feel everything fall into place. She saw broken glass and soot stains and one lie wrapped around another. She pressed a hand to her mouth and Everard caught that movement and glanced up, and the fear flared bright in his eyes.

That was all it took.

Elise flew down the stairs and out of the door. She had Phyll by the elbow. 'You are coming with me.'

Phyll tried to squirm free but Elise tightened her grip. 'I *know* what you did,' she hissed, and she snapped round to face Everard. 'And *you*! You, too!'

Everard took a step back, almost dancing, and knitted his fingers together. 'I'm sorry! Please don't tell my father! *Oh, please, please don't!* He'll *kill* me.'

The tears sprung in his eyes and Elise straightened up, suddenly clear-headed. She saw how scared he was, and how small he was.

'I won't tell him,' she muttered. 'But this stops. No more.'

Everard nodded, stepped back, and Elise kept her eyes trained on him.

'You can't see my daughter again. Do I make myself clear? This is the end of it. Whatever *it* was.'

Everard sniffed and nodded again, blinking fast. He threw a last desperate look at Phyll, who had bowed her head to hide her face, then he turned and ran, and as he ran he kicked up a great cloud of dust that stung her eyes.

Back in the darkened post office Phyll wouldn't look at her mother.

'How could you?' Elise cried. 'How could you do such a dreadful thing?'

Phyll threw back her head. 'What have *I* done? That's rich coming from you!'

Because if Elise's mind had been clicking and whirring, then Phyll's had been spinning at speed. '*Mrs Carey confirms the house is haunted*', '*He was only checking on his little girl.*' Phyll went back through those phrases and she pictured her mother with her eyes closed and her arms outstretched. She stared at the wall, then the skirting board, then the floor. A gaping black hole had opened up in front of her. She hovered on its edge. She didn't want to think of her mother as a liar, but she felt a pull like gravity. We are both liars, she thought, and the ground fell away under her, and the walls crumbled and the roof collapsed. The house she had shared with her mother, the house that she'd lived in, no longer existed.

Elise didn't see the danger. She was too angry to see anything clearly and she'd only remember a blur. She glowered at the top of her daughter's head and she tapped her foot and waited. 'Well, young lady? Well? *I am waiting.*'

But Phyll kept her head bent and her mouth shut. The house she'd lived in no longer existed, so she'd build a new one. She remembered the spell Maud told her: *sweep the floors, shut the windows, close and lock the doors.*

Her mother would have to wait a long time for an answer, possibly years and years.

21

DAILY NEWS

Saturday, 14 October 1933

'SARK CAVE VICTIM NAMED'

The woman found dead in a cave in Port Gorey, Little Sark has been formally identified as the wife of Henry William Howell, a lieutenant in the British Navy, currently stationed in Scotland. Violet Anna Howell, aged 28, went missing from her home in Maidstone, Kent, on 20th September. She had told her husband she was going away for a holiday. His last contact with her was a letter postmarked 26th September.

Lieutenant Howell arrived in Guernsey yesterday on the Southern Railway mailboat. He was shown the clothes found on the rocks at Port Gorey, together with photographs of the dead woman and the clothes found in one of the suitcases, all of which confirmed his worst fears.

The Guernsey doctors have now given cause of death as due to 'injuries, shock and immersion' and Mrs Howell's body has been released by the States Authorities. It will be returned to Sark for immediate burial.

THERE IS AN INTERESTING story about a Sark funeral. It's from around the fourteenth century so it's brilliantly hard to prove. This was back when the island was infested with smugglers, pirates and wreckers, a criminal under-class. Dreadful people. They had become such a scourge on Channel traders that a plot was hatched to vanquish them. Thus, a fine-looking vessel appeared in Havre Gosselin and its crew begged permission from the locals to come ashore, pleading that their captain had died suddenly and they wanted to have his body interred in St Magloire's chapel. The islanders granted this on the condition that anyone who came ashore was unarmed – to which the sailors gladly submitted – and the islanders made ready to raid the ship whilst the crew were otherwise occupied over last rites. But although the islanders searched the crew, they didn't think to check inside the coffin, which contained nothing dead, but a dead weight of weapons. Once the sailors were inside the chapel, they armed themselves and turned on their hosts, slaughtering them all.

The motto of this story is not to trust appearances, but we all know that.

The funeral is set for noon and the husband won't be coming. He believed his wife was on holiday with family and she had written him a letter saying that she was 'looking forward to coming home'.

John de Carteret thinks it is a very poor show that they must bury a lady they don't know, but at last they have a name.

'Violet,' says Gil softly. 'It's a nice name.'

He and the other men who recovered the body from Port Gorey will act as pall bearers. He has dug out his father's moth-eaten jacket and oiled his hair especially, and once he is inside the church he even removes his cap, which he hasn't done in public in twenty years. Most of the pews fill up quickly and Reverend Severy, whose once grey hair is now snow-white, is more than satisfied with the turn-out. The Toplis family come in with arms linked, as do the Vaudins and the de Carterets and the Bihet cousins. Even the Hamons, who are notorious heathens, bring a wildflower wreath.

Edie had been excited to attend the funeral and rehearsed it with her toys last night, but after the first hymn is over she starts to fidget. She sits with her mother at the front so must constantly twist her head round to look at everyone else. She scours the pews for possible murderers, identifying several shifty-looking fellows who are actually journalists. She also notices Elise, who comes in late and sits on her own at the back, some distance from Phyll, who arrived early with Maud. Edie assumes this is because Elise never comes to church and secretly worships the Devil. She sits tight and hopes for something terrible to happen.

Something terrible did happen, but that was last night.

As we mentioned, the finest Sark houses have metre-thick walls. This means nobody heard the violent row between mother and daughter. Phyll was understandably upset with Elise as regards ten years of unposted letters and postcards to Everard Hyde. She made a lot of not entirely human noises, damaged two chairs and broke five plates. Elise, caught off-guard, denied all knowledge. When that didn't work she played the 'Mother's Duty to Protect Her Child' card. 'I was only trying to protect you. That boy was no good . . . The trouble you two caused.'

At this point Phyll was so angry she leaned right over the kitchen table, gripping its sides. 'We were *children*! You weren't trying to protect me, you were trying to *control* me!'

For a second Elise had a glimpse of Phillip hovering there – the black fury of him – and she had to swallow hard to smother her fear. By then, Phyll had flung herself back and was pacing haphazardly, swearing at her mother in unprintable language. Finally and conclusively, she spun round and tapped at her forehead. 'Have you seen the scar? Have you seen it? His father beat him so badly he had to take him off the island!' She narrowed her eyes and jabbed her finger. 'And that's on *you*!'

Elise was baffled. 'Rubbish!' she said quickly. 'The journalist in you, looking for scandal. I'd know if that happened.'

Phyll threw up her arms in despair. 'You don't know anything!'

She is right. Elise doesn't know anything. She doesn't know why or how the poor woman died, nor why she is being buried here. She doesn't know why Everard came back, or why Phyll left her job and what it is that still ties them together. Elise doesn't understand any of it, and it's fascinating and infuriating. This is why she sits with her head bent and hands clasped. To all intents and purposes it looks like she is praying.

By the way, contrary to childish rumours, Elise does believe in God, she is just not a fan of organised religion. She thinks people only come to church to be seen doing the right thing, or because they have a guilty conscience, or because they are afraid of dying. Come to think of it, those might be the only three reasons people do anything.

This leads us neatly on to what happens after the service.

Elise sees Everard pacing round the outer edges of the graveyard. He seems to be talking to himself, perhaps even arguing, since his mouth opens and closes as he moves. When she calls out his name he stiffens and spins round like he is still that small boy expecting a slap.

She lifts a gloved hand. 'Please,' she says. 'A word.'

She walks over with her hand still raised, and soon they are facing one another and the first thing she notices is the scar through his eyebrow. She tries to stop herself from staring at it, but now it is all that she can see. She lowers her hand.

'I am here to apologise,' she says. 'My daughter wrote to you and I saw fit to intercept every single one of her attempts.' She looks down, she looks up. 'It was absolutely wrong. *I* was wrong. I am sorry. I should not have interfered.'

Everard absorbs this information and then gives a weary shrug. 'You were probably right to do that, Mrs Carey.'

Elise bristles and lifts her gaze. This is not the response she expected and she can't help but feel annoyed. Doesn't he understand that it has taken a great deal of effort for her to come over and say what she's just said? She never admits her mistakes, not to anyone, and she certainly never says sorry. It is entirely unacceptable that he doesn't just take it. A genial nod is all she'd ask. She purses her lips and glances over both shoulders. Somewhere a dog keeps barking and barking. Sark dogs, being all male, are foul-tempered. Only the Dame is allowed to keep a female dog because female dogs are a distraction. But this is also a distraction. Elise shifts uneasily and lifts her eyes to the sky. She's aware most of the congregation have long left the churchyard, which is what she hoped, but now Maud has come to stand by the side of the church. She locks eyes with Elise and gives a nod of encouragement. Elise narrows her eyes and turns back. Without further fuss, she delves into the deep side pocket of her oilskin. She draws out the brick of postcards and letters, the edges slightly curled. Welcome to ten years' worth of adolescent correspondence.

She would like everyone to know she has put them in date order. You see? She does have a heart.

'I *was* wrong,' she repeats, holding them out. 'Look, just take them. It was all a long time ago. Seems like a lifetime. I had my reasons but I am not sure they were the right reasons.' She sighs heavily, emptying her lungs. 'They were right at the time.'

Everard hesitates, then takes the brick and holds it close to his face to peer at the writing. He smiles. Elise uses this moment to study him afresh. She narrows her eyes and tells herself there is every chance he is still a bad person. Yes, he was young, but she knows what boys are like and if he is anything like his father then . . . She stops. *Wait*, she tells herself.

'What happened to your eyebrow?' She points. 'What is that? A scar?'

Everard lifts a hand self-consciously and turns his head to one side. 'Oh . . . I fell . . . out of a tree . . . years ago.'

Elise breathes in the damp air.

'A tree,' she repeats tonelessly.

She remembers what Phyll told her, so why is he now lying? She wants to call him out on it, but they are standing by Albert's grave, which makes her self-conscious. Albert was an honest, pillar-of-the-community type who'd never have read anyone else's letters or called them a liar. Elise can picture him shaking his head at her and feels a creeping shame. She glances again over her shoulder. Phyll is standing in the space where Maud was. Oh dear.

She turns back. 'It was the way you left that made it so confusing. Phyll was just . . . ' she struggles for the word, gesturing, '. . . *forlorn*.'

Everard is nodding. 'I understand.'

But Elise doesn't think he can. It was a lovely summer and then it was spoiled. They wouldn't talk or look at each other, and she remembers how quiet the house became, hours passing without a sound. Then every summer afterwards was a reminder. Phyll hoped for Everard to come back and when he didn't she was sad. There was a rhythm to it, with Phyll watching the new arrivals off the boat, peering at anyone the right age, who looked faintly like him. It was unbearable to see the hope dwindle and fade.

Of course it might have died a natural death but Elise didn't like to take chances. She needed to control it, like she needs to control everything. That might have made it worse, because the minute she decided to block the letters and keep the cards she made them more important. The more you deny something, the more power it has.

She leaves Everard, making her way back to the path. She wishes she felt better – why doesn't she feel better? – and because she's looking down she doesn't see Phyll walk towards her. She lifts her head at the last minute and smiles. She wants to say, *Ah, you see I am not all bad, I kept the letters and now he's got them!* But Phyll stares straight ahead and passes by. Not a nod or glance. Elise turns to watch her go and the scene has a strange dream-like quality, with all the movements slowed down but feeling oddly inevitable, like something pre-ordained.

Everard holds up the bundle when he sees Phyll. 'I have so much to read,' he says. His eyes dart from side to side. 'And before I forget.' He shifts the bundle of letters into one hand and reaches inside his coat. 'I got this for you.' He hands over a small brown package and pink streaks appear on his cheeks. 'Sorry it's taken this long.'

Elise watches from a distance as Phyll takes the package with both hands, testing the weight of it, then she starts to peel back the wrapping. She stops. Elise can see it is a book. A green clothbound cover, the smooth gold lettering. She knows what it is. It's the book of poems, the book they gave to Mrs Williams. She swallows hard.

Everard watches Phyll's face. 'I thought you should have your own copy,' he smiles, then he sticks out his hand like he wants her to shake it. 'I am nobody,' he says. '*Who* are you?'

Phyll takes the hand. 'I am nobody, too.'

So. A boy and a girl in a churchyard. Let's leave them there.

But we haven't finished with the letters. There is one remaining. Elise walks back inside the empty church, where candles are still burning on the altar. As she walks briskly up the aisle she reaches into the pocket of her oilskin. She first checks that she is alone, then she takes out the envelope, the one that arrived last week, and shoves it under a flame. Once it is alight she lets it fall on the stone floor. She stamps it into dust. The actual letter she will read one last time.

Dear Phyll,
 I am writing to clear the air. I thought we understood each other, but you are not a child anymore, so please don't act like one. I'm sorry if you put me on a pedestal but I certainly never acted like a saint. You wanted it to happen.

As I said at the time, it was just a bit of fun, and I was happy to put the whole business behind us. Now I hear you wrote to Miranda and told her. How dare you! What right have you to come between my daughter and I? When I think of all the months we let you share our adventures. You had no excitement in your life – you were this sad, rough, ill-mannered creature – and we tried to improve things for you.

You must be very jealous of Miranda to try this tactic. I have told her it is all embellishment, that you have let your imagination run wild, as you often did. I said it was because you didn't have a father.

To think I once cared for you. How wrong I was to waste my emotions. You have no idea about the real world, my dear. You are stuck with your cold fish of a mother on that small-minded island. Write whatever fantasies you like in your diary but don't write to us again.

If we come back to Sark this summer – and I don't yet know our plans – I don't expect to see you there. Miranda shan't be coming in any case.

Goodbye, you silly child.

Paul

Elise stares so hard the words blur together. She feels her throat constrict, the blood drain from her body. She shakes her head. Paul Cecil. She pictures him in her mind, his shirt always untucked, a cigarette dangling from his fingers. All these years he's been coming to the island. She knew he had a reputation, but she never for one moment thought he'd interfere with her daughter. She shudders and looks again at his snivelling excuses. How he tries to shift the blame! A man old enough to be her father, saying it's because she doesn't have one. Elise thrusts the paper under the candle. The flames quickly creep to her fingers and she sees Miranda's name before it all turns black.

Poor Miranda, she thinks. But Miranda had a right to know. Elise drops the letter and watches it burn. She feels so angry. If *she* had been in that studio in Paris, she might have pushed Paul out the window herself.

Then she wonders, she really wonders, if maybe Miranda did.

22

Les Boutiques Caves

(Situated at the north end of the island and accessed by Eperquerie Landing. Leave an hour before low tide. Sensible shoes, a torch and short rope advised.)

22 August 1923

THOSE WHO WISH TO BE THOROUGHLY acquainted with the peculiar beauties of Sark must not be content to traverse the cliffs, but climb inside them. The island is one thing on the surface but another underneath, and secretly riddled with holes, tunnels and caverns of baffling depth. We are personally not fans of being underground but for the adventurous traveller with sensible shoes, we recommend the Boutiques: a network of caves extending two hundred feet into the cliff. It is an excellent place to hide treasure, and also to ambush someone and kill them, but that's just a rumour from a long time ago.

Miranda had no desire to go to the caves, none at all, but she was sick of feeling left out. She was often left out by her parents, who spent their lives distracted by impossible views and interesting people, so she wouldn't tolerate this behaviour from other children. She had expected Phyll and Everard to spend the summer fighting for her attention. This had not worked out at all. If she was feeling generous, she could blame it on the age gap. She was fourteen, but could have passed for older. Her mother kept telling her father to paint her, and she wanted that, too. She wondered what dress she would wear. Probably this one because the yellow matched her hair and the skirt stopped on her knee and showed her legs.

The breeze picked up and she rubbed her arms. 'Did you bring a torch?'

Everard shook his head but kept it bent. He had hardly said a word on the way down the cliff and Miranda assumed he'd had a fight with Phyll. She wanted to tell him not to worry, that Phyll got cross with everyone, but then she thought: why bother? They stood at the mouth of the first cave, which had a high ceiling and smooth, dry walls. Miranda walked towards a shaft of daylight.

'Did you hear what happened yesterday?' She glanced over her shoulder. 'Mrs Williams found a book that had belonged to her husband, that he had brought over on his honeymoon. She went quite loopy over it.'

Everard felt the knot tighten inside him. He was pretending to explore the edges of the cave, but all he could think about was Phyll and the mess they'd made. He wanted to go back and apologise to Mrs Carey. He could try to make it better.

Miranda was still talking about Mrs Williams. 'Sylvie thinks she's in love with your father.' She laughed. 'What do you think about *that*? Would you like your father to remarry?'

Everard couldn't think of anything worse. He was feeling very cold and unhappy and he just wanted quiet. All these worries swam and tangled in his brain, and he had to get away, so he turned into one of the openings that led deeper into the cliff. The temperature dropped, and the air was thick with salt and seaweed. He felt safer in the dark and walked on.

It took a second for Miranda to notice that he'd gone. She called out, 'Everard?' But only her own voice echoed back.

She waited a moment, breathing in the damp, cold air. She blamed Everard for not bringing a torch. Had he done that on purpose? Was he trying to trick her?

'Everard?'

After a moment she heard: 'Here!'

She bent her head and followed where his voice had come from. She walked slowly, using her hands to feel the way. It was eerily quiet, a kind of sealed-in quiet, and one of her plimsolls squelched into seaweed. She cried out, a sort of gasping sob because it was so cold and disgusting. The smell was putrid. She wanted to go back and she was going to say so when she reached Everard, but after ten more steps the ceiling dropped and she had to bend over. It was like the tunnel in *Alice in Wonderland* and she was worried there'd be a sudden drop.

'I don't like this!' she called out.

'It's all right,' Everard replied. 'Just watch your step.'

Miranda carried on and after a few metres the tunnel widened and she could stand straight again. She pressed her hands against the walls, which dripped with water. The air was damp and still, and she saw a shape ahead.

'You!' She walked quickly forward – too quickly as it turned out – and her foot hit water where there should have been rock. She was suddenly up to her waist in icy water. It was a huge rock pool and the seaweed brushed against her thighs. It was only seaweed but she screamed. She tried to pull herself up but her foot was trapped. Just for a second.

'I tried to warn you,' Everard said. 'I did.'

Paul Cecil found them at the top of the cliff, soaking wet and scowling at each another. Miranda blamed Everard for not bringing a torch and made a great fuss over her ankle, which she said was sprained. Because she blamed Everard, her father did, too.

Paul shook his head and said, 'You should have been more careful.'

Everard didn't answer back. He felt a constricting pain in his chest and neck that made it difficult to speak. He later thought he could have said something clever, about how Paul should be more careful, too. That might have helped, because the anger was building inside him. He ran back to Beau Regard and all the time he was thinking how he'd run away from Phyll, how he'd left her to face her mother and agreed not to see her again. He felt like such a coward and tears filled his eyes. It was still very hot and he was by now red in the face. Perhaps it was the sun that did it, or maybe it was how these adults spoke to him, or maybe it was Miranda and the lost torch, but after that all he could remember was standing by the clock as his father slammed his face into the wall.

'It was a nasty business,' Paul said later. 'Miranda claims that Everard just left her in the dark!'

It was still light when he came to the Bel Air to collect Sarah and Sylvie. They were expected at Beau Regard for drinks and dinner. Ann had decided to stay behind and look after Miranda, although her ankle was only twisted, not sprained. Paul was secretly pleased with the outcome and made a great show of offering Sylvie and Sarah each an arm and declaring himself very lucky to have two such beautiful females to himself.

Sarah Williams did look especially beautiful. She wore a pale cocktail dress with a low waist and stepped hem, very fashionable but not the kind of thing she normally wore. She felt much lighter but also nervous in it, and even after they reached Beau Regard she had to keep moving, wandering over the lawn with Sylvie. She couldn't quite believe that this evening had finally come. Paul fixed them bitter cocktails. Dr Stanhope arrived a little while later and began a lecture on electrical therapy. 'I believe there is untapped energy in the universe,' he said. 'Not unlike that held in a battery . . . life's vital spark . . . now if we can store one kind of energy, why not another?'

Sarah stayed close to Sylvie, who had kicked off her shoes. The evening was still so warm and there was the sense that they were all just waiting. Sylvie plucked a rose and crushed it close to her face, inhaling deeply. Sarah thought Sylvie terribly Bohemian, and she liked the Cecils, too: their informality, the way they threw people together.

'The great and the good gathering to commune,' called Paul, lifting his glass and tilting it towards them.

Sarah finished her drink, then wiped her lips, smiling. The Major nodded to her and raised his own glass. It felt like the first time he'd noticed her and he looked terribly handsome in the evening light. He held her gaze for a few seconds before looking away, and she stepped back and smiled up at the house. This could all be mine, she thought suddenly, and she blushed and pressed her fingers to her lips.

Sylvie sighed beside her. 'It *is* beautiful, isn't it?'

Sarah turned and gestured down the length of the garden. 'The view is incredible,' she gushed. 'And so peaceful! It's like there is nobody else in the world but us.'

Sylvie draped an arm over her shoulder, drawing her closer. 'We can do as we please,' she said. 'It *is* the full moon, after all.' She smiled and turned her head towards the terrace, calling out to Paul: 'When is it witching hour, then?'

Paul laughed. He didn't believe in witches any more than ghosts. He thought the evening would be a bit of fun, and now that Ann was out of the way, he looked forward to having some time alone with Sylvie. As the sky darkened he busied himself curating the room, pushing back the other furniture to make way for the card table, around which he set the dining room chairs. He placed a single candle in the middle and lit it, stepping back to admire the effect. The wick flickered and made a soft circle of light. The room looked very sketchable, he thought.

Eventually people came inside and he fixed them all more drinks. Sylvie closed the doors and drew the curtains. She was wearing a red dress that hung low around her bosom and as she approached the table she smiled because she knew Paul was watching her. She passed him with her eyebrows raised, running one hand along his back.

'The Major should sit first,' she said gently.

Hyde looked dazed. He had been thinking so intently about the plans for this evening it no longer seemed real. He held tight to the moment and tried to forget what had happened hours earlier. At least now Everard was locked in his room. Hyde drained his whisky. He told himself nobody need know, and he would take the chair facing the fireplace.

He wanted a good view of his photographs, especially the one of him with Evelyn during Cowes week. It had an extraordinary feeling of life to it. With the two boys standing together, it looked like they were friends. He fixed on it as he sat down.

Paul took the seat opposite and stubbed out his cigarette. 'Are you quite all right, Earnest? You look very pale.'

Hyde cleared his throat. His hands were aching and he had the beginnings of a headache. 'Absolutely.'

Sarah sat down beside him without making a sound. She was conscious of all these faces near her own, of warm bodies breathing. 'How do we do this?'

Dr Stanhope pulled out the chair next to hers. 'Have you ever used a planchette, my dear?'

Sarah turned her head very deliberately to look at him. 'I don't know what that is . . . '

'A piece of wood,' Paul explained. 'A pencil is set at one end and the other end has a wheel. People place their fingers on it and ask questions. It's a way of communicating.'

Stanhope nodded and sat down. 'I have seen it done. Quite interesting. But for now we should simply see if some lines of communication may be established. It is a matter of making contact.'

'All we must do,' smiled Paul, 'is empty our minds and join hands.'

Sarah stared at the doctor's sweaty palm. 'And we think of our loved ones. Isn't that how one does it? We think of the persons we want to contact.'

Paul's eyes flicked to Hyde, who very slightly shook his head. 'I believe a blank state is better,' Paul said. 'It's why many people receive messages at night, in their sleep, it's when our conscious mind is relaxed and there are no distractions.'

Sarah was now holding hands with the Major. Because of the dark she didn't notice the red marks on his knuckles, but the pressure of her touch made him sit more upright. Paul laid his hand over Sylvie's. 'Under no circumstance must we break the circle,' he said. 'Focus on the light.'

They had now all joined hands and they waited, watching the flame flicker, and soon they were breathing together, in time.

Hyde was feeling very calm, almost emptied out, and as he waited the room filled with a heavy atmosphere. The atmosphere of a secret. It was really very beautiful, he thought.

But for Sarah it was frightening. She pressed her tongue against her teeth. Time passed. She was aware of her chest rising and falling, rising and falling. She thought of Cyril although she knew she wasn't meant to, and she started to believe it was his hand she held. Then she didn't have to imagine it because she felt sure it was true. She closed her eyes and he was here, in the room, standing just behind her. It was a huge feeling, swelling like water behind a dam. She wanted to turn but she didn't dare. *He is there, right there*, she thought.

'Whoever comes we must welcome them.' Dr Stanhope spoke in a dull monotone. 'Let them know we are not afraid.'

Hyde had become conscious of a buzzing vibration running up his arms. Sarah was gripping his hand very tightly, and he tried to work his fingers free but she only held on tighter. He tried to pull away and the table shuddered, which was her fault. His fingers were throbbing and he let out a sigh.

Sarah jerked towards him. 'Is there someone behind me?'

She felt something tapping on her shoulder, a small hand that was light and quick.

Hyde looked at her for a moment and then looked over her shoulder. Beyond them it was entirely dark. He could not even see the furniture. They might have been floating in space. He looked back at Stanhope, who had kept his eyes fixed on the candle. The shadows under his eyes were like stains. Sarah had again tightened her grip and Hyde felt her wedding ring digging into his skin. Her eyes were closed now, but her eyelids were fluttering. She passed her tongue over her lips and left her mouth a little open. Again, he tried to inch his hand away.

'Don't leave me,' she said, with her chin tilted up. 'Oh, don't leave me.'

Hyde's head was hot but his arms were cold. It was Evelyn speaking. *Don't leave me*. Of course. It had been a full moon when he died, and here he was again.

'I shan't,' he said.

'You cannot break the circle.' That was Paul, his voice impatient. 'We want to speak to the lady. Is the lady there?'

Hyde closed his eyes.

'Young lady, are you there?' Stanhope cleared his throat. 'May we help you?'

'Yes!' That was Sarah. Her gasp made the candle shiver. 'There is someone outside. Can't you hear?' She had opened her eyes and was twisting her head first to the left and then to the right. Everyone turned to look at the curtains. They didn't move, but Sarah stared at the large windows and waited. She was acutely aware of a presence outside. She believed it was Cyril, but she imagined him vaguely and mistily.

'Someone is trying to get in,' she said.

Nobody moved. It was suddenly very hot in the room. A pure, dry heat like that from a fire. Sarah felt her flesh being picked up and pinched. A scream shuddered under her ribs. She tried to stand up but her hand had been pinned to the table and she stared at it in shock.

'You *must* sit,' someone told her.

It was the Major. She saw his face close to hers, pale, puckered with concentration. She sat back down and turned her eyes back to the candle, but she had split in two, and a part of her was walking round the room.

It pleased Hyde to see her frightened. He thought she was like an obedient child, that she would yield to his will. But then he wondered if there wasn't someone behind him and he twisted round to check. The room seemed distant, as if viewed through the wrong end of a telescope. He turned back to the table and felt dizzy. Sylvie had thrown back her head and closed her eyes. She appeared to have gone into a trance. Her neck glowed yellow from the candlelight. She opened her mouth and a small sound came out, a sort of moan.

Hyde swallowed and focused on the candle but the nightmare feeling grew. He felt the sweat on his face, around his hairline, along his lip. Beside him Sarah sobbed quietly, but he couldn't loosen his grip. His heart began to twist like a corkscrew. Something *was* circling them. The pins and needles spread from his fingers into his arms. The smell from the candle grew more sharp, pungent. He didn't understand what was happening. The boy was locked in his room so whatever happened now would not be down to him. He'd fooled them all, but not anymore.

'Is anyone there?' That was Dr Stanhope.

Sarah kept turning her head. She couldn't keep track. Cyril would come in from the garden, she was sure. He was coming to fetch her and she wanted to fling herself back. She looked around the table one last time and she felt like she was under restraints, like a lunatic or a prisoner. She was going to speak, to insist they open the doors, but the room suddenly erupted. There was the sound of glass breaking and something dark hurtled through the air, crashing onto the table. Everything went black. Hot wax scalded her arm. Someone was screaming. Was that her voice she heard? She was falling backwards through the dark and it seemed to happen very slowly but also very fast. She had time to throw out her arms and then she hit the floor and she still couldn't see. It was pitch-black, another world, but there were people moving around her, swarming over the floor. Her skin crawled with the horror of it. They'd been invaded. There were shouts and a thump-thump-thump and then doors opened and slammed and opened again. Sarah rolled onto her side and something sharp pressed into her palm and she screamed out, and then she heard another voice and that voice was scared, too.

Someone said, 'Get the lamp!'

But it was all happening at once, this cacophony. She couldn't understand it so she screamed and that felt better. Soon her face was wet with tears. She thought of Cyril. Where was he? Where had he gone? She had got so close but now she'd lost him. She had lost him all over again. She tried to sit up but the ground was rocking and lurching. She felt hands on her lifting her up. Many hands, she thought, and she fought them and sobbed. She didn't want to be carried and she shuddered and twisted her body, resisting. There was the outline of a man, his shape like a halo of light, and then she didn't see anything at all.

23

GUERNSEY EVENING PRESS

Tuesday, 17 October 1933

'SARK CAVE MYSTERY: SECOND BODY FOUND'

P. Carey writes: There was a startling development in Sark yesterday afternoon when the body of a man was found close to Port Gorey. George Vaudin, a local boy who has been keeping a careful watch of the island's cliffs, spotted the man's body through his binoculars and raised the alarm. Young Vaudin then climbed down to the beach and waited until Mr Gilbert Baker arrived by boat with the deputy constable. The body was recovered without difficulty and brought into Sark harbour, where Mr Baker reported that he believed this to be the man he had first encountered with the deceased woman now known to be Mrs Howell. Sark's new doctor, Stephen Greener, attended the harbour and agreed that it would be in everyone's best interests for the body to be taken directly to his colleagues in Guernsey.

There were upsetting scenes at the quayside, where Sark islanders took exception to the rabble of pressmen gathered there. All the national newspapers have in recent weeks dispatched representatives to Sark and their behaviour has left much to be desired. As a result, Chief Constable John de Carteret ordered Mr Baker and Mr Remfrey to continue on to Guernsey, where the authorities were notified and standing by.

Regarding cause of death, we await the findings of the medical examiner. There are naturally questions to be asked about the time lapse between the discovery of the two bodies. It seems remarkable that a whole nine days has elapsed between the finding of Mrs Howell and her male companion, yet both came ashore close to the place where their clothes were originally found, within a short distance of each other.

DOLLY TAKES A DISHCLOTH and twists it round and round in her hands. She should clean some glasses, tidy the bar, keep herself busy, but she's in a kind of daze. She had to walk down to the harbour to see the man's body and what shocked her most was seeing his face. He looked just like she remembered him.

'Yes, that's the man I served coffee to,' she said, covering her mouth with her sleeve.

Oh, she feels sick. There's a smell that lingers still. Could he really have been in the water all that time? Gil, who was with her, talked about the cold water slowing down decay and about ebb tides and the Atlantic. Dolly didn't understand a word. Did the man and woman die together? She remembers when she saw them in the garden, how unhappy they seemed. She supposes it was good they didn't have children. No little ones left behind.

Dolly would quite like children one day, as long as they are nothing like her brothers. She bites the inside of her gum. She feels the presence of something, a shape, a shadow, lurking in the corners of the verandah. She takes a ragged breath and then another. Last night she dreamt she saw the woman's face hovering above her and she tried to get up but a weight pulled her down. It reminded her of the dreams she used to have when she worked at the Bungalow. She wants to sleep more now but she's drunk so much coffee her heart is fluttering wildly, like a bird in a cage. She wonders whether Dr Greener will come in later. He's been coming in most days and she looks forward to seeing him. She likes him better than Willis Hamon who she will only meet in secret, in a field. Willis Hamon is sometimes rough. Dolly is not sure why she thinks this is all she is worth.

She broods about the poor woman. She was obviously unhappy in her marriage and hoping to escape. She ran away, and if only she'd kept on running. Why did she choose another man? Why do women do it? Dolly leans on the railings of the verandah. Perhaps there are only wrong men. She could walk out to his farm right now, face up to Willis Hamon and tell him: 'No more.' Then what? She turns to the steps and stares down across the garden. She is poised for flight when she sees the woman waiting. She is sitting alone at the table, with her face turned away. Dolly knows it's her by the hair, of course, the beautiful, long brown hair. She braces herself against the railings. Dolly holds her breath. She says it's her mind playing tricks, but it feels absolutely real. The woman is looking down the valley. She is waiting for the boat. She's made up her mind to go back to Guernsey. Dolly feels her heart pumping, the blood moving around her body. She must tell the woman to hurry but the wooden steps are slippery from the rain. She's suddenly tumbling forward.

'Go!' she screams. 'Go!'

Then she wakes. She's in her chair on the verandah, a shawl draped over her shoulders.

Phyll also had a dream, but she didn't dream about the missing man and woman. She dreamt about Everard, or at least she thought it was him. She dreamt that she woke in the night to find a shape at the foot of the bed, and she thought it was Everard, or the boy he used to be. He hid his face from her and he was hunched over and soaking wet and shivering from cold. What had happened? Why was he wet? Phyll never got to ask, and when she woke up she smelt salt from the sea. Maybe the wind brought it in, but even so.

Everard was with Small George when he spotted the man's body in the sea, but George told Phyll that Everard had explicitly asked for his name to be kept out of the *Press*. Phyll wonders why. Everard was so determined to find these two people, these two people he never met. The search for them kept him here, and now it's over will he go? She doesn't want that. There is still so much to say, so many questions she must ask. When she sees him on the Avenue she doesn't miss her chance. She runs downstairs, flying out the door.

'Stop,' she almost shouts, holding out one hand and blocking his path. 'Just tell me: what did I miss?'

Everard pulls up short, eyes glazed, face tense. He is wearing the same clothes he wore to the funeral. 'What did you *miss*?' He shakes his head. 'I don't understand.'

Phyll keeps her eyes fixed on him. 'Yes, you do.' She lifts a hand, carving the air. 'Every time I ask you a question I see this, this hesitation. You're like an actor going over his lines, trying to work out what's safe. Everard, I *know* something's going on, I know you are keeping things from me.' She pauses. 'Maybe that's your right. I mean, why trust me? It's been years! But you are here and whether you like it or not I care.'

Everard blinks and looks down, his shoulders relax. 'Thank you for not mentioning me in your article,' he says.

The wind comes gusting up the Avenue and pushes Phyll's hair into her eyes. She nods and pushes it back. 'But why? They think the man drowned. It has nothing to do with you.'

Everard stares back at Phyll and she sees relief pass over his face, but then there is doubt and fear. She wants to take him by the shoulders and tell him to stop hiding.

'I know *something* happened,' she says. 'I don't know if it connects with what is happening now, with these two people. Please just talk to me. You're keeping secrets and you're obviously upset. Just tell me everything, and let's start from the beginning, from ten years ago. What happened to you that didn't happen to me?'

Everard breaks eye contact and lifts his head to look at the sky, which is both dark and bright at the exact same time. His breath comes out in a pale plume. 'You're asking *that* now?'

Phyll rubs her arms, which are studded with goosebumps under her coat. She fiddles with the hem of her cuffs. 'Why not? Something terrible happened, didn't it? Before . . . before you left.'

'I didn't leave!' Everard says angrily. 'My father *took* me. It's *not* like I had a choice.'

Phyll stands there, hesitating, unsure what to do. 'Exactly,' she says. 'So. What happened?' She waits. 'Tell me.'

Everard ducks his head and swerves around her and she thinks for a minute that he's walking away, but then he glances back. He wants her to walk with him, and it's like the first time they met. She can almost see the children they were running ahead, looking back. She feels giddy, but maybe that's all haunting is: time catching up.

They don't speak again until they reach the churchyard. Everard veers off the path, kicking his way through wet leaves. 'Do you remember Sylvie Price?'

Phyll narrows her eyes, registering the name. Sylvie Price. She sees bright lipstick and shiny black hair. She nods. 'What's she got to do with it?'

Everard swallows and presses his lips together. 'She was sleeping with Paul Cecil. I saw them together.'

Phyll feels the breath catch in her throat. It's like she's been punched. She blinks and looks at her shoes, at the rust-coloured leaves under them, at her arms folded over. She feels light-headed and unsteady. She doesn't know what to say, so she says nothing.

After a minute she hears Everard sigh. 'I was too ashamed to tell you.' He has come to stand in front of her and she sees the front of his shoes, which she notices are tide-stained. 'I wasn't spying . . . I was waiting for you and they just *appeared* on the road. Or no, Sylvie was waiting for Paul, and then they were together and I was shocked and I didn't know what to do.' Another sigh. 'It brought back bad memories. I could have told you . . . I have often thought that if I *had* told you, or anyone, it might have changed things.'

Phyll is still far too stunned to speak. Every part of her is being shuffled and re-shuffled. Sylvie and Paul. So Paul was like that even then. But of course he was. She can see it now so clearly. She finally raises her head and meets Everard's eyes. How she wishes he had told her. If only he had told her. So many things might be different. She shakes her head slowly and keeps her arms folded tight.

Everard turns a little, first to the left and then to the right. 'I nearly told Miranda. She was always so smug, don't you remember how smug she was?'

Phyll thinks of Miranda, her friend, who she trusts.

'I am not sure,' she replies.

Neither of them speak. Everard looks across at her, or rather his eyes pass over her. 'I went to the Boutiques with Miranda. You were meant to come. I was trying to act normal, but,' he pauses. 'But we were both in strange moods and she started to tease me.' He bows his head and runs a finger over his eyebrow, over the line of white skin where hair won't grow. 'I walked off and she fell into a rock pool. Mr Cecil blamed me.' Everard shakes his head, almost laughing in disbelief. 'He blamed me! It made me so angry I ran back to the house. I thought I could do one last trick. If I could stop the clocks, wouldn't that be something? I was so *sick* of the ticking in that house. But I didn't hear my father come in. He caught me red-handed and went mad and started hitting me, I didn't think he'd ever stop.' Everard rocks slightly, as if the ground is bucking under him. He balls his hands into fists. 'The next morning he took me to Guernsey so nobody would see the state I was in.'

Phyll presses her palms to her cheeks; comforted by the pressure, she weaves her fingers together over her mouth. 'So that's why I never saw you.'

Everard refocuses on her. 'You wouldn't have wanted to see me.' He shifts nervously. 'That night, that was the night it all went wrong. Afterwards something happened: I let something in, something evil.'

There's the sound of cracking wood close by. Everard snaps round. 'Who's there?'

Phyll turns with him to look and two magpies crash out of the closest hedgerow, a flurry of black and white feathers. Everard staggers back, arms outstretched. He turns in a slow circle, peering into the undergrowth.

Phyll watches him, not moving. She is still trying to process what he's told her. She lifts a hand and lays it flat on her chest. 'It was nothing,' she says. 'Birds.'

Everard stands straighter, tensing, looking over her shoulder. 'You'd better just go.' He drags his hands over his face. 'You don't understand, Phyll. We thought we were playing all those years ago, but our games and tricks triggered something, something evil. Maybe it's my fault or maybe it's that house, but something awful *did* happen there, and now it's happened again, and I couldn't stop it. It must be my fault for coming back.' He swallows. 'I don't know how I can fix this. I just think I must be cursed.'

Phyll is so shocked she almost laughs, but she can see by his face he means every word. She drops her hands to her sides. 'Don't say that. Bad things happen, yes, but . . . but . . . what's just happened would have happened whether you came back or not, and it isn't connected with what we did before. I mean, if you think you're cursed then I must be, too.'

But Everard doesn't seem to be listening. He is scanning the graveyard, moving his red eyes without blinking. Phyll tries to see what it is he sees, peering at the shadows and the trees. 'Everard? Did you hear what I said?'

He turns back to her, but it's like he's somewhere else. His face is set, his gaze faraway. Where's he gone? He is squinting at something by the wall. 'Don't you feel it?' he asks in a low voice. 'She is *here*, Phyll. I have seen her.'

Phyll tries to keep her voice calm, but she feels like she might cry. 'Who?'

Everard lowers his head. 'The woman my father saw. The Stranger Lady. It must be her. She's back . . . maybe she never went away. And she knows me.'

Phyll gulps air. 'No. She's not real, Everard. This is my fault. I filled your head with stupid stories all those years ago. I didn't know what was true and what was a lie, but that's just what children do. We turned it into a game to trick people, and I encouraged you, because it was fun and I was excited to have a new friend. You've had a shock. You're upset . . .'

Everard looks at Phyll and his eyes come into focus. He takes a step forward and reaches for her hands, holding them in his own, curling his fingers round hers. 'I made such a mess of this,' he says. 'I'm sorry, Phyll. I wish we *could* go back . . .'

Phyll bends her fingers. 'I don't. I was so awkward. Nobody liked me.'

'That's not true.' Everard frowns at her hands, cradling them on his chest. '*I* liked you.'

The words have a powerful effect, as if something clicks into place, and before she can stop herself Phyll leans in and kisses him. It's clumsy and dry-lipped and it's over in seconds. She pulls back, untangles their fingers and cups his face firmly in her hands.

'Listen! You didn't let anything bad in that night, Everard. It was me. *It was only me!*'

24

'Night-time Rambles'

23 August 1923

BEAU REGARD LOOKED bigger in the moonlight, the grass shimmered under it. Phyll stood on the lawn, wondering what next. She'd snuck out of the house and come all this way, but she didn't know how to get Everard's attention. Of course it was a risk but it was also exciting. It was like *Romeo and Juliet* in reverse, which she'd think about later when she got round to reading it.

She walked over the lawn and climbed the steps to the terrace. There was proof of a party scattered about: a table full of empty glasses, an ashtray, the remains of a cigar. Phyll twisted her hair to one side and bent over, examining everything with care, like a visitor at a museum. She gingerly picked up a glass, sniffed and sipped at the sticky liquid left in it. The taste was vile and she pressed her lips together, wincing. She picked up another glass to see if it was better. This one had dark lipstick on the rim and smelt of Sylvie's perfume. Phyll smiled to herself and used her finger to take a little of the colour and dab it on her lips. That taste was better, interesting.

She counted chairs, glasses, cigarettes in the ashtray, and all the while she listened out for any sounds from inside – she was braced at any time to make her escape – but the windows were shut and the curtains closed and the house seemed strangely vacant. There was not even a sliver of light sneaking out from any edges. Phyll wondered where everyone had gone. Had the party ended? She knew there had been a party because Nancy had mentioned it to her mother in disapproving tones. Phyll stood alert, but all she could hear was the sea murmuring far down the cliff. She was close enough to the windows to study her outline in the glass. She saw the moon bright and full behind her, filling the sky. She turned her head and gently pressed her ear to the pane.

There was never a plan, let's be clear about that. Phyll wanted to come, but she had no idea what she was meant to do now. She remembered the layout of the house but she didn't dare try to go inside. She stepped back and looked up at the windows. She knew Everard had the guest room round the side, above the kitchen on the second floor. It was the smallest guest room and the furthest from his father's room. She couldn't tell if the curtains were open on the upper floor, but without making a sound she made her way round to the kitchen, then she positioned herself right under what had to be his window and tipped her head back.

Now all she had to do was wait.

Well, she also squeezed her eyes shut and said his name in her head. Phyll genuinely believed that would work. She pictured him in his room, maybe lying on his bed. She was sure they could communicate telepathically, and even if Everard didn't hear her thoughts clearly, he'd at least sense her presence and come to the window. Minutes passed and Phyll imagined this thread connecting them.

Unfortunately nothing happened. She opened her eyes and sighed. She looked left and then right. She took a step back, clasping and tugging her fingers.

'Everard?' she hissed. '*Everard . . . are you there?*'

More minutes passed, which by now felt like hours. Phyll made her hands into fists and banged them together. She chewed her lip and stared at her feet. She wasn't sure what to do, but she had come all this way and she wasn't going back without seeing him. She turned and walked to the closest flowerbed and scooped up some pebbles. She made her palm flat and chose the smallest stone from the group and then turned back. She tossed it up lightly, but only hit the bottom of the windowsill. She tried again and this time the pebble touched the glass. It made a light 'ping' and she crouched down, waiting. She really thought that would do it, and Everard would appear. She was ready to jump up, like a jack-in-the-box, and she grinned as she imagined it. Ta-dah! How happy he'd be.

But where was he?

Where. Was. He?

Her legs grew stiff so she straightened up. She was getting impatient now.

'Ever-ard!' she called hoarsely. 'Ever-ard?'

But the window stayed shut. She turned and looked about the garden. The rosebushes made odd shadows on the grass and she looked past them to the trees and the sea. Maybe he was out already. She stepped back onto the lawn. What if he had come to the post office? No. That wasn't likely. He was too scared of her mother. Unless. What if he was with Miranda? Phyll felt her stomach clench. Everard and Miranda. They had gone to the caves without her. Now *they* were going to become best friends without her. He'd probably told her everything and they were inside now, or they were somewhere, doing secret things. Oh no. Oh no. Phyll bent her head and pushed her hands together. This could not happen. If only she'd kept the book. If only she hadn't shown it to Everard. She pressed her knuckles to her face. She wanted to shout. This wasn't fair. It had been his idea to leave it on the bench, but now he would forget about her and go off with Miranda. Phyll bent over. She pictured Miranda and Everard together, dressed in white of course. They were sitting on a lawn with Everard's mother and they were having tea and cakes, and everyone was looking very happy because Miranda was the sort of girl Everard should play with and that was really that.

Phyll dug into the grass with her fingers. She found a little stone with a sharp edge and she pressed it into her palm, needing the pain to shift her focus. Then she stood up, turned around and threw it hard at Everard's window. This time it rapped against the wooden frame.

Stupid house, she thought. Stupid house and stupid people.

The drumming in her chest spread to her head, and she bent and took three more stones, throwing them up at the exact same time.

Of course nothing happened. They rattled off brickwork and glass and bounced back down.

Phyll marched up to the scullery door and pressed down on the handle. It was locked. She shook it a little, just to check, then she pressed her nose against the window. All she could make out was the sink and two pairs of boots on the floor, the doorway through to the kitchen. She stepped back and slowly made a circuit of the house, looking for an open window, pressing at them gently, turning handles. Everything was shut or locked. It was as if it had been locked up for the winter.

By the time she came back out to the garden she didn't care if she made any noise. She took up a fistful of stones and threw them haphazardly, and they bounced off Everard's window and fell like hail around her.

Phyll felt her breath quickening. She turned and stalked back over the grass. She was going to leave. She had had enough, she was absolutely going to leave, but something made her turn. One last chance, she thought, as she stared back at the French windows, at their perfect rectangular panes. They stared blankly back at her and she felt something shift. *They are not away, they are hiding. They are sitting on velvet cushions, drinking from glasses that I will never drink from.* Phyll retraced her steps and without knowing why she picked up a large stone from the rockery. She liked its jagged edges and how they cut into her hands. She bent her elbows and held it under her chin.

I am going to do this, she thought, *I am really going to do this.*

She didn't wait to see where it landed although she did hear the glass break. She was already running away and she didn't stop to catch her breath until she was home and safe. When she stood in the cool of her kitchen, she wasn't even sure what she'd done. Nobody had seen her, so it was like it hadn't happened. Nobody would know. She stared at the door, the table, the walls. She counted down from twenty, waiting for the adrenalin to drain out of her body. She stuck her hands out and fluttered her fingers, letting the cold air settle. She walked through to the hallway, treading lightly on the balls of her feet. Her mother was fast asleep upstairs. Phyll thought about waking her up, whispering: *Don't you want to know what I did?* Her mother, who ruined all her fun, who had stopped her going to the caves and seeing her friends. She deserved this.

Phyll breathed in and then out. She had hoped she would feel less angry, as if sneaking out of the house might be a kind of cure, but now it all seemed so unreal, like a dream. She walked into the parlour and stood for a minute in front of the two chairs. She remembered her father sitting there, his body spilling out of it, then, automatically, her brain veered away from the memory. She turned and climbed the stairs.

It was as she reached her bedroom that she sensed somebody waiting there. The door was a little ajar, just as she'd left it, but someone was moving behind it. Phyll stood very still, her eyes fixed on the door. So her mother was awake and waiting up for her. In some ways, Phyll was glad to be caught. But as she stood on the landing she heard the sound of Elise turning over in bed. Phyll caught her breath. That meant someone else was in her room. Her mind jumped erratically. Could it be Everard? Had he snuck out to come and see her? It would explain so much! Phyll pushed her bedroom door open and peered around the edge of it.

'Everard?' she whispered.

The smell hit her straightaway: the air was heavy and sour, it was the smell of damp or rotten clothes. She took one step over the threshold and balanced on a silent floorboard. She felt suddenly so cold that she had to clutch her arms and press them into her sides. She blinked and blinked in the darkness. Her bed looked the same. The window was closed, the curtains half-drawn. It was all as she'd left it. But there was something else. A pause. A pulse. The shadow at the end of the bed seemed to flutter and reform itself. Phyll looked at it and then looked away. She swallowed and lowered her eyes so that it was only in the edge of her vision. She walked towards the bed, clutching her elbows. Normally she would take out her box of charms and count them out and kiss them. She wanted to, but she had started to shiver. She looked again to check the shadow was there. It was like a cloud of insects, swarming. Phyll was very cold now. She climbed into bed and pulled up the covers but she stayed sitting up, hugging her knees.

She watched the shape and the shape watched her. She even heard the mattress creak – just a small movement but a weight as solid as flesh. She wondered if it was her father, and that scared her. But it didn't seem big enough. She wanted to reach out and touch it, but she couldn't lift her arms. She lay down on the pillow but curled her body round so she could keep her eyes trained on it, daring it to move again. After a minute she lifted her chin.

'Do you know,' she whispered, 'I have done something really awful.'

For a second all was still, then the strangest thing happened. The shadow seemed to hear because it shifted again, and if it had a head, it turned a little way to look at her.

Then it nodded slowly, she was sure, as though to say, 'Me too.'

25

DAILY GAZETTE

Wednesday, 18 October 1933

'SARK CAVE MYSTERY: DEAD MAN NAMED'

The body of a man recovered off the cliffs of the Channel Island of Sark earlier this week has now been formally identified as Thomas Sutton, aged 32, from Essex. His parents had become concerned for his safety after receiving a letter from him, and alerted local police.

We learned this morning that Mr David Sutton, the brother of the missing man, travelled to Guernsey. After inspecting the suitcase left at the docks Mr Sutton confirmed that the contents belonged to his younger brother. He was then able to view the body and give a positive identification.

The enquiry continues.

IT IS LATE IN THE DAY. The rain has stopped and the air is still. It's like the eerie quiet that follows an explosion. The island feels empty, and of course, it is. There are no more men in mackintoshes prowling the Avenue, peering in windows. The journalists have left. They have followed the body, and the story, to Guernsey, and for the first time in weeks Sark feels at peace.

Edie and Small George went down to the harbour to wave the last of them off. As they sat on the breakwater Edie told George her news.

'I caught Phyll Carey and Everard Hyde *kissing* in the graveyard. They have been madly in love all this time, which explains why they both look so miserable!'

Edie wasn't spying – she was visiting the woman's grave and just happened to see them there – so naturally she hid.

Small George was mortified. 'Oh no,' he groaned. 'We had better keep an eye on them. They are bound to do something stupid.'

It is getting dark when Marie comes looking for her daughter. She strolls along the Avenue, muttering words under her breath.

Elise stands at her door. 'Edie is with George,' she calls out. 'They are good friends to each other.'

Marie turns, surprised, and manages a small smile. Elise smiles back, which she never normally does. Marie finds it hard to blink. She cannot look away. Elise is never nice to her, so clearly something terrible is about to happen. 'Is something wrong?' she asks.

Elise shakes her head and persists with the smiling.

It feels highly suspect, but Elise is trying a new tactic, exuding tolerance and warmth. She accepts that in the past she has been too quick with her judgements, too sharp with her words. Whether it's because of the dead couple, or the business with Paul Cecil, or whether there's some deeper seismic shift occurring underground, let's just go with it.

As the grey sky darkens into evening Edie leaves George and hurries home to her mother, and Elise takes herself off to check on Maud. Some people enjoy the night-time – those dark hours of quiet where the mind roams free – but in Sark the nights can feel infinite, so it is good to have company. At the gallery, Lisl Drake is pacing the cold, concrete floor. Eric jumped on a boat with the last of the press men, claiming important appointments in London. Poor Lisl. She does not take well to being left. She's sick of the empty days and the constant rain, and she's been brooding over the dead woman.

Elise is walking back from Maud's when she finds Lisl smoking on the gallery steps.

'I don't know much about art,' she says, 'but I think you are a study in sadness.'

Lisl looks up and it takes a second for her eyes to come fully into focus. She frowns and then laughs. 'Well, Mrs Carey – for once, we won't disagree!'

Elise holds her hands together and stares past Lisl to look at the pictures on the walls. She has so far refused to set foot in the gallery, but now Lisl steps aside. 'Come on in.'

Well, well. The world has become very strange indeed. Here is Elise Carey strolling about inside what she called a concrete carbuncle, nodding in approval at the size of the rooms. She takes everything in, including the half-drunk whisky bottle on the table by the staircase, and the bottle of pills beside it. Elise doesn't think Lisl should be drinking alone, and certainly not mixing alcohol with sedatives. She walks to the table and picks up the pill bottle, then she tries to make her voice casual.

'Tell me, why do you have Major Hyde's pills?'

'Oh,' Lisl gives a vague shrug. 'He gave them to me when I told him I was having trouble sleeping. He's going soon and said he won't need them.' She wrinkles her nose. 'I don't like him much. He was all over me the other night. He leers terribly.'

Elise nods. 'Men of a certain age. Rather like Paul Cecil.'

Lisl pulls a face. 'Oh yes, I suppose.'

The two women regard each other for a moment, then Elise tests out her new smile.

'Why don't I make us some tea instead?'

Nobody will later believe this, but Elise and Lisl talk for quite some time. Elise asks lots of questions about where Lisl worked and studied and why she married Eric, and what she still hopes to do. By the time the tea is drunk, Lisl will be seen handing over spare keys to the gallery. She's decided to leave, at least for the moment. They agree that Phyll can check in on things from time to time and Lisl should stop doing what Eric wants and follow her own ambitions.

Later on, the islanders will wonder how Elise managed it: she never liked Mr Drake's pesky artists and now she can take some credit for dispatching them. They will assume she issued some grim warning or dire prediction and poor Lisl fled in terror. Of course Elise did no such thing, but it is odd, the things people prefer to believe.

Readers might be intrigued to learn that the last person to be officially tried as a witch in the Channel Islands was in 1914, which is not that long ago. She was a pregnant single mother who made some money reading tea leaves. She just happened to push her luck when she sold some 'charmed powder' which turned out to be flour. Everyone was outraged, but until that moment they had trusted this woman and followed her advice.

Our point is, the power of any witch is the power people invest in them.

Which brings us back to Elise, and to Phyll, who is waiting for her mother in the kitchen.

'You need to stop reading other people's letters.'

Elise leans against the kitchen door. It's like icy water thrown in her face. She thinks she will fall over but she steadies herself there, pressing her hands into the wood. She stutters out a breath, then another. Things had been going so well, and now this! But she should've seen it coming. It was only a matter of time. She stares at Phyll, her daughter. Her clever child. Of course she's worked it out. How could she not? Elise lifts herself off the door and clasps her hands together. She could try and fight back, defend herself and deny it. She should puff out her cheeks and act outraged. But there are things she needs to explain. She takes another ragged breath, and the words pool and gather in her throat.

Phyll shifts in the chair, her eyes oddly glassy in the half-light.

'I've known for ages, Mum, so please don't deny it. You look in people's parcels and eavesdrop on their lives and you pretend to have some special power. I should have said sooner, but it was too . . . ' she lowers her eyes and frowns. 'It was too *sad*,' she says, almost sighing. There's an uncomfortable pause. She looks up. 'When I was little I used to think you were a witch and I think I'd still prefer that. Better a witch than a . . . ' She can't finish the sentence.

Elise pulls out a chair and sits down. 'Better a witch than a busybody,' she says. 'Better a witch than a fraud.'

She is still looking at Phyll as she lays the gallery keys on the table. She wonders how she can do this, how she can even begin to explain. A breeze lifts the hair at the back of her neck, making her skin prickle. She lowers her eyes. 'I *did* have powers,' she says. 'I truly did. But then, one day, I didn't.'

Phyll exhales slowly. 'Ah.' She waits. 'I wondered.' She waits again. 'What happened?'

Elise presses her hands down hard on the table, feeling the lines of the grain. What happened? That's normally the question she likes to ask. She takes a deep breath in and casts her mind back. This might be the hardest thing she will ever have to do, but she has to do it. She has to admit the truth. So she closes her eyes and starts talking and she talks quickly without pausing to think how it sounds. She tells Phyll that she did feel things once, and she dreamt things and it was shocking and frightening. Mostly, she was right. Mostly, she hated it. The War years were the worst when the news was never good. Death and pain everywhere.

'And then your father came back.' She opens her eyes. 'I was pleased, of course, but he was different, like a stranger. He scared me and I wonder if the fear did it.' She hesitates, watching Phyll's face. 'When he left I had no idea where he went. I assumed he was dead but I never felt anything. I never saw his presence or had any dreams about him. He just went out that night and was gone. I waited and,' she sighs, 'waiting became its own routine.' She shakes her head. 'I never meant to pretend or trick people.' Her voice rises higher. 'The problem was, they kept asking me for things, and everyone was anxious and needed some comfort and I honestly thought it was better. I didn't want to let them down and I thought if I carried on then maybe, in time, things would go back to how they were.' She stops talking and stares at the table, spreading out her fingers. 'I realise how bad this all sounds. I lied to everyone, and the lies trapped me.'

Elise told herself that she did it from habit, that she only did what people wanted. But it was also about power. Women have so little power, and it's always fleeting. She needed to feel in control. Of course she is ashamed, but as she talks she feels a huge relief. It is as if she is shrugging off a heavy coat after a long journey.

Phyll listens calmly and waits for her mother to finish.

'But Everard and I were only playing,' she tells her. 'We were just children. To us it was a game, a joke . . . children *do* play games.' She pauses. 'But you went to the Major's house and you lied about feeling a presence, and the Major beat Everard senseless when he realised it was all a trick.'

Elise has knitted her fingers together and now she pulls them apart. 'That had nothing to do with me. I never spoke to the Major about it. I know I came down hard on the pair of you. I was so ashamed. I said I was protecting you but I was protecting myself. I think I am just always afraid . . .'

Phyll leans forward, head lowered. 'Afraid of what?'

Elise swallows hard and realises that she's started crying. She brushes off a tear and sniffs. 'Of not being needed, maybe.'

She realises she is holding Phyll's hands. She doesn't recall reaching out for them, but Phyll responds to the pressure of her fingers and thumbs.

'But I'll always need you. Maud will always need you. People love you. *I* love you.'

Elise sniffs and nods. 'And I love you, too.' She needs to wipe her nose but she can't let go of Phyll's hands.

Phyll smiles. 'But you must stop reading the letters. It's so wrong. Can you stop?'

Elise nods quickly. 'I already have.'

This is true. Paul Cecil's letter finished her off. She cannot face it anymore.

Phyll brings her mother's hands together. 'Good. Because I lied, too. I hated Southampton and I hated the job, but I never told you because I couldn't bear to let you down. When I was here, all I ever dreamt about was getting away. I thought I'd run off to England and become this new person. But I just felt like more of a misfit. So I acted like an ungrateful brat and dug myself into a hole and made one mistake after another.'

Elise looks up sharply. She is tempted to say *I know* but instead she shakes her head. 'You're not ungrateful.' She sniffs again and brings Phyll's left hand up to her cheek to wipe another tear. She's not sure what else to add. She might try an: *I just wanted you to be happy*, but she's not sure that's right. She has never valued happiness since happiness doesn't last. No, what she wanted most of all was for Phyll to be free, and to have the choices she didn't have. She wonders why love has to be so hard, so consuming. She can't get over that she has a daughter, that she made this creature. It terrifies her. Perhaps that's why she sent her away, because she couldn't bear to have her close. To love someone is always a risk, you risk being disappointed and rejected. Elise hated that risk.

It is much easier to die for someone than it is to live for them, in the same way that it is easier to push them away than it is to hold them close.

She lowers her head. 'Do you know how much I love you?'

Phyll lets out a little laugh. 'You make it sound like a threat.'

Elise almost chokes. She stands up quickly and moves around the table and draws Phyll into a hug, wrapping her arms around her shoulders and kissing her head.

Phyll stiffens, and then, after a few seconds, she lifts her arms and hugs her mother's waist. They stay like that, locked together, and Elise strokes Phyll's hair and wills time to stop. She closes her eyes and wants to bottle this feeling.

It's Phyll who moves first, shifting her head to look up.

'We are on the same side, Mum. I'm not trying to fight you. But there is something else.' She keeps her arms tightly wrapped around Elise's waist. Her face looks still and carved in the half-light. 'Everard thinks he is cursed and it is connected to what we did all those years ago. He says it is all happening again, and I can tell he's scared. He says *she's* come back.'

Elise narrows her eyes, not understanding. 'Who's come back?'

Phyll hesitates. 'The woman, of course. The Stranger. He says he saw her. He says she's in the house.'

26

Beau Regard, Little Sark.

23 August 1923

SARAH WILLIAMS WOKE TO THE shutting of a door. She heard someone walk away, but the sound was swallowed by the ticking of a clock. She tried to open her eyes but they seemed to be glued shut. She took a breath in and then out. She was lying in bed, flat on her back. She felt terribly sick. Had she been sick? She prised her eyes open. She didn't know where she was, and she wondered for a moment if she'd died. But the pain was real, pressing into her skull. Was she in a hospital? *I have been very ill*, she told herself, *I have had an accident*. Did she bang her head? Echoes of conversations came back and she realised she was still in the house. The Major's house. She remembered smashed glass and falling back and the dry ache of her own screams, then Dr Stanhope standing over her. Oh, it was too much.

When she woke again the room was glaringly bright, she had to lift a hand to shield her eyes. She tried to sit up but nausea rippled through her body. Yellow curtains fluttered around a blue sky. If she moved her head, she could see her dress, draped neatly over a chair. She squeezed her eyes shut and remembered walking on the lawn with Sylvie and the smell of the roses. Now she smelt of tobacco and something bitter and chemical. She tasted it, too. She breathed in and then out. She strained to make her brain work, but a part of her didn't want her brain to work, because she was in a strange room wearing only her underclothes. She felt helpless, ashamed.

She slowly lifted her arms. Her fingers felt stiff and swollen, as if she'd soaked too long in the bath. She tried to prop herself up but she still didn't have the strength. Anything physical was at a distance, as if her mind was elsewhere. It was also strangely blank. What had happened? What had happened? She closed her eyes and shifted through the darkness. She saw the table with the candle. She remembered holding hands around it. She'd felt someone touch her and she felt them again now, holding her wrists. Her eyes flew open and she stared at the ceiling. Something bad had happened but she couldn't say what. She had this terrible feeling of an overwhelming presence, of hands invading her. She looked around the room. All so clean and tidy. She clenched her eyes shut. A bad dream. She thought she could hear Sylvie's voice somewhere and she remembered that Sylvie had helped her to bed. That was it. She had screamed and wept and made a scene, but Sylvie had been there.

Sarah pressed a clammy hand to her face. The men had called her hysterical. She could hear Dr Stanhope very clearly. Hysterical. It was what she had been called as a girl, and after Cyril died. Sarah opened her eyes. *Cyril.* He had come back. She raised one arm and started plucking at the skin, where he had touched her. It felt both bad and good. Had she gone mad? She watched her skin turn red and waited.

The clocks recorded the seconds and the minutes. The window let in a little breeze. She propped herself up and reached for her dress, dragging it over herself. She had to make herself presentable – this single thought now hung in her mind. She held up the fabric and studied it. As a child she had refused to wear any dress with the smallest stain: she'd shriek and rip it off and drive her mother to distraction. Sarah felt a sudden pang to see her mother. She would go to her as soon as she could. She laid the dress over her body.

There was a creak on the stairs and fear filled her mouth. 'Help,' she called out. 'Is there someone?'

It was Nancy. She'd been in and out several times that morning, but 'My poor dear lady' had slept very deeply. Nancy didn't mention that she'd twice leant over her to check that she was even breathing. She talked quickly because she was anxious, her words running together. 'How are you feeling? Shall I get you a basin? You've had a terrible shock. Would you like tea? Water?'

Nancy was the only one who had a full account of the evening, which was ironic considering she hadn't even been there. She was of course relying on the version of events recounted by her employer, who had gotten her out of bed at some unearthly hour, apologising profusely over this 'appalling business'. Major Hyde had explained to Nancy that Everard had been tricking them all along, playing at ghosts, and his pranks had reached a climax with the smashing of the windows.

'I am so ashamed, Mrs Dolbel. But there will be no more of it! I am taking him off the island on my boat.'

So Everard had been taken away at first light and Nancy was in charge of the mess that he'd left. And what a mess.

There was broken glass all over the drawing room floor, making it a veritable death-trap. Someone could have been blinded. A throat might have been cut! The windows would have to be boarded up until new ones were made, and heaven knows what that would cost. Nancy organised for the two Hamon boys to make temporary repairs, paying them with the day-old lobster salad. She was deeply offended that nobody had even touched the food she had spent so long preparing. She was sure all that drinking on an empty stomach hadn't helped.

Dr Stanhope arrived in time for a plate of food, which he dearly needed. He looked very ill. The shock of last night had stayed with him. He had given Mrs Williams Chloral Hydrate, then gone home and dosed himself with brandy. He assured Mrs Williams that she'd feel better soon, but she accused him of 'manhandling' her, which he found rather shocking. He had only done what any doctor would do.

Nancy told him not to worry. She had been against this idea of a séance from the off. You do not go round inviting ghosts into houses. It is not a form of entertainment. Stanhope nodded, and admitted that he too had had grave reservations, but felt obliged to attend in a professional capacity, in case of an emergency. And wasn't it a good thing that he had?

But Sarah Williams was unable to accept what had happened. She felt that the spirit of her dead husband had returned, she said, along with something more malevolent.

'Well, it *was* malevolent,' Nancy sighed. 'It was the Major's son. That little lad! Who would have thought?'

It was late afternoon when they returned Mrs Williams to the Bel Air in a carriage and Nancy stopped in to see Maud to tell her what had happened. She wasn't spreading gossip, you must understand. She had the idea that Maud could make a purgative for the poor lady, something to flush the toxins out. Dandelion and burdock, that sort of thing.

Nancy didn't mention the blood because she didn't know about it. She spent most of the day in the downstairs rooms, sweeping and mopping, then she climbed the stairs to strip the beds. Everard's room was still dark, the curtains tightly drawn, so she smelt it before she saw it. She flung open the window, knocking two pebbles that were stuck on the ledge, then turned and let out a low gasp. There was a rusty-brown stain in the middle of the pillow, almost the shape of a head. She pressed her hands to her mouth and stared at it, then she saw the blood on the sheets. Nancy folded her arms over her stomach. She felt faint and then she felt sick. She'd smacked her boys a few times over the years, but she'd never drawn blood. She was surprised that Dr Stanhope hadn't mentioned it.

Nancy did her best. She scrubbed until her wrists ached, filling basin after basin with water turning red, but the stains had soaked through to the mattress. She did worry about Everard. Wouldn't it have been better to make him stay and face up to what he'd done? Wasn't that better than a beating? But then she remembered Mrs Williams raving about someone in the room as she slept, about feeling 'invaded'. Nancy scrubbed and rinsed and thought some more, and her thoughts crowded together and made it hard to see. She stood on the landing, arms folded, and she stared at each door, and then she paced between them. Her mouth opened and closed and she muttered words quietly, afraid to say them out loud. Was it possible that

Everard had spied on Mrs Williams? Was *that* the explanation? But he was just a boy, so that's all he would have done. Nancy pressed her hands to her chest. The house was so quiet since he'd left – the boy who had played all those horrible tricks.

She didn't want to think more about it, and soon she wouldn't need to. When Maud called at the Bel Air in the morning with her tonic, Mrs Williams had already settled her bill and left on the earliest boat. Maud found this very curious. She wanted to tell Nancy but first she told Elise.

'It's very worrying,' Maud muttered. 'I hope she is all right.'

Elise shrugged. 'Well, she's gone now so there's nothing you can do.'

Elise was not in the mood for more drama – Phyll refusing to talk to her, blaming *her*, of course – and she didn't want to hear another thing about Beau Regard. She'd vowed not to get involved with outsiders and hadn't her instinct proved right? All the trouble came and went with the visitors. She naturally felt guilty about Mrs Williams because of the book, but *only* because of the book. She wouldn't tell Maud about it. She wouldn't tell anyone. No. Better to swallow it like a bitter pill and forget. She sat down heavily, facing Maud.

'So, Mrs Williams has left. I can't say I blame her. It was a terrible idea, to have *a séance*. What were they thinking?'

Maud arched her eyebrows and stared into space.

'But,' she said. 'There *was* something in the house. How else could it have happened?' She turned her gaze on Elise. '*You* told me it was harmless.'

Elise straightened her spine. She didn't like the note of challenge in Maud's voice.

'I don't recall my exact words,' she countered. 'But if it was the boy making mischief for the father, then it was *his* presence I felt.' She tilted her head and lowered her gaze. '*Most* people would consider a small boy as harmless. This *chaos* was his revenge.' She paused again. 'Mrs Williams – poor thing – was caught in the middle. You say Stanhope gave her Chloral after her fall. It sounds like she had a bad reaction.' Elise stared at the bottle that Maud had prepared. 'Or maybe he gave her too much – that man can't be trusted. It is his fault, perhaps. Let us hope she will be all right. What's done is done.'

But Maud couldn't take her eyes off Elise and her gaze was intense and engulfing. 'But *what* about the boy?'

Elise gave a small shrug. 'He has gone. Good riddance.'

She meant it. She had barely said five words to Everard and even that was too much. She felt a huge relief. She could file him away in her bureau, label him 'trouble' and forget. He'd had some fun at other people's expense but now he had been caught, and thank heavens she'd managed to keep Phyll out of it. She only regretted allowing them to be friends at all. She would need to be more careful in future. Boys like Everard would come and go, always go, and it wasn't a healthy kind of friendship for Phyll to have. Things would never be equal between them, and Phyll would end up left and hurt. Elise lifted her eyes to the ceiling. She pictured her bleary-eyed daughter hunched in bed upstairs. She was upset now, but she'd get over it. She was young, and the young had great powers of recovery. They had their whole lives ahead of them.

Maud wore an odd look that Elise hadn't seen before. Her face was creased with thought and her eyes were small. Elise watched her for a moment, wanting her to stop.

'No. This isn't right.' She shook her head. 'It doesn't feel right at all.'

Elise held her hands in her lap. 'Come now, Maud,' she said reasonably. 'Why involve ourselves in someone else's business?'

Maud stopped twisting the bottle and looked up, a look of unguarded horror. 'If it happened in that house then it *is* my business,' she said. 'It is your business, too. It is *all* our businesses.'

Elise frowned, a little uneasy. 'I don't see how.'

Maud waited a moment. 'Then I have to tell you. Let me explain.'

27

'An Island Legend'

WHEN A STORY IS REPEATED it will change. It's like when a house changes owner. The structure is the same but a lot of things are different. At first, you think it is just the furniture, but then a door appears or there are new windows and extra rooms. Certain things remain the same but it might take time before you realise what they are and what has happened. Maud always feels like that now, which is one of the reasons she likes to walk. She has to find her bearings. It is why she tramples gardens and peers through windows.

Actually, that's not why.

Let's go back.

It was the afternoon of Saturday, 30th September and she was on La Coupée when she saw the man and woman. (Yes, she did see them.) She thought they looked very smart from a distance, as though dressed for an occasion, but as they drew close she had that dread feeling. The woman bent her head and the man held her at the elbow, the way men sometimes do. Then he stopped and talked to her in snappish jolts. Maud stood to one side to let them pass but she lifted her hand and circled it vaguely.

'Did you miss your boat?'

It was a perfectly innocent enquiry. She was not being snide. She just wanted the man to look her in the eye.

He did and then he almost bared his teeth at her. 'Mind your own business,' he hissed. 'You old witch!'

Maud's eyes drifted out of focus and she raised a hand to her cheek. Did she look like a witch? That did sound familiar. She pressed her skin, kneaded her flesh. It wasn't always so slack, but had that made a difference? She took a deep breath in. She was still on La Coupée, but the railings had gone. They'd not so much fallen away as never existed. Hah! She could see straight down the cliff to the waves and it gave her a giddy feeling of freedom. It was later in the year, a different year entirely. She lifted her face to the needling rain. Clarrie Baker. That was it. Clarrie had had a fever after the birth of her second child, a little girl they'd named Ellen. Maud was back and forth to Little Sark every day to check on them – no easy task when the wind was up, like today. She saw the house ahead of her and frowned. She didn't know the gentleman who was renting it. For a long time it had been empty – considered too remote. The new tenant was an artist and liked the isolation. He was tall with flinty eyes and small teeth, and he always smelt of a heavy cologne. You could follow his trail wherever he walked on the cliffs, like a dog leaving its scent. Maud tried to avoid him, but there was something about his wife. Maud liked women. She was interested in how their minds worked, and how they talked about their lives. This woman had long dark hair that she always wore loose, and her skin was strikingly pale. People thought she must be foreign since she never spoke. She wore a loose-fitted, hooded coat and the way that she walked, with her head bent and her hands tucked inside her sleeves, made her look like a penitent. Sam Baker, Clarrie's husband, said there was talk of a nervous illness, but Clarrie just sighed and rolled her eyes at him.

'She's nervous, all right,' she tutted. 'She's scared of her husband.'

Maud saw that, too, and so whenever she saw the woman again she made a point of smiling and nodding and speaking a few words. The lady always turned her face away, but Maud didn't take offence, she just tried harder. One evening she almost ran into the woman on the cliffs and she clasped her hands. 'Oh! What a day to be out! You need some gloves.'

But the woman shrunk back, her eyes skittering anxiously to the other side of La Coupée. 'You must not talk to me.'

She bent her head, as if to hide it. Poor thing, Maud thought, but she had a busy time ahead with two more babies due within that month and no time to spare. She was relieved when Clarrie's fever passed and she wasn't needed on Little Sark so often. Maud saw the lady one more time, on the cliffs one dark afternoon. Despite the driving rain the woman wore only what looked like her nightdress. Maud veered off the road, shouting out that she'd catch her death, but when she looked again the woman was gone.

Maud knew she was too late.

We used to say an old maid attended the body because that sounded better, but Maud wasn't old, not then. The husband sought her out because she was young, in fact. He called at the post office the next day, announcing that his wife had died in her sleep. He didn't seem that upset, but then he explained his wife had been ill for years.

'I had hoped the clear air would've helped somewhat, but she wore herself out with walking.' He shook his head slowly and sighed to himself. 'She had some kind of fit or seizure in the night.'

Since Maud was a nurse, she had to go and help. The house on the cliffs was much smaller than Beau Regard. It was set back, banked by hedges and trees. The rooms were sparsely furnished and all dark wood. The woman was laid out and waiting. She looked more like a wax model than a once living thing, but Maud noticed the wisps of baby hair in the corners of each temple and the mole below her right eye. She also noticed the red marks on her chest, at her neck, the old bruises on her wrists, her ribcage, her legs.

We carry with us so many versions of what we like to call the truth. The artist had his version: that he had tried to revive his wife, that she'd been unwell before, that there was nothing he could do. Maud was filled with doubt, but she was still very young and lacking in experience. If she'd been older, she might have stood up to him and trusted her first instincts, but she didn't want to cause trouble and she had no real proof.

Contrary to some accounts there was only a wooden cross, two roughly hewn sticks nailed together, like a signpost stuck at the head of the grave. When Maud saw it she felt dizzy. There were sentences in her head, but she didn't know how to say them, and the words stuck in her mouth. Murder was a terrible thing. A serious crime. It seemed too outlandish, too unlikely. People would say *she'd* gone mad – that was the danger. In a small community there is always gossip, and she had to take care. She didn't want to stir up trouble.

Maud didn't know what to do, how to go on. She loved her work and it meant she was welcome in every family home, and all the women trusted her. But it was *because* the women trusted her that she felt she had to speak. When she next came back to Little Sark, just crossing over La Coupée brought it back. She walked up the path to the Baker cottage and saw mother and baby sitting in the doorway, looking fine and healthy. She should've felt relieved, but she just wanted to weep.

She put down her bag and let out a long sigh. 'Clarrie, I have to talk to you. It's about your neighbour. I have this terrible feeling it's not what it seems . . .'

Clarrie, who was rocking Ellen in her arms, looked at Maud. 'You think he killed her? I feel it, too. He killed her and he's going to walk free.'

But they were just two women. What could they do?

Let's go back to the wooden cross. It is a far easier thing to remove than a great granite headstone, you'll agree. A day later it was found on its side. The gravedigger blamed the softness of the ground after rain, but it happened the next night. Then on the fourth day it was found some yards away with the wood all splintered, as if it had been thrown with real force. By now the rumours had started, as rumours reliably did. Sark women have always been an excellent news network, although do give us credit, we are much more than that.

Come on, catch up. By all means call Sark 'traditional' and 'timeless', but don't be fooled about who's in charge. The men might do the fighting and the fishing, but women do everything else. We run the households, we care for the livestock, we do the cooking and cleaning, the nursing and rearing. We care for the sick and the old, we card and comb the wool, we milk the cows, we churn the milk. The women are in charge of everything, from births to deaths and the bits in-between. Men don't like to admit it, of course, but this is not some secret club or underground movement and no, we don't meet in groups of thirteen.

We women just do what we do. Which is everything.

So you would not want to cross us.

Because then we will come for you.

Maud remembers the artist in the churchyard one lunchtime, trying to thrust the splintered wooden cross back into place. She only saw him do it the once, but it gave her a satisfied feeling. He was filthy and sweating hard when he saw her, and then he had the gall to ask if she'd seen it move. She looked appalled and shook her head. The only thing Maud had seen was the line of dirt under Clarrie's fingernails. She warned her to wear gloves when it was next her turn.

You would perhaps like to know how many of us were involved, but we don't dig and tell. And what about the husband, the widower. Shall we call him the murderer?

Now the fun could start.

A ghostly shape was seen at the tip of La Coupée – a woman in white standing, overlooking the cliff. She was seen by several people, including Clarrie, who made a great show of trembling and weeping in public, and asking aloud what it meant. On a later evening a pale figure was glimpsed through the trees of Dixcart Valley. Three visitors walking up from the beach had the shock of their lives but did not get close enough to be sure what they'd seen. The story was repeated and embellished. Some people called her the White Lady. We preferred the Stranger Lady. Nice and mysterious. Maud reported seeing her twice and the second time seemed significant: 'She was on the brink of telling me something then she looked very scared and ran away.'

Ghosts, as we know, carry a message from the dead to the living, they return because some business remains unfinished. Everyone wondered what the Lady had to tell them. Her husband was understandably perturbed. The next time Maud walked by the church he seemed to be loitering, keeping watch, and he caught her by the wrist and twisted her arm so violently it made her skin burn.

'You did this,' he hissed. 'You are all the same, you little witch!'

Maud wasn't a witch, of course.

If she had been, she could have spoiled his milk or infested his house with fleas or frogs, since, according to court documents, that's what witches do. But those kinds of witches don't exist: they are a fantasy, a fetish.

Maybe now, when a man calls a woman a witch, it's a good sign. It means she has power, that he is scared. Maud knows what she did was wrong, but a lot of the time nowadays she can't remember what she did and so her days pass in peace. It was when she stood on La Coupée and that man called her a witch that a door in her mind unlocked. She raised her hands to her cheeks and the memory fluttered free. Did she look like a witch? Maybe now she did. Well, that's fine.

She had to laugh, she really did. 'There are worse things than meeting a witch,' she called after him.

But that poses an interesting question: what's worse than meeting a witch?

The answer, dear readers, should be clear.

There is only one thing worse than meeting a witch and that would be meeting her coven.

Hello.

28

JERSEY EVENING POST

Friday, 20 October 1933

'BROTHER'S LAST LETTER'

Thomas Sutton, the man found dead in the sea around Sark, had apparently written to his parents, saying that he had to go away 'to save everyone further heartbreak'. His brother, who has now been thoroughly questioned by police, maintains that nobody in the family was aware of his association with the dead woman, now identified as Mrs Violet Howell.

David Sutton states that his brother had not mentioned any new relationship and remains as baffled by recent events as everyone. The inquest was held in Guernsey late on Tuesday afternoon in the company of island officials and representatives of the press. Mr Sutton confirmed that this was his brother, who had lately written to their parents informing them that he had to go away, but assuring them that he was 'happy with his decision' and that it was 'the right choice'.

Thomas Sutton worked at Hills and Son, a local manufacturing plant in Colchester. He was seen by his parents on 17th September when he seemed quite his normal self. His landlady last saw him on 24th September. She told police he left in his best clothes, with a suitcase, saying he was to have a short holiday. His employers received a telegram from him saying that he was sorry but he would not be returning to work and that he hoped his absence would not inconvenience them. A neighbour reports he had seemed very agitated in the week prior to his disappearance.

What followed is all reported, and yet still not understood.

WE ACCEPT IT MUST BE HARD to see how the pieces fit together, how choices made years ago can shape what happens now, but history has its rhythms and repetitions. If we could walk backwards through our lives we'd see the inevitable connections. Nothing exists on its own and there are always repercussions. Some people call them curses. Curses are not real, but they fill a real need. To call someone cursed is to surrender control, to say their fate is bound up with what's happened before. Everard thinks he is cursed but it's not the fault of a ghost or a witch. It's not even about what he did. It's about a memory, a memory from a summer night, ten years ago.

He was locked in his bedroom, lying on his side, cheek stuck to the pillow. The head bleeds a lot, please remember, and the smell smothered him. As his father greeted guests downstairs, and as Paul Cecil made cocktails, a twelve year old boy lay very still and waited to die. He really did think he was dying because it hurt so much to breathe. As per later medical records, his right arm was broken, three ribs were cracked, and that's to say nothing of the mess of his face. He should have seen a doctor straightaway, but the doctor was downstairs and didn't have a steady hand.

Everard lost consciousness twice and the world was quiet. He dreamt he could walk downstairs and out of the house and he wasn't scared or bleeding, and the moon was huge and full and he saw a large crowd of people moving away. He tried to catch up with them and hear what they were saying, but they didn't see him and he wondered if he had died and become a ghost, and he smelt smoke but he never saw what was burning. That was when the noise woke him.

It was a sharp, tapping sound from outside. Tap, tap. Then a pause. Tap, tap, again.

He was awake in an instant. He tried to turn his head but his cheek had stuck to the pillow. His eye was throbbing and he thought he might be sick. He lay back and let the nausea pass. Did he hear someone call his name? Was that Phyll? His heart squeezed painfully, as if someone held it. Oh no. Let it not be Phyll, because if his father caught Phyll he'd kill her, too. There was nothing worse. Everard rolled slowly onto his back, and the pain drove up his shoulder. It felt like knives digging under his ribs. He gasped and winced and took a few shallow breaths. It was all too much. Hot tears flooded his cheeks. He licked his lips and sniffed.

'*Just go,*' he whispered through his teeth, '*give up and go . . . please!*'

After that, there was silence. He told himself Phyll had gone and she was safe, which was something. It was good. He thought he could write to her from London, and maybe invite her to visit. They'd have fun and his mother would like her because she liked girls and would make a fuss. These thoughts calmed him down and made him breathe slower. He wondered what Phyll would think of all the streets and houses and people. His house in London was never silent: you could hear sirens and milk carts in the morning and his mother was always rushing down the stairs, calling out for her hat or gloves. He started crying again. He wanted to see his mother. He thought of her French perfume and the way her hair would brush his cheek when she bent to kiss him goodnight.

A sudden crash shook the house, then screams and shouts and slamming doors. Everard lay very still. Another dream. A bad one. Maybe someone would come and get him. There were footsteps and men's voices and a woman weeping.

Everard couldn't remember the rest. He told himself to forget it and was amazed to find that he did. It is always interesting what people forget – the events we can't give words to. Time helps, of course. Time heals, they say. It is like the action of the waves eroding the rocks, smoothing down all the sharp edges. You just need to watch out for the cracks, though. There are always cracks, and the waves make them wider.

It is through those cracks that ghosts slip free. Sark has a lot of ghosts, as we've mentioned. Let's just say, we have been waiting.

Jump forward to Saturday, 30th September, 1933. Everard was, there, all grown up, standing on the dock. He disembarked the *Joy Bell II*, but it was half past eight in the morning and there were only a few people about. He could have booked into the Bel Air and then Dolly would have known, but he didn't plan to stay. He was going to walk over and see his father and make him sign the papers, these important papers, and then leave. Earnest Hyde had procrastinated out of spite, but the idea was, when confronted with his son, here, in Sark of all places, he would relent. Everard had it all planned – he was still a careful planner. He wanted to make his father as uncomfortable as possible. He was also now big enough to hit him back.

So Everard walked up from the harbour and took the road to Little Sark. He did not meet anyone on the way. No, he did not pass two people wandering over La Coupée in the opposite direction. He did not hear the man raise his voice or tug at the woman's arm and demand that she stay. He did not meet Maud, or Small George, or Phyll. He did wonder about Phyll, but she'd never replied to his letters and she might've long left the island.

He was sombre and business-like when he arrived at the house.

'If you sign now,' he told his father, 'then I can get the next boat and we need never see each other again.'

Of course Earnest Hyde had to read everything carefully and so Everard went for a walk. He walked fast with his head down, fighting the wind and to some degree the wild weather distracted him. He went further than he planned, reaching the Gouliot headland. He even peered through one of the windows of the Cecils' locked studio, rubbing away the grime with his coat sleeve. He remembered the last time he'd been there, with Miranda limping beside him. It was strange, being back, as if he'd been thrust into a parallel life. He wanted to be back, but back there. The wind had picked up and the sea was very rough, creating pits and hollows and crashing into the cliffs. Everard realised he'd have to stay. Just one night. We would like to think a part of him was pleased, as if a choice had been taken from him.

He didn't want to go back to Beau Regard straightaway, so he called at the Bungalow to see if there was a vacant room, but it had closed the week before. That's when he met Nancy Dolbel on the lane.

He took off his hat and held it to his chest, and Nancy, who had known he was coming, saw the scar on his eyebrow. She looked away. 'I can make up the bed in your old room,' she said, then her mouth dropped a little because she remembered all the blood.

Everard thanked her and said he'd stay out of the house until she was ready. 'I caused you enough trouble when I was here before. I hope you know I am so sorry for that.'

He was on Gorey Common. There was a moment at around four or five o'clock when the dying light made the rocks shimmer, and the greens and rusts of the bracken seemed to glow. It was beautiful in its strange, wild way. Everard was so busy taking it all in he didn't notice the man and woman on the path higher up. He didn't see the man walk ahead and the woman hold back and glance over her shoulder. They were retracing their steps to the shed.

Maybe this is where it starts.

Tap-tap-tap on the window. Everard. Are you there?

He woke in a panic, surprised to find he'd slept at all. He was back in his old room at Beau Regard. He had waited as long as possible before coming back inside.

That noise. *Tap-tap-tap*. What was that noise?

He stood up quickly, almost falling forwards, arms outstretched. It was pitch black but he was no longer a little boy scared in the dark. The noise came again and he turned towards it. He thought it had been Phyll at the window all those years ago, but it couldn't be her now. That would be too ridiculous. He walked across the room and pulled back the curtains and pressed his nose to the glass. He could just make out the lawn and the shape of the trees, nothing else. His breath misted the glass and he wiped it with his sleeve. He sighed and stepped back. Why on earth had he thought of Phyll? Because he wanted to find her. She was the still point on the horizon. He didn't even know if she was on the island, but tomorrow he would maybe go and look. He scratched his head, sighed and turned back to the bed, but then the tapping came again. Frowning, he looked out of the window again, cupping his hands over his brow.

There she was. The white dress, the long, dark hair blowing up in the wind. It wasn't Phyll. It was the Lady, it was the lady his father had seen all those years ago. She was moving across the garden then she stopped when she reached the fence. She turned and looked up at him. Everard jumped back from the window and held his breath in his throat. He slapped his hands on his cheeks to check it wasn't a dream, then he tipped forward and looked again. She was still there, waiting, then she turned towards the cliff.

Everard was out of the room, running down the stairs, pulling on shoes and stumbling onto the lawn. He wanted to shout, 'Wait!', but the wind stole his breath and buffeted him back. He staggered and corrected himself. There were no stars, no moon, so he had to be careful. He walked fast with his arms out, trying to watch where he stepped. He had to catch up with her. She was the one who'd started it all – the ghost he never saw – and now she was here like an answer to a question.

He was more excited than scared, and he tripped, his shoes pushing into the mud one minute and hitting rock the next. Although he remembered the way he was careless and fell badly. His knee collided with a rock and he threw up his hands to shield his face. He cried out with shock and rolled onto his side and the cold gorse seeped into his clothes. He was up again. He could hear the sea roaring and he wondered if the woman was leading him off a cliff. The sea sounded very close and he had the sensation of being pulled strongly towards it, as if hands were on his shoulders, urging him on.

He was scared now, but just a little way ahead was a shed where he could stop and take shelter. He was at the entrance when he sensed something or someone was there ahead of him. There was a muffled shape on the floor. He drew back, pinning himself against the outside wall. He didn't know what it was, so he waited, holding his breath.

That was all it took.

He listened and he waited, and he suddenly remembered it all. He remembered the night his father beat him, the doors slamming, the women crying. No, one woman crying. He was in his room and these noises came at him through the wall. After the crying stopped there was a long silence and he was relieved. Some time passed and then this other noise started. The bed next door creaked and there was a dull thud that repeated, over and over, like it was being rammed against the wall. Everard heard it and hated it, covering his head with his pillow to try and block it out. A rhythm and a repetition. Then it stopped and he heard his father gasp.

Everard stood very still, back pressed into the wall of the shed, and the ground under him rippled with the aftershock. For years he had buried it completely, but now it broke through to the surface and it was clear and fresh, like a body embalmed. His darkness – the explanation to everything – was not what had happened to him ten years ago. It was what had happened to someone else, just next door, and he had heard it through a bedroom wall.

He closed his eyes and turned his head, pressing his cheek to the cold, rough wood. He had to get away, but then he felt someone standing beside him. The woman was there, facing him, barely inches away. He stared into her eyes and he felt an icy hand over his mouth. He couldn't move, he couldn't cry out. He tasted cinders and saw black.

The next thing he remembered, he was staggering back to the house. He just wanted to leave – it was all he could think about – and he ran upstairs and packed his bag. But what use was running away? He couldn't keep on running. He'd come here for a reason. He walked back downstairs and paced about. The papers he had brought were still on the desk, still unsigned. Everard sat at his father's desk and stared out into the garden.

The sky was lightening slowly and he watched it through the window. Maybe he'd dreamt it all, so he went back outside, calmer now, and walked back down the garden. He slipped through the gate and onto the headland. He wasn't sure what he was doing but the common was deserted. He found the shed and circled it cautiously. He stepped inside and saw the crushed fronds on the ground where two bodies had lain. Two real people. Good, he thought, I haven't gone completely mad.

The rain was starting up again, a light patter drumming on the roof. Everard turned up his collar and walked back outside. So two people had been here but where on earth had they gone? He carried on to the cliff's edge, eyes fixed on the dark horizon. There was a thick bank of cloud and the sea churned under it. He was turning back when he saw someone down on the beach. It was a man and he was stripped to his vest and shorts. Everard struggled to make sense of it. The man would get swept out if he stayed there. The currents were dangerous – didn't he know?

Everard shouted: 'Hey you!' but his voice was snatched by the wind. He waited a minute, debating what to do, then he started down the rocky path to the beach. 'Hey!' he bellowed. '*Hey!*'

The man still couldn't hear. He had his back to the cliff and stood with hands on hips, staring out over the sea, so Everard carried on down the path, watching his step as the stones were wet and slippery. Every so often he'd stop and look up and call, 'Hey!' But it was like he was trapped behind glass.

The man was up to his calves in the water, struggling to stay upright against the push and pull of the waves. What *was* he doing?

Everard had made it to the last run of steps and yelled: 'Get back!'

He thought his ribs would burst out of his skin, and then he saw something else, something out in the waves. A black cloud, a flash of white. It was a body. A woman's body.

Everard sucked in breath. He felt like he'd been winded. 'No!' he shouted. He scrambled down the last steps, and the man turned around now.

Everard hit the shingle and felt the icy water curl around his feet. The two men stared at each other.

Everard gripped him by the shoulders. 'What's happening?'

The man's eyes came alive. 'It was an accident,' he said.

Everard didn't believe him. He turned to look out to sea and just at that second he felt a hand at the back of his head, shoving him down. The man was stronger, pushing him into the water and he was slipping on the shingle. With one arm flailing he got hold of the man's vest and wrenched him down, too. A wave slammed over both of them and dragged them under, and the shingle fell away like a shelf. Everard was peddling with his feet but the cold water invaded his clothes and froze his skin. He broke through to the surface, gasping for air. He had to keep moving, trying to find something firm to touch down on but all he could see was sky. He squeezed his eyes shut and thought about cycling, cycling over La Coupée with his eyes shut, with Phyll holding tight to his belt. He had thought they'd die, but they didn't. They didn't. He opened his eyes and pushed out with one foot. He touched down on something and pushed himself off, propelling himself forward. There were jagged rocks and seaweed. Another huge wave picked him up and he hit solid rock. The tide pulled away but he clung on desperately and then scrambled up higher. His clothes dragged him down but he climbed higher.

He'd been taken by the tide and pushed back onto the rocks below the pier, and now he could see that he could climb around. He spat water and gulped air and it burned his lungs. His teeth chattered manically and he couldn't make them stop. His fingers were bright-red and numb but he was back by the path. He sat down, breathing fast, and looked out. The tide had rushed forward, covering the shingle with foam, leaving everything altered afterwards. He saw no one in the water. No man. No woman.

He staggered backwards. He didn't understand.

He had to get help, he knew he had to get help, but then he realised how this all looked and that he'd be blamed. It was happening all over again. He would always be guilty of something.

29

THE PEOPLE'S FRIEND

21 October 1933

'SARK MYSTERY: FAMILY APPEALS FOR "FAIR PLAY"'

Mr David Sutton has made an appeal for 'fair play' on behalf of his family. 'I feel very deeply that a great injustice is being done to my family' he said. 'The Guernsey doctors told me that the injuries to Mrs Howell were received before death. When Mrs Howell's body was found there was no trace of my brother. The question of foul play naturally arose at that time, but since he has been found we should be satisfied that they died together.

I would like it to be known that my brother had a weak heart following a childhood illness. Our family doctor has assured me that even the shock of a cold bath would have been sufficient to induce heart failure. I think it is probable that my brother got into difficulties and Mrs Howell, being a good swimmer, went to his aid, but dived in and struck her head as she entered the water.

That is what I believe, and it is the last I shall say on the matter.'

AS WE'VE SAID ALREADY, there's never one version of the truth. Everard is waiting when Elise opens the front door. He looks tired and dishevelled, like he's been out all night.

'I need to know what you think I did,' he says. 'All those years ago, tell me exactly.'

Elise stares at him, not understanding, then she feels herself flinching and looks left and right. The Avenue is deserted since it's still so early so she opens the door wider and brings him inside. They stand together in the dark hallway. Everard is the same height and build as his father, but he stoops to make himself smaller, pressing his back into the wall. Elise glances over her shoulder, checking for signs of movement upstairs. Phyll, she hopes, is fast asleep.

'I need to hear it,' Everard says in a low voice. 'I need to be clear in my own head.'

Elise folds her arms. She should invite him into the parlour but she doesn't want him to stay. She thinks very carefully about what she can say.

'You tricked people.' She stares at the wall, at the skirting. 'It was a strange time and people were grieving and you children, you didn't understand and you took advantage.' She pauses again. 'It was *so* cruel. I realise you were young, but . . . think about that poor woman, Mrs Williams. She had lost her husband and you made it worse. You went too far. The poor thing, she was scared witless . . . '

Everard looks up. 'Mrs Williams.' He repeats the name slowly. 'But all we did was give her back her husband's book. I don't think that scared her.'

Elise purses her lips. He is still playing tricks, only admitting to part of it. He is a good actor, she will give him that. She looks at him squarely with her hands on her hips.

'The book,' she says, 'was just the start of it. You *know* what I am referring to. The broken windows? You could have killed someone. Mrs Williams collapsed and Dr Stanhope had to sedate her, and then what?' Elise waits, almost tapping her foot. She puffs out her cheeks in frustration. 'Well, I don't know exactly, but someone was there, in her room, tormenting her even in that state.'

Everard draws his head back. He looks horrified. 'What? But I was locked in my room. I heard glass breaking but

I couldn't do anything.' He lifts his hands, palms up. 'I don't know what happened, but it wasn't me. I couldn't have . . . ' He gestures to his forehead. 'I lied to you about this scar. My father beat me.'

Elise folds her arms and shifts the weight of her body from one foot to the other. 'Your father,' she says.

Everard nods and draws a hand across his face. He looks suddenly older. 'So what happened to Mrs Williams?'

Elise wishes she hadn't started this conversation. She hears movement overheard: the slam of a drawer and the creak of a bed. Phyll is awake, and any minute she'll come out onto the landing and see the two of them.

Elise leans towards Everard and lowers her voice. She speaks slowly, watching him. 'Mrs Williams was very unwell. She collapsed and had to be sedated and she had this idea that her dead husband had visited her. Someone was in the room with her . . . touching her. Can you imagine how frightening that must have been?'

Everard looks back at her. His gaze is direct and unwavering. 'Yes, I can, Mrs Carey.'

Elise thinks he's about to confess. She hears more noise upstairs: Phyll opening her curtains. Time is running out. She leans closer. 'Well?'

Everard pulls away from the wall, lifting himself up to his full height. 'I heard it through the wall,' he says flatly. 'I heard it through the wall and there was nothing I could do . . . I was locked in my room . . . there was only one other person in the house . . . '

Elise holds Everard's gaze. She doesn't understand what he means, but then, very clearly, she does. It is like a trapdoor opening. The ground is gone and she is falling. She sways backwards and the hallway feels smaller, the walls are pushing in. She reaches out to push them back.

'Your father,' she says. 'Your father?' She can see him. The Major. That man. She sees how he walks and talks and acts, as if he is above them all. She can't believe it's possible, but then it's blindingly obvious. Damn him. The lies he told. Why didn't she see it? How could she miss it? Her of all people. After everything she went through. She resists it even now, this pull of the inevitable. She wants to force it out of her mind but she can't. That man! She can't look at Everard any longer so she turns and swings up the stairs, taking them two at a time. She bursts through the door to Phyll's room. She doesn't know what to say at first. She wants to shout, but she swallows it down.

'You!' she squawks. 'Phyll. Was it you who smashed the big windows at Beau Regard that night?'

Phyll straightens up, startled by the urgency of her mother's voice, the intensity of her gaze. She shakes out her hair. 'Yes. I thought you guessed.'

Elise rests one hand on the door and the other on the doorframe but the whole house is pitching like a ship in a storm.

'I think . . . as we have already established,' she whispers, 'I am *not* psychic.'

She has to press her spine into the edge of the doorframe. She is going to be sick. She remembers feeling only the relief that the drama was done with, that the boy was gone. Why didn't she realise? Why didn't she question it? She stares at the ceiling and swallows hard. This is her fault. She was always so determined not to call herself a victim, not to name it as abuse, and that meant she couldn't see it anywhere else. She had to turn a blind eye, trying to keep herself impervious. What a fool.

'So you snuck out and went to see Everard and you smashed the French windows.'

Phyll nods.

'And *did* you see him?'

Phyll shakes her head. 'I threw stones at his window first and when he didn't appear I picked up a bigger stone and . . . ' Phyll stops mid-sentence and stares at her mother. 'So you know now. I was too scared to own up. You were already *so* angry . . . '

Elise glares back at Phyll. She wants to say that's not fair, that's not true, but she's always been angry. She's been angry for as long as she can remember, simmering at a steady heat for years and years and years. She pushes herself off the doorframe and stands on the landing, swaying uncertainly. She needs to think, to walk, to think some more.

She starts down the stairs, calling out over her shoulder, 'Everard's here.' She reaches the bottom step and barks, 'I am sorry!' (She is not sure who she is saying that to). 'I am so sorry!'

A minute later Phyll finds Everard waiting in the kitchen, warming his hands by the stove. 'What a morning.' She glances about. 'My mother keeps saying sorry.'

She's trying to make light of it but Everard doesn't smile. 'Well, I am sorry, too,' he says, turning to face her. 'I was an idiot in the churchyard. You took me by surprise.'

Phyll feels embarrassed and looks down at her hands, clutching at the sleeves of her cardigan. There's a thread dangling free from the cuff and she tugs at it. She pictures the sleeve unravelling and stops. She folds her arms over her waist.

'I don't know what I was thinking,' she says. 'It is all so confusing, isn't it?'

She's staring down at her feet. She's always embarrassed by the state of her brogues, but his are worse. He sniffs loudly and pulls her attention back to his face.

'I want you to know that that summer was the happiest time of my life,' he says. 'Thank you for being my friend.'

Phyll should smile back, but she can't. He sounds like he's saying goodbye. She pushes her lips together, then shakes her head. 'But I wasn't a good friend; I let you take all the blame.'

Everard draws his eyebrows together, thinking hard about what to say next. 'I don't think it matters now,' he replies. 'Everyone wants happy endings, don't they? It's why we like stories. But real life isn't like that. There might be happy starts and happy middles, but endings aren't ever happy. The ending is the same: people die, things fall apart. Look at my mother and father, or that man and woman who came here, look at *us* . . . There can only be happy beginnings and middles and we had that . . . I will always remember sitting in the tree by St Peter's, and seeing you through the leaves. A part of me will always be there.'

Phyll clutches her sides. She understands what he means but it makes her anxious because it sounds like defeat.

'But so much is ahead. You can travel and do what you want. You are young. *We* are young. We're still at the start.' She glances over at the window, which glistens with last night's rain. She thinks of her mother and wonders where she's gone. 'We've all made mistakes,' she says finally.

Everard steps towards her and draws her into a hug. He does this very gently, very slowly, and because he's taller she presses her face into his shoulder. It feels like they fit, and Phyll closes her eyes and is comforted. They stay like that for a moment. Everard runs a hand through her hair and she wraps her arms around his waist. It's as if there's one heart beating between them. Then he pulls back and kisses her on the forehead.

She doesn't realise, but he's had just enough time to slip one last letter into her pocket.

30

'A Note on Witches'

26 August 1923

READERS MIGHT BE INTERESTED to learn that there were more witches in the Channel Islands than anywhere else in Europe, if the number of witch trials is anything to go by. Perhaps this is proof of how rooted in the past we are, how bound to tradition and history. As recently as the Great War, there were many letters in the *Guernsey Press* lamenting the persistent belief of the 'Dark Arts' on these islands, naming Sark as 'the worst afflicted'.

But in times of strife and trouble people need someone else to blame. Scholars have found that the early witch trials happened in clusters, coinciding with outbreaks of plague and high taxes. The people persecuted were most often delinquents and troublemakers. Once you see a pattern it's hard to unsee it. Witchcraft is meant to be oh-so-mysterious, but there is nothing mysterious about singling out a scapegoat. It is usually easier to blame women or children – vulnerable people who don't have the resources to fight back.

Leave it to the men of authority to pick out the good from the bad.

And on that note, let us eavesdrop a while on Earnest Hyde and Percy Stanhope, sitting in the surgery, a bottle of whisky on the table between them. It was a decent single malt that Hyde had brought back from Southampton as a gift after 'that unfortunate business'.

The Major looked very well: his hair was oiled and he was impeccably dressed. He shook his head and stared at his glass.

'The boy is essentially evil.'

He liked the word evil as it was suitably vague and implied the supernatural. He already had his story, having worked it out carefully in the days since the séance. It was easy to blame Everard since Everard wasn't here. He told everyone he'd sent his son back to England in disgrace. Hermione Hyde remained in the south of France and a letter wouldn't reach her for another week or so. Hyde shook his head, muttered: 'unforgivable' and poured out two more measures. Naturally there'd been gossip but he'd paid Nancy a generous bonus and assured her the boy would not come again. By next summer there'd be new visitors and he'd make a few donations to different causes. He looked down. He looked up. 'You know, I often wonder if he *is* even mine . . . I think that is the crux of it.'

Stanhope glanced over at the window, thinking he saw someone look in, but it was only a shadow obscuring the sunlight. He drained his glass, feeling the sweat under his armpits and at the collar of his shirt. His clothes were too tight, every button straining. He didn't feel himself – hadn't for days. *Evil*, he thought, *yes, it was something evil*.

'Mrs Williams seemed to temporarily lose all reason. I did not realise she was quite so unstable. I recommended that she go back to England, to her parents. Let us hope she recovers quickly, poor young thing.'

Hyde wet his lips. 'We could not have known the ghost business would so excite her.'

He tried to look sincere but Stanhope didn't notice. He was toying with his empty glass. He put it down.

'It is tricky with these young widows,' he said. 'Their hopes for the future have been snatched away and they are quite adrift, there is a vacuum, nothing to look forward to. I think that is what makes them so vulnerable to delusions.' He shook his head. 'I even wonder about that book now . . . whether she planted it there herself?'

Hyde nodded slowly, eyebrows raised. It was an interesting idea. He might repeat that to Nancy when he had the chance. A subtle, '*Well, you know what old Stanhope thinks . . .* '

Hyde looked about. Stanhope's surgery was tidier than usual; the papers on his desk were arranged in neat lines, his medicine cabinet gleamed in the sunlight.

'But it wasn't all invented,' he said. 'I am still finding bits of broken glass. A bloody awful fright, that was, and it will cost a *fortune* to repair.' He sighed. 'The boy must really hate me. It's his mother, of course. She has poisoned his mind.'

Stanhope opened his eyes wide and shifted in his seat. 'Well, I never saw him.' He kept his eyes fixed on the glass.

Hyde let out a strangled laugh. 'But he admitted it. Once I had thrashed him, it all came out.'

Stanhope suppressed a shudder. Nancy had told him about the blood on the sheets. Not that it helped to brood. What's done was done. He stared at his glass. He would not have another drink. Not yet. He shifted uneasily. 'Mrs Williams was convinced someone had been in the room with her. *Was* it the boy, do you think?' He looked at Hyde. 'Did you check on her? I should have stayed the night, I realise now.'

Hyde gave a slight shrug. 'Oh, I'm sure you did everything you could, old chap.'

Stanhope nodded and shifted forward, bulging out of his waistcoat. His brain was foggy and his heart began to race. 'It is a shame. I had the impression that you and Mrs Williams, well . . . I think Ann Cecil was hoping that . . . ' He paused again. 'There might be something of a romantic attachment forming between the lady and yourself.'

Hyde looked shocked. 'Good grief, man.' He leant over, resting his elbows on his knees. 'No, I don't think so. I made no overtures towards her. She was a sweet enough thing but you saw how hysterical she became. No, no. I married once and once was enough.'

Stanhope nodded, leaning back. There were beads of perspiration all around his hairline. He reached for the bottle and poured himself more whisky.

Hyde stared into space. He felt no guilt for what he'd done. What use was guilt? He pictured Sarah lying there, her head to one side, her mouth slightly open. He smiled. He had done the unthinkable, the unforgivable, but it was like he hadn't done it, and he would survive because that's what he did. He could do it again if he was careful, he might have any woman he liked and not even have to pay. Blame the spirits, he thought, and he almost laughed, but he noticed Stanhope's eyes on him, so he checked himself and frowned.

Outside the sun was still shining, but it had, at last, lost some of its heat. Phyll walked along the Avenue, oblivious to everything. She understood that Everard had gone but she still couldn't accept it. She walked to the church and paced the graveyard. She thought, perhaps, he had left her a note in some secret location, so she turned over stones and peered under the bench where they'd placed the book. She even wandered inside and checked between the pews and climbed into the pulpit. Once she'd done that, she climbed Everard's tree. She was fearless now, scrambling over all the branches, scrutinising every inch of the trunk. But there was nothing. Not a trace. Phyll hugged her knees, closed her eyes and willed Everard to come back. She asked for a sign, like a breeze that made her skin prickle. There was a breeze, but it just meant evening was close.

Phyll would never admit to smashing the windows at Beau Regard. She had been blamed for the book, and that was enough. She knew it wasn't fair that Everard had been blamed, but she didn't entirely understand what had happened, and it didn't help that each time she walked into a room the adults fell silent. She pretended not to care and turned on her heel, and she was getting good at slamming doors. Her aim was to slam a door so hard it came off its hinges. She had already started a letter to Everard. She would write to him at school so nobody would know. She wouldn't mention the windows. She would just say, 'I hope you come back soon'. She was sure he'd come back eventually and things would be fine. People would forget. And it wasn't like they'd killed anyone.

Phyll sighed and tilted her head back, staring into the leaves.

'Will you come down now?'

She plucked a leaf, and let it go. Then she tore off a larger twig with three green shoots. She imagined ripping off all the branches. Then she thought, no, don't blame the tree. She laid a hand on the rough branch.

'Not your fault,' she said.

'Are you talking to a tree?' Miranda called out. She was leaning against the wall, watching her friend. She sighed loudly and shook her head. 'Honestly, Phyll. I can't believe you!'

Miranda decided to wait – she had nothing better to do. Her parents had found some new rapturous view and she was really very bored of them. She walked around the tree and plucked at some pink campion. She could make herself a crown and pretend she was a princess. It was low-grade fantasy but it would help to pass the time.

'You know, it is probably as well that Everard has gone,' she said, tilting her head back. 'He was horrid to me when we went to the Boutiques . . . he was rushing *and* it was his fault I hurt my ankle and he didn't care. He just left me.'

Phyll drew up her legs and hugged them. 'You are trying to make Everard sound mean. Maybe you are doing it so that I feel better. But nothing will make me feel better. *Nothing*.'

She pressed her chin into her knees. She could feel her heart beating. Did hearts still beat when they were broken? She thought she'd made a friend for life and now she'd lost him. She wanted to cry out loud about losing him. Why did people have to leave? It made her feel horrible. She banged her forehead against her knees. She knew this was the end of something, that if her life was a book this would be the closing of a chapter. She lifted her head and sighed, emptying all the air out of her body.

'I will never be happy again,' she said.

(Slightly melodramatic, we agree, but she was only twelve.)

She shut her eyes, gripped her knees and held her breath. She willed Everard to come back, to escape whatever boat or train he'd been bundled onto.

She would need to wait a long, long time.

The sky turned to a deeper red and Miranda busied herself making a crown out of ivy and pink campion. She twisted the stems round and round, making it wider and thicker. She was annoyed that Phyll was this upset but she had a good plan to snap her out of it. She kept adding to her creation, using daisies now too, until she heard a rustling through the leaves. Phyll landed with a thud at her side. Miranda didn't look up, but turned slowly and laid the crown very gently on Phyll's head.

She stepped back, smiling. 'You know, you *are* pretty when you smile,' she said, and then she started to bunch and twist Phyll's hair round over her left shoulder. 'I have a dress that I've grown out of. If you want you can have it. Maybe you'd look better in a dress? Why don't you come to the studio and let me *improve* you.'

Phyll wiped her hands on her trousers. She didn't want a dress and her head felt heavy with the flowers sitting on it. She sniffed. 'He didn't even say goodbye.'

Miranda gripped Phyll's shoulders and peered into her face. 'I know what you did with him, by the way, the silly ghost business.' She looked hurt for a second. 'It explains why you were always whispering behind my back.'

'Oh.' Phyll frowned. 'I'm sorry.'

Miranda didn't say anything for a minute. 'It doesn't matter. I won't tell anyone, because we are friends and that's what friends do.' She ran her hands down Phyll's arms and their fingers interlaced. 'Let's not mention it again,' she sighed. 'But on *one* condition.' She met Phyll's gaze and held it. 'I want you to promise me that we shan't keep secrets from each other again. My parents keep secrets and I can't tell you how much I hate it.'

Phyll thought about this for a minute. 'That sounds good.' She gave a firm nod. 'Miranda, I will always be honest with you. No secrets, I promise.'

It was the sort of promise someone makes when they are twelve years old, when they have no idea of the consequences, nor the responsibility. But it was one promise Phyll didn't break.

31

DAILY GAZETTE

22 October 1933

'A MINIATURE GARDEN OF EDEN'

Sark is very much in the public eye at the moment due to the tragic deaths of a man and woman whose bodies were recovered from the sea some weeks apart, but let us not forget that this island is still one of the loveliest places to visit, with safe bathing at low tide and beautiful walks to be had. Our nature editor, who has himself visited the island during the milder months, writes to reassure us: 'If not quite so primitive as Eden, Sark is surely the closest I have found to it, a fact which accounts for much of its charm.'

If recent events might deter visitors from water pursuits, be assured that there is still much to see in this miniature paradise. Indeed, Sark has for years been a favourite place for botanists, such is its rich array of flora and fauna. The wild, wooded areas are their own fairy kingdom, where rare plants and shrubs grow in abundance, and the more cultivated Sark gardens are such to rival Hampton Court.

The Dame of Sark herself has now returned from America and will soon be opening her gardens at the Seigneurie for all to visit and will offer tours of her greenhouses, where many exotic plants grow.

So let us remind our readers of the very many good things in Sark, and forget the bad.

BUT THERE IS GOOD AND BAD IN EVERYTHING, even simple plants. Take foxglove, or *Digitalis purpurea*. It was here in Sark that famed botanist Thomas Knowlton recorded a variant with white flowers. The plant itself contains digoxin, which is very useful for medicines of the heart, but just two leaves can kill a child. It's the same with henbane: the roots, seeds and leaves contain alkaloids such as hyoscine, hyoscyamine, and atropine. They depress the central and peripheral nervous systems. So useful! But in the wrong dose they can cause a painful, seizure-like death.

Even so, henbane has been used to flavour beer, with the added benefit that it made the drinker thirsty so they'd drink more. Now, such facts might not seem immediately relevant but let's just store them away somewhere, like jars on a shelf.

Maud has cut herself on something, she can't recall what, and she walks into the bar of the Bel Air with blood dripping through her fingers. Everyone jumps up, including Stephen Greener. Dr Greener remains devoutly teetotal but he's been coming here most nights. He likes the smoky, convivial atmosphere and yes, all right, he's in love with Dolly, who makes her own fresh lemonade. It's possible Maud knew he was there as she doesn't seems surprised when he runs to her, takes her hand to examine the wound, and steers her to a chair.

'You poor thing,' he says. 'Just as well I brought my bag.'

Stephen Greener brings his doctor's bag everywhere. It is a thing of talismanic importance, possibly the reason he chose a medical career, and his instruments are gleamingly clean, which is a relief.

Maud explains that she was making a tonic and her hand slipped.

'The natural remedies are often the best,' says Dr Greener. 'Passed down through generations, I am sure. Someone told me you make an excellent rosehip syrup for the winter months.'

Dolly, who rushed to fetch a basin and water, pours a generous measure of brandy into a glass. She holds it to Maud's lips, but Maud clamps her mouth shut, like a child refusing medicine. Maud never touches alcohol and Dolly knows this but has forgotten in the excitement. She now remembers and lifts the glass to her own lips, enjoying the sensation of the warm liquid coursing down her throat. Dr Greener has already plucked a thin shard of glass from the heel of Maud's hand. He holds it up so that it catches the light and everyone applauds, then he drops it into the basin Dolly thrusts at him. He feels as if he should take a bow, but instead he asks her to fetch a bottle of antiseptic from his bag.

Dolly nods. She likes being useful and immediately pulls out several small bottles, lining them up on the table. Dr Greener has meanwhile fished out two further fragments of glass to wide approval. Jim Remfrey watches, tankard raised.

'I will buy you a pint after this, Doc,' he says.

Dr Greener nods genially. The wound is superficial and he doesn't mind an audience. He rests a hand on Maud's shoulder to check she is calm. Everything seems to be going smoothly until Dolly pulls the stopper off one of his bottles.

'Ugh!'

She grimaces and shakes her head, covering her mouth and nose. 'Is this the stuff you gave me? My, it was horrible. It made me feel like lead!'

Dr Greener is busy applying pressure to Maud's wound. 'I am sorry to hear that, Dolly. Chloral isn't for everyone.'

Chloral. The word drops into Maud's brain like a pebble in a pond. She jerks her head round. 'You gave her Chloral?'

Her eyes became small and sharp as pins, and Dr Greener feels suddenly uneasy.

'Dolly was having trouble sleeping, isn't that right, Dolly?' He glances over in her direction and smiles, but Dolly has an odd look in her eye. He turns back to Maud, frowning now. 'I just wanted to help.' He thinks it sounds perfectly reasonable but the way Maud glares at him, it is as if he has crossed some invisible line.

Dolly makes an odd noise and gives a little shudder. It's been bothering her for days, this thing dragging at the back of her mind. She presses the bottle under her nose again. 'Do you know what it is,' she says. 'This stuff tastes like the water in Little Sark. I have always said the water there was tainted. There's only that one spring and they should test it. It leaves the same bitter taste. What if it's connected to what happened to those two people? Maybe it sent them mad.'

Dr Greener thinks this is all very eccentric. He has bent Maud's arm at the elbow and raised her hand so that it is level with her chin and with his other hand he reaches for some gauze.

'But Chloral is a drug,' he says in his best doctor's voice. 'The water won't be tainted with a *drug*.'

He chuckles to himself, but the bar is suddenly quiet, as if everyone is holding their breath. Dolly stares at the blood and water in the basin. 'When I worked at the Bungalow I got the most fearful headaches, and this sick feeling . . .'

It's unclear who she's talking to, and then there's a whirr and a click and a breeze. For those unfamiliar with the doors of the Bel Air Inn: they are twin doors with a spring function, and so to make a dramatic entrance it is best to place oneself at the centre and take a door in each hand. It is helpful then to stand for a moment with both doors open. This allows the requisite gust of air from outside to enter with you. Elise has done this many a time to great effect. Invariably, in years past, she would sweep through these doors in search of her errant daughter. Elise never approved of the amount of time Phyll spent in the hotel kitchen. She felt it gave the impression that her child was some kind of waif and stray, and that her cooking was terrible (oh, but it was). Elise also felt Dolly was a 'morally dubious influence'. We women must support each other, but we can't always like each other. Elise used to find Dolly too frivolous and uninhibited and she cannot understand why her bosom must spill out of every dress that she owns, but this isn't a moment for a critique of current fashions and Elise in her gum boots is hardly one to judge. No, today, let's keep to the matter in hand: Elise has come looking for Maud. She found broken glass and blood in Maud's kitchen and was alarmed. She also has excellent hearing and a habit of listening at doors. What this means is she has heard the exchange as regards Chloral and certain ideas are now at the front of her mind. She gazes directly at Maud, who twists her head round and stares back. Something is happening: a memory stirring, things linking together. Elise walks over to Dolly and takes the bottle of Chloral out of her grip. She does so gently, prising it from her fingers as if taking a grenade off a child. She removes her glasses and reads the label closely, then she sets the bottle down.

'You think you had this before?'

Dolly starts to bite her already bitten lip. 'I don't know. But like I said, when I was at the Bungalow . . . '

Her cheeks and neck flush pink. Elise can almost feel the heat from them. She reaches for Dolly's hand. 'When you were working for Major Hyde, you mean.'

Dr Greener is busy securing the bandage. Once he is finished he steps back to admire his work. It takes a while for him to sense the change in atmosphere, the yawning quiet. He can't even hear the wind. He glances up and everyone is looking downwards, their faces frozen. It is like an oil painting, though he can't think which one.

He turns to Elise, but she makes him so nervous he can't meet her eyes. He nods at her left ear lobe. 'Will you be seeing Mrs Pratt home?' He tries to sound jovial but his voice is as shrill as a choirboy. 'You should check the kitchen for broken glass. She was making something.'

The doctor is about to bend down and ask Maud *what* she was making and he will enunciate his words slowly and at such a volume we will wince. Thankfully Elise lays a hand very firmly on his shoulder and is strong enough to steer him aside.

'I will clean up. I know what she was doing.' It's as if she is dismissing him – she doesn't even look at him – she simply turns from Maud to Dolly and back again. 'Ladies. I will take it from here.'

32

'An Island Legend, Updated'

LET'S BE CLEAR ABOUT ONE THING, whatever version you hear, whatever version you're told, the ending is the same. Let's go back to the artist, who is now a widower – or we could just call him the murderer – living on the cliffs of Little Sark. The house was battered by storms and the noise kept him awake. He began to drink heavily. He'd be the first and the last in the bar of the Bel Air and he'd often end up sleeping in a chair.

Maybe he just wanted to forget, but the best way to forget was to leave. He decided he would quit Sark before his lease expired and made enquiries at the harbour. It was a period of bad weather so it gave us a bit of time. Much as we wanted the man off the island, we also needed to see him punished. If a person is not punished for their crime, then there's every chance they will repeat it. What if another poor woman fell under his spell and was killed? When would it end?

It wasn't just Maud who was worried, as by this point we were all involved. We women stick together – what else could we do? What we needed was for the man to admit his guilt, for an arrest to be made and justice served. It didn't seem too tall an order.

Remember that fun fact about henbane? It was used to flavour beer. A small amount of the plant boiled down has a bitter flavour, but not unpleasant. It creates a solid thirst, at first, and then it all depends. Maud had the idea. Her plan was to drug the artist just enough. He'd get confused, disoriented, and say something careless. She really thought it was possible. So she made a special brew and left it at the Bel Air. But she had no idea how much this man could drink, and she waited in vain. (We should explain that she was not then the expert in plants that she would become. We could call this whole unfortunate episode a steep learning curve.)

Never mind! Maud made a stronger brew and that worked very well. Maybe a little too well. If there had been a doctor resident at the time, he might have diagnosed 'a mania' because the artist started convulsing and then (unfortunately) foaming at the mouth. Maud was dragged from her bed to come and help. Imagine the scene, Maud in her nightdress running through the door. The artist reared up, rigid with horror.

'No!' he screamed, his face contorted. 'But I killed you!'

To be fair, with her dark hair untied, Maud did look a bit like his dead wife, and it was later noted that a number of the island women had long, dark hair and a loose, pale nightdress, so any one of them could have made a similar impression.

Let's move on.

So there it was. A confession of sorts. Maud should have been delighted but she felt numb with shock, and the artist fell backwards. He smacked his head on the side of a table. Blood everywhere. The head bleeds so much!

We thought he was dead.

But now the story will change, depending on who takes hold of it.

The island men stepped in and, frankly, it was time. Albert – dear Albert – volunteered to take the chap to France. Sam Baker offered to help and went to get his boat.

They left at first light and Maud climbed the cliff to watch it battle the waves, and as she stood in a daze of exhaustion she resolved to teach herself more about plants and pay more attention to her doses. But the heavy feeling in her chest only grew, because the sea was very wild and there was a real danger that the boat would go down.

The morning advanced but the sky didn't lighten. Maud was rooted to the spot, feeling herself getting colder and colder as if she were turning to ice. Then she sensed something beside her and she managed to turn her head. The woman was there. She really was there – it wasn't one of us dressed up or pretending – it was the stranger's wife. She wore the same white dress she was buried in and her long hair fluttered behind her. She stood a few yards away, staring out to the sea. Maud turned to face her. She wanted to say, 'I am sorry'. She wanted to say, 'He's gone'. But suddenly it was raining, and the rain came down with surprising force and splashed into her eyes and ran into her mouth and she couldn't see anything at all.

When the boat returned to the harbour later, the crew were badly shaken. They never made it to France, they said. The artist had woken up, goggle eyed and spitting blood, and before they could stop him he had lunged overboard. Sam Baker swore that he'd been screaming about a woman in the waves.

Some of us wondered about that. We thought that the men might have killed the artist and told this story so it relieved them of the guilt. We wouldn't have blamed them. In a way, it was another invention, like when we dug up the cross or flitted about, dressed in white. It's funny to think we pretended it once and now we are dead we don't need to.

But the men were traumatised by what happened. Sam Baker became obsessive with his rituals, which he duly communicated to Gilbert, his son. Albert, too, was greatly affected. He wouldn't talk about it for a long time, but he'd wake in the night shivering and soaked through with sweat. He always worried the artist might come back, in some form, and he sat up some nights, keeping watch over Maud in the darkness.

One of her lasting memories is him sitting, shivering, at the end of the bed.

Dear Albert. He is still there.

Maybe that's why we love ghost stories, because the end takes us back to the beginning, and so we begin again.

33

THE GUERNSEY PRESS (MORNING EDITION)

22 October 1933

'STORM WARNING FOR BAILIWICK'

Guernsey, Herm and Sark have experienced the wettest October for seven years, according to official records, and gales around the coast continue to cause trouble for shipping. Strong winds of up to 40 knots are expected later tonight, with severe downpours and thunder and lightning. All ferry services between the islands have been suspended until further notice. Islanders are advised to stay off coastal paths and make no unnecessary trips.

BEAU REGARD SITS on the cliffs where it always has, but its white painted walls are cracking like capillaries under the skin. The glass doors that lead to the garden are rotting and let in the wind. After they were broken, the Major had the frames remade using smaller panes and now they resemble the bars of a prison. Although it's still daytime he pulls the thick curtains closed and walks over to his armchair. He can still hear the wind – it sings down the chimney towards him. He sets down his glass on the small side table and struggles to bring his double vision together. He holds both his hands out in front of him. Four hands and all tremble. He blames it on the cold and the wet. He will head south as soon as possible. There have been too many disruptions. First, the boy arriving, and then this business with the dead couple.

Hyde has never killed a woman, but sometimes, the way they lie there, makes him think that he did. Of course it's just a fantasy. They are unconscious, lost in a deep, drugged sleep. He smiles to himself but then the smile fades. Too much has been written about Sark these last weeks, too many people coming here and asking questions. He doesn't know how he endured it. He looks down at the pile of newspapers at his feet. They should make a decent fire.

He yawns and sits back, staring straight ahead. He's trained himself not to look in the corners of each room. For a while he assumed it was Evelyn, then he thought the shape was more feminine. He wondered if it could be his mother. It hardly matters now. Why be scared of a dead woman? She is dead, so there is nothing she can do.

He lifts his glass and drains it quickly. The alcohol will warm him up and he enjoys the burn in his mouth and throat. It blocks out the smell of damp wood and soot. He leans forward and rotates his shoulder, which is still stiff from when he slammed into the deck. Everard's fault. That stupid boy. He has been nothing but trouble over the years, but now the papers are signed, so it is done. He will be rid of him. It is annoying to have to hand over the money, but it is the only way. Hyde moves his shoulder harshly, hearing it click, enjoying the sound, and pours himself the last of the whisky, shaking out the final drops from the bottle. He needed to finish it before he left. He might have stayed a few more days if Lisl Drake had hung around, but now she's gone there seems no point.

All he needs is a calm and clear day.

The clock chimes on the hour and Hyde eases himself forward. He feels ready to start the fire. Nothing like a good fire, as his father would always say. He lowers himself carefully onto his good knee and sets to work laying some twisted newspaper in the hearth, making it into a neat little pile. He adds dried pine cones and a touch of kindling. He can hear the wind in the chimney and it sounds oddly human. He adds a few coals and leans back, satisfied, but a gust of icy air comes at him and a photograph flutters down from the mantelpiece. It lands by his knees, facing up. Hyde doesn't recognise it. This is not one of his photographs and he has never seen it before.

He picks it up with a trembling hand. He frowns at the three children crouching on the sand. There is the young Phyllis Carey, unsmiling even then, squatting beside Everard, who looks just like his mother. Standing behind them is Miranda, and just behind her is the blurred figure of a woman dressed in white. Something catches in Hyde's throat and he thumps his chest hard and spits. He wipes his mouth, tasting soot. Of course he remembers Sarah Williams. He remembers her dark hair and the long pale stretch of neck. He licks his lips. His heart is beating faster now, and he is amazed to find that he is also in the photograph. He's turning away, his face almost hidden under his panama. It has an oddly disorienting effect to see himself there and Hyde leans himself against the armchair. He doesn't remember the photograph being taken nor does he understand why it's here now. Had Paul given it to him? But when? Another breeze makes the curtains bulge and shift. Hyde turns his head to look at them, challenging them to move again.

The room is still.

He pulls himself up to standing and scans his eyes along the mantel. There are eleven framed photographs and if he were to move any one of them he would see the shape they had left in the dust, as clear as a negative imprint. This is deliberate. He doesn't allow Nancy to clean certain surfaces so that he can check for disturbances. He presses two fingers of his left hand onto the mantel and then lifts them off and inspects the amount of dust. In his right hand he is still holding the photograph. He looks at it again and wonders where it came from. Was it tucked behind one of these frames? It is possible that Everard left it here to taunt him.

Hyde casts the photograph onto the coals and bends over, reaching into his pocket for his matches. He's crouched over the hearth when another burst of wind comes down the chimney, and brings a huge cloud of soot. It smacks him in the face, making his eyes burn. He gasps it in and chokes. He can't breathe and he can't see and he's flailing against the chair. He waves his hands frantically in front of him and wipes his eyes on his jacket sleeve. The soot stings and he blinks and tries to spit, but the taste in his mouth is vile. He searches for his handkerchief.

'Damn it!' he splutters, feeling the rasping sting in his throat.

He wipes his face. The handkerchief is quickly covered in black and his shirt's the same. Quite ruined. He keeps blinking and spitting out grains of soot. The air is foggy and smells of ash. Then a hand reaches down to him and he feels himself being lifted into the chair. Someone is here to help him and it's a woman so he assumes it is Nancy. In fact, it is not one of Nancy's days. It is Elise. She has always had a solid grip.

'Major Hyde. What's this?' She keeps her tone business-like. 'You need to get your chimney swept.'

Hyde, who has allowed himself to be helped back into his chair, is quickly indignant. He wrenches his arms free. He's not an invalid and he wasn't expecting guests. Shock silences him for half a minute and he repeatedly wipes at his face.

'Mrs Carey?' he finally says when he has pulled himself together. 'What do you want?'

Elise smiles and her eyes glow like small electric bulbs, but perhaps that's just the darkness of the room. The wind has quietened a little. She starts saying something about a fire and the Major is too confused to notice her take the photograph from the hearth. He is frowning at the mess on the carpet and asking himself when the chimney was cleaned and what day of the week it is and why is this woman here. He is still pressing the handkerchief to his nose when he's handed a full glass of something. He thought he'd drunk all the whisky, but apparently he was wrong. He glances to the table at his elbow and there is a new bottle. A gift, she is saying. Hyde is covered in grime and the taste of soot is disgusting so he drinks quickly, greedily and wipes again at his mouth.

'A gift from who?' he asks, after a moment.

Elise, coming more clearly into focus, avoids answering. She is making some joke about the drama of the last weeks and sits down facing him, as if she's been invited.

'Do you mind if I sit?' she asks pointedly. 'You see, I wanted to come. That's not so peculiar, is it?'

Hyde thinks it is but he drinks anyway and Elise crosses her legs, the same peaceful smile still fixed on her face. She clasps her hands in her lap and looks at his empty glass. 'Oh you've had a nasty shock. You should have some more.

I'll give you a bit of time to collect yourself before I explain what I have come for.' She pauses and cocks her head ever so slightly, arching her eyebrows. 'I think you have the *time*, don't you?'

The fire in the hearth seems to have started all on its own. The newspaper pages burn well. 'The Sark Cave Mystery' is going up in smoke. For weeks the English public have been gripped by its possibilities. Accident or murder or suicide, they asked. It was a puzzle just out of reach, like one of those classic mysteries where the victim was someone they didn't know or like, and therefore don't care about.

It is interesting that in popular fiction the victims are usually poisoned or shot. Poison is appealing because it does not involve violence. It's more popular with women.

Well, well, well.

Shall we leave it at that?

34

THE GUERNSEY PRESS (LATE EDITION)

22 October 1933

'NEW GUIDEBOOKS TO BE PRINTED'

We are delighted to announce the *Press* will be publishing a new series of illustrated guidebooks to each Channel Island in the coming year. Responding to popular demand, we have commissioned local writers to supply the content, to guarantee the most up-to-date information and 'inside knowledge'. There will be maps, timed walks, sections on best beaches and local landmarks, lists of restaurants and hotels, and chapters devoted to our rich history and culture.

The first guidebook to be published will be on Sark and authored by fresh, local talent P. Carey, who has already begun work on the opening chapters and says he is greatly looking forward to the challenge!

THE SKY IS A HEAVY, unbroken grey, as if winter's already come. Phyll blows on her fists to warm them and thinks about how she'll start. A view of Sark from the sea, the arrival at the harbour, then she'll describe the Avenue. She breathes out and dances from one foot to the other. She'll have to list the best walks, and what about maps? It is exciting. She can write this guidebook in her sleep, in fact her mother said as much. Phyll was surprised that Elise was so calm about it.

'Better you do it than anyone else,' she smiled. 'A local talent indeed.'

Phyll wants to tell Everard but he's not here yet. She's standing by the entrance to St Peter's, by what he calls 'their tree', and as she waits she starts to get worried. It's as if there's a thread between them that's stretched taut. She wants to tug it and pull him back in. She looks up and down the lane and rocks on the heels of her shoes. That's when the feeling starts: a bad feeling. The trees know it, too, and their branches shiver and creak above her head. She hunches a little. She doesn't want to look so she studies her shoes, holding her elbows. Something small hits her on the top of her head and a cold liquid feeling seeps down her scalp. She runs her fingers through her hair. She has that lurching feeling she's had before, like missing a step on the stairs. She has to balance against something solid so she reaches out for the wall.

The branches shift and groan. She takes a breath and looks up. She sees two sharp eyes she knows so well, the messy hair falling over the face. It is herself, crouching over, younger.

Phyll presses her back into the cold wall. The edges of the stones push into her shoulder blades. She studies her own face until it becomes a burning hole in the centre of her vision. It's not the shock it should be, but what does it mean? She lifts herself off the wall. The wind tugs at her coat and pulls her hair over her face. She digs her hands into her pockets, bowing her head, and she finds a piece of paper. It is the letter Everard wrote to her. It is the letter where he explains everything that happened, or what he thinks happened. Phyll reads fast.

'Dearest Phyll, it's over. My life is over before it really started but you were the best bit of it. I don't want you to

miss me. I want you to go back to the time when we sat in the trees dropping leaves on people. I want to go back to being young and safe. I can't bear to see the terrible things people do and I can't risk being like my father.'

She shouts, 'No!'

Small George and Edie, who have been trailing Phyll at a distance, now run into the road.

'What's wrong?' Edie asks. 'What is it?'

Phyll looks down at Edie and then at George, who has wheeled his bicycle over.

Phyll grabs the crossbar. 'Everard is going to do something. I need your bike.'

George jumps back as though scalded. 'Take it,' he flaps his hands. 'Go!'

'Should I, Dad?' Edie asks.

Phyll swings her leg over the saddle and kicks off. 'Yes!' She twists her head round. 'Get a boat. We need a boat. At Port Gorey.'

Everard is on the beach already. He has been watching the seagulls climbing high in the sky. They scream and circle the rocks, as if warning him. He could stay here forever but he knows that it's time. He walks into the water quickly, braced for the shock of it. If he'd stripped there might be some confusion, but he has kept all his clothes on, even his shoes. He needs the weight of them. The freezing waves catch his legs and drag him in. He's reminded of what happened before, when he saw the woman in the water and ran to rescue her. He fought the man, or at least he tried to, and then he was pushed under. It's happened again now and this time, he doesn't fight back. It's so cold he feels like he's being flayed alive. He expects the numbness to take hold and he closes his eyes and mouth and waits. *So this is what it feels like*, he thinks, but it's hard to think because the icy grip of the ocean stops everything. He's thrown upwards, gasping for air, twisting his head back to look at the cliffs.

He knows he should surrender. He had wanted to slip away peacefully, let his muscles freeze up. He swallows water and lets himself go under again, but every time he does, he's pushed up. There is something about the water; it is almost too black, thick as oil, as if it's pushing against him. He closes his eyes. He just wants to rest, to sleep, but the waves won't let him. He has the idea they are pushing him back to shore, they are telling him he is wrong. They don't want him. Why not? He opens his eyes then, thinking he will see the woman who drowned, the woman he couldn't save. Maybe she will save him.

He looks up at the sky for what should be the last time. It is streaked with grey clouds but the sun streams yellow rays beneath them so that parts of the water sparkle. He can't focus on anything very clearly now, there's too much glitter everywhere.

He's turning in the water when something snags in his blurry vision. There is someone on the beach, running over the stones. She pulls off her shoes and her coat and jumps into the water. There is no hesitation.

Phyll doesn't think of the danger, and she doesn't think of her mother or her father or what she's doing. She is simply moving, launching herself into the sea and thrusting with her hands and kicking with her legs. The cold stuns her, it is so cold it burns, but she's a strong swimmer and she can see him – his dark head bobbing up like a seal's. A violent swell pushes him back and his mouth is open like he's calling her.

'Everard!' she shouts. 'Here!'

If she had the time and the breath she would say, '*Don't. Don't become another ghost.*' She wants him to live, but she wants him to want to live. She wants him to fight for himself, and then maybe for her, so they can fight together.

'Everard!'

They're catching different currents and the waves are bringing them close to the rocks. She can hear how the waves smack into the cliff, the rush and swell. She thinks of the man and woman getting caught and not having a chance. It could have happened like that. Phyll ducks down and pushes on, going under, the cold water numbing her face. Drowning can happen in only a few minutes: you hold your breath until forced to exhale, and then you gulp water. As your lungs are flooded, there's no oxygen to the brain. Phyll is underwater when she sees a woman's face. It is turned three-quarters away but the hair fans out behind her. She bursts up through the surface, crying out, and something snaps Everard back into himself.

'Phyll!' he gasps. 'Phyll!'

He forces himself through the water, pushing his arms out, reaching for her. He feels shredded and raw but his arms still work and there is Phyll looking towards him. He gasps and she grabs him and he is stunned by the tightness of her grip. He realises he wants to live, he wants to live as fiercely as she does.

'Got you,' she gasps.

Elise has let herself out of Beau Regard and stands for a second on the overgrown path. She shuts her eyes and pictures bricks crumbling, glass shattering, a building returned to dust. She lifts her face into the wind. It is over, she tells herself.

James Earnest Jolyon Hyde cheated death many times, as his obituary will later note. The death certificate will say it was a heart attack. Barbiturate overdose can cause coma and respiratory depression. It can be a rather painful death, a bit like henbane, we might suggest.

Elise is walking fast – a brisk trot, nothing too conspicuous – planning what she will say. She just wants to get home but she should call in on John. She will explain how she was simply delivering the post when she found the Major slumped in his chair. At first she thought he was asleep, and then she realised he wasn't breathing. He was holding a photograph of his son, which could be meaningful. But oh, Elise needs to find Everard. She wouldn't want him seeing his father like that. She assumes he is with Phyll, which is good. She plans how she could tell them both together and mutters the story, nodding to herself.

She crosses La Coupée without looking back, without turning her head left or right. She does this because she's lost in her own thoughts but also because she doesn't like the sheer drop and the way the wind bullies her. She doesn't hear the frantic whistling of George Vaudin, nor does she notice two small boats out at sea. She's in shock, not registering anything. The next few days will not be easy. She doesn't want to be a murderer, to have that on her conscience, but it was the only way in the end.

She has reached the other side of La Coupée and a thick mist has settled on the road ahead. She looks from side to side but everything is grey. She walks on, head slightly down so she can concentrate on the path. She hasn't gone far when she senses something ahead. It is the Lady. She is standing perfectly still. Elise sees the white of her dress, the black of her hair. Elise will have to pass right by her. She keeps moving. She feels her heart rise and sink, the valves fluttering, opening and closing. Her nerves are alert at once. As she reaches the Lady's side, she finds she can speak.

'Thank you,' she says, without turning to look. 'You come for me, to warn me. I understand that now.'

Phillip would have killed her if he'd stayed, and the moment Elise grasps this, it's over: the fog thins and the woman has gone.

Elise walks on, blinking quickly, wondering if this is some kind of dream. She holds her hands together at her waist and keeps her head slightly bent. Should she tell Maud? People *should* know. The woman is a warning, so let people be warned. She is still thinking about this when she turns onto the Avenue. She is surprised at how fast she's walked, as if she's been carried on a wave. Her pulse is still racing. She feels an odd tingling along her arms and prickling over her scalp spreading down her neck. She is beginning to feel queasy. She cannot see anything clearly. She stares along the road towards the post office and it's a view she knows so well but everything is blurred, like a lens smeared with grease. She blinks and blinks and thinks there must be something in her eye. Or maybe it's the shock. She tells herself it's the shock. She manages small steps but she's worried she will faint before reaching home. She has to stop and rest her shoulder against the signpost, the one Albert made. How embarrassing to faint in public, she thinks, but after a minute she levers her body straight and looks up at the post office, her post office. Immediately she sees what's wrong: the front door has been flung wide open. Elise feels the hot pulse of fear. Who is here, she wonders. She staggers forward and has to work hard to make it to the threshold. She peers into the hallway, pressing a hand onto her heart. There are wet footprints glistening on the flagstones. Elise gasps and almost chokes. It feels as if someone's hands have pushed up inside her skin and are trying to pull her ribs apart.

'Who is here?' Her voice quavers.

No answer comes, and she stands at the threshold of her own home, suddenly not her home. She leans on the doorframe and rests her forehead on her knuckles. It's all too much.

'Phillip?' she calls softly. 'Are you here?'

Although it is dark in the hallway an icy breeze comes at her, and he is there, right there. She smells the sea and has to stop herself from falling back. There is the sound of splashing water and he comes at her. He is a huge black shape filling the corridor and blocking the light.

'I got them,' he says.

Years later, whatever else changed in the story, Elise was very clear on this. She saw her husband. He walked straight into the hall and then straight through her. 'I got them,' he told her.

Elise lunges forward and breathes in the sea. 'So you are back,' she says, although it doesn't sound like her voice. She closes her eyes and feels his hand brushing the hair from her face and she sees only a small figure. 'We got them, Elise. It is all right.'

'Gil,' she gasps. 'Gil?'

The old man is shaking. 'I pulled them out of the water. I didn't think I'd ever have the strength.' He lifts his hands and stares at them, his expression strangely rapt. 'I learned to swim. Did I ever say?'

Elise doesn't understand. 'You got them? *Who?*'

Gil looks up, blinking. 'He went in first, she was trying to save him.'

Elise leans forward, taking Gil by the shoulders so that he can hold her up, and then John comes out of the kitchen. 'There you are.'

Elise looks at him. 'John?'

She doesn't understand why these men are in her house but Gil is still talking, telling her how he taught himself to swim in the Venus Pool after Phillip died. 'I didn't like feeling helpless.' Then he looks over at John and taps a finger in the air. 'And John here got in a boat for the first time since I don't know when.'

Elise looks back and forth between John and Gil. She can't think what to say, so she takes Gil's hand, which is rough and bony, and they walk through to the parlour. Phyll and Everard sit hunched by the fire, hidden under blankets. They look so small, like they are children again. Elise feels her gut clench and she stutters out a breath. 'What did you do?' She goes to Phyll and stares at her wet hair, sinking down onto her knees. She wraps her arms around her shoulders, then she turns and does the same to Everard, pulling him in. 'What happened?'

Everard has a blanket gripped right under his chin. His teeth are chattering and his lips are blue. 'So sorry,' he whispers. 'I never meant for all this trouble.'

Elise grabs the blanket and pulls him in, pressing her forehead against his, breathing hot air into his face. 'You're not the one she came for.'

Everard can't stop shivering. His chest feels tight, like there is a hand inside, gripping his heart, but as Elise says those words, the hand lets go. He starts to breathe slowly, in, then out.

Phyll stays silent. She's numb, catatonic. It seems incredible to her that Everard is here, sitting with her, that they have made it back alive. When she saw him in the waves she was sure she'd lost him. She keeps thinking this is a dream. She saw herself in the trees. She was a ghost then. She tells herself nothing else matters beyond this, being alive, but then she stares at her mother's grey hair and notices for the first time that it is not grey at all but black and white, small strands meshing and curling together, and when Elise turns her face Phyll sees the expression of pain. She has never seen her mother so distraught, so destroyed. She starts to cry, and the crying helps as it gets the blood moving.

Elise can barely see through her tears but she looks back and forth between them. 'Listen to me, both of you,' she says. 'There's no curse. But something has happened.' She gathers herself, remembering the story she'd already rehearsed. 'I have to tell you. Let me explain.'

Epilogue

Final Hints for the Stranger

THE POSTSCRIPT OFTEN forms the most important part of a letter, the marrow of the bone, and it is also a ploy to prolong the parting. This is not a happy ending since your journey's just begun. If you come to Sark, you will be sure of a warm welcome. Dolly Bihet, now Dolly Greener, presides over the Bel Air Hotel, but if you wish for more seclusion we recommend the Bungalow, where Nancy Dolbel is in charge. Should you wish for a private tour of the island we suggest you enquire at the post office. It is now situated in the building that was briefly used as an art gallery. Here, Mrs Elise Carey sells tourist guides, maps, herbal remedies and select works of fiction. She would like to make it clear that she no longer reads private letters. She reads novels and feels better. She's also an excellent proofreader.

'A bit flowery,' she mutters, handing the pages back to Phyll, who has closed her eyes to the afternoon sun.

Mother and daughter are resting against a boulder, facing out over the gorse-covered cliffs. In front of them the sea shimmers with a brassy, hard light. It is autumn again, a whole year has passed, and some things are the same as well as being different. At their feet is a basket full of ripe, juicy blackberries. Phyll bends over and picks up two and tosses them into her mouth.

'The descriptions are important,' she says, sucking her fingers, 'because people can read them without coming here.'

'Ah, I see.' Elise nods with more enthusiasm. She would of course prefer that and Phyll grins because she knows.

Elise clears her throat. 'You know, I am so very proud of you.'

Phyll's guidebook is being revised and reprinted. We are pleased to report that *The Stranger's Companion to Sark* has sold surprisingly well.

'Hey, you two. No slacking! We don't have all day.'

Closer to the lane, over a stretch of brittle grass, Mule Toplis arches her back and checks her watch. It's been several hours since she abandoned her father with his easel on the other side of the island, and he doesn't like to be left alone on the cliffs after dark. Mule deposits her full basket beside Maud, who perches on her overturned wheelbarrow.

'Not a bad crop this year,' she says.

Just then a sudden gust of wind catches Maud's hat and flings it into the air. Edie runs to fetch it and after much giggling and shrieking, returns triumphant and lays it in Maud's lap.

She grabs a handful of Mule's blackberries as a fee and narrows her eyes.

'So . . . Everard *is* coming back?'

Maud nods. 'They are going travelling, apparently, to Europe.'

Mule clicks her tongue. 'Lucky them!' She pats her trousers, searching for her cigarettes. 'I am glad it's working out.'

Maud holds tight to her hat and looks down to where Phyll and Elise sit together. She can't see them perfectly, but their blurred outlines are sufficient. Just in front of the wheelbarrow she has neatly folded their two coats and Phyll's cardigan. She does like to be tidy. Maud has long forgotten finding the clothes cast aside at Port Gorey, but it was she who collected them and carried them up to a ledge, laying the coat out to dry and folding the rest. Later, she did the same with Phyll's coat when she went into the water after Everard. Now the two events have muddled and merged together. Does it matter?

Maud closes her eyes and feels a breeze lift her hair. She wants to let her old mind drift, but Edie clambers onto the back of the wheelbarrow, rocking it gently from side to side.

For the tenth time she asks: 'What are you going to *make* with all these blackberries?'

Maud glances over at Mule, who lifts one eyebrow.

'Jam,' they both say.

Edie plants her hands on her hips. She persists in her belief that these women are witches. She has no proof, it is more a gut feeling. She is sure that eventually they will let her join their midnight meetings, but in the meantime, she straightens up and pretends that she is the masthead of a ship. She stretches out her hands and flings back her head. Nobody notices and after a while her arms are tired so she lets them drop to her sides.

Edie watches the sun sink lower, touching the sea and turning it gold. Even the gorse seems to glitter and dazzle her. Then she sees two women. They have walked up the cliff path and stand silhouetted against the sun. One wears a long dress that's so pale it seems to reflect the light, the other wears a jacket and skirt. Edie is confused. It is not Phyll and her mother, and it's not Mule, because if Edie stands on tiptoes and rotates her head, she can locate Mule by the hedgerow. She frowns. The women at the bottom of the field are strangers. They belong to a different time: a different time to now and a different time to each other. Edie crouches down very slowly, bending her body over.

'Maud,' she whispers. 'Maud. Do you see them?'

Maud has been sitting as still as a statue, turning her hat in her lap. She gives a tiny nod. 'Yes,' she replies. 'I am glad it's not just me.'

Mule, who has wandered back into the field, points her cigarette like a dart. 'Who *is* that strange woman?' she asks. 'And who is her friend?'

But once she says it, she knows. You just know.

Time is like a wave pulsing forward, sweeping back, but the sea holds everything in. The two women incline their heads towards each other. It's a sign of tenderness, as familiar as the cliff where they stand.

And Elise and Phyll are standing now, staring back at them. It is a curious sensation to see the dead. Elise feels it like a jolt through her body, but Phyll is frozen, locked in place, then comes a slow pulse of calm. The two women do not need them, and in that same instant they've gone. Phyll turns to her mother, blinking. 'What was that? Did you see that?'

Elise bends down to collect the sheets of the manuscript she's dropped. 'I did. I think it's good.'

Phyll doesn't understand. Her thoughts are blurred, unclear. She stares at her mother's grey head. 'How is that good?' Her voice sounds thin and stretched. She looks at the empty space. 'Did I see a ghost? Did I see two?'

Elise lifts a hand and lightly touches her daughter's cheek. 'We saw two, and that *is* good.'

Phyll blinks. '*How* is that good?'

Elise smiles. 'Because they are together.' She hands Phyll back her papers. 'The Stranger won't be lonely anymore.'

Author's Note

The Stranger's Companion was inspired by a real event. On Sunday, 1st October 1933, the clothes of a man and woman were found neatly folded on the cliffs of Sark, with no trace of their owners. 'Island Riddle' ran the headline of the *Guernsey Weekly Press*. It printed a description of the clothes and appealed to the public for help, but days passed and nobody was reported missing. The English newspapers swiftly picked up the story and soon the 'Sark Cave Mystery' was making front pages in the *Daily Mirror* and *The Times*, as well as smaller regional chronicles and gazettes up and down the country.

It was a puzzle that had to be solved, like a piece of detective fiction, and each day brought fresh hints or clues. There were reports the man was a war veteran and the woman his nurse, that the man had left Sark separately with a new set of clothes, that the abandoned clothes were a 'suicide hoax'. But after nine days the missing persons case became a murder enquiry. A woman's body was recovered from the sea, close to where the clothes had been left. Now someone came forward. Chief Petty Officer Harold Britter had only recently returned to England from Hong Kong, and after reading about the case began to worry that the woman was his wife. She had gone for a holiday, he believed, and his last contact with her had been a postcard from Guernsey.

Beatrice Britter was thirty-seven and a mother to three young children. There had to be two inquests as the doctors were unable to agree on cause of death. Beatrice had sustained terrible injuries to her head and neck, which some felt were caused before her death. The first verdict was 'found drowned', then corrected to death by 'injuries, shock and immersion'. Harold Britter maintained that his wife was an excellent swimmer and would never commit suicide, and he knew nothing about a male companion.

Reading through the newspaper archives, I was gripped by the daily updates, but unlike the islanders at the time, I could skip ahead. Police continued their search for the missing man, who was presumed on the run or in hiding. He was soon identified by a suitcase left with porters in Guernsey as one Leslie Bradley, a thirty-year-old electrical apprentice from Kent. It would later transpire that Lesley had met Beatrice at a Rochester dance hall and their passion for dancing had blossomed into love. Leslie had warned his parents that he needed to 'disappear' for a while, so it was clear he and Beatrice had run away together, but then what?

A whole nine days after Beatrice's body was recovered, Leslie was found drowned. Doctors debated whether they'd gone into the water at the same time, but why then the time lapse between the discovery of the bodies? As a mystery the case caught my attention, but as a tragedy it stayed in my mind. I began running through different scenarios for what might have happened. Had it been murder or an accident? What if Beatrice wanted to return to her children, but Leslie saw no way out? Was someone else involved? That is how *The Stranger's Companion* began. The press cuttings at the start of chapters include original reporting of the case as well as my own embellishments, and I borrowed headlines to reflect how the 'Island Enigma' gathered momentum in the press at the time. I changed names and certain details, because I realised early on that the only way to write the story was through fiction.

That said, there's plenty here that's not invented. James Cachemaille really was the vicar of Sark and a friend of Peter Le Pelley, the Seigneur who funded the silver mines. Cachemaille's articles on the island were first published in the *Guernsey Magazine* and then brought together in the book *The Island of Sark*, published in 1928. Similarly, William A. Toplis was a much-admired landscape painter who made Sark his home. His painting *The Venus Bath, Sark* was exhibited at the Royal Academy in 1910, and now resides in the Guernsey Museum. Toplis also exhibited at the Sark Art Gallery, founded by Eric and Lisl Drake. Other books that helped me with my research were *Sark as I Found It* by Captain E. Platt, who describes his own encounter with a ghostly woman on the cliffs, and Sybil Hathaway's autobiography, *Dame of Sark*, which refers to the tragic events of 1933. There is also Barbara Stoney's biography, *Sibyl, Dame of Sark*, which recounts how Sybil's daughter, Douce, pranked tourists by dressing a family friend as a ghostly monk.

All these books can be found in the treasure trove of local history that is the Priaulx Library in Guernsey. I encourage everyone to spend a few hours there (and please leave a handsome donation!) before they then go on to Sark and see its beauty and mystery for themselves.

Acknowledgements

First of all, thank you to Elizabeth Sheinkman, my beyond wonderful agent, who loved the women in my book as much as I did, and found us the perfect home at Baskerville. Thank you to Jade Chandler, my brilliant and inspiring editor, and to Zulekhá Afzal, for her unstinting enthusiasm and support. Thank you also to Ellie Bailey, Anna-Marie Fitzgerald, Alice Herbert, Drew Hunt and Diana Talyanina. It's wonderful to be published by Baskerville and I very much hope I can continue plotting murders for them for years to come! A huge thank you also to Neil Gower for his stunning artwork for the book's cover, and to Etienne Laine for accompanying me to Sark's steepest cliffs and taking such wonderful photographs.

I am so grateful to Georgie Byng for giving the best advice, as always, and for her constant generosity. Special thanks to Marina Warner, Lisa Appignanesi and Susie Boyt for their support and encouragement along the way. I also owe a huge debt to Christie Hickman, who was an early reader of the book and really helped focus my ideas.

I also can't forget these excellent women: Chloe Aridjis, Devorah Baum, Marie Darrieussecq, Marion Deuchars, Allison Devers, Anouchka Grose, Lucy Heyward, Rachel Kneebone, Vicken Parsons, Ali Smith, Eleanor Tattersfield and Sarah Wood, who have helped, hugged, prodded and encouraged me.

The book is dedicated to my mother, a font of knowledge and ninja proof-reader, but I must thank the aunties, too: Fiona, Kitty and Victoria, and my sister Sarah. A proper coven, right there, on the Sunday family zoom.

Last but never least, thank you to Darian, who remains unfazed by my darkest ideas and likely caused some of them, and my wonderful kids, Jack, Iris and Clem, who I mention not just because I love them more than anything, but because I consider it my duty as their mother to embarrass them.

HAPPILY EVER AFTER

Nobody told her that marriage
would be murder...

Discover Mary Horlock's
electrifying new novel
of suspense, love and lies.

ORDER NOW

BASKERVILLE
An imprint of JOHN MURRAY

HAPPILY
EVER AFTER

Nobody told her that marriage
would be murder.

Discover a killer new book
about living happily ever after —
at her expense. Love it to life.

ORDER NOW

BASKERVILLE